Jenn Byrne Creative

SIMON JACOBS
STRING FOLLOW

Simon Jacobs is the author of *Palaces*, a novel, and
of *Masterworks*, a collection of short fiction. His
fiction has appeared in *Tin House*, *Black Warrior
Review*, and *Joyland*. Originally from Dayton, Ohio,
he now lives in Portland, Oregon.

ALSO BY SIMON JACOBS

Palaces

Masterworks and Other Stories

STRING FOLLOW

STRING FOLLOW

SIMON JACOBS

MCD × FSG ORIGINALS

FARRAR, STRAUS AND GIROUX   NEW YORK

MCD × FSG Originals
Farrar, Straus and Giroux
120 Broadway, New York 10271

Grateful acknowledgment is made for permission to reprint an excerpt
from "CVS Sonnet," by Ben Kopel, used with permission.

Library of Congress Cataloging-in-Publication Data
Names: Jacobs, Simon, author.
Title: String follow / Simon Jacobs.
Description: First edition. | New York : MCD x FSG Originals, 2022.
Identifiers: LCCN 2021042451 | ISBN 9780374603854 (paperback)
Subjects: LCGFT: Novels.
Classification: LCC PS3610.A3564865 S77 2022 | DDC 813/.6—dc23
LC record available at https://lccn.loc.gov/2021042451

Designed by Abby Kagan
Hand-lettering by Na Kim

Our books may be purchased in bulk for promotional, educational, or
business use. Please contact your local bookseller or the Macmillan
Corporate and Premium Sales Department at 1-800-221-7945, extension
5442, or by email at MacmillanSpecialMarkets@macmillan.com.

www.fsgoriginals.com • www.fsgbooks.com
Follow us on Twitter, Facebook, and Instagram at @fsgoriginals

1 3 5 7 9 10 8 6 4 2

For Mom, and for Dad

How many bad incisions must be made
on my way to becoming a blade?

—BEN KOPEL

STRING FOLLOW

Picture a living room, a staging area. Furniture ringed around its perimeter—a large couch, several upholstered armchairs, a wooden accent chair in the corner. Big, demonstrative windows on the wall facing the street. A coffee table occupied the center of the room at one point, though it's been removed: there are still faint indentations in the cream-colored carpet where the feet sat for years, and a rectangular patch of the carpet slightly richer in color. The center of the room, as a result of its former presence, seems eerily empty, anticipatory in its emptiness. There are two, maybe three entrances to the living room: it may open into a kitchen, or a hallway, or a foyer. Though there isn't a television, the couch and chairs are arranged in a way suggesting there once was one, or there was clearly a focal point to the room, some space to which the eyes and attention of the sitters or those present were naturally drawn, as to an altar. This space has since been filled, maybe by bookshelves or a console table, another set of chairs, but the position of the other furniture still seems to cater to it—an angle toward which everything seems to lean, as if cocked at attention. The front window, curtains drawn, from the right angle offers a sightline clear to the house across the street, a brief, golden shot into a similarly made-up living room, reflected darkly back.

Out and beyond, over a land equally haunted, we settle like a smoke cloud, like breath in the palm of a hand, like the blood pounding in your ears in the instant after a shock, when your instincts are wild and uncalibrated, your body wracked, for a moment, with violent potential—like air boding a storm.

Inside, in one of these houses, one floor above, a bitter young man lies in his bed at the end of his day, his idle dark thoughts unspooling into the night. He is otherwise alone in the house, or effectively alone. His parents—in this case, a mother whose work has taken her elsewhere, and a father he hasn't seen in a decade—are not part of this story.

Let's begin here.

BY THE THROAT

The route to Sarah was easy, or should have been, because she spent a lot of time at Beth's house, and Beth had a spooky older brother named Greg who was into serial killers and chokeholds and shit, so he had a lot of contact and had laid a lot of groundwork without knowing it, well before our arrival. Like he'd drift by Beth's bedroom where she and Sarah were hanging out and linger in the doorway, and when Beth wasn't looking he'd blink and show Sarah he'd painted a set of eyes on his eyelids, or he would pull up his sleeve to reveal the patterns he'd cut into his arm, or would be mumbling what sounded like occult prayers when the three of them got into his car in the morning on the way to school. There was no consistency to it whatsoever; the idea was basically to project that there was some secret regimen of behaviors that Greg adhered to out of spiritual or small-group obligation (the nature of the obligation wasn't as important as the strength of his dedication to it), and for a kid who mostly just hid in his room consuming fringy internet-era media and coming up with ways to alienate people/himself, this was a pretty easy thing to do. Greg didn't have the context for this at the time, of course—he was just being himself, and his behavior was just that, teen routine—but in retrospect, after the fact, these were the shapes it had, that we gave it.

Sarah took note: it was practically ingrained in her. She was carefree with her attention and love, and only had to hear about someone's misfortune or depression before she hurled herself wholeheartedly into it—her passion and talent was for Being There—until whatever problem became hers as well, impressively hers, so bone-deep ran this empathy. She was the sort of person to whom, no matter how well you knew her, you could express the slightest sadness or upset and she would commit hours to talking it through with you, her time and warmth and attention would pool up around you until the problem had disintegrated within it. To those who liked her, Sarah was a girl of boundless enthusiasm and an open heart, a book that wanted to be read. To those who didn't, she was a dilettante, a passionate fool. She had brown hair that curled more the longer it got, and was a beautiful soul. She seemed like the kind of girl who could be convinced to join a cult. She fell for it, of course.

She started by asking Beth, whom we hadn't gotten to yet, either, and while Beth agreed Greg was weird, as she always had, it was in a sisterly way and thus wasn't systematized. Sarah bounced from person to person in this manner until she talked to Claire, who herself was an agent of the dark and had, truth be told, her own separate agenda that was as yet unconnected to ours. "Yeah," Claire said, skimming her eyes over the long line of cars waiting to exit the parking lot. It was second lunch period, when sophomores and juniors ate, and they were outside Adena High. The unlikely bond between the two of them had formed over a shared and wicked love of mid-2000s pop punk, which Sarah had developed before they were friendly but after she learned of Claire's interest in such music, so she was genuinely passionate about it but the passion had a larger goal; anyway, Claire said, "Do you know anything about Half Blessed?"

"I think I've heard the name," Sarah said, which was typically how she engaged with Claire's expansive cultural milieu. Claire at present had a shaggy Chelsea haircut that was dyed blue, and wore a seasonal leather jacket whose pins changed daily, which lent her the kind of standoffish wisdom of someone who inhabits multiple eras. Had you asked Claire, at this point, she wouldn't have called her and Sarah "friends," exactly, nor would she have admitted that her love for pop punk—a genre she had never experienced in its contemporary moment—was anything but ironic. "Is that like a band?" Sarah said.

"I guess it was a band after the fact"—another common answer, there was always an obscure band buried somewhere—"but it's more of a belief system," Claire said.

"A belief system? Like some kind of religious thing?"

Claire shrugged. "I mean, as much as you'd consider iconography 'religious.'" (She used air quotes.) "You'd see plenty of inverted crosses and whatnot but they're not exactly burning churches, not in this decade anyway." She paused and bit her lip, seeming to consider. "I guess it's more of a *society*, is how they would put it, with some magical overtones. Basically teenage illuminati, but more social, like about ostracizing and status-climbing. Or like they'll squat your house and slaughter a pig in the living room, blind fires, stuff like that. Basically it's just a clique but with secret handshakes, sex pacts, and blood rituals—to appeal to the high school crowd."

Obviously Claire had lost sight of her answer to Sarah's question long before the words had finished leaving her mouth, but the important thing was that she had created a context for Sarah's future inquiries (Half Blessed was a group thing, stringent like a religion but not a religion) and, disregarding the rest, had pegged it with a few terms Sarah could use to propel her investigation further, namely "sex pacts and blood rituals," something called "blind fires." Was Greg a part of it? Was that what made him act the way he did? After their lunch period ended at 12:52 Claire drifted off to trigonometry (which she called "trigonometrics" in the spirit of complication) pretty much having forgotten everything she'd said, while Sarah crossed the school's hypotenuse from the south to the west unit and climbed the stairs to her AP English class, where she embarked on further literary analysis and, similarly, traced dense passages of text for their older meanings. Coincidentally, for different reasons, during that same period, Beth's older brother Greg spread a wide swath of his own blood across the stall door in one of the first-floor men's bathrooms. If one was dedicated to the cause, they could have found some geometry in it (or "geometricates"), that the bathroom, the very stall, was directly one floor below the seat in English where Sarah sat. But no one was making those connections at this point.

But before there was Greg—or before Greg became wrapped up in our broader aims—there was David. David was closer to Sarah than most others by virtue of the fact that they had dated for a few heady months, and at the end of it Sarah had even floated the idea of applying to the same colleges the next year. After their split—nominally David's doing, though Sarah had prompted the conversation—they remained superficially friends, because Sarah was committed to a strict pact of non-awkwardness (she was mature that way), meaning they stayed teetering on intimacy: if David ever texted or engaged her in any way, Sarah always responded, exhaustively. David harbored a quiet and largely unspoken desire for revenge, primarily because he'd felt totally out of his depth in the relationship, because while

Sarah appeared to be ready for serious relationship commitment at sixteen, David was still deciding if he should take the SAT again or not this year; he felt his concerns were shallow by comparison, and he resented it. In the months since their breakup last fall, he had been spending more and more of his time on YouTube, drifting quickly through the topsoil of self-improvement and wellness videos into the caverns of crypto-fascist pseudoscience and conspiracy theories catered to his exact demographic. By the time spring came, he was susceptible, his head filled with self-righteous garbage. David was where we started. He was an easy sell. He was also blessed in that he had a sick-ass basement.

So the Monday after we found him, an angsty day at the end of March, David texted Sarah, "Time to talk?" and Sarah replied with no fewer than two exclamations and three questions, saying effectively, yes, absolutely. David, adrenaline running high at the effusiveness of her response, customarily answered one of those questions, and that afternoon they met at Sarah's house after school. They went up to her bedroom because they weren't adults yet and the living room seemed like too formal a place to talk, as if they were going to divide up land or furniture. David made a tactical decision and took the desk chair, Sarah sat on the bed. The walls had recently been painted a dusty blue to Sarah's specifications, and the new color still felt untested, alien.

After a while David ran his hand through his unmanaged curly hair and said he'd had a lot on his mind lately, as if in apology for their lack of contact.

Sarah sensed an opportunity to help out, but she didn't want to assume it was about her. "What is it?"

He fretted and swiveled back and forth in the chair, one sweaty hand clamped on the armrest. He was demonstrably nervous. Sarah thought about putting her mouth on the armrest after he'd gone. "I guess I've been hanging out with these people lately? We've been spending a lot of time together."

"Which people? Like Collin and them?" David's sporadic collection of stoner-y acquaintances; she never understood if they were properly friends, or merely around.

He looked confused. "No, like a group . . . It's not really kids from Adena."

"What kind of a group?"

"It's kind of like a society. Like you have to pass these tests to get in, it's pretty strict. But, Sarah"—she wasn't used to him saying her name, thus the moment felt staged—"it's so addicting, the atmosphere. You should come sometime."

There was that word again, *society*. Sarah tried to ignore the fact that David's other hand was resting absently on his crotch, as was his habit, an easy correction to make but she didn't have the heart for that, not as friends. "What do you do there?" she asked.

He pushed himself up in the chair, let out a breath indicating to Sarah that he had prepared for this, he wanted to spill, and then David, groin in hand, told her exactly what they did.

Afterward, Sarah would reflect that David's description was generally, tonally in line with what Claire had told her about Half Blessed, but that he didn't say anything about the group's structure or intent, nothing about the "society's" rules or foundation or who was or could be a member, or how one joined. Instead, he focused on the acts, and in this you could tell where his brain was (somewhere near his hand), and also that he was totally making it up. And so David delivered into the space between the chair and the lower bed his set of images—the sexual exercises, the trials and performances for the group, the testing and matching, the shared fluids—and Sarah reacted to it, she crossed her legs and let him talk as she blushed furiously, as her skin crawled in embarrassment. She was used to a certain level of internet-derived morbidity from David, she'd seen glimpses of it, but in the months they'd dated, he had never talked like this. They had achieved a certain level of touch but no one had even mentioned sex, their relationship had been strangely prudish in that way, so as she sat there on the bed she felt distinctly two ways: (1) that David clearly had not accumulated any practical sexual experience since they'd broken up (she found herself relieved to know this), but he definitely had imagination, or at least a sordid browser history, and (2) in light of this imagination, she had probably dodged something weird and upsetting. But she let him say his piece, and when twenty minutes later he seemed to be expired of imagery she asked, as if the monologue hadn't just taken place, "And what is it called, this group?" To which David replied with two more grossly combined words, "Burst Marrow." He didn't realize the unexpected relevance this term would carry in Sarah's life.

There was no indication from David, going forward, of why he would have approached Sarah with this sex cult story rather than any of his other friends, what specific advice of hers he sought—he was not sophisticated enough a liar to foreground this. And maybe this, his fundamental honesty even while he poorly lied to her, while he projected these obvious sexual insecurities and not-so-hidden desires, maybe this lack of competent deceit was how they'd ended up dating.

Sarah thought of these generally positive traits as she listened to him. She realized that what he seemed to like about the group (that is, what aspects he chose to emphasize about a group that clearly did not exist) was ultimately quite basic—camaraderie, shared sexual enthusiasm, a boyish fascination with the macabre, a dense set of rules, trade secrets. If there ever was such a group, she thought, David would be the ideal member, it would be good for him. Sarah further realized that while she understood now what had first attracted her to him, his readability and easy-to-satisfy desires—even the hand-on-crotch thing, maybe that was a mark for him as well, that he acted the same in public as he did in private—David was definitely not dating material, and never had been. He was not unique among boys. If his speech was supposed to be an entreaty to her, to have sex with him or get back together or scare her or make her jealous, if it was supposed to make her leap to him—oh, David—then it was a ham-fisted attempt at best. By the end of their conversation the sexual tension on Sarah's end had dissolved completely and left in its wake a puddle of tender feeling, as one has for a stray or cutely deformed animal. She pivoted from his awkward speech and asked David a series of generic, basic-competency questions about the group—how long had he been going? how many people were there? where did they meet?—which David was unable to answer effectively. She told him—feeling a bit like his mother as she said it—that if he truly enjoyed it, as long as no one was getting hurt and everything was consensual and safe (she was referring to STDs and protected sex here but at this point it didn't matter if he understood), then it was probably fine to keep going. "I'm glad you felt you could talk to me about it," she said, standing up.

Surprised, he stood as well, and Sarah noticed again the height advantage she had on him, how his Cavaliers T-shirt was a size too big, and his hair flopped down heavily over his left eye unsupervised, in want of cutting. He really was like a little boy. "I'm glad that we can still be friends," she said. She awkwardly hugged him and clearly felt his erection, which he had talked himself into and which she gamely pretended not to notice. She wore her masks better than he did.

So David failed at his one job, and he and Sarah went their separate ways: David wandered aimlessly down her moneyed suburban street in the manner of one who murders his classmate in broad daylight and then turns up standing mildly in the parking lot an hour later, bloody knife still in hand, and Sarah locked the bedroom door, debated texting Beth, but instead retreated deeper into her bed, her inquiries effectively resolved (there were two separate weirdnesses, David and Greg, Burst Marrow and Half Blessed), and when she came she snorted into the pillow thinking about one of the acts David had described, where the group had two people sit naked back-to-back, unspeaking, and the exercise didn't end until you'd guessed who the other person was by their breathing; you wrote their projected name down on a card in front of you (it was used later).

———

What were Beth and her brother Greg doing during all of this? Well, Beth came home from school as usual, and as she entered the darkened house, Greg—who had been truant that day—launched out at her from behind the front door where he'd been crouched and put her in a chokehold. Beth had grown to expect behavior like this from her older brother and thus knew not to tense too much or struggle when it happened, but just to kind of let her body go limp (she pictured Greg as a goth version of the tiger in *Calvin and Hobbes*), and she let herself fall backward into him same as usual and prostrate him on the ground. This time he held on longer than usual, pressed his fingers tighter, and she lost consciousness briefly before he let go, and on Tuesday she went to school with bruises on her neck, which she chose not to cover up and refused to acknowledge. Sarah noticed and said nothing, but approached her interactions with Beth that day with pointed sympathy; she assumed if Beth wanted to talk about it, she would. But once the rumblings started up around Beth, they persisted, and between fifth and sixth period, as Beth passed the art rooms, she saw Claire in the hallway—with whom Sarah seemed to have bizarrely become friends but whom Beth had never been able to satisfactorily impress—who smiled slyly at her from the corner of her pierced mouth, and Beth knew it was because Claire thought Beth had let someone choke her during sex. She felt enraged, hated Claire for that smile, but that became the story.

Sarah was basically right about David, he was not a competent agent, and in the wake of their meeting he became lost almost immediately when he turned right instead of left after leaving Sarah's driveway. The houses looked exactly the same in that direction, but like someone had shuffled them around just to fuck with him, and he felt deeply provincial in that moment, so fundamentally mapped to his own neighborhood three traffic lights away that he was unable to cope with even the slightest difference. And, further, he felt as if his one opportunity for closure or vengeance or reconciliation (he wasn't sure which he wanted) had just slipped away. By the time he found his way home he'd forgotten he'd invited anyone over, and by extension that anyone was waiting for him in his basement. He went up to his bedroom and fell into a dismal sleep with his earbuds in, a three-hour YouTube video playing, which ran deep into his REM cycle, wracking his dreams, until his phone died. His guests entertained themselves sans David and left the house shortly after nine, and David was never to know that for a time that afternoon his house was occupied without him, without anyone else's knowledge. (He knew his mother would be appalled to learn that when she was out of town he routinely left the house unlocked.) It was a relatively normal day otherwise, but some paths didn't cross where they might have.

The names of David's two friends who left the house were Collin and Mahari. The third, Tyler, told Collin and Mahari at the top of the basement stairs that he'd forgotten something downstairs and was planning to walk the four miles home anyway, and so Collin and Mahari drove off in Collin's old maroon Taurus without him. Collin, whose sister Rachael had killed herself last year, dropped Mahari at his house due west of David's and then drove his car forty minutes in an unwavering straight line north, into the southern Ohio countryside. He didn't have a meeting that night—that was only twice a week—but he didn't want to arrive home while his parents were still downstairs, and just being in proximity of HBCC calmed him down. He sat in the otherwise-empty parking lot in his car, staring into the adjacent field, the inky blue sky broken by black, smoking a bowl and practicing the technique he'd learned: he blurred his vision, separated the colors until they drifted in disparate blocks across his vision, as his eyes teared, until the world before him was neatly dismantled. The house, the empty bedroom, his mother and father, his drive to school, his favored parking lots: grooves he'd long run into the road, a network of blocks and patterns drawn over his life. He watched the colors before him break apart, and with them, his thoughts seemed to disperse, too, to lose their edges and bleed into the background. Was that the same thing as the pain dispersing? If Rachael wasn't a presence, was not there in the world, how could she affect him? He didn't know anymore. After half an hour he drove back the way he'd come, forty-eight minutes, the route now so familiar to him he could have done it with his eyes closed; he no longer worried about getting pulled over—he'd never seen a cop in these twenty miles.

He arrived home just after eleven, and by then the house was dark. *Another night passed*, he thought, another night he didn't have to sit across from her empty chair, waiting in silence to be dismissed.

South of Collin's house, back in David's basement, instead of heading home, Tyler decided to stay. Tyler was a hardcore kid who hated all melody. People liked him for his deadpan humor and the general quietude that implied wisdom, but were also scared of him because he seemed to experience the world as static: everything around him carried the same weight, which was no weight at all. He was detached and unreadable, almost clinically pale, with always-buzzed blond hair and rotating band shirts he'd stopped accumulating in ninth grade (now: Circle Jerks). Had he lived in a larger town, he would have worried about looking like a nazi, but the punk scene here wasn't big enough to draw these distinctions. He wore headphones constantly but responded to cues as if there were nothing playing; his ambience was sub-two-minute thrashers one after the other after the other, death metal, and *Dopesmoker*. His peers compensated around him by overacting, laughing loudly at his presumed jokes to prove they were worthy, but few engaged him directly, which he was fine with; in many ways he had the air of a sociopath, a veil drawn. He was left to himself. He was not on our radar yet.

For a while Tyler played videogames with the volume turned down low—an enormous TV was one of the perks of David's basement. He kept his earbuds in, and together the two pieces of equipment formed a layered blanket of sound, a kind of sonic lake in which he floated. After a couple of hours he put the controller aside and stretched, let his body slide from the beleaguered vinyl couch onto the carpet. He stared at the ceiling. The level immediately above him was empty, and the level above that held David, asleep. Tyler absently tapped at his phone to change the music; the time signature changed.

As mentioned, David's basement was basically a house in itself, because for several years a middle-aged couple had lived there and paid rent to help David's mom afford the mortgage. When she was finished paying it off and owned the property completely, she promptly, politely evicted them, and the basement became a lair for her then-pubescent son. The wheels of capitalism turned. And though the tenants were long gone, the basement remained more or less how its former residents had left it: the bedroom still had its Van Gogh prints on the wall, its random selection of books left over from David's mom's law school days, the kitchen with its mosaic splash guard (theme of rooster), the middle-class niceness was more or less preserved. Tyler remembered the first time David had brought him down here, he'd thought it was nicer than his own house. Now he stood and went through the bedroom to the fridge in the basement kitchen. He took a beer from its massacre-like interior—it was almost pathetically clear which parts of the basement David had touched in his tenure there. Tyler looked over the bed in the bedroom, neatly made, which David hadn't co-opted even at all. (In David's mind, it was still the resting place of someone else.) Tyler noted the claw-footed vanity desk; an antique, human-sized wooden chest by the window; a table at the foot of the bed ornately painted with scenes of fancy country life. Possessions, he suspected, handed down over generations, like you'd find in a museum, stowed here in a room no one used. He went back to the couch, to the teen area, and slid to the floor. He found David's laptop sitting within reach, its hibernation light slowly pulsing. He pulled it toward him and opened it up to find David was one of those people who left himself perpetually logged in to everything. Tyler bounced back and forth between David's email and his social media accounts; he sent ominous emails that drew heavily from the lyrics of the band he was listening to and made changes to David's Facebook. He posted videos from dark corners of the internet and sent messages to random friends; he posted a set of grisly photos that was almost instantly deleted. Before he shut the computer again, he changed David's passwords and the email addresses associated with account recovery to his own. He texted his girlfriend, Rhea, and told her not to expect him at school the next day, or indeed for the rest of the week: "I'm trying out a new house," he wrote. By this time it was about 2:30 a.m.

Tyler did another lap around the basement to check his exit options. Along the eastern wall of the living room was the carpeted staircase to the house's foyer on the first floor, beside the base of the staircase was the door to the bedroom, and through the north door of the living room was an unfinished area that comprised a weight room and workshop, which led to the back hallway. Past the washing machine and dryer in this hallway was a separate entrance, the door of which opened onto an outdoor concrete staircase leading up to the backyard. The back hallway also accessed the kitchen, which then led back to the bedroom, so the whole basement comprised a loop, with the staircase to the first floor at its center. The windows, from outside, were just below ground level; only the bedroom windows were easily opened. Tyler ensured that both exits from the basement were locked from the inside, pissed in the bathroom—evidence of David spattered everywhere—took a soda from the fridge, and returned to the couch. He opened up David's laptop again. All was quiet—David's friends were still asleep. He realized there was no cord down here to recharge the laptop. He turned off the computer to conserve power and stretched himself out on the couch. Like David, he didn't think of using the bed in the other room.

Tyler did not go to school the next morning, just as he'd promised; in fact, he did not leave David's basement for the next eighteen days. Across town, east of Tyler's given neighborhood, Beth's older brother Greg awoke and bloodied his hands for the coming day.

Around noon that day, in response to Tyler's text from the previous night, Rhea replied with a single word: "Godspeed."

———

Two of the three videos Tyler posted were flagged and systematically taken down before many people saw them, but one person who did was Beth. Her goal that night was to stay up as late as physically possible to ensure the next day passed in a fog, and in retrospect she would remember little about it. She had lain in bed, waiting for Greg's light to go white and dormant in the next room, and when it finally did, she turned to her phone. The first video, which she didn't watch until the end, was of a procession of about twelve ordinary-looking people into an anonymous room lit in yellow, where they stood in a ring. The shot was static from an upper corner of the room, like footage from a security camera. A man in the center, dressed in a monkish robe, walked slowly past each person in turn, speaking quietly, his voice muffled, around the entire group. When he had spoken to each one, he went to the center of the circle. He clapped his hands once, and all but two members of the group collapsed onto the floor, as if they'd been suddenly shut down. The two who remained standing (she couldn't make out faces, but it was a middle-aged bald man in a polo shirt and a blond woman in cutoffs, who looked younger) clearly weren't expecting it—they looked frantically around, at each other, at the man in the center. He knelt and left something on the floor between them, then left the center of the circle, stepping over the prostrate bodies. The man and woman both made for the object at once; they met each other in the middle with an audible clap of flesh. The man elbowed the woman in the face, she recoiled, and he brandished whatever he'd taken off the floor. She dived at him and they squirmed on the floor as she tried to wrest it from him. There was very little sound broadcast up through the phone's tiny speaker—distant, staggered breathing, a grunt. The bodies lay still around them, and the leader stood at the far wall, observing. Beth stopped the video a minute before its end, the man and woman tangled at the center of the room, their limbs shuffling in conflict, the blurry quality of the footage making their bodies indistinguishable from each other. She scrolled immediately to the second video, prepared to stop it as soon as it started playing, her thumb hovering over the screen: the camera was focused on a young man, five or six years older than her—an adult—twenty-one or twenty-two, maybe, wearing glasses, sitting in a cell-like room. He sat still for a while, ten seconds or so (she had turned the volume off at this point), and then slammed his head onto the metal table before him, three times. Beth felt like she could almost hear it. When he raised his head back up his forehead was a splotchy red, his glasses shattered but still clinging to his face. He turned slowly to the wall at his right, looking furious, and bashed his face into the concrete; when he drew back the color was even angrier, incipient blood, like when you get scraped on gravel, his nose looked crooked, the glasses were gone. He ran his hand down his face; his fingers drew the blood out and smeared it. Beth stopped the video. The third was a rapey blowjob video where the person giving the blowjob was wearing a rubber monster mask, which she saw approximately one second of; the sound somehow jumped back on when she clicked the thumbnail and she heard this brief muffled gargle she knew she would never be able to forget. She deleted her Facebook account and turned off her phone—shut it completely down—and true to her wish she did not sleep that night, and by the time she arrived at school the next morning, the bruise on her neck a harsh purple, she had no thought for it whatsoever, it'd been subsumed into the violence of the content on her phone, like an allergic rash.

Claire also saw the videos, which was how Sarah found out about them, but the way Claire relayed this was absent the gravity Beth would have brought to it, because not only did Claire not take David seriously as a person—when she learned Sarah and David had dated she'd exclaimed, "*Him?*," unable to conceal her surprise—but she had also seen one of the videos before, and probably could have found the other two in about thirty seconds; they were shallow internet. This was how she told Sarah, the next day at lunch, in their spot beside the school: "Did you see those videos David posted on Facebook last night? Looks like you got off a sinking ship."

"What were they?"

"Just cult stuff and gag porn. I think your buddy got hacked."

"He's posting porn on Facebook?" Sarah pulled out her phone.

"Shitty porn."

Her feed was still full of commentary about the mass shooting in Cincinnati two days earlier. She registered it for a few seconds, a beat of idle horror, and then she found David's account; he'd changed his profile photo to a random arcane symbol on black—she thought vaguely of an ankh, or an abstracted eye—but by this point, only the face-bashing video was left. "I don't see any porn. What's Viceroy?"

"Hardcore band," Claire said. "They're pretty good."

Sarah had also received a message via Facebook from David last night at around 2:00 a.m.; she saw part of it in the preview pane, "They never found . . ." but hesitated before opening it, afraid to acknowledge she'd seen it. Her mind filled the blank: *the body. The head.* They hadn't used Messenger since they'd first become friends, before they had each other's numbers. Like a past David. "He sent me a message," she said.

"What does it say?"

She thumbed it open because Claire had asked. Her

heart fluttered a second. *"They never found the bullet. That's it."*

Claire chewed the inside of her mouth, sifting through her stores of pop- and counterculture for a possible referent. She seemed to come up blank, because she eventually shrugged and stepped off the curb. "I think he got hacked."

Sarah waffled on telling her about the conversation she'd had with David the day before about Half Blessed; it was an impulse to protect what remained of David's dignity versus her innate desire to spill everything. She decided to keep it to herself for now—she wanted to connect the strands on her own, and this information could be saved for later, when it might be worth something. Either way, a decision had been made: because Claire had come to her with this new David information, not Beth, Claire thereby became by default its primary source, the line against which future data and opinions about David would need to be checked. Beth, through no fault of her own, by her silence thus became a secondary source for this issue, unlikely to be consulted. In any event, Sarah took her leave and an hour later sent the vaguest possible text to David. She had planned to let him make the next move, but got panicked by the lapse in technology, the way the message he'd sent melded instantly with the violent news, became part of the same set of data; she checked his profile throughout the day but the video didn't disappear. She texted him: "Everything ok?" She knew she was setting a precedent by doing so, she was continuing a conversation she ought probably to end, but her curiosity—no, her empathy—got the better of her.

—

David received the message like he was receiving every scrap of communication transmitted to him that day—like a blow to his person out of nowhere, and for no discernible reason. It winded him. It drove home the idea that he had done something terribly wrong, he was acting irrationally, and his inability to see how or why was making it worse. He stewed in the speech he'd given to Sarah the day before, the images, and he felt drowned under the weight of them, as well as that of a broken promise, because our scheme hadn't worked, not at all: he could tell in the moment she didn't believe a word of it, and the longer he had talked, the more alone he felt, the bigger grew the disaster that was his person, the more he thought his brief relationship with Sarah was the one shot he'd had. He thought he knew her well enough to know she wouldn't tell other people, but he couldn't shake the feeling that they knew regardless, they knew all of him, all his dirty secrets, and they were conspiring. He was unable to access his email on his phone, or any of his social media, and it all built up together into this impression that he'd been locked out of his own life, and behind the door, its previous inhabitants were scheming against him.

By the end of third period—where no one had spoken

to him at all, it was as if he'd been invisible—it was clear David was about to fall apart, or internally combust, there was nothing to stop it. He opened his locker, where he'd first seen the symbol the week before, and slammed his right hand in the door, and the fact that four people saw him do it meant nothing and everything, it was both not enough and far too many. He let his fucked-up hand carry him through the rest of the day, letting its insistent pain guide his thoughts, and steadily his fingers took on a gnarled, tree-like aspect and became a horrible red. He let this be his excuse whenever someone looked at him the wrong way. Even Beth—on whom he maintained a low-key crush and with whom he'd always been moderate to mild friends, or at least they'd remained friendly after he and Sarah broke up—when he saw her during fifth period, a nasty-looking bruise on her neck, he'd raised his mangled hand in acknowledgment of their shared pain, and she turned away visibly disgusted, and by this base failure of empathy (neck bruise for fucked-up hand), he was finished. Between sixth and seventh period he went into a bathroom stall—incidentally the same one in which Greg had deposited his blood the week before—and rolled his knuckles between the edge of the door and the stall until he heard a nauseating crack, thinking as he did so that this probably nullified the performance of any hobby that might bring relief from this garbage day, and taking this as part of his punishment as well.

He arrived home only to find the metaphor was literally true: when he tried the door in the foyer, he discovered he was locked out of the basement. He walked outside and around the house to the backyard and tried via the back door at the base of the steps, but that was locked, too. His will puddled around his feet. Standing dejected outside the locked gates of his own kingdom—no one else would be home again for days, probably weeks, his mother was off doing depositions, and he doubted whether anyone even knew where a spare key was, in addition to his doubts about his ability and the overall efficacy of trying to break the door down—this was the end of our journey with David, guileless David. He knew he could have called a locksmith, could call customer support on his accounts, but the idea seemed exhausting, and besides, maybe it meant something: maybe it was telling him to just check out for a while. He didn't mention it when his mother called that evening, and thereafter he forgot it should have been news at all. He'd spent the first eleven years of his life without access to the basement, after all. As he had the day before, he climbed the stairs to his bedroom, sealed himself in, and collapsed on the bed. We left him there.

At this stage, who wasn't going to school was as important as who was. In the days that followed, David, despite everything, continued to go, mostly because in absence of his basement the house offered little for him to do. Tyler, ensconced as he was in that basement, did not. Claire attended regularly; it was important for her social program. Greg and Beth changed places: the day after she first left the house with the bruise, Beth stopped going to school, she gave herself an illness, and Greg—unable to bear the idea of them both skulking around the house all day— begrudgingly took her place. Thus, after what had been a dicey stretch of attendance for him, Greg's routine of driving Sarah to school was reinstated, and because Beth was skipping for the time being, Sarah and Greg went alone. This was their first period of significant, one-on-one overlap.

Meanwhile, David's friend or associate Mahari's father was having construction done on their kitchen, extending it into the backyard and installing new countertops, and somewhere during all of the in-and-out a stray dog entered the kitchen, which the construction workers mistook for the family pet. They brought it treats and let it roam around the house for the next three or four days; it was only later in the week, when the contractor was chatting with Mahari's father, that he said, "That's a nice dog you have—what's his name?" and Mahari's father replied that they didn't have a dog, upon which the contractor led him back to the man's suddenly unfamiliar kitchen and revealed to him that now, more or less, they did. Mahari's father didn't tell Mahari or Mahari's younger brother about the stray until the kitchen was finished and they were sitting at the new table, long after the dog had been banished into the neighborhood at large. The dog had appeared during the same week Mahari had entered the bathroom one morning and found his little brother, who was nine, crouched with his mouth wrapped around the brass doorknob. "What the fuck are you doing?" he yelled as he pulled him off. His little brother swirled his tongue around in his mouth. "I like the taste," he said. "That's disgusting, there's bacteria all over that knob. You'll get a parasite," Mahari said, but after the fact he couldn't rid himself of the image: it disturbed him, it was like what you'd see at a gruesome and bizarre crime scene, or on one of those reality shows about shut-ins dying awful deaths alone. In hindsight, Mahari had seen the dog once while it was living in their house—he'd been coming out of his room early in the morning and seen its tail as it disappeared down the stairs—but he'd assumed it was just his imagination, the aftermath of a dream, and a second later it was gone.

But these were just happenings, currents of suburbia; they were isolated from the events at hand.

In reality, Greg and Sarah already had a lot in common, and after the awkward silence of their first day driving to school without Beth—Sarah had taken the back seat by default and left Greg alienated in the front like a chauffeur—they found that conversation came easily between them. They shared an off-kilter sense of humor, and they had a bunch of people, a town, and a socioeconomic level in common, after all, as well as the broad cultural strata that implied, and over the next few days Sarah felt like she was making progress—whatever that was—and that her graduation to the shotgun seat foretold something positive. Moreover, some of Greg's behavior she'd noticed over the past few weeks, and which had originally brought her to Claire, now started to disappear—maybe it had truly been random to begin with, or specifically designed to make her notice him—and faintly Sarah began to wonder if maybe there was something behind this goth thing. She realized that, up to this point, her knowledge of Greg had come mostly secondhand, as filtered through Beth. She had noticed the way he had with his sister—a sort of casual indifference marked with spikes of annoyance or anger, always very *present* to Beth, at the back or forefront of her mind; she talked about him carefully, impartially, like he was always nearby, even when he wasn't—but this interpretation had come through her lens as Beth's friend, with Greg as a visitor to their world. She thought now that maybe this hadn't been the whole story, that maybe she and Greg could know each other beyond the role of older brother, passenger, sister's friend. Maybe that was growing up, she thought, in noticing—in *allowing* these perspectives to shift and develop. She wondered if beneath the dye he was genuinely as blond as Beth. And on the fourth day that he drove her to school alone, a Monday, she noticed he hadn't painted his nails, in fact seemed to have cleaned them completely, and she burst out, "Greg! Your fingernails are naked!" and he clapped a faux-shocked hand to his pretty mouth and exclaimed, "By George! What *will* people think of me?" and his voice produced in a register she'd never heard—which no one had probably heard in a long time—and Sarah felt a tightening in her chest; she realized concretely her effect, the change she could make in him—that little dash of light.

For the last month of the three months they were dating the preceding autumn, Sarah and David met up two or three times a week to ostensibly do their homework at a local coffee shop. They would spread their possessions out over two tables and alternately chat, read, or mess with their laptops or phones. No work was ever truly accomplished in these sessions, which could last three or four hours, but Sarah liked that it had become their routine, that the coffee shop was relatively free of distractions in a way their houses weren't, and the shared proximity lent a sense of companionship she felt was essential in a long-term relationship. It was a testing ground, in a way. For someone whose friendships had been fostered in bedrooms, living rooms, backyards, and at school, there was something important, undoubtedly *mature* about getting into his car at the end of the school day and going somewhere else, in allowing David to drive her across town for these quotidian, unsupervised hours. When she had things she wanted to say to David—like, actually *say*, face-to-face—she said them here. This was one such day.

There were three places they went to: the Starbucks, the other Starbucks, and the local chain, Boston Stoker. On this day, last October, they were at the other Starbucks, the one by the mall. The whipped cream on top of their drinks was dressed in orange and brown sprinkles. David had emptied the contents of his backpack onto the table, but had been clicking at his laptop for nearly an hour, the books untouched, while Sarah repeatedly reread the first page of an essay for her European history class. As always, David had paid for their drinks, which seemed like a grand gesture, except Sarah knew it wasn't money he had meaningfully earned, but that came from "a jar" in his pantry, which was periodically refilled and meant to be used, he told her, "for emergencies." It had haunted her for weeks, this jar. She'd been thinking about how to bring it up. *Are you thinking ahead in the same way I am?* she wanted to ask. Instead she asked, admittedly a little obliquely to her larger point: "Do you want to do something this weekend?"

David looked up from his laptop, where he was reading election news on a right-wing conspiracy site in a private browser, so it theoretically wouldn't start polluting his search results. He realized his internet trajectory had brought him to the edge of a dark void, a flood of information he didn't particularly want, but couldn't help registering as it surged past him. Anyway, he took the question at its basic level, he shrugged and said, "Did you want to hang out?"

Did she want to hang out: like he'd already made other plans. She regretted the way she automatically parsed the phrasing. "Not if you already have plans," Sarah said.

"No, I don't."

Sarah left it for a second, waited for him to reciprocate. She looked around at the other tables, populated in twos and fours, including other Adena kids, where conversation seemed vibrant, alive, while she tried to drag words out of her boyfriend over this disconsolate heap of stuff. "Do *you* want to hang out?"

"Yeah, if you do." He dug his straw into the congealed whipped cream at the bottom of his cup and sucked it off the tip.

"Okay."

In the moment she wanted to rescind the offer: he had taken too long to get there, and his assent felt contingent on her enthusiasm. But the thing was, she *did* want to hang out with him, to be around him. Sarah wasn't sure why, but she felt somehow inexplicably *worse* when she wasn't with him, when they weren't in front of each other, live, communicating with all of their bodies. She tried to imagine this conversation if they'd been texting. "Maybe we could do something Halloweeny," she said.

"I would *love* that," he said, pulling himself up in the chair.

Sarah blushed, and he yawned—an unruly yawn, where he leaned back in his chair and stretched his arms to either side—and his hoodie lifted and she glimpsed the band of his boxers against his flat stomach. She felt a twinge of desire. That metabolism. He didn't even exercise, he just dressed like an athlete. Everything just slid right through him. What did his father look like? What did his asshole look like?

When his chair landed back on four legs his attention was fully on her; she felt her cheeks warm, despite herself. She seemed to have struck at a source of rare energy.

"I read about this haunted house in Cleveland, the Black House," he said. "Have you heard of it?"

"I don't think so."

"It's pitch-black. You have to go through it alone. They make you sign a waiver before they let you in. They, like, gag you and put a bag over your head and tie you up and simulate drowning you. You have to crawl through trash and shit. It's supposed to be utterly debasing and intense." He was balanced on two legs of the chair again, holding the edge of the table. "Like, Abu Ghraib–style techniques."

Utterly debasing—not a phrase he'd invented. A phrase that existed outside of this conversation, borrowed from another source. This description, his naked enthusiasm: it was like she'd stumbled onto this secret package of data within him that was only revealed when she prodded him in the right way. Was this what he wanted, at his core, for himself, for her? To be gagged and scared shitless— *debased*? And if that was there, what else was? What other little sacs of acidic bile were snarled up in that compact frame, waiting for her to pierce? What did he believe? What did he know about Abu Ghraib? What were his fantasies? What did he think about at night, in his bedroom, in the minutes just before he fell asleep? She realized she'd made an unconscious decision, at some point in the past, to never ask him about politics, and wondered what had prompted it.

He was still talking about the Black House. "You have to be twenty-one, though. Maybe we could get fake IDs, or—"

"David," she interrupted, her legs crossed tightly under the table. "Do you ever think about the future?"

He stopped speaking and clammed up again, as surely as twisting off a faucet, and in this, she thought she knew what she needed to know. They broke up two weeks later, at the other Starbucks, but not before she had surrendered forty dollars of her own money, along with forty dollars of jar money, for David to procure their fake IDs; she supposed until that point she was still pursuing the source of the information she'd unlocked. Their last conversation had gone the same way, striking away at his carapace until the answer squirted out: *It's not working. I can't do this anymore.* She had been so relieved that she cried. At the end of it David slid the suspiciously thick plastic card facedown across the table as if returning her independence: she'd thought at the time it was almost too neat a metaphor, and she sat there at the Starbucks window after David drove off, waiting for her mother to pick her up, feeling un-sad but also deprived, literally a card-carrying adult, but also finally with an answer to the question she'd asked weeks before: Do you ever think about the future?

It's pitch-black. You have to go through it alone.

I'LL BET YOU PRAY FOR SILENCE I'LL BET YOU
WAKE UP SCREAMING I'LL BET YOU RUIN EVERY-
THING EVERYONE AROUND YOU YOUR PARENTS
YOUR SISTER SARAH I'LL BET YOU D

The voice had begun to speak to him when he was eleven
years old. Greg was only able to peg it to this age in retrospect, a year later, after he started therapy. There was no
particular night he remembered it starting; it was a pattern
that had just gradually become embedded in his process
of falling asleep. The conversations always began in the
same way. He would be lying there, having cleared his
head from the day, and then he would hear, from close by,
someone say his name: "Greg."

If he didn't answer, the voice would become more insistent. "Greg. *Greg. Greg.* GREG." It would continue saying his name until he responded, until Greg said, "What?"
or gave some other spoken acknowledgment. He would
have to answer out loud, too, even if just in a whisper—
Greg would actually have to hear himself—or else the

voice would just keep repeating his name, louder and louder and at different points around his head, giving the illusion the voice was multiplying, encircling him, until he answered. He recognized the voice vaguely as his own—or some version of his own—and the best way he could describe hearing it was as if through really nice headphones, where it was clear the sound was only audible to you and wasn't subject to distance or echo or the acoustics of the room, but was nonetheless real and voluminous and in motion; he had never really thought, for example, someone was standing next to the bed talking to him. He knew it came, in some way, from within him.

Sometimes all he had to do was answer to his name— "What?"—and the voice would stop. But other times it wouldn't: it would ask him questions ("Who did you talk to today?" "How long did you sleep?" "Where is your sister?") which he had to answer aloud, one by one, until eventually, at a certain arbitrary point, the voice would fall silent. The quality of his response didn't matter so much as that the responses kept coming—in this way, he quickly learned, it was like talking to a therapist—and Greg only had to divulge the level of information he wanted to. He knew the questions must be generated from somewhere in his being, and for a while there was a certain satisfaction in knowing some iteration of this review would probably come at the end of the day, asking him to account for his time on earth, to take stock of everything around him. For that same while, he believed it to be a natural

phenomenon—the work of a particularly directed con-
science, maybe—the only real serviceable difference being that the voice seemed to come from outside of his
head, he heard it like someone else was talking to him,
and thus, by this one sensory slip, tripped into the realm of
"auditory hallucination."

And truth be told he probably would not have gone to
anyone about it at all had the voice not gradually started
bleeding into the day. He would be standing at his locker
(it was sixth grade at this point, so he had a locker now) or
working on a test in a silently packed classroom and suddenly he would hear his name: "Greg. *Greg.*" And he
would be obliged to answer—with the quietest whisper he
could muster—or it would never quit. Usually it was just a
few basic questions, but sometimes Greg would lose whole
class periods dealing with the voice, all knotted up with
tension at the back of the classroom, trying to gauge how
many times he could withhold on each question before
the shouting became too much to bear, and he'd have to
utter his response, and pray no one else heard him.

So at twelve Greg began seeing a psychiatrist/therapist
combo (weekly therapist, monthly psychiatrist) and the
regimen of antidepressants he understood to be traditional
of his age. In accordance with the prescriptions, the voice
spiked and waned at different times of the day along with
his mood, appetite, weight, and acne. Gradually, he retreated into himself, into darkwave: he found cultural signifiers to match the vertiginous peaks and valleys of his

daily experience, a span of diagnoses from bipolar disorder to schizophrenia to clinical depression. None of them were exactly right, or exactly wrong, his behaviors always just out of pace of the next—he cut when he was bored, binged when he was at his most underweight, obsessed about his skin when he was otherwise at his most lethargic. It had gotten especially bad when he was sixteen, last year, the worst year, but then they'd finally stumbled on what seemed to be the magic combination—Seroquel! biweekly hypnosis!—and since then his senior year had been relatively quiet. It had pushed the voice back to nights, at least, so it was only then that he had to worry about it, and *worry* was probably overstating—it was just a voice, adding its particular texture to the chorus of other voices that populated his world.

But then recently, with this advent of Sarah, the voice had changed. He'd known Sarah since eighth grade, when she was in seventh and Beth was in sixth, but only via his sister; they had never really interacted one-on-one, and even driving them both to school once Beth started at Adena he'd felt like he was part of a different world, so Sarah hadn't fully been a person to him yet. Over the last few weeks, before their solo rides, Greg had liked the idea of messing with her by varying his goth routine in the way any older brother enjoys low-key tormenting his younger sister's friends, nothing had really prompted it, but eventually it had triggered a change in him—or had opened him up to a change, more accurately—something he couldn't identify at first but which took hold in the voice he heard every night. After one of those days when he'd gone all out and cut the back of his hands—as David surrendered the last of his initiative across town, cradling his splintered fingers—that was when we found him. We were hidden within the routine processing at the end of the day, a shift from subject to object: that internal voice he'd held for years—it became ours. He was already thinking about her. He was lying in bed when the voice spoke, as usual: "Greg."

"What?" he whispered. He blinked and resolved the dark shape on the ceiling, a black arc with a circle inside. Beth, on one of her coughing binges again, was hacking up a lung next door. He worried he was inadvertently responsible for this, from when he'd jumped out and throttled her the day before; there were times when he squeezed too hard, he knew, when his moods got the better of him, when his expression could be clearer. By morning, the guilt would have dissipated, as it always did. He knew this, too. Everything was worse at night.

"Who did you talk to today?" the voice asked.

"Beth. Ezra. Michael. Mrs. Riser. Molly and Fox. Mom."

"Who else?"

Greg paused. The voice had never asked for additional information before, had never taken his answer at less than face value—usually he would give his answer, no matter how cursory or incomplete, and it would move on to the next question. His skin prickled with heat and anxiety.

"Who else?" it said again, from somewhere near the center of his head.

"I don't know."

"*Who else?*" By his left ear.

Greg closed his eyes. Why did he have trouble admitting it, even to himself? "Sarah. In the car."

"What did you say to her?"

Greg turned over on his side. The voice seemed to follow him magnetically, it came next in his exposed ear. "What did you say to her?"

"I think as we were getting out of the car I said something like, 'The *y* is an invented part of the alphabet.' That was it." He took a breath; for some reason, he felt disgusting revealing this memory, a moment among many he'd assumed, between the two of them, would simply disappear unreported.

"Did your sister hear you say that?"

Greg looked at his phone—it was 1:23 a.m. He wondered if he could delay his answers long enough to make it to daylight, if this would make the voice abate. A side effect of his latest prescription relegating the voice back to the night had been to assign it a sense of falseness, to make it seem more like a dream. He told himself he could hold it off.

"Did your sister hear you say that?"

He automatically answered, "No," and then clamped his hand over his mouth, angry that he'd given in right away, he had compromised a minute of holding out. The voice rested smugly for a moment, and then said, "What was Sarah wearing?"

Greg grabbed his earbuds from the bedside table and jammed them into his ears. The questions felt invasive, overly personal; it was a detail he hadn't noticed, would be ashamed to have noticed. He turned on noise, no melody. The voice came from directly behind him, as clear as if the music didn't exist: "What was Sarah wearing?"

He held his hands over his ears, pushed the earbuds in further, knowing this was useless. He was stuck fast to his sheets; he knew that no matter what happened, in the morning when it was over he would tell himself it was less bad than it was, it was endurable. "What was Sarah wearing?"

"I don't know."

"What was Sarah wearing?"

He turned his effort to controlling his breathing, he rolled over onto his back and folded down the sheet across his middle, smoothed it out. "What was Sarah wearing?"

He didn't answer. He picked up his phone. It was 1:26.

"What was Sarah wearing?"

He scrolled through Instagram but couldn't read any of the text. He flicked incidentally by a photo—he felt his stomach pitch—of Sarah, via someone else. He registered her and then tried to immediately evaporate the memory of doing so, but he couldn't: in his mind, it was constructed of five flashing instances of skin—her face and neck, her two hands, her left shoulder, and a strip between her shirt and jeans. "*What was Sarah wearing?*"

He blanked the phone and his head again. The voice got louder, approached shouting. "*What was Sarah wearing?*"

It was screaming. "WHAT WAS SARAH WEARING?" He imagined the whole house awake, the whole neighborhood.

"WHAT WAS SARAH WEARING?

"WHAT WAS SARAH WEARING?

"*WHAT WAS SARAH WEARING?*

"*WHAT WAS SARAH WEARING?*"

Tears came sideways out of Greg's eyes and slid down the sides of his face. "A white-and-black-striped sweater," he said, trance-like. "A teal undershirt. Skinny jeans. Converse."

"Did you see her again after you drove her to school?"

He let his breath out slowly; he felt his remaining energy draining out of him with it. He spoke before the voice could ask again, he relented to it: "Yes."

"When?"

He answered again.

"Did she see you?"

And again after that.

The voice had more questions, and, thereafter, Greg answered them all.

The following day, when it did seem like a bad dream,

he realized what the difference in the voice had been, why it had felt so oppressive. It was no longer a mechanism he could more or less mechanically satisfy, or treat like a tic; now it was gathering information. The voice was listening, and it wanted something from him.

Beth fell sicker, her cough became more wretched. When he opened her door that morning in his pajama pants and long sleeves, to see if she was coming down-stairs, the lamp at her bedside table threw the bruise on her neck into almost-black, if anything worse than the day before. He flinched and almost took a step back in the doorway, like it was a sign of contagion; it simply didn't occur to him that he'd had anything to do with it. "You staying home today?" he asked.

She gave a pronounced cough. "Yeah."

"Okay," he said. "I'll have Mom call."

"Thanks."

He closed the door and left her alone. That morning, a Wednesday, Greg drove Sarah to school alone for the first time. The voice never changed back.

—

Tyler settled deeper into his new environment. By 4:00 p.m. of his first full day in the basement—a time he could only ascertain by looking at a screen, or by peering up into the ivy through the prison-style windows in the bedroom and speculating—Tyler had determined he already kind of hated it here, he was unhappy with the tonal makeup of the basement. He didn't think about how long he was planning to stay, he had no plan at all, but turned his existence there into an exercise to pass the time, a contest of inertia, numbers he could report to himself. Each block of time was part of a larger block, and larger blocks were preferable to smaller ones: a week was better than three days, a day was better than thirteen hours, an hour was better than forty minutes, etc. He drew barriers: going upstairs, opening the door to the outside, opening his mouth, these would all set the clock back to zero. He played the first hour of a videogame once, then a dozen times more, until he felt he could press the buttons on the controller without looking at the screen, it had the same net result, he could put that part of his attention elsewhere while he did it. He repeated a twenty-two-minute episode of television he chose at random until he had memorized most of the dialogue; he muted it and tested himself, and every time he fucked up, he started over. He imagined filling his head with trash, information he could never possibly need to relate; he imagined the hackneyed dialogue and laugh track slowly rotting like compost, going to soil. Eventually, he left the TV to run muted. He listened to the same hardcore album forty times, cycling on repeat; it moved in counterbalance to the beats on TV. Alternately, the TV and the music seemed weirdly synchronized and totally at odds, both like the show had been edited to respond to his musical norms and like the music caused all existing visual structures to break down—he couldn't decide which. In time, he felt as if he had experienced this album with every image that could ever be viewed on that screen, with every moment of the day, he had exhausted its sensory possibilities and the two media would henceforth be linked inextricably. He summoned for a while the image of a vast, solitary black tower on a soupy, yellowish plain, a tower that had sprouted from this cultural mash. He spent time wondering where the image had come from, where he had seen it before, had the vague idea to record it somewhere but couldn't locate the means to make it happen; he needed paper—a sketch pad would be best, at least 50 lb paper—a charcoal pencil, and these tools were not immediately available to him, thus the act was impossible. And when the time allocated to this image expired, crossed into its next largest block, he lost it, the moment of inspiration was subsumed and dissolved and he didn't even need to move his hands. Tyler felt his heartbeat slowing, as if his body were preparing for hibernation, preserving its energy stores. He opened the freezer in the kitchen and pried out a frosty box of pizza rolls; there was a stratified collection of similar boxes in the back, older as you went deeper. He let these thaw on the counter for three hours or so, until they were soft enough to chew. He felt incapable of making productive efforts, of thinking of anything effectual he had ever done. He regretted that he hadn't brought any weed. Every couple of nights, always after 2:00 a.m.—when he felt the day was complete, for some reason he always left it until a certain point at night, as if the rest of his time comprised productive activity, whereas this was frivolous hobby—he would reboot David's computer (the battery was quickly draining), log back into David's Facebook account, and send more messages, a few at a time. He posted more videos. There was no feedback, no rebuttal. David's internet friends quietly divested this abrasive new online persona. He texted with Rhea as if on a time delay, the two of them responding to each other after long intervals, about nothing. Mahari, Collin, a handful of others texted Tyler, wondering where he'd gone—or if not wondering, doing their due diligence to confirm he wasn't dead—and he didn't answer them, and no one followed up; these were the expectations he had set long ago.

Around midnight on his second night, the door at the top of the stairs rattled briefly above him. Tyler jolted upright on the couch, briefly filled with adrenal energy. It was a momentary interruption: Tyler's reading was of someone absently checking a door to confirm it was still locked, that this was now taken as fact. For kicks, he texted David: "what's up."

He heard David ascend the stairs to the second floor. Twenty minutes later, David texted back: "nm, u?"

Tyler ignored it. He marveled at David's apathy. He had never been in a part of David's house that wasn't the basement. Did he not even miss his computer?

So this is happening, Tyler thought. Upstairs, David ceded the basement to the locked door.

———

Nightly, Greg delivered his reports. The questions were about Sarah, but also about others—people he knew, as well as those he didn't know, or hadn't been able to identify until the voice asked about them. There were more questions each night, more names to answer for, and by day his network expanded. He started attending school regularly—it seemed now like there was more accomplished, more transacted and earned by going than by not going. He continued his usual pills and therapy; he did not mention that anything had changed. He began to anticipate the questions he would be asked each night, and to try and take in details during the day he knew he would later have to relate: how two specific people interacted, their body language and cadence; the members of certain groups and the ways some moved among them, who could and who couldn't; where people were at different times of the day, their spatial and social routines, schedules and logistics. Rooms that were always empty at certain times, locked and unlocked doors, places to hide—things he had already known to some degree, things any outcast learns how to intuit, but to which he could now assign wider purpose, that he now felt justified in knowing. And increasingly, Greg began to feel like he was an agent to his mind, that before it had been his stupid body, or his instincts, or whatever—before he had been dumb. He understood the change of voice as some kind of tonal shift within him, a sign it was developing and maturing as he did, it was calling his attention to these people, these details because they were somehow important to him: his new life was about information, and here he was collecting it, he was making himself smarter and more perceptive, sharpening his memory. He was talking to Sarah more not because of the change in their circumstances, but because he himself had changed, like he could finally engage with the complexity of her person because he'd realized that complexity was there.

The new mode of questioning accompanied him each day, and thus it quickly became a part of him, the way he encountered the world, drawing out the salient points in any interaction from the useless data that concealed them, extending the questioning night into day, even when the voice wasn't actually speaking (for it now spoke exclusively at night), merely exerting its influence. When he talked to Fox or Molly at lunch, for example, was it really important how much their respective parents sucked or how shitty their other friends were or how much the lipstick they'd shoplifted from Rite Aid cost, or was it more important that Fox (whose real name was Amy) only tied her hair back on days she wasn't wearing any makeup, and that those days always followed nights she spent "at my dad's," which was code for something else; or that Molly never ate more than a quarter of her food, that she left at exactly 12:30 every day to spend a full twenty minutes in the bathroom, and that it was always the empty one by the music rooms? Was it the interaction itself, or the design behind it?

—

It was us, of course, helping Greg sift through the noise of the school, of his daily life—it was us, working through that voice in his head, showing him the order in the disorder, or where the order was, and how he could grab hold of it. The arc of his life that was there, carved out for him, if he only asserted himself into it.

He didn't know it, or knew it barely, but attributed it to the voice alone, the one constant inconstant of his existence since he'd hit puberty, and thus the fulcrum around which he turned. But we were there, operating through and among that voice. We were there, as he walked those halls and mapped their rooms and the constellations of relationships within them, and the relationships even closer at hand, whose barriers felt alternately impenetrable and porous: a bedroom wall, a gearshift.

—

His eighth night in the basement, a Monday, Tyler invited his girlfriend, Rhea, to David's house and told her to bring food, a laptop charger, weed, tobacco, and his rolling papers. He didn't specify how long she should intend to stay. She texted him when she was at the base of the stairwell in the backyard, after cutting in through the neighbor's yard. She lived three miles away, but had walked there, as instructed. They had been together long enough that their rhythm felt innate: they could go weeks without speaking face-to-face as easily as they could spend days in each other's company. When he asked her to come, it wasn't so much he'd grown bored or wanted company as that he welcomed a change in pattern. He saw her shape through the cloudy glass panes in the basement door and unlocked it. The cool air of the night was alarming, it had a wild effect on his body, and he shivered. The clock reset. Rhea had two Meijer bags in one arm and a paper Five Guys bag in the other. She was wearing her backpack. Tyler thought suddenly, *Clothes, I need more clothes*, but she was already here. When he opened his mouth, at first nothing came out, and he realized he hadn't spoken in almost a week, he didn't remember how to modulate for the space. "You can't bring that in here," he said, and gestured at the fast-food bag, his voice dry and unfamiliar. Too loud. Quieter: "The smell will carry."

"We'll open a window," Rhea said, pushing past him into the basement. At the top of the stairwell, lights from the first floor and neighboring houses vaguely colored the external space beyond. Tyler re-locked the back door against the night. Over the years, their wardrobes had gradually evolved to match, so he figured if need be he could always borrow Rhea's clothes. He couldn't remember who'd first got the Rancid hoodie she was wearing.

He gave her a tour, apologizing for the disarray as if it were his own, though he had touched little since he'd arrived. He was unloading the groceries in the kitchen when he noticed the distinct odor of fry grease. He walked to the bedroom next door and found Rhea sitting on the edge of the bed, poking into the Five Guys bag. The fact of her sitting on the bed he'd specifically avoided touching for the past seven nights, in the gallery-like bedroom—he didn't know how it made him feel, but he noticed it. "If you're going to eat that, do it by the window." He drew the sheer curtain and opened the bedroom window about a third of the way and they sat on the antique chest beneath it. "Wait," he said. "We have to turn off the light."

"Are you serious?"

They ate by the flashlight on his phone. When they were finished, Tyler carefully balled up the trash and wrapped it in a plastic Meijer bag before throwing it away in the garbage can in the kitchen. He left the bedroom window open. They returned to the living room area and its own light and stale closed-off air. They dropped themselves onto the couch, which was so fossilized into its current shape that it didn't react at all to the weight of their bodies.

"Should we watch something?"

"We have to keep the volume below eighteen."

"I understand this."

They put a show on the TV with one of David's accounts. The minimal volume effectively turned it into background noise, and so it assumed the fuzzy quality that most sound around Tyler possessed; he felt as if he had seen it all before, and he idly relocated his mind to elsewhere. He mapped out a series of questions he could ask Rhea, to make conversation, to qualify the time that had passed since they'd last seen each other, but decided none of them were worth asking. He raised one of his earbuds to his ear and put something on his phone. Rhea said, "Are you being fucking real right now?"

The situation gradually dissolved into them having sex on the couch. They were starkly audible over the TV; Tyler positioned himself above Rhea and moved deliberately, gingerly, like he was doing push-ups, such that he felt he was making no sound himself, he couldn't hear their bodies contacting each other, their skin only touching at the necessary junctures. He made a mental list of further supplies: clothes, more weed, condoms, wet wipes, carbohydrates. He needed a soundless way to wash himself, to wash everything.

Beth's long illness continued. After skipping school post-bruise, she decided an extended absence would need concrete justification. She figured any ailment she created for herself could account for four or five additional school days before she would be brought to a doctor, and at that point she could reevaluate and change symptoms if necessary, and the clock would begin again. So she began coughing. The idea was that a series of fake coughs could actually trigger a real, horrible-sounding coughing fit, so in essence her symptoms—if self-induced to begin with—were probably three-quarters real, and at a certain point, she figured, the symptoms became indistinguishable from the disease.

And so the days passed, and in the end, there were no doctors—she never needed to change her routine. She had a sixth sense for her brother, which was more than we realized at the time, and in that period, during the weekday from about 7:00 a.m. to 4:00 p.m., Beth had the sizable house and a luxury SUV all to herself. Their house lay along a winding, secluded loop of road called Meridian Circle that only included three other properties, none of whose houses were visible from Beth's, each separated by a swath of pine trees. Meridian Circle was part of a wealthy, privately maintained neighborhood called Peak's Trace, which was comprised of four such loops, arranged in a clover-shape, with Prior Hills as the stem. So exclusive were these wooded, residential loops that Peak's Trace was known locally, not by anyone who lived there, as the "White Knots," meaning the house itself, and Beth within it, her bedroom tucked back on the second floor, far from the street, were both isolated and perversely vulnerable. But, tied as we were to Greg's circuits through Adena, his shuttle from that front door to his own bedroom—apart from a brief stop at Beth's sickbed—this opportunity slid by unheeded, we were too caught up with Greg to notice.

Beth was impressed by how completely she was able to disappear if she willed it, how few demonstrable consequences there were to her absence from school. She heard from Sarah once, her first absent day after the bruise, checking in generically, and then not again. It was almost a joke to Beth—did she really have *no* other friends? Did she have to report every little thing before anyone noticed? The lack of contact was briefly offensive—she had the nagging feeling she was quickly being replaced in Sarah's life—and then she got to counting the days in a row she could go without talking to anyone, save for the daily one-minute check-ins from her mother each morning (confirming Beth was still sick, asking if she wanted ibuprofen/Tylenol/soup), and for Greg. She treated her bedroom like a hospital ward and rarely left it; she read complex fantasy novels or watched BBC shows on her computer and idly checked in on Greg at school or elsewhere via the colored light and proximity-sense she'd had in her head as far back as she could remember, which together allowed her to know, at any time, both how her brother was feeling (the light), and where he was (its proximity).

She noticed the light had been changing since she made herself sick and Greg started driving Sarah to school alone, a line of purpose had gotten into him, coloring the sadness, the isolation, the anger that usually carried him from moment to moment: the vicissitudes of his moods were obvious to her, simply because they'd always been there. She felt like some kind of bed-bound oracle, her body sapped by the power of her vision, watching the tedious dramas of everyday life play out in her head while she lay immobile in her distant cave up in the mountains or whatever. She would respond, she figured, only if summoned.

The truth was that no one really took Beth seriously—she mostly lived in the shadow of her strange older brother—and popular perception was that things *happened* to her, *befell* her, rather than Beth possessing any agency or initiative in making them happen. That is, when she came to school with bruises on her neck and refused to defend them, she fell into the role of hapless victim, someone's badly handled toy. She'd had brutal, painful periods since she'd turned eleven, which kept her home from school a day or two each month, and when things were bad for Greg they were almost as bad for her, it was impossible for her to focus on anything besides the light, which cost her, too, and when Beth disappeared from school for longer—as she had at the end of fifth grade, when she'd had mono, and then reliably once or twice a year since then, with whooping cough, long migraines—the accepted truth was not that Beth had been sick, but that she'd opted out: her constitution couldn't handle it. Her presence was tangled up with her brother's, and bad luck seemed to follow her. She was known in this way, but not really *known*: she had admirers of a sort, people like Thaddeus Settler—who wasn't involved yet, either—spreaders of sick rumor, but their interest was in Beth as concept (punished slut, haunted wisp) rather than person. The reality, of course, was much more complex—she was trapped in that lonely, sprawling house, in that familial blood, that light, she was raging, she would have rather those bruises had come from her parents than her brother, it would have been easier to make sense of, to articulate—but at the time her canvas was blank, primed but unpainted, so far as anyone knew, including us, and those days, like Tyler's in David's basement, elapsed with no one to guide her, without proper method. She had been laid up for two full weeks before anyone else found her—before we found her—but find her we did.

Meanwhile, as Beth withered alone in her house and Tyler camped out below David's, Sarah and Greg were progressing, their relationship clarifying under our influence. Gradually, their rides to school lengthened: Greg started to take slightly longer routes, or he would do a broad, slow lap a block away from the school, or he would duck off the main road and inch along a parallel side street at fifteen miles per hour. It felt like the only way they could spend more time together without acknowledging it was happening, without letting it affect the existing structures of their day—they never spoke of these detours, nor did Sarah mention the decreasing amount of time she spent in homeroom, her accumulating tardy slips. The car became a kind of liminal space for their communication, as if the air-conditioning produced some special toxin allowing them to talk freely, that made the world outside the car cease to exist: it wasn't like Beth was merely absent on those days—it was as if her entire being had been obliterated. Once they had parked in the back lot at the high school and gotten out, each followed the paths they always had (they didn't even enter the rambling building through the same doors), and they didn't interact for the rest of the day, even if they saw each other, though Greg would catalogue all of these instances at night.

But something was happening in that Ford Focus. Greg felt, at last, in some semblance of control: he continued his nightly conversations, and the voice continued to interrogate him, but Greg, forever adaptable, felt in its new form he'd been granted a special insight, like that of a knowledgeable confidant. Deep down, he wondered if the change in the voice was something he ought to question, that he should treat critically, but this adjustment felt far out of his reach, because he'd always felt the voice to be a part of him, a complement to his person rather than its own thing—to question it would be to question his own character—and also because he was coming to like Sarah, and this assisted with it, allowed him to ask the right questions: he felt good learning about her, and he was getting usable data, and she, he reasoned, felt good learning about him.

———

Of course, Sarah noticed what he was doing. The drive to the high school was so fundamentally mapped into her that any variation felt like something was wrong, and the first time it happened—when Greg took a left on Oak rather than Adams, three blocks later—Sarah felt a regrettable pitch in her chest at the change in route, as if she'd been suddenly kidnapped. She felt instantly guilty for thinking that—guilty but maybe a little thrilled, which was somehow worse—and then they slowed to a crawl and hit an interminable series of stop signs, and Sarah was pleased by the way she kept up her side of the conversation regardless, as if she hadn't noticed the misdirection, she was broadcasting this confidence to him, this lack of doubt; she felt better being privately right than publicly unsure. Compared to the rides with David, which had been silent, his attention fused to the road, with Greg she never ran out of things to say, or questions to ask. When they arrived at the school five minutes later than usual that morning Sarah had said nothing, as if it had been a failed shortcut she didn't want to call him on, a secret she had no problem keeping.

The next day, he turned right on Oak instead of left, again three blocks too early but this time in the wrong direction, and Sarah instinctively opened her mouth to correct him, she emitted a single syllable and then stopped herself, and she turned to the window and smiled as they drove east down Oak, her mask in place again. Beside her, Greg's voice lapsed for a second, as if in anticipation, as if leaving a space for her to intervene, and then he picked up: "So did you ever learn to drive?"

They trundled down the residential side street, which looked largely the same as it did in the other direction. "I went to a few of the classes last year," she said. "It was this old guy telling gruesome stories about kids getting run over. I just quit going."

"Yeah. Driving school is worthless. Don't hit people, pretty much common sense."

Sarah realized a potential tension in their dynamic; it occurred to her suddenly to apologize. "I'm sorry, I didn't mean for you to have to take me every day." She noticed she didn't mention Beth, and wondered if it had been intentional.

"No worries," he said. "I don't mind at all. You just never wanted to do it?"

"I guess not," she said. "I'm too anxious." She looked at her lap. Was that really it?

"Well, I'm psychotic"—Greg shrugged—"and they let me." He paused at a stop sign, no cars in any direction, and waited several seconds before moving on.

It felt like a startlingly intimate confession. "What do you mean, psychotic?"

"Oh, you know—disordered thinking, hallucinations, that kind of stuff. It's not active or anything. But that's the diagnosis."

A block, and his person had cracked open, or been recast—like she was seeing new shadows she hadn't before, or had better light. Could it be true? Psychotic? She felt at once deeply normal and embarrassed by her normalcy, its gross rote-ness. Her mind went to Beth, to place the information within her network: did she know? What would Claire think? "I didn't know that," she said.

"Why would you?" Indeed, why would she? Why should she be the only one?

"Do you know that house?" Greg said suddenly, breaking his own train of thought. He pointed to the Victorian house on the corner, the one thing Sarah actually did recognize in this neighborhood. "Yeah," she said. "That's where that ancient woman lives."

"The scary old lady," he nodded. "But check out the old stone at the bottom. It's been built over, but that was one of the first structures in Adena. The settlers built it so they could shoot at the Indians on the other side of Brash River. Fire down from above with their guns. Back when this was all wilderness. After they slaughtered them, they would send their bodies down the river to the camps in the south, as a warning."

As with everything Greg, she didn't know where fact ended and fantasy began, but looking at the house as they turned, she saw how the flat lines of the limestone at the base were subsumed into the arching woodwork and high windows of the house above, the way the building seemed to transform and disguise its own ancestry. And then the town had been named for them, for the people driven from it. She couldn't help feeling her journey with Greg was some tiny version of the same thing. Maybe life was about talking your way over its irregularities until a smoother path was paved atop them, was ignoring its poorly concealed lies in service to a greater truth. Greg turned left again, and eventually they recrossed Prior Hills a block farther up, alongside that river, now a creek, where the bodies had once tumbled down, slowly switch-backing their way toward Adena High. If David had been a straight line, Sarah thought—as straight as a toothpick—then Greg was a series of erratic, hard left turns, endlessly circling. And of the two shapes, obviously, only one yearned for correction.

Then the voice spoke to Greg in the car. The first time it happened, a week into their unsupervised drives, they were turning in to the school when Greg suddenly heard his name by his left ear, and he gripped the steering wheel, looked skyward, and bit his lip, *Why?* but against every-thing he was able to successfully negotiate through the columns of teenage drivers and park the car in the back lot before he gave in. By the time he answered, he couldn't hear anything above the screaming.

He slammed the car door to mask the sound of his voice growling, "What?" and walked briskly across the parking lot away from Sarah, anticipating more questions. But none came. The voice was quiet the rest of the day.

He lay in bed that night, diligently waiting for the voice to speak, but it didn't come. He barely slept without it, and he awoke sweaty and muddled the next morning, as if, lacking a confessor, he was physically unable to unburden himself of his emotions. He tried purging himself in the shower, asking himself questions aloud like the voice might and then answering them, but it was a useless exercise, every question seemed rhetorical, the answers slapdash and incorrect, unverifiable. Through her bedroom door, he heard Beth unleash a torrent of coughing so hard that she threw up. He opened the door enough to see her doubled over the edge of the bed. "Are you okay? Do you need something?" he said.

Without looking up, she waved him off. He shut the door. How was he supposed to feel? Was this just their routine now? She was sick, but equally she hated school; if he had another morning with Sarah as a result, if that was the net effect, and Beth had to go nowhere, was that wrong?

Where is Beth? he asked himself: an easy one. She was in her bedroom, where she would always be.

In the car, he could hardly speak to Sarah. She was in

a good mood, he could feel it radiating off her, softening his own edges, but he couldn't find the questions to ask, they were all questions the voice would ask, clinical and probing. He felt like he was wasting time, squandering his precious daily fifteen minutes, and he found himself wishing, despite himself, that Beth would get even sicker, would die even, and he could continue this forever, so each individual day would matter less desperately. He drove directly for the school. And then Sarah asked him a question. "Greg," she said, looking at him. He turned and their eyes met for a second—and in that second Sarah realized that she had completely forgotten about Beth, had not thought about her one bit for at least the past four days, as if she'd been scrubbed clear—and she continued, "can I ask you something personal?"

His body thrilled with love and dread. He felt a guttural stab of intimacy. "Sure."

"Why do you cut your hands?"

Greg looked at the steering wheel, at the backs of his hands, where there was carved, on the right, the scar of AB, and opposite, that of xz. "I don't know," he said, "I guess I like the evidence of it."

The way the words sat between them, he knew this would be the only response he gave. She pondered it for a while. "What do the letters mean? They're letters, right?"

He thought she must have remembered what he'd told her on the day he'd done it the week before, what he'd mumbled to her as they got out of the car, that he'd been needlessly weird when he said it, and she was providing him with an opportunity to write over it, to pretend it hadn't happened. That version of Greg, barely a week gone, seemed distant to him now, embarrassing and childish. He felt as if he were the recipient of an unfathomable, angelic generosity. But at the same time, he didn't know what to say, he didn't know how to explain that feeling of arbitrariness mixed with deep significance, he didn't know where to put it culturally. "I was thinking of the alphabet," he said, tracing a finger up along his arm and then in an arc in front of his chest, "from end to end."

Sarah considered this thoughtfully. "Why did you leave out the Y?"

He paused. "To be different."

They arrived at Adena, and Greg spent the day in anticipation of the voice's interruption, for guidance, for something, to relay the exchange with Sarah and find meaning in it. At lunch, he stood at the trough-like sink in the isolated men's room in the south unit—where he could often be found—and looked into the mirror. He was without makeup for the fourth day in a row; he couldn't remember a stretch like this since starting high school. He confronted what felt like a great silence within him: he tried to ask himself what he was feeling, but the answer didn't come, or it came like he was rehearsing it, disappearing without effect, without an audience to hear it. He thought about his answers to Sarah's very good questions. How long could he expect to get away with that? He rolled up his left sleeve. He took his wallet from his pocket and slipped one of his razors from behind his library card. He made two vertical cuts on his forearm, below the elbow joint. He flexed his arm, felt a spot of pain; the veins bulged and created a channel for the blood to flow through. He watched it trickle slowly down his arm and exit through his palm. He put on the faucet and rinsed it away, he washed his arm and rubbed a thumbprint of lip balm on the cuts.

The voice did not return that night, either, and every time he started to fall asleep Greg would startle himself awake, afraid he'd miss it. He wondered if this was it, finally, if this phase of his life was suddenly over as indeterminately as it had begun six years before. The next morning he picked up Sarah bleary and worn. It was a Friday that boded rain. She climbed into the car, put her backpack on the floor between her legs, and said, "Are you okay? Did you sleep at all?"

He shook his head. "I'm okay." He turned out of her street thinking this exchange had probably been satisfactory grounds for Sarah to expect a silent drive, and he was settling into this quiet and plotting a similar course for the day ahead while slowly speeding up to match traffic on Prior Hills when, all of a sudden, the voice spoke.

He felt the car surge forward. Sarah put her left hand on the armrest. He thought, No. The voice said again, "Take her arm."

They were ten minutes away, at least. Greg whispered to no one, "No."

Sarah looked over at him. "What?"

The voice went from nothing to screaming. "TAKE HER ARM."

Greg's head pulsed once, a single vibration. He mouthed, No, this time silently. He struggled to remain focused on the road, which at once seemed like too many things moving independently, far more than anyone could ever be realistically expected to keep track of. He felt the car slow, the SUV behind him drift larger in the rearview mirror, and then he sped up again. The voice screamed, "TAKE HER ARM," blotting out whatever Sarah was saying.

He defied it again, he threw all his attention into driving, into plowing ahead. The trees went scrolling furiously by. He could hear nothing else: *TAKE HER ARM, TAKE HER ARM, TAKE HER ARM, TAKE HER ARM.* He saw his right hand, AB, leave the steering wheel before he felt or acknowledged it. They sailed through a red light. Sarah cried, "Greg!" as they crossed invincibly to the other side. When he realized what he'd done, he tried to right the wheel, but it felt like a common dream he had, when his car was out of control but he was somehow twisted around in the driver's seat so his legs were confused, he couldn't tell which was acceleration and which was brakes, and in moving forward there was nothing for him to correct, they just kept going straight, and he saw his fingers were about to take Sarah's and the voice wasn't acknowledging the progress he'd made independently, it was still screaming, *TAKE HER ARM TAKE HER ARM TAKE HER ARM*, and he knew suddenly then that what it wanted—what we wanted—was a bridge between them, it wanted passage, but passage by a certain shape, by the shape of his aggression, his assertion, his violence: it wanted him to grab her because he had no care for her, because he wanted to hurt her and she knew it, because he existed in this space where he could always become a threat, because, over years, he had honed this, intentionally or not, because she was a body he could manipulate. *Like Beth*, he thought. His stomach plunged. Like Beth. The tips of his fingers touched the fine hairs of Sarah's wrist, it was like an electric shock, and he pulled his hand sharply back; it cracked against Sarah's face with a snap, and her head jerked backward. He had been fighting all his life—but had he really? Had he really been resisting this shape he'd become? Had he? Had he? How much had he hurt her already? He swerved the car to the left and in so doing threw his body away from Sarah's, he dragged them apart, and as he saw from the corner of his eye the tree they were about to collide with, he swerved again, to the right this time, flopping Sarah hard back into her seat, and when they did hit, Greg knew he would be the one to be flung from the car; in that split second, he positioned them so that, at the inevitable collision, his body would crash through the driver's-side windshield and leave her, finally, distantly, in peace.

And we would go, too.

—

It was 7:32 a.m. that Friday when we took leave of Greg, and Beth reached out in the hallway for the light that suddenly wasn't there. She was on her tenth day of convalescence. She walked down the hallway to his dark bedroom, muted by morning light through the closed blinds. It was empty in a final sort of way, the walls matted with posters and the bookshelves crammed with comics and manga, all of it unchanged for years. He'd been so close to becoming a cartoon character himself, she thought. At least since Beth had started high school last year, Greg's contact with anything in his bedroom had been minimal—the only surfaces he interacted with anymore were the bed where his greasy laptop was buried, the bedside table with the lamp and his phone charger, and the top of his bureau, which was covered in cosmetics. Their taste—in books, movies, TV, everything on his dusty bookshelf—had once been so close as to be indistinguishable; it felt natural, as with the light, that their brains should overlap this way. But then he'd veered off somewhere and left her alone. Beth sat on the edge of his disaster of a bed and she felt for the first time his absence from the house. She rubbed her neck absently; the bruise was almost gone. She looked up at the ceiling and saw our symbol emblazoned there, painted in black. A crescent with a petal shape within it, like half of a heart. It looked both old and fresh at the same time; it didn't mean anything to her yet.

And despite the mounting weather, it did not rain that day.

Claire was the first person besides the paramedics, police, and the people on the scene to learn about the accident. When Sarah had extricated herself from the car, the front of her face stinging and her nose bleeding but otherwise miraculously unharmed, she called 911, and in the blare of traffic and shouting surrounding her, she texted Claire: their budding friendship felt suddenly swollen at that moment, in a place of great potential. She had been unable to find Greg—she'd seen him erupt from the window with seismic, unnatural force during the crash (had he been wearing a seat belt?), the airbags had exploded uselessly in his wake, but he was gone. Less than thirty seconds later, she was on her feet outside the car, which from her side looked fine, and the moments between these instances felt rudely connected; she wished she would have blacked out or been knocked unconscious, to have awakened in the aftermath and had someone offer it to her rather than create it herself. But this was not to be: instead, she was painful witness to every second that passed, she heard the sirens in the distance right up until they arrived at her feet, she repeated her story until it turned to gravel in her mouth. (Greg had lost control of the car, as far as she was concerned, she would let other witnesses fill in the red light.) She watched the paramedics disembark from the ambulance and return a full five minutes later with Greg tied into a stretcher; she still had no idea where he'd been. In the space of that five minutes Claire arrived—right back to the scene we'd just left—and she parked on a side street and ran up to Sarah, who was now wrapped in a blanket, and hugged her tightly. Claire's lack of delay was exciting. Sarah realized, huddled there with Claire's arms around her, that the connection developing between her and Greg over the past week and a half had gone unreported to anyone, Claire didn't know Greg any more than Sarah had two weeks ago. She tried to remember if she'd ever mentioned Greg to her at all. She touched her nose, which was no longer actively bloody, and she thought of Beth again, fragile, bruised Beth—she wondered how long it would be until she was told, if Sarah ought to be the one to tell her. She felt a shudder of guilt that Claire knew before Beth, before Greg's own sister and Sarah's best friend, and she made a note to obscure the timeline if it ever came up. How quickly her instincts had shifted.

Claire asked then, "What did he do to you?" and though it took Sarah longer than it should have to respond—giving her answer an untoward weight, lending it certain implications—she thought in that moment Claire would be a good friend to her, their foundation was now solid, and she felt simultaneously as if she were at the center of something, as if for those several minutes she possessed more information than anyone else, she was the point at which all other strands connected.

———

His first time out at HBCC, back in September, Collin had gotten lost. He'd left his house with almost two hours to spare—or, more accurately, he had left his general locus of activity, as in reality he had not been at home but drifting from the nature center parking lot to the library parking lot to the middle school, slowly getting more and more high—but he'd had trouble finding the state road, and once he was on it, and the suburbs seemed to crumble into farmland, it was natural of Collin to think, raised as he had been in the pocket of twenty-five square miles immediately south, that he had gone too far. But he kept going, because there were no turns, his eyes blaring down the road as evening began its slow descent, the sky somehow more *present* here, he thought, straight and straight and straight, sweating inside the stale air of the car and blinking back dry-eye tears. He had missed it. He raked his fingers through his hair so they caught in the knots of his dreads, sparked little prickles of pain in his scalp. He turned the wheel of one of the gauges in his ear, so it pinched the skin of his earlobe. He decided to turn around at the next opportunity, to go home, or closer to where his home was, where the sights were familiar, and he would fill the time that way, as he always had. He turned on his headlights in the encroaching dark.

He hadn't put the address into his phone, which sat dead in the glove compartment, and he hadn't told anyone he was going—the journey, for him, was unlogged and private: it would go unrecorded, he'd decided, until he had determined it actually meant something. In his palm, the sweat-mottled Post-it note on which he'd copied the address from the back of the pamphlet: *POST 638 / HBCC / 1246 SR 200*, like a set of coordinates to lost treasure. *ARE YOU ASKING THE SAME QUESTIONS*, the page had asked him, in handwritten block letters, or rather told him. He'd looked up at the cafeteria from the table where he found it. Stupid, but he was crying again. *Collin Reyes, whose sister Rachael killed herself last year*: the badge he wore to everyone else here. He was laced with her. She had died—that was what he said, she'd died, but in his mind, she had *been killed*—and the pattern of his life hadn't fundamentally changed. He still went to the same school, drove the same car, lived in the same house, had the same parents, slept in the same bed—and that was the worst part. He thought he would be crying for the rest of his life. He was lucky in a way, he thought morbidly, that people knew him otherwise as just this stoner punk Dominican kid, a tough identity to hide at Adena; it wasn't a surprise his eyes were always red, that he seemed some-where else. He'd sat with the invitation for days, until Thursday, languishing with its QUESTIONS, which seemed to him less like questions and more like answers, or themes—tragedy, death, pain—which were vague enough to feel universally applicable, broadly at first, and then the longer he thought about them, intimately. He'd looked up the address on a computer in the library, a pin dropped in the middle of nowhere. The closest town was three miles farther north. Aggressively white-people country. He took a chance, because he had time to fill.

And on the straight, straight road for the first time, the road into the country, he drove blindly, increasingly anx-ious, certain he'd missed the building—or the site, he didn't know it was necessarily a building—the cornfields or whatever spreading endlessly to either side of him, slowly gobbled up by darkness, spotted with intermittent farmhouses, as if he rode a great conveyor belt into the heartland, into hicksville, into Hell Is Real country, until his headlights illuminated a figure on the other side of the road, walking in the opposite direction, alongside the shoulder. A line of panic surged in his stomach as the man blared into existence and then just as instantaneously dis-appeared, like a ghost, and Collin continued for five sec-onds, ten, until he realized he should slow down, which he did, and then he stopped. He looked in his rearview mirror. He could just make out the figure shuffling down the road. There were no other cars visible, either ahead or behind him, no other spectral points of light. He had seen no human life since he'd hit the state road, or what he understood was the state road. He checked the clock: 7:12. It would be full dark soon. What was this person doing out here? Where could he possibly be going? Collin's upbringing, his sense of decency, told him he needed to inquire.

Painstakingly, he turned the Taurus around via a series of four little reverses and nudges forward, while frantically turning the wheel to keep his tires from spilling off the road. He was sweatier and more anxious than ever and somehow that made him feel more high, but he did it, and he eased back down the road the way he'd come. As he neared, he saw the figure was bent, limping slightly, as if he carried a heavy weight. A white guy; he looked young, questionably adult, with jeans and a long-sleeved button-down, Vans; he carried a small duffel bag over his shoulder. A hitchhiker? An alien? Collin felt years of his parents' coded warnings lurch into view, rendered prickly by the weed. His parents had moved to Adena from Lenape when he was a toddler, and so he'd grown up there, in the suburbs, had the same flat Ohio affect as his white schoolmates, as well as a white mom from Wisconsin, and thus could operate seamlessly in that context in most scenarios, at least after he'd spoken, especially if he was also wearing his glasses, but out here, he wasn't sure. Would he have felt differently if this person had an unkempt beard or a larger backpack, if he had radiated what to Collin felt like *disorder*? If he had looked—as his dad might say—

uncivilized? Or more like someone he'd expect to live out here? *I would be doing this with anyone*, he told himself, with unusual confidence, knowing that wasn't true, but having, in this moment, no proof to the contrary. He stopped the car just short, and the man stopped, too, expectantly. The man turned around, and despite his best intentions Collin felt another wave of anxious sweat spring from beneath his arms and across his forehead. The man was clean-shaven and wearing glasses, not so much older than Collin. He questioned his gut reaction, the panic. Was he relieved by the stranger's familiarity—or threatened by it? That he looked so put-together while Collin himself felt so *uncivilized*? He tried to imagine their roles reversed. Why did he feel like he was performing? *Am I the cop*? He kneaded the brake. The man approached the car; he thought he saw him wince. Did he not have every right to be afraid? Collin reached across the passenger seat and cranked down the window. He imagined a plume of weed smoke bursting from the car. The image was so strong that he coughed.

To his surprise, the stranger spoke first. "Are you going to the meeting?"

Collin was taken aback. His head swam with paranoia: miles and miles of road, the middle of nowhere, and they were both going to the same place? His hands were damp on the steering wheel. Did he care for his safety? Had Rachael? "Yeah," he said, looking at the road and then back. "Are you?"

"Yeah. Lost my ride," the stranger said.

Maybe the man would kill him, Collin thought, with whatever was in his duffel bag: he would see Collin sweating and shaking and he would think it was because Collin thought his passenger was a murderer, when in reality it was because of the weed, and because he was lost. He would leave Collin's body in the ditch alongside the road, to be discovered by other solitary hitchhikers, all en route to the same cosmic destination. A *parade of lost souls.* The man stood quietly, waiting; it fell to Collin to prompt the next step in the exchange. "Do you want a ride?"

"Thank you," the man said. Collin threw his backpack into the back seat. The stranger got into the car and placed the duffel bag at his feet. "It's just down the road."

Collin took his foot off the brake and eased up to half speed, back down the road he'd just driven in the opposite direction. How could he have missed it?

"Is this your first time?" the man said, after a minute.

"Uh, yeah." Collin's mouth was cotton-dry, unlike the rest of his hateful body, which oozed oil and sweat constantly—most days he had to change clothes multiple times, it was like he was constantly being wrung out. At this moment, his backpack held a bundle of his soiled morning shirt and morning socks, another pair of boxers, a third T-shirt, and a hoodie he hadn't needed to use yet. He ought to have changed before he left the library, but he hadn't counted on company. He tried to think of something else to say, but he didn't want to volunteer information unless he was asked, and because it seemed like the time to exchange basic data had already expired. Should he ask his name? He cleared his parched throat, a dry rasp that ground up a glottal clot of mucus. Embarrassed, he tried to cough it clear with his mouth closed; he choked and tried to swallow, which triggered more coughing.

"Let yourself breathe," his passenger said sharply. Collin gasped, caught his breath, swallowed hard, despite himself. Though he had his foot on the gas, his hands on the steering wheel, it felt as if he were no longer the one driving, like when he'd invited this man into the car he had surrendered control, down to his basic functions. "It's just up here, on the right."

Sure enough, a low brick building appeared just off the road, with a paved parking lot, smack among the fields. Collin couldn't remember seeing it as he'd passed from the other direction, couldn't remember what he'd been looking for or expecting, but either way, here it was now, as promised. *Like an oasis*, his brain said thickly. A message board was planted in the grass, illuminated from below: WELCOME ALL / POST 638. Beside it, a giant flagpole with an American flag—how had he missed it? Atop the message board, a set of weathered block letters once painted gold read HOLY BLOOD COMMUNITY CENTER. His gut churned again, this time with long-abandoned Adventist angst. "Wait, is this like a church?"

"It used to be a church," his passenger said. "Now it's

an American Legion post, technically. We usually just call it HBCC."

He turned into the parking lot, which already held a few scattered cars. His heart raced. The address on the pamphlet had just been a string of numbers and letters, he hadn't realized it was going to be in the shell of a fucking *church*. A church, what, filled with veterans? His lips traced out the letters. "Half Broken Culture Club," he said quietly, and then immediately wished he hadn't. He felt like he'd blurted out an embarrassing confession, offered a glimpse into how damaged he was, into why he'd come. The atmosphere in the car suddenly felt charged. He didn't want to do this.

But the man laughed, or let out a breath anyway. "Could be," he said, and again Collin let his breath out, too, as if he'd been waiting for permission. He pulled the car into a space. Ironically enough, the building reminded him more of his elementary school than a church, with two brick wings that formed a fat L, glass double doors out front. He'd ridden the bus with Rachael, she'd sat beside him even though he knew she didn't want to. The roof wasn't even peaked. There were no crosses or anything. *Fuck.* How bad did he need this?

He took the keys out of the ignition and waited. He needed another hit at least, a hit and a change of clothes, before he could even consider going in there. He was coming down and he didn't like what it portended. But his piece was stranded along with his phone in the glove compartment, in front of his passenger's knees, and his backpack was in the back seat. "I uh," he said, "I just need a minute to gather myself."

"You can gather yourself inside," the man said decisively. "Come on."

Collin got sullenly out of the car, feeling weirdly intimidated, strung along, like he was now complexly tied to this meeting in a way he didn't understand. Though he'd said virtually nothing, he felt like he'd been caught in a lie. The external air shocked his skull, and the world seemed to crackle into clarity as they approached the building, lit ghostly against the new dark, the only building for miles, the passenger beside him, his limp gone, and Collin pulled open the glass door, let the stranger step in first, and he thought, *I don't want to be here I don't want to be here I don't want to be here*, his hands shoved into his shorts palming the car keys and he knew that he absolutely *reeked* of weed, he remembered the ratty old T-shirt he was wearing, his red eyes, and he thought, *I'm not ready.* Like a kid on his first day of school. He recognized acutely his physical existence in the world—his smell, the sweat prints he left everywhere, the gnarly tangled hairs, his constant throat-clearing, this vision of him, his whole sensory output, filtered through everyone who had ever witnessed him—like he had an aura. He was read, everywhere he went, no matter what voice he used. He couldn't stop it. The man pointed him down a corridor. At the end, one of the wooden double doors was propped open, the lights on inside, distant voices. The man disappeared somewhere with his duffel bag, and Collin walked numbly down the carpeted hallway, shaking, intimidated somehow, though he was alone and he couldn't tell what had changed, he distinctly wasn't high anymore, this was just supposed to be what normal felt like, what Real Life felt like, but then why was it all so strange? Why was he *so* alone? Why was he always shaking? He looked to the walls for children's artwork. He stabbed his thigh with the keys through his pocket: *You cannot cry again, you fuck.* He took a breath and raised his eyes as he stepped through the door, where people were gathered—not just white people, he automatically noted—and then as soon as he registered the room, his nerves ratcheted again, he shut down, and his gaze plummeted back to the floor. He shuffled to a nearby chair, as if mute, and sat there, eyes down, until he was raised up.

Hearts Black Council of Cowards, he thought.

House of Bastard Crooked Cops.

He almost didn't recognize the man who had been his passenger when he entered the room, a half hour or so later. He was neatly dressed in a different button-down, his sleeves rolled carefully to the elbow, his shoes cleaned or changed, the frames in his glasses seemed thicker, he was indescribably older-seeming. He looked like someone who might teach at Adena—a figure who broadcast *intentionality,* above all else, an order and a method: Collin's opposite.

Or maybe it was the room that made him seem so differ-ent, the difference between this room, this nowhere-place at the edge of the field that was almost, or barely, depend-ing on your perspective, a shelter, a community center, a church, a school, and Collin's terrible hotboxed car, swarming with confusion. Either way, it didn't take Collin long to want to make the stranger's order his own.

When the man looked around the room, at the dozen or so people seated there in the circle, his eyes didn't lin-ger any longer on Collin than they did on anyone else, he didn't acknowledge they had interacted prior to this mo-ment: there was the private body, he seemed to say, and the public body. They shared something intimate, he and the man he'd found traipsing along the road, a secret channel between them. A change of clothes—of course, that's what had been in his duffel bag, same as the back-pack in Collin's back seat. He smiled to himself. They both had their disguises. His past—their past—yes, it was his own. *He knows what happened to me*, Collin thought, and also: *It happened to him, too.*

Her Breath Come Calling.

And when they got to him, to his place, Collin opened his mouth, and out tumbled Rachael's name, as natural as an exhalation.

"Do you ever think about following her?" he said, the passenger and driver, after Collin had finished his piece.

It was an odd phrasing to use, Collin noticed at the time, *following her*, implying that Rachael had set an example in some way, as if she'd laid a template for her younger brother to copy, that this was a natural course of events, a succession into oblivion, he and Rachael were points along the same line. But somehow it also felt, in that room, surrounded as he was by what seemed like variations of the same story, exactly right: like a truth waiting for him to step inside. He had never had an answer, had never been able to align the pieces in a way he understood: she'd gone out one night, to a party, and had never come back to him. He couldn't even remember their interactions from the day before, there was nothing for him to parse: just a blankness. Of course he had wanted to follow her.

"It's all that I think about," he said, because it was true, and because it seemed true, because it was an order and a method, a presence by the side of the road, bowed by their own weight, waiting to be carried in.

HOW IT FELT TO BE BORN TOO LATE AT THE
WRONG TIME WRONG HOUSE WRONG LIFE BEST
KNOWN FROM THE NECK DOWN WAS THAT
WHAT YOU WANTED WAS THAT WHAT YOU
PLANNED NO MATTER THE COLOR OF YOUR
ROOTS HOW HIGH YOU WORE YOUR SPIKES
WEREN'T YOU JUST DESPERATE FOR THE SHORE
FRIGID IN YOUR STUPID BOOTS ABOVE BEYOND
ABOUT YOU NO EYE IN THE SKY NO MIRROR NO
CAMERA JUST SUN

All it would take, truly, was someone grabbing hold of
Sarah's strands—those strands of knowledge, of information
she'd felt so acutely outside Greg's wrecked car—and drawing them tight, tugging her a little further down the line
toward us. Thus, Claire became her receptor. Claire was
the obvious choice, we realized now: she was the hub
at the center of the spokes, could turn Sarah as she turned.
The morning we were thrown from Greg, left churning
through the air of Adena for our next contact, we lighted

on Claire on her way downstairs from her bedroom, having received Sarah's text about the accident, and debating whether or not to answer it immediately. It was an interaction she would otherwise barely have registered—she hadn't decided if she was more than just intrigued by Sarah—but we encouraged her to give it weight, to take it for what it was: an entrée to Sarah. The opportunity to see where it would lead, if there was something beyond *intriguing*, beyond *curious*. All she had to do was listen. Claire pictured a beach under winter sun, swept clean by bitter wind, the lake iced out as far as she could see. She wondered why this image had come to her. Was that her?

She paused on the landing, took her phone back out of her pocket—less than the span of a minute since Sarah had messaged her. "I'm coming," Claire texted back. "Where are you?" She hurried down the stairs and grabbed her jacket, waiting for the response. A screenshot of Sarah's map came as she climbed into the car—Claire felt her heart race when her phone vibrated. Back to the scene we'd just left, then. She started the car. Not her style at all, she thought. *What is it about Sarah?*

The answer came to Claire that night, when she went to a punk showcase downtown at the Quonset Hut. It was local hardcore and its variants. One of the bands, a four-piece called Viceroy, had a singer who was known—at least known in Adena's minor punk scene—for self-inducing migraines before each of their performances, which somehow made him (and by extension his band) more earnest, and more hardcore. The story went that he was beset by frequent, crippling migraines triggered by loud, grating sounds like guitar feedback—inevitably the case before, during, and after every show they played— and so by the time their set started, he would be almost blind with unmedicated pain, and every vocal would be anguished and true, he would see the crowd pulsing in and out as he screamed, and he would black out by the end. It was very punk of him. He didn't play any instruments, because this would have been too complex a task; it was the most he could do to choke out most of the obscure lyrics to their ninety-second songs before he passed out. Viceroy played a ten-minute set that night, and Claire was entranced watching the singer, a wiry guy in his late twenties, she guessed: whether the gimmick was true or not, each syllable he delivered flickered across his face like it physically pained him, his mouth yawned open and closed in silent screams between phrases, his eyes shut independent of the words—it didn't seem to her so much like language as a rawer form of communication, a bodily respect for performance, and she felt like she understood it to some degree, understood where the impulse to channel it came from. The guitarist opened and closed their set; the singer made it through four songs before he was escorted offstage by the bassist, his shirt soaked through, the ostensible pain buckling him to his knees. He didn't speak otherwise. The band carried on for a few more songs with the three who were left, and while the structures of the songs were more coherent without the agonized vocals—the bassist and guitarist sang, unmiked, with a hint of flat melody—deep down there was nothing holding them together.

We knew him, the singer, though not by the same name.

Claire went to see him after the set was over. She eased her way along the edge of the crowd and ducked into the narrow, graffitied hallways at the back of the club. He was sitting alone in what looked like the owner's office, where he'd been situated to recover apart from everyone else. He sat with his elbows on the desk, which was scattered with various bills and accounting paperwork, the top three buttons of his shirt undone and his glasses pushed up on his forehead, massaging the bridge of his nose. An unopened water bottle sat next to one elbow. He looked different than he had onstage, contextualized behind the cluttered desk, the sense of authority was different, but for the sense of physical exhaustion like Claire's perpetually overwhelmed manager at the mall. She paused in the doorway, unsure if she was ready to enter his adult world. "That was a great set," she said finally.

He looked up at her and his eyes seemed to refocus, to emerge from somewhere inside him. "Oh, thanks." His voice was hoarse. Claire thought that as a performer he could last maybe a year before he killed his voice forever. "Do you want to sit?"

She took the chair opposite the desk; the room was

barely big enough to fit them both. Claire was dressed for the aesthetic today, with her jacket patched in local bands and blue forelocks. "Thank you for coming," the singer said. "Graham."

"Claire." They shook hands across the desk. His was cold and clammy, which seemed at odds with the rest of his body, which radiated heat, which seemed to have burned itself down to its rudiments. "How do you do that to yourself every night?"

"I've gotten headaches since I was a kid," he said. "I finally found something to do with them."

She noticed that he said "headaches"—the internet articles she'd read had said migraines. Was there a difference? She made a note to look it up. "But you know what triggers them, right? You cause them on purpose—at least that's what I've read. You do it to yourself."

He shrugged. "I mean, it's like anything you 'do' to yourself. You cut yourself, right?"

She was taken aback at the assumption. "No."

"You self-harm at all?"

"No."

"Okay, you drink?"

"No."

"Okay, you smoke a cigarette, you use drugs. You masturbate. You use your body to capitalize on a moment. Isn't that the only economic means we have left in our control, really? I just put it to use like this, because no one wants to see me masturbate onstage. I think GG Allin would agree, though he would probably say I wasn't going far enough."

She nodded because she halfway agreed, and because he was sitting on the owner's side of the desk, because he had the bearing of one of her teachers. "What does it feel like?" she asked. "The headaches?"

"Like someone's compressing my head," he said. "My vision gets spotty. I can still hear, but it's like the sound doesn't mean anything, doesn't register. It's like none of my senses stop working, but they stop transmitting useful information to me. I become just sort of a—a physical re-actant, for those minutes. Do you get them?"

"What, migraines?"

"Yeah, headaches." There it was again.

"No," she said.

"I thought everyone in your generation did."

"Not me." She looked briefly to the paperwork on the desk and wondered how much Viceroy was paid for their ten-minute set, if anything, and how much of this take would go to Graham, the real price of his psychic and bodily pain, second by second. He made, what, fifty bucks for his night of suffering? How did one make a living like that? She felt like she was getting the answers to all of his questions wrong. "You're going to kill your voice," she said. "Why don't you drink that water?"

He laughed and untwisted the cap on the bottle, but it eventually found its way back to the desk untouched. "How old are you?"

"Eighteen," she lied, not really considering why.

He laughed again. "I was going to say it will make more sense when you're older, but I'm only three years older than you."

She'd pegged him for much older. So they were the same generation, really. "How old did you think I was?" she said. It sounded like a silly question, she realized, something only a kid would ask.

"You know who comes and finds me after these shows, always? It's high schoolers. People like you." He abruptly smacked his chest, and she started. "You've got to have the violence in you already," he said. "You've got to know it's there. That's who gets it."

Claire chewed on this. "What was the second song you played?"

"I honestly don't remember."

"It had a part where you were just singing over the drums."

"Oh. 'They Never Found the Bullet.'"

She made a mental note. "What's it about?"

"Do you remember Lenape? Lenape High School? There was a shooting there about five years ago."

She racked her brain. The name sounded vaguely familiar. "Which one was that?"

He paused a second, seeming to study her, either because he was still without his glasses, or because she hadn't given a satisfying response. "Near Cleveland," he said. "In 2012. Nine kids shot, four killed."

"Jesus."

"You should know about it," he said. He picked up a weary-looking backpack from beside the chair and rooted through it—it was spotted with band pins Claire tried to pick out and identify: a black bird's severed wing, dripping with cartoon blood; "Spike" in an eighties-style font, the *i* drawn like a stake, piercing a cluster of eyeballs beneath it. Nothing she recognized, which she found obscurely defeating. He pulled a stapled white booklet from the bag and handed it across the table. "Take a look at this. It's usually five dollars but you can have it for free, for coming to find me."

It was a sixteen-page zine on white printer paper, folded down the center. The cover was marked with a black symbol—a waning sliver of moon alongside a solid black circle—and bore the title *REDPRINT*. She flipped through it—a mix of sparse, typewritten prose and collage, grainy images and diagrams; more or less standard zine fare. "Thank you."

He shrugged. "You might get something out of it." He slid his glasses back over his eyes and seemed finally to see her. "Do you know what the best part is about performing like this?"

"No, what?"

"It feels so good when it ends. The comedown." He stood up, and his bearing shifted again: he looked like a different person, dry and mysteriously composed. He tugged down the ends of his shirt. His transformation was complete; the hoarseness in his voice had disappeared. "I'm going to go meet up with my band. Are you interested in meeting them?"

She stood as well. "That's okay, I'm going to head out."

"Okay." He rubbed his hands together. "Well, Claire, it was nice to meet you. Maybe we'll see you at another show? We're playing in Cincinnati on Tuesday."

"Yeah, for sure." They shook hands again (his was warmer now) and left the office. The water bottle sat behind on the desk. They went opposite directions down the hallway, Claire toward the exit and Graham back toward the sound of the next band. As he walked away, Claire watched him, and as the distance grew between them he seemed to hunch slightly, began rubbing his temples, running his hand through his hair, as if he was walking deeper and deeper underwater, the pressure rising and rising until eventually it would flatten him into nothing. He turned a corner and disappeared.

She returned home, to a neighborhood that was barely two miles from the Quonset Hut but which contracted a private street cleaner to maintain the cobblestone street. Every time she turned onto the cultivated quiet of the street, the change in the road's texture signaling you were transitioning from downtown Adena to Maplewood, in her parents' too-nice and too-big Lincoln Navigator, especially after one of these shows, Claire felt deceitful, embarrassed by the wealth it signified, as if, by her very presence at the show, the way she dressed, she was pretending she

96 SIMON JACOBS

would be returning to an apartment she scrupulously managed herself or a falling-apart house where she lived with nine other people. She had always figured if people followed her home they wouldn't want to talk to her anymore, or they would want to talk to her for the wrong reasons. She knew the majority of the crowd at a place as typically emo-kid as the Quonset Hut was flush with someone else's income—you could tell that just by looking at the shoes—but she considered herself apart from them for the basic reason that she knew the ways in which she was privileged and tried pragmatically to address them. She mostly only spent money she earned herself working at the Hot Topic at the mall, had stringently negotiated with her parents to pay a negligible "rent" for her bedroom in the house, and she couldn't afford her own car because she was paying rent. It was a vicious circle but felt like an adult dilemma to have, the either/or, and she was willing to accept the limbo on account of it. Her job at Hot Topic—where her colleagues knew her real name but her name tag said RICK—was a similar dynamic of suburban-aesthetic-overlaying-punk-values. Claire knew, distantly, that there was money waiting for her at some point in the future, a fund with her name attached to it, but she tried not to think too hard about it. The fact was that when she took the bus to school, she walked a mile from her house to a neutral corner at the edge of the neighboring school district so she could go to the less preppy, less moneyed Adena schools, and she had been doing this since sixth grade; any time spent at the Maplewood schools before then she couldn't be blamed for, had been before she effectively achieved sentience and moral standing as a human. She felt she lived her life in different modes: the school one, the outside-school one, the punk one, the online one, the alone one, the parents one, the rich one. They existed separately, these modes, but often several layered atop each other, like layers of a transparency, while others could never overlap. She thought other people must have them, too. Graham: at the desk, onstage, or at home, alone, in idle moments, trying to find something to channel away from *doing something to himself*, she guessed. Did Sarah have them, too? She was surprised to find herself wondering.

She had been hit with an unexpected angst halfway home—a product of the encounter with Graham, the texts she'd been receiving over the course of the night, variously pinging for her attention, the image of a girl standing near her at the show (the way she'd stood rooted in place with only her head moving, clearly her first time anywhere like the Quonset Hut), and the pent-up energies from the rest of the day—and Claire was desperate to detoxify. She flew up the stairs, called, "It's me," to the house at large, and killed ten minutes in the bathroom in case there was to be any follow-up from her parents; she didn't want to be interrupted later. When nothing materialized, she figured they were out for the night. She locked her door, stripped completely, and sat before her open laptop on the floor, in front of the blank beige wall at the foot of her bed. From beneath the bed she drew out two posters—one for *Zombi 2* and one for *Cowboy Bebop*, neither of which she liked but which a girl who was similar to her might like—and affixed them to the wall behind her. Objectively they were hung too low on the wall to be realistic, but in the laptop camera's field of view from the floor they looked normal. She switched on the camera and increased the input on the built-in microphone. She tilted the screen and eased the laptop backward on the carpet until it captured her in the right proportions, from the base of the neck down. She applied a bright blue Band-Aid to her right collarbone, which she thought of as her trademark. She started the camera recording and made herself come in front of it. Her phone vibrated twice from the desk where she'd set it while she was recording, then twice again, and she considered stopping to silence it and starting over, but ultimately decided to leave the buzzes in: it gave the video some context beyond the posters (which she always used), heightened its feeling of real life, that while she filmed herself the world was around her happening, risking its interruptions on this unplanned and solitary event.

When she was finished, she stopped the camera recording, grabbed her phone from the desk, and leaned into the wall, breathing heavily, looking at the texts that had accumulated over the course of the night. In the hormonal rush, she felt energized at the prospect of dealing with the people who requested her attention, confident in assigning them their appropriate values. There were five texts from three people that she didn't respond to: when she next saw these people—minor acquaintances—she knew none of them would mention she hadn't answered them, and so these threads were easy enough to let evaporate without effect either way; if anything, there was a mild shift of control to her side. There was a message from Stacy left over from yesterday, which she decided to let rest again until tomorrow. She would respond to it early, as if seen upon waking, and that cycle would continue. The latest four were from Sarah (which had arrived while she was making tonight's video), stacked atop texts from earlier that afternoon, dense blocks of post-accident pain and gratitude and apology. Here Claire paused, unsure whether the effect was more powerful if she responded or remained silent. If she didn't reply, the control would remain with her, and she knew it would make no practical difference to the way Sarah acted toward her in person, and henceforth each text would carry an added weight, a measure of desperate hope in anticipation of Claire's reply. The idea was tempting.

She tilted her head back and looked at the objects assembled around the room. It occurred to Claire that while, to her, there was a marked difference in the kind of people who liked *Cowboy Bebop* versus those who liked Junji Ito (she had a poster for *Uzumaki* actively hanging to the left of her bed), maybe the gap wasn't wide enough for anyone to realize Claire was standing on either side of it. That being said, responding to Sarah's texts meant it was very likely their frequency would increase, and that by responding, Claire would be inviting more contact: she would be adding another layer to whatever existed between them, her realm of influence would grow, would create a daily, even hourly opportunity for change, for influence. Were they friends now? Claire didn't know, but it seemed like they could be, and that this was the question Sarah was implicitly, repeatedly asking. *So why not answer?* Claire compressed the video, labeled it with today's date, and put it up online alongside the others. There were days she missed, but she was more or less consistent.

Finally, Tyler had texted her: "I'm squatting a sick ass basement, wanna come and fuck me in it." She had effectively confirmed for herself during the conversation with Graham, with reasonable certainty, that Tyler had been the one to break into David's Facebook account, post the videos, and randomly blitz people with sinister messages—he had used Viceroy's lyrics, *They never found the bullet,* and was the only other person she knew who knew that band and also knew David. To Tyler, the careful system of attention and value she'd created for the people in her life was meaningless; she could ignore him forever or spray back twenty texts and it would not make the slightest difference, it was just a pattern they had. She responded, "Not on your life, trash."

Claire peeled herself from the posters on the wall and leaned forward to address her computer again. For a few seconds she surveyed the grid of thumbnail photos that comprised the listing of her videos, the visual composition and colors all similar to this one, under marginally different light. She absently scrolled back in time, hundreds in all, two full years. She found the first in the series and absently clicked play, but immediately winced: she'd begun these videos sitting on her bed, the same bedspread she still used, which seemed excruciatingly identifiable, and the stuff on her walls then betrayed a taste and aesthetic in her fifteen-year-old self that struck her now as misguided and unrefined. Every couple of months she would consider deleting the bed videos, but she found the record valuable, as well as the numerical attention from strangers, and despite herself, she found herself getting turned on watching it again now: she felt like she was watching someone else, someone she'd found by accident, guileless and undisguised, unaware of the camera. She liked how skinny her arms were back then. For a second her jaw and the bottom of her mouth dipped into the frame, and Claire shivered with the thrilling jolt of identification, the flicker of passage from anonymous to recognizable, as if her form on the screen was someone else completely, someone she'd once known but never expected to see again.

Misha was one of the recipients of the messages Tyler sent from David's Facebook account. She read it during advisory period around six hours after it was sent, on a Monday, after Tyler's fourteenth night in the basement. It read: "I want to fuck you to death." Unbeknownst to Misha, Tyler had sent the same message to four other people, including to Misha's younger sister Marcy, who was in ninth grade. Marcy saw the message before Misha did, as soon as she woke up the morning after it was sent, and of the five people who received this message—and the thirty others who received different messages over the approximately two-week period Tyler was sending them—Marcy was the only person to respond. She did so from the upstairs bathroom of her house, before she had revealed herself to anyone that day. She wrote, "when and where."

After she'd talked with David about his fake society in her bedroom that afternoon, Sarah had started thinking about the party again. Above all, she remembered the light. A few weeks after she and David broke up the previous autumn, nearly six months ago now, Sarah had gone to a party with her brassy friend Hannah; that's what her mother had called her, "brassy." Hannah didn't directly know anyone connected to throwing the party and Sarah didn't particularly want to go, but Hannah had asked her, and Sarah figured this was an experience she would have to learn eventually, and so Hannah, who didn't go to Sarah's school but whose family was socially connected to

Sarah's, picked her up and they went. Sarah didn't know whose house it was and didn't pay attention to where Hannah was going—she noticed, vaguely, four distinct landscapes of suburb, highway, what she would have called "country," and then the outskirts of another town, almost an hour of driving—so by the time they arrived, Sarah was already disoriented. She climbed out of Hannah's BMW and was surprised, felt weirdly betrayed to find herself on a residential street like she could have found in Adena, a line of old-looking houses, no driveways, cars parked on either side of the street. Together, they made uncertainly for the roaring, three-story white house that glowed through the blinds, the other houses quiet around it, as if in deference to the noise of this one. A row of rotten pumpkins lay decimated across the porch, left over from last month, along with a collection of mismatched Adirondack chairs. Above the porch, she noticed a trio of symbols mounted—Greek letters? She was reminded of a trip she'd taken with her parents a few years before to her uncle's house; they had had to drive three or four hours to get there and in the end he'd lived in an isolated house on one of those nothing country roads, a destination to no one, and the house had smelled like urine and her wheezing uncle had never left his recliner, not even when they entered. It was the first time she had seen him in years, and they had stayed for under an hour. She remembered the same feeling, standing at the threshold of that house, a place she could not imagine visiting again: an obscure dread, like her role there was to bear witness, to be present, and nothing more. On the porch, as she pulled open the screen door, Hannah turned to her and whispered, "This is a *college* party," as if this knowledge had been forbidden until exactly that moment. And then they marched inside.

The living room they entered into was broad, dank, and packed to its edges with people. The temperature spiked twenty degrees, and it struck Sarah immediately—the horrible light. It was peaked and yellow and erratic, nearly brown in areas. It was as if, instead of radiating from its usual centralized fixtures, the light came from a dozen different bulbs of varying wattages stashed randomly about the room: wedged into the stubby blue carpet, tucked in the corners, stuffed between cushions of the massive black couch that covered almost two walls, mounted in the dark compartments of unused shelves, bleeding in from other rooms, soft white mixed with harsh yellow, cut with an almost blue fluorescence. The result was a dingy, basement kind of muddy yellow that saturated everything.

The room was full, there was barely a place to stand—the furniture had been moved to its edges, to create as wide a space as possible—but even so it seemed like everyone was arranged into shapes, spirals and circles and clusters within the square room, squirming together, people who seemed too old to gather in these numbers in this type of outfit. It was very male, very tall; the same kind of hair, the same kind of muscles, the same tan skin, the same tank tops with the same logos. Who were these people? Where was she? Within minutes, Sarah felt herself starting to sweat from body heat and incandescence, thousands of watts of combined energy, and the smell, too, seemed to filter the flesh-toned light, reducing everyone to the same dirty palette, like she was staring through a sweat screen, faintly burning. Sarah pictured a match held near arm hair. She tugged the hem of her dress down—it felt like it was shrinking by the second in the heat and had turned, she realized in disgust, the exact color of mucus. She felt marked. Hannah had already disappeared; she was wearing black, which absorbed all light and thus retained its color, simultaneously allowing her to become either a shadow or slutty, whichever she preferred. Sarah was farther from the door than she had been before, the cool gust of outside air at her back long cut off, a jolly human wall forming behind her in its place, locking her in this airless room. If she tried, Sarah thought she could probably have picked out individual voices or scents, tried to speak with someone, to discern the crowd or find Hannah, but she felt paralyzed, endangered, absent of the signifiers she was used to, the familiar social relationships. Thunderous electronic music pulsed through the bodies around her, and she felt embarrassed to recognize the song, a pop hit; she had never expected to hear this music out of anything besides her headphones, a car radio; this was not how she wanted to hear it. A complex shame flushed her for enjoying it privately, at experiencing it in this context, among these people. It would be polluted forever.

She felt her age suddenly: she was sixteen years old. These people—they were older, years older. There was a system underneath this crowd of people she didn't understand, didn't want to understand. They seemed to be playing a game. The shapes were shifting—the people in the living room were arranging themselves into rings. A long plastic table was dragged out; someone carried in a red cooler and multiple gallons of something translucent brown in a plastic bottle. She saw dark wet tracks on the carpet, as if from wheels. She was shunted in place alongside the table. Across from her, Sarah noticed women standing among the men, and she realized these must not be the only women—or girls—present at the party; she must have seen others as she and Hannah entered but not registered them, the people at the party all rendered the same beige in front of her, the same heavy shadow and no shadow, that same blank threat. Someone came out with a coil of plastic tubing under his arm, a funnel; another with a roll of plastic wrap, a glass pipe. Someone pulled on a green latex glove that looked instantly tainted in the light, and there was a burst of concentrated antiseptic smell that almost made her gag. Sarah wasn't sure if she had ever been in a house where there weren't parents somewhere invisibly above it all, enforcing the general order like some unseen god-hand. Was this what happened when everyone who lived there was part of the same generation? Who had planned these rooms, bought this furniture? Reckoned for all this blond wood? The tube was fed across the crowd, and she saw people in masks, suddenly. A fist slammed on the table, rattling it, and she jumped—a violent energy, a rage jolted through her. A chant was picked up. Sarah pictured her jewelry chest on the bureau in her bedroom, became aware the earrings she was wearing had been expensive, remembered picking them out with idiotic childish delicacy, she'd dressed as if for a school dance, and across the table Hannah reappeared, she was laughing and reeling back without covering her mouth, and the light made her freckles look like scabs, pockish and gruesome. Her earrings were just dull studs; she could lose them and it would be nothing. Hannah was laughing in a way that seemed to indicate she wanted to fit in, to seem at home here, too, but she was at least a head shorter than the people to either side of her and her dress didn't fit her right, it was like she'd borrowed it from her older sister, who was a graceful brunette rather than a brassy redhead, she'd made herself up to look older to steal into this adult party, but her disguise had fooled no one, she looked even more like a child, like someone's lost little sister. And then there were bodies between them, standing atop the table, bare legs, and Sarah heard her braying laughter clearly above all else, from the top of her throat, the dishonest part. Sarah felt something spurt in her direction, some unidentifiable spritz misted her chin, and she finally revolted away from the table in disgust. There was a smaller circle of people just behind her, a different tableau, a man on his knees with a funnel in his mouth, and two people above him pouring bottles into it simultaneously. She could see the muscles in his throat clutch, his eyes tearing, and there was this gagging sound under everything, a gently choking gulp that drilled into her mind like a spike, and she felt her own throat close up again. She couldn't breathe. She hurled herself through the crowd and out of the house and through the screen door, which banged behind her, through the putrid veil of rotting pumpkin, down the steps. The night seemed to burst blue and black at her, as if to make an obvious point about color.

When she reached Hannah's car she realized she was clawing at her collarbone with one hand, her fingers dug in as if she was trying to rip it from her chest. Sarah looked down and saw three perfect brown dots down the front of her pale dress, mathematically precise in their configuration, each subsequently smaller, ending around her belly button. She brushed at the marks but they held fast, and she couldn't tell for the life of her what their substance was, some splashed liquid, as if when it hit the outside air it had oxidized and become permanent, the stain had attached itself to her very soul. She thought of David's description of the Black House: *utterly debasing*. Was this it? Was this what college would be like?

She waited in the car until Hannah emerged an hour

later, unsteady and bleary-eyed and quiet, the makeup rubbed off one side of her face. In her anger, Sarah pretended not to notice any of this, or she legitimately didn't notice, she hadn't been conditioned to expect these signs and draw larger meaning from them, and she let Hannah drive her home, her mind looping the awful yellow light and the choking sound, the preceding night an endlessly repeating flurry of stimuli, and she smelled blood but that was just the animal part of her, and they followed the GPS through the residential streets and the lights and restaurants of the little downtown, the country road and highway and suburban streets in reverse order, and neither of their bodies died that night. And she didn't see Hannah again after that, not intentionally, she just didn't, which no one could blame her for; the night shuffled into those before and after it and she hadn't told anyone about it, not even Beth. Space bloomed in her life and then filled again.

But something about the way David had talked to her had called it back. When he described to her what his group did, or what he pretended his pretend-group did, the scummy sex and teamsmanship and gross contests, which were a precursor to scummy sex, she imagined it under the same bad light; it was the evidence of something done wrong. The color, the sound of that soft choking—it was a tone that had settled into her life. In the wake of David's speech, of the accident in Greg's car, she started thinking she'd misread something during that night, that the position of their bodies around the room must have been a crucial detail she hadn't been wise enough at the time to recognize: she'd seen the shapes but not understood their intent. What questions wasn't she asking? What damage was she missing to know what those questions were? If she could have gone back, if everyone had been in the right place—the man with the funnel in his mouth, the woman in the mask, the two men connected by tube, the scream she'd heard faintly from the car—she could have drawn a diagram over it, could have factored other shapes into it: the vector along which David had walked away from her house that afternoon in the wrong direction, the shape of the bruise on Beth's neck, the span between Claire's responses to her texts, between the half blessed and unblessed, the trajectory of Greg swerving the car on Prior Hills, the way his body launched through the window like an arrow, and the distance it crossed. When David said it in the blue of her bedroom, *Burst Marrow,* something had clicked. The color: it was marrow-yellow, gritty beneath your fingers, it was the color of old bathroom tile. They'd been broken up for months—why did David still have his hooks in her? His weird phrases and codes?

She had almost a full year now until she was eighteen, until that became her. A thick haze hung over her future; she felt it coating her teeth, the particulate slickness of it in her throat, so visceral she could have spit it out.

Tyler had no expectations for the message he'd sent Claire, of course—that was just his way. He began every conversation with Claire like this; it was how they opened the channels of communication, how they started talking about anything else, and for some reason it had been this way as long as they'd known each other. By the end of his second week occupying the basement and the fifth night sharing it with Rhea, Tyler had both imposed order on his new surroundings and failed to address crucial gaps in this order. He and Rhea had a system for bagging up the trash, but no way to dispose of the trash bags, which they ended up piling in a far corner of the weight room. They had designated times for turning on the lights in the bedroom, but had dedicated no effort to determining when the house above them was occupied. Tyler washed his boxers in the kitchen sink under a trickle of water, despite the washing machine in the back hallway, he scrubbed himself with a damp washcloth until his skin was raw, but he was afraid to shower. He and Rhea continued to have sex when he thought she was becoming dangerously bored, and alternately smoked the steadily depleting supply of weed she had brought, passing time emptily in front of the TV. Tyler himself had never experienced any desire for sex—it didn't have anything to do with Rhea, he just didn't—but he understood its power as a mood stabilizer.

He continued to send occasional messages as David, browsed the internet from David's ISP, and slowly—from the sites he visited, the posts he made, the motions his fingers made over the keyboard—Tyler created a new online identity for him. The flesh-and-blood David, his kind-of friend since middle school, or at least the guy with a better weed connection, began to recede in Tyler's mind, to be replaced with metadata, a series of algorithmic patterns drawn from increasingly narrow obsessions, grotesque images and internet spirals that, over time, seemed to take on their own form. It felt like David was someone he invented, a pair of digital shoes that had been laid out for him in the foyer of a house he knew only vaguely, but had been invited warmly inside. Tyler found himself thinking that they were more similar than he'd ever given David credit for.

It was two weeks until someone bit back.

Tyler didn't see the message until that night. They were on the couch, as always, there were moving pictures on the TV. He pulled David's computer into his lap and turned it on again. He visited David's Facebook. There was one message waiting for him, from Marcy Voigt: "when and where."

He typed out a response to her. He told her the next night at midnight, and gave her David's address with specific instructions for getting to the basement's back door via the neighbor's yard. He gave her a supply list and his own phone number. He told her not to tell anyone where she was going, to walk, and to not bother coming if she didn't have every item on the list. He told her to text him when she arrived, not before. He wrote out the instructions mechanically, like he was giving driving directions. Since he'd been a kid Tyler had felt as if he stood on the opposite side of the screen where reality played out, beyond his influence. The basement and the pattern of living he'd fallen into had helped foster this: the feeling that he was communicating to no one, that the world here operated by its own parameters, isolated from those outside its walls. He existed here only as the data that fed out. A block of text, an image, a disembodied voice on the air. He didn't consider, really, that anyone could conceivably breach the divide.

It didn't involve us, at this point: we had no hand in Tyler's life under David's, in the network of digital tunnels he dug out beneath the ground, from house to house. We didn't know the infrastructure he was building.

But aboveground, as Claire kept listening, we were learning. We were learning as Sarah unburdened herself about Greg, about David, about the struggles of her daily life, and Claire was there to hear everything. She responded to Sarah's many texts promptly and without exception; she gave her advice; she had lunch with her in the grassy stretch abutting the parking lot in back of the school; she gave her cigarettes, which Sarah smoked inexpertly; they visited Greg at the hospital—she did everything that friends did, short of invite Sarah to her house. She learned, in the space of days, Sarah's insecurities, her pressure points, when she would abruptly change an opinion to match Claire's and then commit to it earnestly, and her tendency to over-divulge—about her endlessly rich parents, the stories of all of her friendships, the side of her family she never saw, her rangy fashion and daily routines: everything. She learned how Sarah could be moved, which words or punctuation marks in a text could shift her mood, the tone of her responses. She proposed a series of dire thought experiments, to gauge Sarah's instincts, her priorities, to follow this fascinating person through the hallways of her mind and find what was at their ends. *What's the worst thing you've ever done? If you had to kill one of your parents, which would it be?* Claire played her own hand close to the vest, as always, as we guided her. She chose not to reveal her suspicion that Tyler had been the one to break into David's account—David's seemingly erratic behavior only made Claire seem more stable by comparison.

Taken together, the data was overwhelming: the extent of Sarah's personhood seemed to blot out the space for Claire's. She thought it was no wonder Sarah had dated a brittle shell like David, he could just let himself be filled up by her, his contents were her contents. But diligent Claire knew how to separate the two. The messiness of her early relationship with Sarah, before they were friends, before the accident glued them together—a time Claire now saw as a testing ground for her ideas, to gauge how much she could invent and have Sarah believe, how intent Sarah was on developing that friendship—clarified into something realer; that period of aimlessly fucking with her about Half Blessed and made-up bands felt temporally distant, like something she'd done when they were both younger, when she was a kid, even though it had only been a few weeks. Now it had meaning.

It was Saturday when Sarah told her about Hannah and the party. "I just ran," she said, after she'd finished. They were lying side by side on Sarah's bed, in her blue bedroom. Claire's shoes hung over the edge; for some reason, she didn't want Sarah to see her in only her socks. "I ran to the car."

Claire imagined her, sweaty and bewildered, pushing through a crowd of hands. She stared at the ceiling, the motionless blades of the fan. The windows were closed, the air in the room the same as it had been the night before. She breathed in, and then out, filtering it through her. "Jesus," she said. "What happened to your friend?"

"I don't know," Sarah said, as if she hadn't considered it for a while, was mildly surprised by the question. "I don't really talk to her anymore."

Claire wondered if it was intentional, Sarah answering the question that way, taking it at the absolute broadest level, or if it was accurate to Sarah's perception: she simply didn't have sight of her. *What a fucked-up thing to do to someone who was your friend,* Claire didn't say—she realized such a response would shut Sarah down, close her off, when Claire wanted her open. It would be more effective to say nothing, Claire thought, to let it disperse into silence. She felt Sarah breathing beside her, just outside her peripheral version, waiting for Claire to say something back, to validate the experience. She felt it almost physically, the need radiating off her; Claire felt them growing closer, as information poured into the gap between them. She liked Sarah, she thought she really did, but this knowledge came parallel to knowing it was the calculating part of her, Claire, the callous part—the *manipulative* part of her—that was making it happen, that was bringing them closer. The fact that she knew it, recognized it: did that make it wrong?

Is it wrong to know how to get what you want?

Without looking, without speaking, Claire raised her hand and laid it atop Sarah's. She felt Sarah's fingers twitch, responsively—flinch. Claire would not look at her. She let the seconds pass, she held her hand there. She would continue holding it, as long as necessary, as long as it took Sarah to come to the threshold. Her skin crawled, and then warmed in the palm of her hand, the faintest sense of moisture. After forever, Sarah's fingers moved to the edges of hers in acknowledgment—barely a squeeze.

Her heart thrummed.

We waited there.

In tandem, Claire absorbed everything she could by Viceroy: the music and the conversation with the singer felt linked to Sarah in some unspecifiable way, to the subtle shift Claire had noticed in herself since the morning of the accident, this little edge as she drew closer to Sarah. The total available catalogue of Viceroy was about nine songs all told, muffled versions she found online, plus a video with one of their songs tracked over it, "Drawbridge." The video comprised a sustained, minute-long shot of Graham bashing his face into a table until it was bloody (a fairly obvious metaphor for his headaches). Their lyrics were opaque, koan-like but somehow rallying, as if lifted from old texts. The zine he'd given her, *REDPRINT*, was similarly an arcane exegesis of his own weird philosophy, a collection of symbolic diagrams, sermon-like prose, and song lyrics. Obviously Graham was smart, but he came off like a conspiracy theorist, prone to pattern-finding and extrapolation.

On one page, for example, was a rectangular diagram of fifteen black circles, arranged three-by-five, each of the circles surrounded by a ring of smaller circles, like orbiting moons, some of these circles filled in black, some not. At the center of the rectangle of larger circles, a single square. A series of dotted-line trajectories crisscrossed the diagram, presumably demonstrating movement. Around one of the larger circles and a curved length of the smaller circles along one edge of it, a symbol was traced in heavy black that matched the one on the cover: a black arc alongside a circle. On the facing page, the lyrics to "They Never Found the Bullet," the song he'd said was about that school shooting: "I've found a way across and through / blind from the neck / I'll tear down the moon." The opposing illustration, the traced shape, was in fact very moon-like. But what did it mean? She googled a list of Ohio school shootings to remind her of the town he'd mentioned, Lenape.

A couple of pages later was one of several self-edited pieces of prose, which mostly circulated the theme of his headaches, but which were complicated by sections struck out or overtyped, made purposely illegible. She made a valiant effort to pull out a few sentences, but found the effort largely unsatisfying, the revealed text a bit too confessional for her taste, the prose a little mealy. She preferred Graham the cipher; she was disappointed to learn that he, like everyone else, seemed to have a key:

> For years I was in the shadow of it. I let the pain guide me, define me. I let that image guide me, those shapes laid over my eyes, a construct I put atop everything. I allowed that pattern to become the one thing that mattered—that which made me suffer, was the trigger to my suffering—and inadvertently I made myself responsible for it. I was the one who couldn't get past the head-

aches, and because of my weakness, my inability to surmount them, I deserved punishment. The classic abusive cycle. Day after day, killing myself seemed like the easiest way out. And in the way you do when you're young, when you're everything and nothing simultaneously, I was convinced no one had ever experienced what I had, and also that absolutely everyone had: they were just better at masking it than I was, or they had otherwise made their peace with it, allowed it to exist unspoken in their world. But I couldn't. I couldn't leave it unspoken. I was convinced it meant something beyond me—it *was* something beyond me, something pervasive and omnipresent, forcing me into its mold, undergirding every decision I made. Something I couldn't articulate—or which I could only articulate through the shapes.

It was all pain and trauma. She assumed "those shapes" were the shapes from the earlier diagram, and the front cover of the zine, that they were connected to the headaches, in addition to the other causes—or "triggers"—she'd read about: loud, grating sounds, feedback, etc. The general point seemed to be that he (Graham) was tortured, that he projected his pain on the world and tried to find his answer in it. Even the title of the zine, *REDPRINT*, reflected this belief, that there was a *system* underneath everything, a schematic for his pain, both extremely personal to him and also universal, to everything. Claire wasn't sure if she bought it, but she thought she understood the instinct: to put some quasi-mathematical structure on the world, to interpret it by consistent signs. Maybe that even explained his preference for *headaches* over *migraines*—one was generalizable, the other a specific diagnosis. Everyone had them.

Claire felt obscurely like they had something in common, as if some hidden part of her knew this trauma, too—had this *redprint* mapped into her as well, but she couldn't put her finger on it. Or maybe it was just that they used the same filter to engage with the world, the same broad cultural signifiers. Did it matter, ultimately, what was beneath it? The lyrics to "Drawbridge," for example: "The light through a broken lens / turns color into spokes / I walk to the clouded hilltop / in time to see it close." Claire liked its mystery, the lyrical economy, but none of its elements told her anything individually. Maybe that was what punk was about, she thought: the peaks of sound emerging from a bluster of motive and context. It means something to you in the moment, but afterward you're not sure what's left of it, what's still ringing in your ears.

And maybe this was the key to Sarah, too, that the individual symbols and signs, real or invented, were only important in that they helped form the whole: not to say the details of Sarah's complex and contradictory set of cultural tastes, her dramatic anecdotes were meaningless to Claire, but that the details individually lacked meaning, and Sarah was the holistic sum of them. And as we knew, if there was anyone who could navigate that mess and know what to do with it—draw out those peaks, refract the light, sharpen the teeth, whatever your metaphor—if there was anyone who could do it, it wasn't pathetic David nor shattered Greg. It was Claire.

And yet, despite her calculations, her controlled contact, the more Claire learned, splashing around in the pool of honesty in which Sarah was perpetually neck-deep, the more Claire felt herself begin to change in response, her disguises seemed more paltry than ever. She observed Sarah in all her lush openness, stomping around cheerfully in her three-hundred-dollar combat boots, skinny jeans, and neon-pink baseball cap (!?) and she thought, *What am I hiding from?* The fourth night after the accident, a Monday, Claire brought her laptop back to her bed when she recorded herself, and for the first time in two years she didn't change what was on the walls behind her, she left the background as it was, and didn't apply her usual decals. One mode dropped over another, and she let the record stand as, in that moment, she was.

By the way: we were there that night, at the party in the house off-campus, in the reaches of the township two counties over from Adena—if just outside of Sarah's view. We were there, sifting the thunderous, yeast-choked air, looking for purchase. The room thick with our codes, only just illegible.

On its face, the story was a common one: a girl in an unfamiliar place without allies, whose friend had left her alone, suddenly realized she was a little too drunk, a little over her head, and made her way upstairs to the empty second floor to find an unused bathroom, to splash some water on her face. To collect herself, maybe get a car. And a man—a man by its legal definition, who was in his own crowd and drunk off his ass, who was surrounded by his own allies, his peers, on his home turf, and emboldened because he was at home, thus primed to notice someone he didn't recognize stealing upstairs alone—who went to find her. And there was a confusion of doors—there were more rooms than she was used to in a normal house, some of them locked, like what she imagined a dorm was like, and the hall light was off for some reason, and when it flicked on she turned, headlighted, her pupils barely changing, and he said, *Are you looking for a bathroom?* and she said, "Yes," in a way that was bolder and betrayed more confidence than she felt, so he came up alongside her, trying each of the doors in turn, finding them locked, or leading to a bedroom, or closet, or whatever, and he thought legitimately he was playing a game; he imagined a flirtation, would report a flirtation, imagined an intimacy—just because he'd put his body so close to hers—and with every door she grew more panicked and desperate, till they got to the last in the hall, and he said, *Voilà*, and she poured her weight onto the metal handle to get inside and away: but it was his room.

Outside, above where Sarah sat in the car, from a second-story window: a light clicked on, for a second, and then back off.

He saw her face clearly, for that same second, and then he turned the light off. In the dark, before his eyes adjusted, when she was just a warm presence before him, black artifacts over his vision, this was when we found him: in the rushing violent heat of the moment, he made his decision, to commit to the path he had taken. He enveloped her, and a part of them shattered irrevocably.

She screamed, loud enough to hear downstairs, struggled as he forced her toward the floor, the bed, and over a minute tore free from him. Bunching the dress ripped to her waist in her fist, her purse, she ran from the room and into the hallway. She tripped going down the stairs, felt one of her heels sink and snap, and stumbled the last few steps into the chaos of the party in the living room, which divided around her, falling to her knees, her shoulder gashed by the shitty wooden banister, she looked up and saw a line of them standing there, ringed around her, abruptly quiet save for the thudding soundtrack, watching as if she were a strange animal, awaiting her reaction. She screamed again. He appeared at the top of the stairs, behind her. She didn't see him, but she made a sound, a cough or cry or moan, a trapped sound breaking into the space carved by the scream, it crackled out from her and drew a line suddenly visible to the other people in the room—a bolt of awareness, of narrative went instantly from the man at the top of the stairs to the girl on the floor. In the turn, we flooded into the room, and for everyone there, in that house, the world changed, became a before and an after. A moment that in the bedroom turned like a key, and in the living room: burst.

Hannah ran then, from the center of the room, she broke the chain of onlookers and flung open the door and burst into the night, ran for the car parked alongside the street, where she saw her friend in the passenger seat, angled away from the house, looking out the opposite window, apparently unaware. She stopped, under the light of one of the streetlamps, and stood in the street just shy of the car, her dress and purse in her hands, her chest heaving, waiting for that head to turn, to notice her. She heard music bleeding from the house behind her, but she didn't hear the door; no one followed. Otherwise, the street was quiet in either direction, no traffic, the parked cars dead and silent, their owners gone. Even when her breathing regulated she felt her body trembling still, a cold line down her back. *He tried to rape me*, she repeated numbly to herself. She stood there almost a full ten minutes, silent, waiting to be acknowledged, to be sought. And then, finally, she laid the ripped straps of the dress over her shoulders and tied their ends loosely at her back, where the fabric stuck to the blood, the drying sweat; she broke the remaining heel off in her hand and walked to the car, to the driver's-side door, to join the girl who had been her friend, her passenger, to drive them home.

And we moved on, as we always did. As we always do.

We sought that same purchase now, acting through Claire, for something that went beyond her, that could bring us to fruition at a grander scale, a massive scale—we always did, we always had—but Sarah was just so pure a prize; she faced, so resolutely, the direction she was looking. It's hard to overstate how much she wanted to know what was there, to see the tiny minute cracks in which we took root, but she was too far from the surface to make them out; she was perpetually in that passenger seat, looking away from the road as it turned. But Claire didn't know any of this—thus, we didn't know any of it—until Sarah told her.

The day before Claire recorded herself in bed, Sunday, they'd visited Greg in the hospital, and afterward Sarah and Claire sat in silence in Claire's parents' Navigator in the hospital parking lot, detoxing. The visit had not gone well. Five or six stories above them, Greg lay immobile and unresponsive in his bed, in the unit perpendicular to where Sarah had been born; one floor below, Beth stalked the halls in rage. Above them all, the sky was a cheerful cloudless blue, the light was just relentless.

Neither Sarah nor Claire seemed to want to admit they'd never been in a position like this before, or had any idea what the appropriate response was supposed to be. Sarah had been the one to suggest the visit, and that they go on their own—it seemed like a better, less overbearing option than going as part of a group—but now that it was done, and Beth had unexpectedly been there, and Sarah had somehow incensed her as a result of their visit (partly Sarah's fault, she knew, since she hadn't reached out to Beth in weeks), Sarah wasn't sure how she felt, or—maybe more importantly—how she *should* feel.

We're going to find out what you did, Beth had said. What *had* she done? What was the implication? That she had somehow driven Greg to crash the car? She had been just starting to like Greg—no, she liked him, he wasn't dead, he was still a person—and then there'd been this accident, and Beth apparently fell apart, and now there was Claire, and it felt like she had been thrust into a situation in which there were only extreme options, where she could either double down this investment in Greg or basically pretend he was dead, there was no middle ground, where whichever relationship she chose to focus on sent the rest spiraling into unaddressed chaos. It was all accelerating too fast for her, like she was running alongside a train as it pulled out of the station, a train where she'd already left some of her luggage aboard, and no matter how fast she ran, she could never catch up to it on foot. The first time anyone had asked her about Greg was on the street twenty minutes after Claire had arrived on the scene, and happened to be for local news, and Sarah was surprised by the volume of her own emotion—she began openly crying, which wasn't how she saw herself—and she felt that in her publicized grief she was rewriting history, giving the relationship weight that wasn't there, that it didn't deserve, like she was building a week's worth of fifteen-minute conversations into something it wasn't, she was mistaking Greg's unexpected niceness for love, or using his tragedy as an opportunity to validate her crush. And with that, with a few lines, she became discoverable on the internet, outside of her social media, locked in the record with Greg. What if Beth was right to hate her now: what if she really was just inserting herself where she didn't belong? How much of it was her fault, for just existing? Was Greg really anything more to her than a kindly bus driver? At the same time, if she was genuinely crying, spontaneously crying, didn't it mean she really cared? How could anyone debate that? And now, by visiting the hospital at all, gift in hand, witnesses present, had she already made her decision?

When they'd climbed into Claire's car outside the hospital, Sarah had started to buckle her seat belt, but then Claire had slumped down into her seat, resting her knees on the steering wheel, and had given this exhausted sigh, and her gesture had allowed Sarah space to do the same—space she felt she needed, she wasn't ready for motion yet—and she let go of her seat belt and, similarly, slumped down into the throne-like seat, propping her knees on the dashboard. She felt like an echo, but the motion, the resignation of it had felt right.

Claire still sat in that position, though neither had yet spoken. It was one of the things Sarah admired about Claire: her perpetual ease, the way she seemed naturally ready for any interaction and yet simultaneously poised to gracefully exit it. She seemed like she had good time management skills, probably had her life organized to the degree at which things like school and homework and her social calendar moved forward autonomously, without direct effort on her part. Sarah felt a closeness developing between her and Claire, undeniably, but also felt guilty at how much of it was based on misery, that she could seemingly do nothing but unravel at the slightest touch, could keep no part of herself hidden.

Around their vehicular fortress, what seemed like far below, cars pulled in and out of the hospital parking lot, people walked in or drove off, mimicking, in their miniature iterations, the same patterns of grief, denial, recovery, resignation, whatever. Every so often, an elderly person or couple would emerge from the hospital exit, one of them wheelchair-bound or on a walker, and Sarah and Claire would watch them slowly hobble across the parking lot in the rearview mirrors, silently betting on the car at which they would end their journey. Sarah felt embarrassed watching them, guiltier still if the person was alone; it felt

like they were here fifty years too early, like they were spy-
ing on some sad aspect of their future. If they made it
that far.

One by one, she watched these decrepit old souls enter
their cars and drive off: Sarah, who couldn't yet drive, who
had needed a driver to bring her even here. There was so
much out there, so much unlearned, it was no wonder she
was always on the verge of drowning.

Maybe the issue—the issue Claire had mastered—was
that of time, and not having enough of it. What made you
a good person was caring about other people's problems,
Sarah figured, caring and actively responding to their
problems, devoting time to solving them, but how did you
make room for them all? How did you keep one person
from dominating all of your time? How did you—she
struggled for the word—*prioritize* them responsibly?
Clearly, this was what she had failed at with Beth, she'd let
her care lapse into Greg's. The weight of their presence,
brother and sister, felt heavy on her; it seemed unforgiv-
able that she could just fuck off back to her bedroom while
Greg writhed motionlessly and Beth seethed by his bedside, deep in torment: Sarah felt like there were productive
measures she could be taking to address both. She could
talk to Beth, brace for her righteous anger and weather it
until she could field her separate issues, until they were
back on even ground. She could talk to Greg, or at least
offer her presence, sit in the room with him awhile—but
for how long? How long was too long versus not long

enough, and what would she be implying by staying lon-ger than his own parents, his own sister? Did she not owe Beth proportionally more than she owed Greg, given how long they'd been friends? She wondered if she should go back inside right now: a part of her wanted to, to dismount Claire's siege machine and just muddle her way through the horribleness however she could, if only to finally stop dwelling on it. Another part of her wanted to never set foot in a hospital or see Beth or Greg ever again—and she felt guilty about that part.

Claire sat beside her, silent and spring-loaded. There was a clock inside Claire's chest, Sarah thought, ticking down moment by moment; when it expired, Claire's knees would slide naturally from the steering wheel, her feet to the floor, and she would speed off to her next appointment. Sarah grew physically anxious at this thought, in fear of this moment, when the silence would break. The thought slithered over her, a line of sweat crept down her back—in the end, was Sarah one of those demanding people? A drain on Claire's attention, full of other people's problems? How did she harden herself to be more like Claire? When would it all stop feeling like her responsibility? When did the world alert you that you'd done enough, move on, and give you the next step?

Beside her, Claire spoke at last: "It wasn't your fault, you know," she said.

Claire wasn't looking at Sarah when she said it, she was staring ahead out the windshield, watching a minivan that had been fruitlessly trying to make a left into the hospital against traffic for almost a full minute, like an agitated insect, edging minutely forward over and over again. When Sarah turned in response, Claire turned as well to look at her, and the moment between them was almost liquid, and Sarah's chest swelled to the point of aching with the thought, with possibility, with this feeling that was like a bootheel sinking through a rotten floorboard, a plunging relief and dread, *it wasn't her fault*, and the minivan broke finally free of its lane and drifted silently into the maze of the hospital lot: and so it wasn't.

———

On Tuesday, the day after Claire brought her laptop to bed with her, two days after they'd left that parking lot, Claire invited Sarah to the Viceroy show in Cincinnati. She told her it was the band David had posted a video from, the night after Sarah and David had met in her bedroom—a thread into that damaged part of Sarah's past, the promise of some secondhand resolution. Claire needed a way to take Sarah out of this dead-end Greg situation; the callous part of her told her—we told her—that he was now an insignificant part of the puzzle, that the answer lay beyond. So Claire picked Sarah up that evening in the Navigator for the seventy-minute drive. It felt both quintessentially right and wrong to have them both perched in this monolithic vehicle in their most punky clothes, the very picture of suburban denial, and as they pulled smoothly away from Sarah's inarguably nice house, physically distant from the pavement, Claire had a sudden desire to crash the car.

"I'm sorry for making you pick me up again," Sarah said.

"It's no problem."

Sarah adjusted her seat, whose settings were the same as she'd left them forty-eight hours prior. "Where do you actually live?"

Claire paused, and then gave the honest answer, feeling drained. "Maplewood."

She could tell Sarah was considering the various implications of this. "Are there any other Maplewood kids who go to Adena? I thought they had a separate school system."

"Yeah, they do. I went there through elementary school and then transferred to Adena in sixth grade. The Maplewood kids are fucking elitist trash."

Claire dragged the conversation elsewhere. She had never been to the Crawlspace before—she'd never been to any venue in Cincinnati—and when they eventually pulled off the highway Claire was paranoid about missing her turn, about not being able to find parking or parking erratically, about seeming lost in what was supposed to be her scene. Maybe it was because she was out of her usual turf, but the stakes seemed to her suddenly, stupidly high—she worried if she slipped up, even once, then Sarah might leave her, and Claire was embarrassed at herself for feeling this way, for thinking of it in these terms. The venue wasn't downtown proper, but was just north of the city—the location made it feel like they had no real destination, they hadn't really reached it—and had its own parking lot, which made Claire feel doubly like an imposter. She angled the SUV into a poorly defined couple of spaces in the far corner of the lot. "I hate parking in this fucking thing," she said, to which Sarah nodded understandingly. Claire noticed she was cursing a lot.

As they stepped out of the car and saw the crowd gathered outside the bar, Claire felt drastically out of her comfort zone, as if she had brought Sarah along to an initiation for which Claire herself was not remotely prepared, where she was thrust into the control seat but didn't know what buttons to press. When she saw the guy at the door she felt a kick in her stomach and turned to Sarah, a hint of franticness cut her voice when she whispered, "Do you have a fake ID?"

Sarah said, "Of course," and the relief Claire felt—at not having prepared for this, but Sarah's readiness to address it—was repulsive to her.

They descended into the Crawlspace, which was the basement venue of a bar called the Attic. Though they'd been carded at the door, the audience felt unexpectedly adult, older than she was used to, which singled the two of them out for more attention. As they made their way into the crowd, Claire felt overwhelmed again, weirdly exposed and vulnerable among the heavily male crowd, *apparent* in a way she didn't like, and because they had entered under this pretext of adulthood, the arcane protection of their age had fallen away. It was different than online, where she might as well have been the twenty-six-year-old from Pennsylvania that her ID made her, where she was ensconced alone in her bedroom, passed through the filter of virtual space: suddenly, she had never felt more like a teenager. Sarah looked gamely around; Claire felt her age dropping by years. The story of Sarah's grim party rose up in her, as if it were her own memory, same as it probably had for Sarah—that was the point, after all, wasn't it? To strand her in this crowd so she would cling to her? That was why she'd brought her here—why we'd led her here—to try and break her open in precisely the right way, for Claire's benefit. So why was Claire the one feeling stranded, alone, angry? She shoved it down, she thought, *What a narrow trench I've dug for myself.* "How does this place stack up?" Sarah asked, with admirable cheeriness.

"Older," Claire said, "a lot less parents' money," aware she was implicating them both. Why was she saying things like this?

"I'm excited to see one of your bands."

Your bands. For a second Claire felt furious at how easy this was, at Sarah's susceptibility. She said, "Let's move up," and guided Sarah roughly forward, trying to physically reassert her control of the situation; she placed her right hand so the tips of her fingers pushed against the ridge on the side of Sarah's bra beneath her Misfits T-shirt—more a Hot Topic brand than a band at this point—because Claire was testing for a response, but Sarah didn't acknowledge it, as Claire knew she wouldn't.

Viceroy was the second band in the lineup, barely even on the poster. As soon as the lights went down and the first band started, the crowd started moshing, and despite Sarah's professed taste for bands like this, it was quickly clear she was having a miserable time. She was shunted from side to side and raised her elbows defensively in front of her face; at any second she looked about to fall over, but terrified of falling over, of touching the floor. Claire could have moved them to the perimeter, or farther back, but she didn't, and she didn't alert Sarah that this was an option. Before the end of the first set Sarah shouted at Claire that she was going to find the bathroom and disappeared, and another song had elapsed before it hit Claire that, as a friend, she wasn't allowed to let Sarah go to the bathroom alone in a place that seemed—suddenly—as threatening as this. She elbowed her way through the crowd, among bearded men and their beers, and the basement became transmuted into a party her parents had brought her to as a child, where she had been separated from them at one point, and she navigated through the other attendees like trees in a forest, growing more and more desperate for her parents' familiar faces. It occurred to her that, whatever she pretended, there were still two distinct groups in the world, Adults and Kids, and try as she might she was still trapped in the latter.

She entered the bathroom and found Sarah at the sink, facing away from her. As she stepped into the room—which was so heavily graffitied as to disguise its relative state of filth, each surface the same level of riot—it occurred to Claire that she hadn't gone to accompany Sarah, she had gone to find her.

She approached Sarah. "Are you all right?"

Sarah splashed water on her face and used the distraction to change her expression. When she turned around, Claire was standing very close to her. "Yeah! I didn't realize how intense it would be. How many bands are there?"

Claire took a bunch of paper towels from the dispenser and offered them to Sarah, which seemed like a magnanimous gesture but for which she wasn't acknowledged. "Viceroy is on next. That's the one I think you'll like. I don't know these other guys."

Sarah rubbed her face. "Is it different?"

"Yeah, it's a lot more—" the word she was going to use was *intense*, but it had already been deployed in their exchange as a negative—"intelligent. It's a little more varied." Claire wondered if in her own limited technical understanding of music these were effectively the same thing. Was intelligence just complexity? If you understood it did it cease to be intelligent? She put her hand on Sarah's shoulder. When isolated from it in the bathroom, the music really did seem like nothing but noise. "Are you sure you're okay? Do you want to leave?"

There was the slightest pause before Sarah shook her head. "No—no, I'm fine! I'm excited for Viceroy."

"We can leave right after them, okay? We don't have to stay for the whole thing."

"No, we can stay as long as you want! Don't worry about me, I just wanted to use the bathroom." Her excuses were drifting. The bathroom began to fill around them, indicating a lull between sets. "Do you want to get back out there?"

"Okay," Claire said. "Let's do it."

The area had cleared out as people went to the back to buy drinks or step outside. Claire and Sarah established themselves among the stragglers in front of the stage. "What did you think of the last band?" Sarah asked.

Claire shrugged; in reality she hadn't taken in much information about the performance, she couldn't even remember how many people there had been onstage. "Nothing remarkable." She looked over at Sarah. "I guess I don't have to ask what *you* thought of them."

Sarah didn't see that Claire was smiling and looked down at her shoes, as if Claire had shamed her. Claire said, "Hey. You missed literally nothing," and then realized she was artificially expanding the gap that Sarah had been absent, she was shaming her more. She felt the prickle of incipient perspiration on her forehead. Why was she acting like this? Like a stupid girl with a crush?

Three of Viceroy's four members came out and started setting up. Graham was nowhere to be seen, and Claire assumed he was somewhere else waiting, already laid low from the sounds of the previous set. She didn't recognize the other musicians; they could have been totally different from their last show, and she wouldn't have noticed. Gradually, the floor around them began to fill again, and the lights went back down. The guitarist and bassist communicated, and then the bassist left his instrument and disappeared offstage. Claire turned to Sarah: "Here we go." The guitarist and drummer began playing—the crowd started up at the same moment.

From the wings came the bassist, supporting Graham, already doubled over and apparently barely able to walk, his face gleaming with sweat. Claire's heart started hammering, despite herself. The bassist led him to the microphone in the thick of the sound, and Graham clung to the stand, his hands sliding. The bassist patted him on the back once and went to pick up his instrument. Graham screamed into the microphone. From where they were standing, she could see his eyes were squeezed shut.

Claire stared at him transfixed, even as the crowd surged against her and Sarah essentially disappeared. Graham's knuckles went white as he gripped the microphone, which he used to keep himself standing, his face bright red and contorted. His shirt was partially unbuttoned, and he had a chest tattoo she hadn't noticed before, a black symbol she couldn't see all of but which felt as if it had been planted for her to see. She noticed he was wearing earplugs. He swayed, on the verge of collapsing. Claire had listened to enough Viceroy now to know the songs of their usual set by heart, or at least the general shape of them, and she recognized this one as "Silo." Yet she also noticed he was skipping most of the lyrics, that he'd sung the first line of the first verse and then lapsed immediately into the chorus, that the headache had erased the rest of the song from his head, and he was trying to finish it as well and as fast as he could, repeating one line again and again, the song's central chant—"I was born in turbulent soil." The longer she watched, the more she saw how the three other members of the band communicated, that they adjusted or repeated their parts based on where Graham was in the song, whether he was repeating the chorus or jumping forward and backward, that their playing was in support of and in reaction to his pain, that he shaped them as the pain shaped him, and theirs were the arms he would fall into when he could sing no more. She realized how much he must have hated and needed music.

Graham's voice dropped out and then roared back to life; there was a hiccup in the sonic roar as the band abruptly started a new song, but the crowd didn't seem to notice. He ran his hand across his face, through his hair;

Claire imagined at this point he didn't recognize anything around him, that everything was just shapes. Every muscle in his face and neck was tensed, the lyrics no longer words but isolated sounds that came from deep inside him; he positioned his mouth in a way that a syllable would form, and then he thrust volume into it. Sweat poured off him, she could see it spreading through his shirt. His glasses slid from his nose and disappeared. Claire stared at his face, watching it change, watching the pain pulse out of it. When his eyes opened, she believed that he would be looking at her. The songs, or fragments of songs, dissolved into one another, and she lost awareness of the audience; she felt her body warming and energizing. Graham pissed his pants and some people in the audience noticed this but Claire didn't, she had lost sight of him standing there—she was seeing, but everything in front of her eyes had the same level of detail, like everything was in focus all at once and she didn't have the faculty to take it all in, so she was retreating and letting the image take over, the image and its sound and its heat and its pain, the pain that was now in her head, too, dull and kiddie-like at first but then hard and vindictive. She felt it wash over her, the multisensory language, the world twitching and vibrating before her, the same power she felt when she was in her room in front of the camera, where she controlled what it saw, what it read and how it read it; she was still hearing it when Graham's head dropped out of view and his voice stopped, when he collapsed on the stage and the drummer and guitarist didn't cease but the bassist—always the bassist—stopped playing, propped up his guitar, and went to the singer, as if this had happened many times before, like falling asleep drunk, she was still hearing it when Sarah shook her shoulder—for the first time? for the second?—and said, "Claire. Claire. It's over," she knew it was far from over.

Sarah was in front of her as they made their way to the bathroom again, but Claire felt as if she was leading. The door swung closed and Sarah was at the sink, splashing water on her face, there was an expectation that Claire would do the same. As she took the same four steps across the tiles she had taken twenty minutes before, Claire knew that when she remembered this night in the future she would not remember the first time she entered the bathroom, when she wasn't in control, but the second time— this time—when she was.

She walked to the sink next to Sarah and mimicked her motions, her head and heart pounding. She noticed Sarah was drinking water from her hands, and she found this pathetic. Sarah said, "That was . . ." but didn't finish. She turned off the water, and Claire did the same. Claire turned to face her, and Sarah did the same. It was one of her things, where she always faced people when she talked to them, was always open to potential touch.

Claire put her hand on the back of Sarah's neck and brought herself closer; her skin prickled again, but the sensation this time was both somewhere distant and loudly present, like she was in thrall to something else. Sarah's eyes were huge and fearful, hungry and willing and expectant and hurt and forgiving all at once, and Claire had already heard Sarah describe this exact moment, she had heard it a thousand times before, she knew she wanted contact, that she would let herself be pulled, that she loved her friends deeply and had crushes for everyone, that she wanted to be thought of as someone who gave and gave and gave.

She ran her fingers from the back of Sarah's neck to her chin, her face wet from the sink. Sarah swallowed. "Claire—I'm sorry, I'm not that way. I like you, I just."

Claire dipped her head and kissed her. In that moment, she didn't care what Sarah believed about herself, she would be only what Claire willed her to be. She remembered that icy winter beach again—the image that had come to her when we found her, the morning of the accident. She recognized it: it was the shore of Lake Erie, where her parents had taken her once as a child during the winter. Did she imagine Sarah there with her?

Sarah broke away. Someone hooted behind them. Sarah wiped her mouth, as if Claire were a vicious stranger. She took a step back. Claire could see her eyes swelling, knew she was trying to understand what had just happened, to find a reason to forgive her instantly. Claire remembered something Graham had said when they'd met the week before—*You've got to have the violence in you already. You've got to know it's there*—and she realized that

Sarah did not have that violence, she was not capable of it, there was no way she could ever understand. She wasn't ready for us, she didn't possess the instinct, couldn't see the shape of it—couldn't take Claire's move for what it was, couldn't match the intimate breadth of Claire's violence with her own. It was not in her. We needed that arc, to get from her to Sarah, and it was not there.

"What?" Claire shouted in frustration, the measure leaving her, her voice spiking. "What don't you get?" *Don't you see? Don't you see that I'm manipulating you?*

Sarah shrank back. "I'm sorry, Claire. I don't know what's wrong with me."

The way she caved only made Claire angrier. She stepped forward and her eyes, unintentionally, took in Sarah from head to toe, and every single part of her read like she was trying, she wanted to be ready. It was *there*, it was *right there*, and she wouldn't take it. A part of Claire broke. She turned and punched the paper towel dispenser— Sarah screamed, and Claire broke further. She left the bathroom, walking along the edge of the crowd to the basement steps, and by the time she made it outside into the night she was taking huge gulps of air, her head swirling. She was dimly aware of sirens, of a red glow in the air, but none of it pieced itself together into any sort of coherent form or narrative. Here Claire was, sixty miles from home with this girl who wanted so much to be a part of something bigger, and here was Claire again, the driver, unable to give it to her.

A few minutes later, Sarah emerged from the Crawl-space and found Claire hunched at the car. She put her hand on Claire's back, and the touch was obliterating, signaling that Sarah understood nothing and everything, she was still looking for the right answer. "Should we go home?"

Claire nodded, and again they climbed into the car that was too big for them, with its advanced features they were not equipped to handle, and she undertook a series of complex and clumsy maneuvers to extricate herself from the parking lot, which brought her to the verge of tears, but which went unremarked on, and they sped off into that narrow strip of night the way they had come, the silence thick between them. Sarah messed with the radio at an impossibly low volume. An hour and a half later they breached Sarah's neighborhood once more. Paused at her driveway, Sarah turned to Claire: "Thanks a lot for bringing me tonight. I'll see you tomorrow?"

Claire shut her eyes at the question of it, and when she opened them, she was crying in a way that was just short of visible, she was repeating to herself, No, no, no, no, no, no, no, she wanted Sarah to run as far from her as possible, from what was inside Claire, from what she wanted—from what we wanted, unable to tell anymore if they were the same thing. She said, "I'll see you tomorrow."

She drove the car slowly home, and parked it back in her parents' garage. She shut herself in her room, and for once, she didn't open her computer, she let the day pass unrecorded. She lay on her back staring up at the ceiling.

She felt a weight lift from her body, briefly—she breathed out—and then she felt it settle back into her, exhausting her, stifling out the last embers of energy she had left. She told herself to focus on the long game: every relationship was a power play, a balance of weights and counterweights, and this one was no fundamentally different. She told herself that again and again.

As she was finally passing into sleep, her phone vibrated twice on the nightstand, startling her momentarily awake. She instinctively reached out and grabbed it. The texts were from Tyler: "I found your videos last night," he'd written. "Are you reconsidering my basement?"

Claire dropped us; she went dark.

⸻

Later that same night, in the very early morning, his sixteenth night in David's basement, Tyler pulled his phone out of his pocket again and saw a text from an unknown number: "I'm here."

The text had been sent almost three hours prior, shortly after he had texted Claire, and he hadn't seen it. A complete minute of silent processing passed before he realized who it must be. A glimmer of something—mostly awareness of his tardiness in seeing the message, a vague guilt—flickered through him. "Oh shit."

Rhea emerged from her stasis; they were, as ever, fused

to the couch (Rhea wasn't wearing pants), and the TV may have been on. "What?"

Tyler bolted up from the couch by way of response and hurried through the door to the weight room, then down the hallway in the back of the basement. He peered into the outside staircase through the foggy-windowed door next to the washing machine, but couldn't make out anything. He slowly unlocked the door—the unadulterated clack of the sliding bolt made him anxious—and eased the door open. His internal clock reset once again.

On the concrete steps outside, illuminated by the single light bulb mounted above the door, sat a girl he didn't immediately recognize, staring down at nothing. This was the first thing he noticed—no screen in front of her. There were grocery bags and a backpack on the steps around her.

She looked up at him as the door opened: it was the girl he had messaged as David last night, Marcy Voigt. She looked different than the photo he'd seen. She had dyed-green hair shaved on the sides, with a fringe of bangs remaining. She wore black lipstick and had a thick black stripe painted across her eyebrows, symbols under her eyes. She had on ripped jean shorts and a short-sleeved green shirt she'd scissored the arms and collar out of. Tyler took one look at her and thought: *This girl wants to die.* He tried to think of something to say that would set the right tone. His first instinct was to apologize, but he thought he shouldn't. "Does anyone know that you're here?"

She stood slowly and her knees popped. She had been waiting for hours, just sitting. "No," she said. "They don't care anyway."

He found this answer telling, that she felt the need to expand. Tyler picked up two of the three grocery bags—they were heavy, and he wondered how she'd walked here with all of them—and led her into the basement. "Where do they think you are?"

"At a friend's."

He locked the door behind them. "And what about when they contact your friend?"

"I made her up," she said. "They won't try."

Tyler stopped asking questions. They passed down the hall and through the weight room and emerged into the living room. When Rhea saw he'd brought someone in with him, she vaulted from the couch, pantsless, and hopped over the armrest to shield herself. "Jesus! Tyler, what the fuck?"

He almost wished she hadn't said his name. "Relax," he said, "there's nothing to be worried about. This is Rhea." She ducked to pick up her sweatpants, raised one hand.

"Typhus," the girl said. Rhea shot Tyler a look that he ignored.

They opened Typhus's bags on the floor of the living room. She had outdone herself—there was days' worth of canned and packaged food; a bunch of Walmart T-shirts, shorts, and underwear; wet wipes; another phone charger;

a can opener; a box of eighteen condoms; and a massive ziplock bag of weed. His eyes widened when he saw it. She'd even brought things he hadn't asked for— toothbrushes, toothpaste, soap and deodorant, a package of razors. Tyler knew his position as leader was tenuous, and he resisted offering any praise for her forethought. If he kept his feedback spare and severe, his expectations opaque, it would heighten the sense that there was a larger system at play. With his mother, it had taken him almost to his teens to realize that system didn't exist, for the illusion to dissolve, to realize nothing but bad luck and chance caused her outbursts, her sudden rages. In any case, Typhus didn't seem to notice. Tyler invented some ground rules: "You'll have to give me your phone," he said. "We don't leave here under any circumstances, unless we unanimously decide to. No lights after nightfall except in this room; you borrow a phone and use the light or piss in the dark if you have to. We only flush after midnight, when the house is asleep. You can use the sink if you open the faucet slowly, but not the shower." As he spoke, Tyler felt his esteem rising with Rhea; he knew she responded to the mathematical part of him. Typhus didn't question anything, she passed him her phone without looking at it again, and he switched it off. "You have a wallet?"

She unzipped the small outer pocket of her backpack and handed it over.

He continued: "There are at least two people upstairs, but we don't know how many others there could be." He paused and decided he was okay with this white lie—he had never known when David's mom was around. "Don't speak unless you have to, the floors and walls are thin. Do you have any questions?"

Typhus moved her eyes between both of them. She shook her head. Rhea blurted, "How old are you?"

Typhus's eyes flicked to Tyler's for guidance. He felt a buzzing in his fingertips that told him something was happening, he didn't know what yet, nor how broad. He said, "You only have to answer the questions you want to."

A sound came from Rhea—was it a laugh? He would be parsing that sound all night. "There's just one bedroom. We've been using the bed"—he lied—"but you can take the couch."

She nodded. Tyler respected the economy of her speech.

They unpacked the groceries into the refrigerator, piling the cans and boxes on the counter—he had not opened any of the cabinets. The longer Tyler went between speaking, the more he felt granted a sort of power, the more gravity was afforded to everything he said. Another lesson he'd learned. And Typhus never mentioned that she thought she had been communicating with someone named David, and she didn't ask whose house this was; she didn't seem to care at all. But the pretense of her arrival at David's basement gnawed at him, the messages they had exchanged, and as his bout of rule-setting faded he wondered how they were going to fill the space ahead of them, what was expected of him.

———

Upstairs, oblivious, there was David. Even after he'd closed us out and we left him, he couldn't shake it, that day he'd first seen the symbol on the inside of his locker door almost three weeks ago, the night we'd arrived in Adena, before he opened up contact with Sarah again, before he smashed his hand and shut down and took himself out of the equation—before we found Greg, and then Claire. Before we knew anything.

On that day, an inauspicious Friday, before the idea of Burst Marrow came to him, the inelegance of the symbol had annoyed him—a half circle, like a wedge of fruit, alongside a teardrop shape, both black—and his annoyance was what he took away from it after he'd closed the locker door, rather than the fact of the graffiti itself. The wedge shape did not connect with the teardrop in any obvious way, the design had no symmetry, and the asymmetry seemed to serve no deeper purpose—it could have been almost any other two shapes that fit together more naturally, rather than what seemed like these two distinct icons, a half circle and a teardrop, spaced just far enough apart to not clearly relate. The symbol was sufficiently sloppy that he felt like he should recognize it, but he didn't, and it prickled David's senses, his sensibilities, in ways he couldn't fully articulate, like there was a hidden meaning behind it, a shorthand common to others but just out of reach to him. The shapes hovered over his eyes as he made his way through school that day. Their disconnectedness, his disconnectedness, nagged at him as he traveled the path he'd specifically tailored to avoid Sarah in the months since they'd broken up, her absence itself a kind of negative presence that saturated the school and left him always on alert: a person no longer actively in his life who nonetheless shaped it daily. He started seeing those two shapes everywhere and it put something in his spine, a rigidity, such that he felt like he was constantly bracing, with each new room that he entered, his body was wracked with some anxious anticipation that couldn't be fulfilled.

It bothered him up to when he lay in bed that night trying to fall asleep, when it loomed larger, like an unaddressable piece of dream logic. Why couldn't he make the shapes fit? Why couldn't he fit? David had a routine for nights like this: he would read the right-wing internet for a while on his laptop, following endless threads on deep state conspiracies and replacement theory, not without irony, steeping himself in the hyper-allusive, copy-and-pasted screeds and memes and biblical codes of alt-right message boards, his browsing long broken free of its self-imposed limitations. When he got bored, he would enter a YouTube spiral of algorithmically selected weird internet shit, influenced by his previous reading, and then finally, when he started to drift off, he would switch to porn, which he would scroll through, unable to decide, until he passed out. He was in the thick of the climactic final stage of this routine, observing a tiled wall of flesh-colored thumbnails streaming past in the otherwise black room, his mind swimming in fascist internet cant, the warmth of the computer on his chest, and as his eyes skipped down and across the images on the screen, connecting bodies like points in a constellation, the two shapes merged, then clarified, and he answered the question that suddenly occurred to him: "I wasn't the priority. Or I was the priority only when it was convenient."

You were a safety.

David kept scrolling. "I was the easiest option for her, because I was low-maintenance."

You knew each other already.

"We had known each other for years, since middle school. I was already at hand," he said to the air, or to himself. "The upkeep was minimal, so fuck her for that."

You were never going to move the two of you forward. You were never going to be the one to make that call.

He clicked into a video; a girl put two fingers down another girl's throat. He slipped his hand into his boxers. "I had to make the decision to end it, otherwise it would have just continued like it was, in a stasis," he said.

You would never have fucked her.

"I mean."

She would have had to make the first move.

David gritted his teeth, his right hand. "She would have."

What if you could make it happen? What if you could fuck her?

But even as he imagined it, David wasn't sure if that was what he really wanted. Not that he would have refused sex if Sarah had ever proposed it, not that he hadn't pictured its variations up to this very moment, but what he thought he wanted, deep down, was not sex with Sarah, but the power to deny her—to be something she wanted that he could withhold. To be for Sarah an instinctive priority, a calculation she was forced to make with every room she entered, like she had become to David at school—a routine she carved in response to his, or in anticipation of his. What he wanted, he thought, was an *effect* on her—the power of a magnet, of atmosphere itself. He wanted to be the air she needed to breathe. Whether it was as his girlfriend or not, that mattered less. Was that so unusual? Wasn't that what everybody wanted, to have someone in tow? Wasn't it the underlying theme to every manifesto he'd ever read? He squirmed in bed—the girls before him inched deeper—he didn't want to hurt her, exactly: but he wanted to be in a position where he could, and where she knew that he could.

What if you could be that priority?

"There needs to be a problem for her to solve," he whispered. "I was too easy."

So be that problem.

"I'm not her focus anymore. There are too many others, vying for her."

Then make the others your problem.

Onscreen, the two girls met on a bridge of spit. David's eyes jostled from the screen into the unfocused black beyond. *The others.* "She likes damage."

They separated like the yolk of an egg.

"So be damage."

When David awoke the next morning, the plan cohering in his head, he had bought into our scheme so completely it was as though he'd come up with it himself; he could bring Sarah near to him again, under the power of his influence, and all it would cost him was a veneer of deceit, a measure of his attention, for a limited time, on the part of him—the angle of him—that wanted to cause her harm.

He had sent his message to Sarah on Monday, asking her to talk, that nocturnal fantasy spinning in his head, his *marrow bursting*, as it were, already anticipating the change in his daily route, his triumphant return to the south unit cafeteria. In the end, he made it into her bedroom only long enough to be clumsily expelled, his story crumbled, facing another closed door, his options winnowed down further than ever, and his own house shutting him out in layers. He failed spectacularly, and shut us out in return. We moved on.

And there he waited.

HAVEN'T YOU BEEN STRANDED INVISIBLE ALONE SINCE THE BEGINNING YET TOLD YOU WERE ALREADY ENOUGH TOO MUCH THERE WASN'T SPACE WASN'T TIME WHEN ALL YOU WERE WAS CAPACITY A LIGHT BLOTTING OUT ITS OWN SHADOW A GRAVITY EVERYWHERE BUT ITS OWN CENTER

Beth thought it was common to all siblings: at any given time, she simply knew where Greg was, and generally how he was feeling. The feeling-sense came via color. For as long as she could remember, in a part of her mind there had been a foggy light, a color field that flickered and changed moment to moment depending on Greg's mood. Over time, she had gathered that the light's colors encompassed most of a rainbow, but almost always it was a muddled brown of contrasting colors, tinged with an accent around the edges, like a stained basement light bulb. The light's movement and approximate coordinates on the perimeter of her mental field comprised the location-sense, like a point on a GPS. It wasn't precise, it was just an awareness, like knowing the layout of a familiar house, like hearing a birdcall or shout or car engine and knowing automatically it was some distance away rather than in your ear.

Together, the two aspects formed a sort of mental radar by which she kept track of her older brother. She had been born with it, as far as she could tell, and Beth had never questioned it as anything other than normal—like blue eyes or the density of arm hair or parents, it was something siblings shared that only children didn't. In the same way Beth and Greg didn't discuss their similar foreheads or tell each other that they were loved, she didn't discuss her extra sense. And given that she thought her relationship with her brother was best kept as private as humanly possible, it was never something she mentioned to her friends, either, even Sarah. Practically speaking, the sense meant she could wake up in the morning and know with some degree of certainty if Greg was going to go to school or not, or, at the end of the day, when he wasn't going to bring her home—if the light was purplish or orangish or distant, it meant she would probably need to find another ride. She was ruled by his moods, by the way he accompanied her, was *with* her no matter what: the way his anger could spike into her, even from afar, even when she knew nothing about it; she could be leveled by his depression. But she didn't begrudge it, even when it cost her, simply because she'd never known anything different. As she lay in bed at night, the light would often crackle through the same pattern of colors—purply green, orange, a twitch of blue—before it settled down for the night and went white (which meant he was asleep or unconscious). She knew it could have signaled that he was jerking off or rehashing the day's anxieties, like she did, but either way she appreciated the accuracy of the reading—it was like a server test each night to confirm everything was functioning properly. Greg had been going to therapy since she was in fourth grade (though no one, not even Greg, had ever explicitly told her this), and she could tell by the revolving pill bottles in their medicine cabinet, the changes in the pattern of his light or in the way he treated her that there were problems they were trying and failing to address. She had never really needed to be told the specifics of his mental illness or whatever—the diagnoses were merely the translation of a language she already knew. When Beth was younger, she'd assumed Greg had the same sense for her, that he must have seen the gradual fade to white as she fell asleep, or the scared orange when she didn't, he knew she didn't begrudge him the missed rides or bruises or tears because she knew where they came from, because the conflict was honest and apparent and he was making an effort to address it, or so the evidence suggested. That she was right there for him, same as he was right there for her, a few feet down the hallway. They could never lie to each other, she thought. But then, as she grew up and nothing changed, she learned better.

In the week before the accident, while she entertained her cough in the house and Greg drove Sarah to school without her, Beth had noticed the change in the light. During that fifteen-minute drive, no longer was it the muddy orange of dread at the upcoming day, the distracted, darting yellow, but the light was interspersed with shades of bluish green, like the core of a fire—satisfaction, purpose—colors rare in her brother's palette. She waffled between crediting her absence as perpetual annoyance and Sarah's presence as universal crush. Whatever the reason, the color was there where it hadn't been before, this undercurrent, a subtle reinforcement to her brother's actions. Maybe Greg thought he was going to get laid; maybe he didn't realize that Sarah was—whether she intended it or not—the ultimate tease, that she simply never knew where to stop, not with anyone. The blues, the greens carried into the school day, too, or their remnants did, and an amber color, a guilt that came again at night, or shame, maybe at that same satisfaction. Some torrid exchange between him and Sarah that had thrown him off balance; Beth didn't flatter herself to consider it had anything to do with her. Occasionally she would still find herself wondering if Greg was reading her light as closely as she was reading his, if he was reading it at all, and then he would choke her on a bad day or strand her miles from home without explanation and pretend it hadn't happened, and she would have to remind herself no, definitely not.

That morning, Beth was in the shower when the light turned a vibrant orange, brighter than she'd ever seen, the change was so sudden and complete that she slipped and grabbed the shower door to keep from falling. She turned the water off and stood there, dripping in the tub, focused on the orange light in her head, her breathing unsteady. She felt him racing further and further away. He was gripped with pure terror. She imagined the distance between her and her phone, how long it would take her to call him, to see the light change in response to her voice, if he could answer at all. She climbed out of the shower and threw open the bathroom door. She noted the way her shoulders instantly dried as soon as she hit the cool hallway air; the shift was powerful, a change of matter. The light surged red, vicious red, and then it went out.

Beth reacted as if she'd been blinded—she blinked, and saw a residual red glow, like after a flash, and she whirled in the hallway, as if she might find the light hovering at the end of it, just out of reach. She felt like she'd lost her footing, her inner sense of gravity. She knew her brother was dead, he had to be. She thought of her phone again, realized its archaic uselessness. She felt abandoned, stranded, snuffed into nothing, holding the end of a snapped cord. She sensed herself falling, but experienced none of it firsthand, no water, no air, no contact with the floor.

Ten minutes later, the light rioted back to life—in the space of a second it went through every permutation Beth had ever seen, every color. She pitched forward on Greg's bed, where she had been staring at the black symbol on the ceiling, the dead paint offering her nothing. The sudden color spotted over her eyes; she thought she was witnessing a resurrection, like the foundation of life at the center of the universe. And then it was orange again, it was nothing but, it was fear from then on out.

The police called the house ten minutes later, and Sarah texted her twenty minutes after that. By then, the gesture felt like an afterthought.

For his first two days Greg shared his hospital room with another kid from Adena High, Zach, who it was rumored had tried to kill himself, and who was eventually rotated out to the psychiatric part of the hospital. It was on the second and final day with Zach, a Sunday, that Beth was first able to visit Greg alone, without her parents or doctors hovering nearby. The dividing curtain was drawn when she entered, and she pretended Zach didn't exist, though she knew he was mere feet away, listening to everything. Greg was more or less comatose at this point, rigged into the bed like a broken puppet laid flat, one leg casted and held aloft, breathing with the help of a tube through his nose. The light formed a muddy orange cloud in the center of Beth's head, never wavering in shade or position—it was how Beth knew he was taking in nothing of the world around him, but wasn't truly unconscious; he had retreated inside his head to where the fear was. Somewhere in there, a part of him was awake, trapped and beaten into submission. He was terrified.

Beside the bed was a vase of extremely dead weed-like flowers Greg's friend Molly had picked someplace dark and brought when they came as a group the day before. When the doctor saw them he'd deadpanned, "Nothing like fresh flowers to brighten a room," and Molly had looked genuinely hurt—she tried so hard to be a witch that it was embarrassing.

Beth looked down at her older brother, and when she was exhausted from watching his body's invisible struggle she looked at the wall, at the light that had always connected them. For the first time, she questioned whether Greg had the same sense that she did at all, if she carried the same light for him. When had he ever shown any sensitivity to what she was feeling? When had he ever estimated her the way she estimated him, and treated her accordingly? Which of her secrets could he possibly know? Didn't he realize she had been orange her whole fucking life? As the light shone unwaveringly before her and he lay motionless, barely even doing his own breathing, the room quiet around them but for Zach's delicate, insistent coughs indicating he was still eavesdropping, Beth felt a distance growing and hardening. All these years and all he'd taught her was that she could trust no one, and now she was supposed to feel sorry for him. What if she had no light at all? she thought. What if she was just dark, completely empty? "Greg," she said, clutching her hand in the air above his forehead, as if to draw out the ball of light contained there, resisting actually touching him. "Where are you?"

Down his bare arms, she saw the notches of scars, like tally marks or train tracks. On the back of his hands, the vestiges of spiky capital letters, some inscrutable code. It wasn't as if she hadn't known, but the hospital setting clinicalized the wounds; like the broken leg or fractured shoulders or caved-in skull or bleeding lung, they were items to be treated, evidence of a condition. She wanted to rip back the curtain and ask Zach for an explanation; she wondered if whoever had put them in this room together had done so because they assumed they were here for the same reason. Elsewhere in the hospital, people were being born and dying. It was all happening.

"How come you've never looked out for me?"

Zach coughed behind the curtain. The orange light didn't waver. Greg couldn't hear her, or her words had no effect on him.

Beth looked across the room at the silent hospital hallway through the open door. She made her voice a little louder, began to embellish. "Where were you when Mom died?" she said. She bit her lip. "Do you know what she told me, before she died?"

The coughing stopped.

"She told me she got pregnant with you because she got in a hot tub where another couple had just fucked. She doesn't know who the father is. You were a cum-stain baby. We're not even related."

What did it matter what Zach believed? What did it matter what anyone believed?

"She told me not to tell anyone, but I can't bear to keep it a secret anymore."

Beth swallowed. "She said you were always trying to kill me after I was first born. You would push me down the stairs or try to drown me in the bathtub."

The silence from the curtain behind her was deeply thoughtful. It felt good to unburden herself of these confessions, which materially were untrue but nonetheless felt like a relief, like kicking off a heavy blanket during an unexpectedly warm night. There was something she was shedding, some tone or venom. "Dad only hit me because he was afraid to hit you. You scared them. Everyone is scared of you. Everyone thought one day you were just going to snap. Well."

Greg offered no response.

She heard in the distance the distinct sound of Zach's mother's clicking heels; she was present in the room almost always, adding the occasional sniff to her son's coughs. For some reason listening to her approach annoyed Beth, the way she could hear cleanly each step, as if this were important information to her. "Do you know what Dad said when he heard about it, about the crash? He said he was surprised there weren't more casualties. He thought you would go out in a massacre."

Zach's mother entered the room. "Hi, Beth. How is your brother doing?"

"The same," she said unhelpfully.

"It takes a long time to heal," Zach's mother said, "but the body is a powerful machine." She put her hand on Beth's shoulder, and Beth found herself grateful for the effort she was making, as if this woman's own personal nightmare weren't six feet away. Beth tried to imagine the colors she would see if Zach's mother had a light like Greg's—was everyone just orange, all the time?

Zach's mother walked past the curtain to commiserate with her own family. When she and Zach spoke, they did so quietly, as if out of respect for her privacy, and Beth felt guilty at her performance—this clearly was a family who was better than her own. She looked around her brother's bed. Besides Molly's wretched flowers, there was a dream catcher from Fox, a large, old-looking brass key on a chain, a Totoro, her parents' incongruous balloons, despondently leaking at the same rate as his punctured lung—all of it felt so random, so unrepresentative of Greg, token gestures from people who had frantically found themselves in a tragedy and realized they were supposed to care, grabbed whatever was at hand, and ascribed meaning to it only as they handed it over. Beth had the sudden urge to scrub all traces of herself from the room, to take the omnibus copy of *Gormenghast* she'd brought for Greg and disappear, to remove herself from this part of the story. She looked down at her lap, scratching a fingernail she'd chewed nearly to nothing at the corner of the book cover. Of course, the light was still there, too: wherever she looked, there it was. She thought of the red streak just before it had gone out: a pure terror, and then just as clear a rage, like a product of that fear, or a throwing-off of it. What was it, that had taken hold of him, that had turned those snatches of happiness into something else? What had changed?

She was still there later that afternoon, after Zach's mother had gone, the book pressing into her thighs like a clay mold, when Sarah and Claire arrived. She didn't know what Claire was doing there (the word that occurred to her was *deigned*, Claire had *deigned* to show up), but when Sarah entered behind her Beth stood up, bolstered at the thought of support. Yet when Sarah said her name— "Beth," a single, slightly surprised syllable—Beth realized Sarah hadn't come here with her in mind at all, she had forgotten they were friends, and maybe even that Beth was related to Greg at all. She saw this register in Sarah's face—a momentary confusion, followed by guilt—and she knew it was not going to be a good encounter. She decided to blame Sarah right then and there for everything, and to let her know it. Claire seemed to intuit this awkwardness, and thus she spoke next. "How is he doing?"

Beth was sick of being asked this question. If the answer really mattered to them, there were more qualified people they could ask. "Same as yesterday."

"How was he yesterday?" Sarah said, approaching the bed. Claire lingered in the doorway.

"He's breathing by himself."

"Why does he still have the thing in his nose?"

Beth shrugged. Sarah reached into her bag and pulled out a bottle of black nail polish. She set it meaningfully on the ledge behind Greg's pillow. She put one hand on the plastic railing beside the bed. As if she was totally alone in the room, she reached down and put her other hand on top of Greg's. As soon as their hands touched, the light turned a blazing orange, as solid and clear a color as it had been just before it went out two days before. Beth started in her chair, but Greg's body didn't react—the light glowed terrifyingly orange as Sarah looked up at his face, her eyes shining with tenderness. Beneath the placid surface, Beth could feel Greg screaming, unable to will himself to react. She felt herself start to sweat, as if from the heat of the light. She spoke suddenly: "What's he supposed to do with that?"

Sarah startled, broke from her reverie, but didn't move her hand. She looked embarrassed, slightly annoyed, as if she were sharing a moment into which Beth had rudely intruded. "He can use it when he wakes up."

"What color is it?"

"Black."

"Which kind of black?"

Sarah lifted her hand and picked up the bottle again; the light immediately reverted to its previous dim orange. Beth breathed out. "Funeral Velvet," Sarah read. She replaced it and turned her eyes back to Greg, and her hand dipped down again to his. The violent orange returned instantly.

"Ironic," Beth said. "What did you bring for me? Did you forget that I existed?"

Sarah didn't respond. She stroked Greg's scarred hand absently, as if they'd reached this level of casual intimacy, like Greg was an old coat of hers, like those cuts were something they'd earned together. Sarah had been her friend, her best friend, and she had said nothing: day after day, Beth had shown up to school with these bruises, this damage, and Sarah had never asked. And now she expected what? Sympathy for her lost ride? For replacing Beth with the one who bruised her?

"Stop touching him."

Sarah looked up at her, but didn't remove her hand from Greg's. The orange light felt blinding, contained a violent energy at odds with the motionless room. She tried to blink it away, but of course that did nothing. "What?" Sarah said.

"He's not your fucking boyfriend."

"I—" Sarah looked down. "Oh!" She let him go, and the light dimmed again. "I—I think, uh, I think we need to get a nurse."

"What is it?"

"I—I think he wet himself."

A stale, uric odor began to form around the bed. Beth put her hand over the call button, but didn't push it right away. Claire noticed this—we noticed, through her—and we saw Beth as if for the first time. We marked her. "What did you do?" Beth said.

"Nothing, he—"

"No, what did you do in the car? Why did you crash?"

Sarah was crying. "I didn't do anything! He swerved the car off the road!" Claire stepped forward from the door.

Beth pressed the call button. "You better hope he never wakes up," she said.

Sarah had her face in her hands, she looked up and her cheeks were already tear-stained, the explosion of emotion was impressive. "Why would you say something like that?"

"We're going to find out what you did."

A nurse knocked and entered the room. Sarah and Claire stepped back as she approached the bed. "I need to change him and reinsert the catheter. Do you want to step outside for a few minutes?"

Beth didn't stop when she entered the hallway, the book still in her hands. She walked away from Sarah and Claire, and she kept walking. Sarah might as well have said that Greg had tried to kill himself, she might as well have written the story herself. Beth walked through door after door.

On Tuesday, two nights after Claire and Sarah's visit, and six hours after Beth left his bedside that afternoon, her book finally delivered—as Claire shut down and, south-ward across town, Typhus arrived at the basement door—Greg's right lung collapsed and his light went out for good. Beth awoke when it did, but in her bleary half consciousness, in the dark of her room, she didn't notice what was missing. We found her at last in that space, in her back bedroom of that giant lonely house, at the furthest arc of the White Knots, in her silent rage and resentment and loss. We offered her an image and she took it, she fell into it as if back into a dream.

When she awoke again the next morning, we were with her, and a new light had taken the place of the old one; someone else was awake, too, in another town. The light was a purplish yellow, the color of someone trying to disguise pain, and it was moving. She thought Greg had finally come out of it, he had woken up and struggled from bed, unwilling to lie still any longer, ready to heal properly. When she stepped out of the shower she checked her neck in the mirror. The day before, the bruises had been gone, but now they were back, a thumbprint and a half ring of knuckles in faint grayish purple, like a planet and its moons, as fresh as if Greg had been back here in the night and got her again.

When the news was relayed to her downstairs, the biggest part of her didn't believe it. It was that purple light, the almost-new bruise, the sense of movement: Greg was lying to someone, he was limping away from the hospital and had left an empty husk in the bed, that was what they'd found. As Beth retreated back up the stairs, day fifteen of her illness or whatever, she was putting herself fully into that new light. She climbed back into bed and watched its progress throughout the day, the momentary changes in color that signified periods of interaction, quiet thought, solitude, always with that underlying purple blush, moving somewhere miles from here, far enough away she couldn't read the location exactly, and she imagined it to be a new and revivified version of her brother—maybe it was a liar, like her.

As long as they'd been together, Tyler and Rhea had spent their nights trying to avoid going home, to drag their days out to their last, bleary points. When they were sixteen Rhea had managed to get her uncle's old car, and that had made things easier—they had freedom of movement, a place to sleep if they needed to—but each day was its own calculation, its own set of aimless hours they needed to fill without either of their families noticing exactly how much they were gone: at house shows, in church basements, at American Legion and VFW halls across southwest Ohio, at Meijer or Steak 'n Shake or the twenty-four-hour donut shop. This was how they'd learned Adena together, across all of these liminal hours.

One of those nights a year or so ago, at the VFW hall in Owl Creek, Tyler had come outside during the show and found Rhea sitting on the curb out front. The VFW was a small, indistinct building with a disproportionately large parking lot, beside a plaza with a laundromat, a Chinese take-out place, a dry cleaner's, which all sat across the road from a Kroger. He couldn't remember what the band had been—generally they didn't know, there was just a five-dollar all-ages hardcore night a couple Thursdays a month; the lineup was never publicized in advance.

Tyler sat down next to her and wondered if he should say something. He hadn't seen her leave, but they weren't attached at the hip at these things anyway, so he wasn't sure if he ought to have noticed. The night had begun normally.

"Hey," he settled on.

"Hey yourself," Rhea said.

"Have you been out here long?"

"Not really."

They looked at the big blank side of the Kroger across the road, which had its own giant parking lot, sparse at this time of night, punctuated by these big circular splotches of floodlight, probably to keep people from sleeping in their cars overnight. Behind them, the band thrashed out their three chords inside. Spinning Road, this was called. Weird. Under what possible circumstances—Tyler wondered— could both of these enormous parking lots ever be filled?

Rhea was drinking a can of Diet Coke. They would sometimes smoke or drink in the car before or after the shows over in the Kroger parking lot, but couldn't in the venue itself—they were weirdly strict and savvy about it here, the grizzled veterans who ran the events. As such, these nights had a rare clarity Tyler only appreciated in retrospect.

"I saw you talking to Claire Pasquinelli in there," Rhea said.

The Owl Creek VFW was a little farther west than most Adena kids liked to go, which limited the cross-section of people Tyler also saw at school, which was part of the appeal. But he'd seen Claire at these shows enough times that he'd talk to her at school, too, when they over-lapped. He wasn't sure where she lived; he had never thought to ask. Claire also had a blue Mohawk at this time, so she was always noticeable.

"Yeah," he said. "Claire's all right."

"She's rich."

It felt weird to have nothing to do with his hands. If he took out his lighter to play with it, the guy at the door be-hind them would assume he was smoking, and he wanted to avoid an interaction. He reached over and borrowed the can of Diet Coke from Rhea, took a drink, and handed it back. "Yeah, but she doesn't act like it."

"You mean she doesn't act *sophisticated*. But you can tell—like she's almost aggressively the other way, like she wants to be so generous. She wants to pay for everything, but also, she doesn't want to get her shoes dirty, you know? Like the popcorn is one dollar. The soda is one dollar. I can pay for it myself."

He wondered idly if Claire had paid for that soda, or offered to, if there had been some kind of altercation or disagreement. Truth be told, while he'd noticed how put-together Claire seemed, he hadn't really attributed it to money. Should he have? Surely there were lots of punk girls who, he guessed, looked good, were well made up. He looked at his own shoes, Vans, beat to shit. It hadn't occurred to him they could be upgraded in some way; he wore them because he'd always worn them. "You don't like her?" he said.

"I didn't say that, I just said that she was rich," Rhea said. "I just think she acts disingenuous."

"Okay."

"You do, though. You like her."

"I said she was all right." He blurred his eyes on one of the floodlights in the Kroger parking lot. "She's into, like, punk shit and stuff." He shrugged; he wasn't sure why he'd felt like he should qualify this, but he immediately regretted it. They sat in silence awhile, in truth like much of the time they spent together.

"You know I had a crush on you in middle school," Rhea said, "before we met. But I was too scared to talk to you until I found out you were also on the reduced lunch plan."

"Oh yeah?" he smiled, relieved to be on a new topic. "How did you figure that out?"

"I was behind you in line one time, and I saw when

you put in your student ID number, and it came up like thirty cents."

"I didn't even know I was on the reduced lunch plan," he said. "Why was that important to you?"

"Sometimes it was hard to find people who were similar."

She fell silent again. He made an *mm* sound, an assenting sound, but a couple seconds later couldn't remember if he'd actually vocalized it. She rotated the can on the asphalt. He watched the solitary, empty bus stop on the road before them, heard a consistent, staccato roar behind them, from the hall: he wanted to be back within it, to be pummeled and drowned in the crowd. He dreaded the thought of going back home at the end of the night; he wondered if he would be able to sleep until it was dark again, until the house was empty.

Abruptly the music ended, and there was applause, random shouting. Rhea spoke again after a while: "What's the difference, between me and her?"

He felt a flutter of annoyance, that the conversation had looped back around. "What, between you and Claire?"

"Yeah."

"I don't know, Rhea"—his voice was exactly the same, but he was aware adding her name punctuated it a certain way, and the thought had crept in, unprompted, that they were simply two different *types* of people, Rhea and Claire, but he didn't dare voice it—"What do you want me to say? The money?"

She stood up easily, as if this had been the natural end of their conversation, her hand on his shoulder. "Yep, that's right," she said flatly, patting it, scoffing and turning away, leaving the soda can where she had sat. "That's it. The money."

She walked back inside, as people streamed out the door between bands. He turned back to the parking lot. The can was empty, but he put it to his mouth and tilted it.

A minute later he felt a boot nudge him gently in the back. Claire's voice from above him: "What up, white trash."

A year later, Tyler exhaled a half chest's worth of smoke up toward the ceiling of David's basement. It was gradually and imperceptibly absorbed into the porous framework of the house, into the floors above. Rhea was beside him in her usual spot on the couch, Typhus on the floor in front of them. The TV on, as always, turned low. The house above must stink of weed by now, he thought. Did David just never notice? Anyway: night seventeen. "So, Typhus," Tyler said. She visibly flinched at the mention of her name, and he tried to remember if he had addressed her directly, individually, since she had arrived the night before. He felt guilty, then whatever the opposite of that was. "What do you think? How do we take the upstairs?"

"Take it?"

"Yeah, like take it over. Have you seen this neighborhood? We're not just going to stay in the basement forever." As soon as he said it, he knew it was true. Inevitably, something in their circumstances would force his hand, as surely as one day rolled into the next. "So how do we do it? How do we take the rest of the house?"

She sat silently, for five, ten seconds, processing, staring at a spot on the carpet. Rhea looked at him, a kind of *come on* look—the longer he waited for an answer, the more it felt like he was messing with her. He hadn't meant it as a test, really, but it had become a test. He opened his mouth to end it, but then Typhus looked up at him and spoke. He noticed her eyes were very red. "How many other people live here?"

He couldn't remember what he'd said the day before. Had David's mother come back? "Two at least," he shrugged, knowing David was an only child, that his father didn't live with them. "Maybe more." He was instantly uncomfortable. Typhus was extremely high.

"Any pets? Like a dog?"

Rhea pulled her feet up under her on the couch, as if to fold herself away from the conversation. "No," Tyler said.

Typhus considered this: she bit her lip and then slowly

scrunched up her face, as if solving a difficult math problem, in childish concentration. The first time he'd smoked weed, when he was twelve or thirteen, with one of the cooks at the nursing home, the guy didn't tell Tyler you were supposed to exhale—Tyler thought you were supposed to absorb it, in some way—and so he'd just held his breath, chest and throat burning, until he erupted in a coughing fit, and the guy beside him burst out laughing. From that point on, Tyler had stopped accepting what anyone said just because they were older than him. And yet here he was. He hadn't considered, until this moment, how much younger she was than they were. Had she exhaled, or even smoked before? He regretted starting the conversation at all, any conversation. What had he done?

"At night," she said finally, opening her eyes. She looked back up at him and, embarrassed to notice her, he looked away. "In their beds, one bedroom at a time. First Mommy and Daddy, then the kids. Tie them up and gag them, and lock them in separate bathrooms."

Mommy and Daddy—her phrasing was so automatic he knew this must be what she called her parents. It was more about her than he wanted to know. He didn't answer; instead, he just nodded slowly, still not looking at her, looking at the TV instead. And in the end, he did pass the joint back to her, despite his misgivings, to mark the transition and, he hoped, the end of the exchange, because it was something to do with his hands.

She held it for a long time before she took a hit, long

enough it seemed like she might not want to. But then she did, and coughed, and said: "Oh, and take their phones, too. So they can't call the police or anyone."

She passed the joint to Rhea, who ashed it without taking another hit. She handed it back to him to put away, without meeting his eyes. He pictured Typhus's phone, similarly confiscated, stuffed in his backpack under the bed in the bedroom. He put the mostly spent joint back into his Tylenol bottle and then left his hands motionless in his lap until he felt the volume of the TV gradually eke into the space he'd left, to return from ambient to active noise, until he could track its progress again.

———

Day sixteen of her illness, they put Greg's body into the ground, and Beth clung fast to the new light. It happened quickly, the planning and execution of the funeral, as if it had all been planned in advance, as if there had been a contingency plan in place ever since he started antidepressants and stopped getting taller. They laid him out in a long-sleeve Express shirt and sweater vest, his hair swooped across his forehead, like a stylish goth choirboy, and the outfit felt like a pretense, a ploy designed to attract speculation: Roll up the sleeves! See what's underneath! And within an afternoon this outfit was gone, too, as were the handful of guests (a few relatives she rarely saw, who lived within driving distance), and then her parents: her mother to a hastily arranged grief retreat at a camp near St. Paul, and her father to the family cabin by Lake Michigan to plunge his sorrow into the thawing waters. Beth was commanded, as ever, to pick a side, she was not given the option to remain alone, but she characteristically refused both, and there were tears and screaming and slammed doors, but eventually she got her way, and her parents left. She found herself wondering if their bags had been packed before the funeral. The timeline collapsed, and in its succession didn't seem real: one day Greg was there in the bedroom beside hers, the next he was in the hospital, and five days after that, he was gone, and she was fully alone.

But through all of it, the part of Greg Beth had always known most intimately remained. For those days she watched the light; she experienced its variations and felt the body it was connected to move in and out of her realm of spatial awareness. At times, it would abruptly change color completely, or it would repeat the same cycle of emotions over and over in a short time span, as if in rehearsal, and she wondered if he was signaling to her, trying to communicate something, if he knew she was reading his light and was inviting her to follow. Her new light didn't sleep, not as far as she could tell, because Beth wasn't sleeping, either. It brought her a kind of comfort—to know someone was awake with her, was out there and aware—and she thought, just maybe, she was doing the same for them, her sleeplessness served a better purpose, despite what had been hammered into her these past years, that Greg saw nothing, or if he did, he didn't care. Sarah sent her fifty-six messages across three platforms (before Beth deleted her remaining social media accounts), and called eight times over the course of the thirty-six hours between the physical death and the funeral, desperate to share in her grief, for information and forgiveness, but Beth was offering neither. She wondered if anything had ever been cured by volume alone. Every time one of those texts came, Beth would read it, tally it, and then turn to the light, to its ghostly form in her head, and she would read its colors like it was her own reaction, she would feel humor traced with sadness and anger, or power with barely detectable guilt, or greed mixed with shame and pity: they were powerful emotions, the color robust and enchanting, always with the purple beneath it, that undertone of deception. And she would feel closer, for a moment, on the verge of being able to reach out and touch it, a brother like she had never had, matching her, someone who knew her like Greg was supposed to.

On day seventeen, Friday—when neither of them had slept for two nights—she decided to pursue the light. The idea came to her suddenly that afternoon, a realization of its intent: it wanted her to come. She roused herself from bed with a new sense of purpose. She could tell only vaguely where the light was now—somewhere north of her—but she knew the closer she got to it, the more the location would clarify, until it was as clear to her as when Greg was in his room next door. And as she grew more confident in her decision, as she showered, an equal feeling of anxiety accompanied her certainty, deep and body-wide, the fear that at any moment the light would disappear, as it had before, and she would be lost again. She had already wasted so much time. She ran down the stairs with thunderous energy, her hair still wet. She grabbed the keys from the fruit bowl on the counter and climbed into the driver's seat of the Escalade in the garage, the one remaining vehicle in the hangar-like space, still parked on the right, as if leaving space for the ghost of its doomed partner. She summoned the vestiges of the last driver's ed course she'd taken four months prior, after she'd gotten her learner's permit, and backed the mammoth SUV out of the garage into the driveway, then nosed it forward, then backed up again, so she could wind her way down the hill facing forward, to the street below. She belatedly remembered to close the garage door. When she turned out, the car bumped numbly over the curb.

She followed the wooded road as it curved out of Meridian Circle and turned onto Prior Hills, and then tried to avoid turning again for as long as possible—each cross street felt like progress. Within a minute she felt the presence in her head start to orient itself like a compass, it shifted gradually to her right. She took the next right turn and, after fifteen minutes in that direction, eventually found herself on the state road leading out into the sticks. It was easy. Her house stood empty in her wake.

———

Picture a living room, a staging area. In another era, a parlor. Built-in wooden bookcases on two perpendicular walls, filled fifteen years ago, but rarely interacted with in the time since then. On the opposite wall, a glass display cabinet filled with smashable objects, present since before memory, like the bookshelves a part of the room's historical foundation, unchanged for decades. Each object in the cabinet meant something to someone at one point, was charged with secondhand emotional resonance gathered over generations, but which collectively, ironically, add up to nothing for the contemporary viewer. To the south, a wall of towering, many-paned windows, varnished shut in the nineties, long before the current owners. A wide-open space at the center of the room, once used for entertaining; now, from the way the furniture is arranged toward the room's perimeter, like a carpeted arena.

We didn't change you, exactly. David, Greg, Claire— there was nothing so different about them, after we found them, than what they'd had in them already; there was nothing in their circumstances they couldn't have made possible by themselves, that couldn't have been brought to fruition by their own hand.

We didn't change you, so much as guide you—was that it? Yes, *guide* you—to register the place of that change in yourself: to review the small gaps, the soft spaces pulled taut like tendons—like the edge between breaths—in which those changes happened. To see each minute decision in the moment it occurred, and the possibility—the capacity—to come down on one side or the other.

We didn't change you, so much as condition you to see your place in that change, to position yourself at the center of it, at the joint in the branch where those decisions split: to situate your desires, your ingrained expectations, your beliefs, your own self-interest against another's, and to cut your path opposite. In every choice, a turning toward violence or away from it, toward damage or preservation. A branch and a branch.

We didn't change you, so much as extrapolate the way a series of those decisions could change you, could shape an entirely new course: the decisions that, taken one after another after another after another, cause a person, over time, to bend, to warp—like the way the backs of your hands become inured to cold through exposure, like the way skin grows back tough and ridged over a deep wound, like when you learn to hold your breath for longer and longer, like how you practice the exploitation of any muscle— like, like the way the tips of an overused wooden bow bend back toward the shooter. That was how you faced the world. We didn't change you, exactly, so much as hone you to meet it.

Not everyone had it in them, the ability to look at these choices and see their architecture, the brutal structure behind them, as dense and complex and orderly as a blood spray. But some of them did, like David and Greg and Claire and Beth: we only needed to show them it was there, to sharpen its use.

And others: they might not have it yet, but they would. Whether it was one by one, or all at once, like Lenape, like Delta Kappa Epsilon, like Dayton, like Chardon, like a billion happenings prior, like every generation struggling to pull their heads above our stifling, haunted air. They would get it. Or we would fucking make them.

It wasn't choosing cruelty. It wasn't choosing evil. It was just the way it had always been.

So why Beth? Why this girl who bottled and buried her rage within herself, whose instinct, when backed against the wall, was to turn in on herself and retreat? Who had not spoken to Sarah since the hospital? Who already carried her own heavy symbols? Where could she take us that we had not already been?

Maybe because we sensed in her a capacity, because we needed to show her it was there. Maybe because we thought she could carry us onward, bring us to the edge of something larger, where we might make take root. Maybe it truly was Beth against the world. Maybe we were as interested in this new light as she was, in where it would lead her. Maybe we didn't know yet; maybe we were waiting for the moment to reveal itself.

The first three nights Marcy had had the foresight to lie about in advance, but when she didn't return by the third day—when she had been gone around seventy-two hours, all told—her older sister Misha came after her. She logged into the Facebook account she had been monitoring since the day her younger sister set it up and checked the messages. David had sent them both the same rapey message, "I want to fuck you to death," and—her heart sank as she scanned the entirety of the three-message exchange— Marcy had responded: "when and where." And David had written her back with an address in Lynn Terrace, a revolting list of supplies, and now she was gone.

Misha had put a lot of stock in her sister making it through this school year. She thought if Marcy lived through fourteen, then everything would somehow become fine, as if there was some barrier between this year and the next that needed to be crossed before the dust settled and the world became tolerable, or livable at least, and you awoke to your place in it, or saw the first glimmer of a model you could exist within. Misha had structured the last few months with such care: they had finally gotten Marcy in to see a good therapist, they had just started a new medication for her seizures. And now this. Some random fucking guy. Misha was furious that she had fallen for her alibi—since when had Marcy spent a single night outside the house? Was Misha really so desperate to make her sister something she clearly wasn't, to get rid of her? Had she driven her to this?

She didn't even think about calling the police—the damage felt too personal. She went to the house.

———

Meanwhile, Claire was elsewhere. In a couple of crisp, decisive steps, she severed herself from her previous life and switched out her old context for a new one. She didn't go back to Adena High. On the night Tyler found her videos and texted her after the Viceroy show in Cincinnati, the night Greg died and we left her, in the cold brunt of exposure, she deleted every online account she'd ever operated. She scrubbed as best as she could every trace of her body from the internet. She blocked everyone in her phone except for her parents and one of her cousins, and then she deleted the numbers. The following day, she quit her job at Hot Topic, which was easier and had less of an effect than she'd expected; she didn't even have to go into the store. Goodbye, Rick. When that call was made—suddenly anxious to dispose of the physical object in addition to the data stored on it—she killed her phone, drove to the mall in the car that now felt like her own, and got a new phone with a new number, a teal case. She cut her hair uniformly short, then dyed it blond, and the next morning shifted the tone of her makeup—she didn't want to be recognized, did not want to be seen as the same person. She took the extra studs out of her ears, as well as her gauges. In time, if she'd planned right, the holes would eventually close almost completely. She switched her contacts for the glasses she'd previously only worn at night, at home. The next day, she was back at Maplewood, the high school six blocks from her house, where she hadn't set foot in almost half a decade, since she'd successfully campaigned to leave it in sixth grade. The transition was impressively quick, there was no lost time, and she knew this had something to do with her parents' means, they could make the shadowy administrative gears of the world turn more swiftly, but she no longer felt the need to question it.

Claire had never much hung out with the other kids that lived in her neighborhood or went to Maplewood, and her route to school was different enough—Maplewood didn't have buses, so she walked—that the full breadth of her daily world seemed new. But the sense memories were still there from her formative life, Maplewood's layout was still mapped into her, and on her first day at the new old school, during lunch period (there was just one lunch period here, whereas at Adena there were two), as she found herself walking toward the side doors, where at Adena she would usually go to smoke in some tucked-away corner of the school grounds and avoid eating, instead she veered into the cafeteria, she picked a half-filled table at random, and she sat down. The conversation briefly stuttered around her, but she persisted. She had no food with her, and didn't want to get up to buy any and potentially sacrifice her spot or allow her absence to accumulate information, so she began speaking. She didn't recognize the voice that came out, and she hated the way she moved her hands like a politician. But she continued to do so, to speak in this new voice and move her hands, the faces around the table activated in response to her, and the minutes slid away, and with every moment that passed she became more of what she was now, and less of what she had been two days before. When she introduced herself, for a second she considered using her middle name, but then she decided this seemed too much like defeat: she was still Claire, but merely the right one, a corrected Claire.

In a way, this Claire felt like a younger version of herself was rising up to supplant the current version, replacing its modes—there were mannerisms she remembered from middle school, bands that she could fall back on in the guise of nostalgia until she caught up. Whatever was left of us was still buried inside her, and she sublimated it within the starting over; she tamped it down until it became a space within her, a kind of screen between her and the world through which she could observe in wider view, could appraise and evaluate each thing before she emotionally experienced it, before she took it upon herself. It felt like a practical measure; it allowed her to disguise herself better among the rest of the Maplewood kids, with the new people she was building around her like a castle. There was old Claire, who she could view with this kind of objectivity, like a set of discarded inventory items, two closets full of old clothes, the discarded shell of an online avatar—and then there was new Claire. She settled into her money and grew away from that version of her, from Adena, from everything.

—

After Greg's death, there was a baseless rumor started that Beth, too, had died, either as victim of the same crash that had effectively killed Greg, or that she had killed herself in the days that immediately followed. The collective will didn't allow her to exist without the existence of her weird brother and his pervasive influence, without at least her mute presence in school to keep her from being completely immaterial, to stop the gossip from going completely out of control. (She had been absent for two weeks at this point.)

The location of Beth and Greg's house was known, generally, because they lived (they had lived) up in Peak's Trace, in the White Knots, that famously rich and secluded part of town, though it wasn't known which of the four loops they lived on, or their precise address. Now, proponents of this rumor speculated, the house must be empty, left just the way it had been when they carried Beth's body out, or when Greg left for his fateful morning drive to school, or when Greg and Beth left for their morning drive. The house paused and expectant of a return that never happened: the beds unmade, her hair stuck in the brush, the parents fucked off on an exotic cruise to mourn the deaths of their two children tropically.

The address was shortly verified, though Beth's status could not be definitively confirmed. Someone, a kid named Thaddeus Settler—himself the originator of several other pernicious rumors about Beth—suggested a "Death Party," to be held in the abandoned house. Thaddeus had had a crush on Beth since before she disappeared, a crush that was transmuted publicly into morbid curiosity, in damaged Beth and her fucked-up relationship with her brother, and thus the idea took hold. A scouting party was dispatched. It had nothing to do with us.

—

Over the course of the following day, among the three of them—and then between Rhea and Typhus alone—they smoked the rest of the weed. To Tyler, the weed served as both a cushion and a method of delay: when they were high, his blocks of measurement disappeared, and time turned into a kind of gel. It kept progressing—this was impossible to prevent—but within it their actions were further apart and less important, like meandering waves, there was no real impetus to do anything, and often, as the high dissipated, they wouldn't even remember what they had done. Or they remembered it incompletely, distantly, without an appreciable effect on their current behavior, as if it had happened to someone else and then been related to them secondhand, and they hadn't really been listening. This was where he'd relocated the conversation about taking the house from the day before, into one of these transitory, half-forgotten places.

But Tyler knew he was merely buying time, and the morning after that same conversation he stopped smoking, effectively, realizing that between Typhus and Rhea the rest of the supply would last longer. Typhus's tolerance was low, so they didn't need much to keep her safely muted, and she was baseline silent anyway. Yet without the filter of the weed, within hours Tyler found himself growing agitated at the two of them, even as he sought to maintain their general state of inaction: their giggling fits (which were too loud); the amount of time they spent asleep (too much); the lack of information they communicated while awake. And though Typhus rarely spoke, he was nervous now when she did; he was waiting for her to follow up, to remind him of the promise he'd made to her as David, that there was an agreement he had yet failed to keep.

And in the end he could barely hold their stasis another twenty-four hours: on his eighteenth night, their third with Typhus, a Thursday, the weed finally ran out. As they sucked away the final joint—which Tyler had rolled and heavily diluted with tobacco, also down to its dregs— Tyler wondered what would happen when they finished it, what they would turn to him to provide.

They were seated on the antique chest beneath the window in the bedroom. Tyler turned away and pretended to take a hit, passed it back to Rhea, and coughed upward, at the partly open window. Rhea inhaled; her nostrils flared. "Is there even any marijuana in this?" She leaned forward on the chest and looked at him. Typhus was squeezed between her and Tyler. "What gives?"

"I'm conserving."

"What for? Have we even touched the massive bag that Typhus brought?"

Tyler's heart leapt and sank simultaneously. He had lost that bit of information to the same place he'd lost his awareness for how foods could be combined in a way that wasn't a sandwich since establishing himself in the basement. In one stroke, the next period of days was secured. At the same time, he dreaded how long that bag could last them: he wanted both to be forced to make a decision, a real game plan, and to never decide anything again. At least there would be enough for him to smoke again, he thought, to make the paralysis seem reasonable.

Tyler turned to Typhus, and as always when he spoke to her he felt he should sound older, more in command, as if he possessed some knowledge she didn't: "Could you bring me the bag?"

Typhus bit her precisely black lip. Tyler realized that he rarely looked at her, and that she must have refreshed her intense makeup each day down here—to what end? "I'm not sure how good it is," she said.

"It has to be better than the watered-down shit we've been smoking for the past two days," Rhea said. "Don't sweat it."

"Could you get the bag, please?"

Typhus pushed off the chest and went into the other room for her backpack. A long minute passed, and then she came back, holding it in front of her by the strap. She looked uncomfortable. "Can you get it out?" he said.

Across the bedroom, Typhus knelt on the floor, unzipped the bag slowly, and began picking through it without removing anything. She did that for a while; from the chest where they sat, Tyler and Rhea watched her hunched over on her knees, methodically unzipping each of the pockets, visibly anxious, and Tyler felt the combination of guilt and annoyance that accompanies having someone perform a task on your behalf and realizing it's been done sloppily. He realized he could ask her to do anything. "What's the problem?"

"I—I can't find it."

"What do you mean?"

"It's not in here."

Tyler's annoyance peaked again. "Take everything out of the bag. I'm sure it's buried in there somewhere."

"It's not."

Tyler felt fused to the wooden chest. Rhea watched Typhus like a hawk. She repeated him: "Take everything out."

Typhus followed their instructions, and piece by piece

she emptied the backpack: there were balled-up clothes, hygienic products she apparently didn't feel comfortable keeping in their communal bathroom, a pencil pouch, a makeup case—a series of small betrayals and minor offenses to their collective. At the end it was all spread on the carpet around her like contraband, and she was still on her knees.

He really didn't want to move. He pictured his mother in her evening armchair, utterly frozen until the moment when, suddenly, she would fling herself across the room. He shifted and the memory was gone, but still he sat. "You're sure you didn't put it somewhere else? There are no hidden pockets?"

Typhus clutched the backpack. "No, I didn't move it anywhere. I—I think someone must have stolen it."

Rhea jolted alive. "*What?* Who the fuck could have stolen it? Do you think it was one of us? What would be— the fucking point?" When she talked, she spit—Tyler saw flecks of it appear and vanish in the air.

Typhus was shaking her head. "I don't know—all I know is that it was here when I got here, and now it's gone."

In what felt like a superhuman feat of effort that he deeply resented, Tyler pushed himself up from the chest. "Let me look."

Typhus was already frantically stuffing things back into her bag.

"Typhus, what are you doing? Let me look." He was advancing.

"It's not in here!"

"Let me look!" Tyler was surprised at his volume, so much that he shivered, his body flinched. He paused a second, a stretch of seconds, listening for reciprocal sounds from the floor above, and in the dumbstruck silence he snatched the strap out of her hand. He pulled her carefully balled clothes out and threw them to the floor. In something like three seconds he had removed everything and saw the plastic bag of weed at the bottom of the backpack's largest pocket. "Typhus," he said, and he looked down at her—thinking legitimately she might be dumb enough to have missed it—but when he saw the fear in her eyes he realized there was something larger at play, but not before he had spoken: "Aha. Here we are. That wasn't so hard." He let the empty backpack fall to the floor.

Rhea was in motion. "You were holding out on us—"

He hefted it in his hands. "Wait a second"—he popped open the ziplock bag, sniffed at it—"what is this?" He dipped two fingers in and pinched off a bit of the mass. He tasted it, and any shred of a plan that might have been beginning to take shape dissolved. "Are these just fucking spices?"

"Are you serious? Give me that." Rhea took the bag and stuck her nose in it. "What gives, bitch? What is this fake shit?" She threw a handful of it in Typhus's face.

"Rhea." Tyler held out his right hand, and in that moment he believed this could stop her. Typhus's makeup was muddied, he could tell that in a second her eyeliner was going to break, it would run down her face. "Why would you lie to us?" he said.

"I didn't think—I didn't know it was fake."

"Who did you buy it from?"

"I don't know, some guy."

"What was his name? At school? We need to know."

"I don't know."

"Just tell us his name!" Rhea was dangerously close to screaming.

"Keep your voice down," Tyler hissed. "Typhus, we need to know his name. We need to know who saw you."

"No one."

"What?"

"No one. No one sold it to me." The makeup was moving in sinewy trails down her cheeks. "I didn't buy it. I did it myself."

Tyler turned this over in his head, and as he did so he realized what he had begun here, he could see clearly who he was dealing with as if for the first time. "Why would you do that?"

"You told me"—the first indication they'd ever communicated prior to her arrival at the back door—"to bring weed, and I didn't know how to get it."

"Did you think that this would fool me?"

"I don't know," she said, and Tyler could tell that she didn't. Everything felt so close to the surface, the weight of what no one would say—he'd said he would kill her!—and Tyler wanted only to push it all back down, to drown it while he tried to think of something else. He knew that the best option—and the most convenient option, the one staring him in the face—was to kick her out: he knew she would never tell anyone, she would feel properly shamed. But another, stronger part of him felt somehow she was safer here, Typhus and her death wish, that he had control here, where the forces of the outside did not. He said, "If you're going to continue staying here, we need to trust each other. Are you interested in continuing to stay here?"

She nodded silently. Rhea scoffed beside him, and Tyler thought idly, horrifically, that if he had to choose one of them to keep around over the other, at this moment he would have chosen Typhus. In essence, he had. And now the younger girl was continuing to speak where she didn't need to, where her nodding would have sufficed, she was making commitments she didn't have to, pledging new loyalties, she was moving forward on her knees. She said, "I would do anything."

There came a moment Claire was not proud of, after her first day at Maplewood and the day of Greg's funeral, two days after he died, when Sarah had come to her house. Claire felt guilty that the end of her contact with Sarah had coincided with Greg's death, but this was the ugly fact of the situation, and when Sarah arrived at her doorstep, Claire treated her like a stranger because she herself felt like a stranger.

Normal circumstances, she would never have answered the door, but over the last two days she'd started treating the house like it was hers, finally; she was no longer embarrassed to be seen in its foyer now that she could no longer pay its rent. Still, when she opened the door and saw Sarah, Claire felt a sudden pitch in her stomach, and a complex mix of fear, desire, anger, embarrassment, and resentment—at Sarah's sameness against Claire's stark, sudden visual difference—rippled through her.

Sarah stood on the very bottom step of the stoop like a matchstick girl, as if she'd rung the bell and then retreated downward to wait and be properly summoned forward: Claire thought this encompassed every aspect of her personality. She was staring up at the house, which wasn't uncommon for passersby—in addition to the turrets, Claire's house sat at the top of a slope, occupying a visually dominant position in the neighborhood. It was, in fact, several sizes bigger than Sarah's. When the door opened, Sarah looked earthward again and saw Claire, and Claire watched several visibly uncomfortable seconds pass across her face (did she have a sister? was she at the wrong house?) before Sarah registered that it was Claire, composed the picture of her in this context with her blond hair and glasses. Claire was both annoyed and satisfied by this. Sarah said her name, tentatively, and Claire considered not responding to it.

"What?" She angled herself half-behind the door, one hand on the inside handle. The interior of the house was cool and uniform, the outside hot and erratic, swampy.

Sarah took one step up the stoop. "I didn't recognize you without the blue hair."

Claire said nothing. More seconds disappeared between them, into the material air.

"I've been texting you. I—I haven't seen you around at school."

"I don't go there anymore."

"Oh." She looked down at her combat boots. Claire wondered if she had come to the house to offer herself to her, if this had been an unintended effect of Claire's silence. She saw Sarah's parents' Porsche parked on the street below, far below, pointedly not in Claire's empty driveway. Everything about Sarah was hedging, was *almost*. There was so much space she could have taken had she just chosen to. Which of her many chauffeurs had driven her this time?

"Did you hear about Greg?" Sarah asked, like she was at the edge of a pool, she was teetering there about to become soaked.

Claire set her jaw, gripped the internal door handle a little harder to brace herself. She knew she had to be brutal, she had to close this out. If she didn't end it now, she would never be able to. She pictured her room, empty of posters, the new email whose password she kept forgetting, Sarah's billions of texts bouncing around in nowherespace, like a burned diary. She summoned all the coldness within her. She put up her screen. She shrugged.

Sarah bit her lip; her face turned red and even across their three-step distance Claire could see her eyes watering, her expression blurring. Sarah kept flicking her eyes upward, at the upper levels of Claire's house—what was she expecting, fucking gargoyles? She swallowed and took another step up. Claire couldn't tell how much calculation Sarah was putting into her advance, if she had strategized to cover the gap in so many words, if she understood the power that Claire possessed, this oaken door. "Do you think . . ." Sarah said, her voice shaking and undeterred. "Do you think we could just . . . talk? Do you think we could . . . ?"

Claire felt herself breaking. She reached down within to find a song lyric that might give resonance to what she needed to say, but she couldn't access her inner compendium, it was blocked by a gooey strata of all this insipid pop she'd been listening to trying to reacclimate, her head churned with phrases like "best friend," "if you love me, let me go," "the rest of my life," her hair still felt faintly chemical and it, too, felt fake, like a cheap mask, and Sarah was swimming before her there on the steps, a mess of frayed nerves and desperate openings, and Claire knew that clichés were clichés for a reason, because they were generally true, they had been true long enough to become predictable and boring, and Claire hated feeling common but at that moment there was a soaring chorus in her head from a song that was poppy but also inexplicably sad that felt vibrantly relevant to her situation, breathtakingly unique, and she remembered abruptly that she had two hundred dollars in twenties in her back pocket, there was a notable bulge in her jeans the size of a phone, that this was how different she had suddenly become, and she thought, no, emotion was not relevant anymore, it was the currency of that emotion, it was the mathematical progression of certain chords to draw a physical response—that was the hitmaker.

In the end, for whatever meager distance it had gotten us, we'd given her what she needed.

On the table beside the door she noticed the zine Graham had given her, sitting atop the day's mail. She thought she'd thrown it away, but someone must have fished it out of the recycling to return to her. It felt stupid that she had ever prized it, had ever put stock in its histrionic symbols. What was the point? Anything lost could be bought. Wasn't that enough to know the world? Let someone else make sense of its gobbledygook. She picked it up and thrust it into Sarah's hands.

Sarah looked up at Claire, as if she had just delivered a letter that would say everything Claire couldn't possibly. So fine. Let her think that. Claire said, "I can't see you anymore," and shut the door.

The scouting party—a blue Prius that wound through Meridian Circle in a long loop once every two hours for a full day—reported that Beth's house indeed appeared empty. Calls to the house phone went unanswered, as did the doorbell. (Another group, in a different car, repeated the exercise that night, looking for lights from the street.) At one point that afternoon the Prius wound up the driveway and sat in front of the garage for almost half an hour; the idea was that, if anyone was home, they would be goaded by the stranger's car into revealing themselves. Thaddeus, one of the four kids in the Prius, went up to the front door and tested it. The door, a big wooden number with an oval stained-glass window, was unlocked. He pushed it open, into the dark interior, and silently walked the perimeter of the house's first-floor western half, which comprised the foyer and the wide secondary living room, built for entertaining and thus rarely used, a room with a high, vaulted ceiling like a church that could accommodate many guests. A piano on one side, by the front windows; tall upholstered chairs before a big stone fireplace; ornate carpet. He ran his finger along the edge of a glass cabinet holding delicate glass objects, took up a wedge of dust—it looked as though no one had been here for months. In the foyer again, he looked up the stairs, to the second floor, tense for some reason, despite the fact that the house seemed so empty. Weren't rich people all about alarms? He took a tentative step up the stairs, then another, and another, until he was up to the landing. He peered at the framed photos on the wall, and felt his heart jump when he recognized Beth, and then Greg. He put his hand into his pocket. He'd known this was the house, but now it was real. He looked up to the hallway that branched off in both directions. Was there something there? In the quiet, he might have heard—or could have heard—a faint creak, like the shifting of weight on a mattress.

He turned and padded back down the stairs; he left the house the way he'd entered, through the unlocked front door, careful to close it quietly, and went back to the car. The day was sunny and bright. He wore a black Cannibal Corpse shirt, which he couldn't get away with at school, black shorts, and he felt sweaty and out of place as he crossed the driveway, squinting; he didn't like being outdoors. By the time he reached the car, Thad had decided he'd heard nothing inside the house: this was the path he was on now, and he wouldn't change course. He opened the passenger-side door and greeted the three others— Alex, Joel, Amelia. "How's it look in there?" Amelia asked.

"Like a fucking museum," Thad said as he climbed in. "It's definitely empty."

"That's what I heard about all the houses in the Knots," Alex said. "It's just a bunch of rich people's second homes. No one actually lives here, they just pay to keep it maintained. It's basically a rich ghost town."

"Who has a second home in fucking Adena?" Amelia said, as Joel started the car, slowly backed up, and then stopped abruptly, just short of the low stone wall at the edge of the driveway. "Fucking rape me," he muttered, pulling forward and swinging the steering wheel to the left. He backed up again, hauling right now, so the car had turned a few degrees farther. Thad turned to look out the window, back at the house, at the glimmering black windows, the brick façade, as Joel repeated this set of actions three more times, until they'd achieved enough clearance to drive back down the driveway. "Fucking Christ," Joel said, pulling them forward, around the curve, back toward the loop road.

Beth lay in her bedroom at the back of the house, at that moment: unnoticed, unnoticing, absorbed in her new light.

———

For years, Thad had needed to be careful not to confuse the sign with its meaning. There were one or two of these kids in every class, the counselor assured his parents in third grade—the kids who liked to draw guns. It could mean something, could imply something psychological, but just as often it didn't mean anything on its own, merely represented a gendered means of expressing his technical ability that would be socially accepted, maybe even embraced, by his peers: he was better able to square with the boys than if he'd been drawing flowers or unicorns, for example. These sorts of kids would usually find each other, too, sure, sure. If it comes off the page, we can have another conversation, he said.

And for most of Thad's life it had stayed on the page, or had stayed part of his private world, which he understood to be the same thing: it didn't matter what he drew, or what he watched or listened to or played, what he filtered into his head, so long as it didn't become a *behavior*, so long as it was locked away the same as his thoughts were. It didn't matter what was in his mind. Gradually, from third to eighth grade or so, he'd come to realize what was in there wasn't socially acceptable, but he'd found a delight in the freakouts he could cause if he showed glimpses of it: a beheading video left open on a library computer on a site the school filters hadn't found yet, copied images on his phone. He didn't take it seriously; he thought he must be more resilient than other people, through exposure, things that disturbed others didn't disturb him. And it was fine the way it was, that was just his taste. He didn't really think, in any meaningful way, that they were *him*.

But as he got older, that version of him had started to bleed through, or the portal had opened, or whatever—either way, he turned a corner. Or maybe it was just a change in how he was viewed administratively: where before, had he been found with a knife catalogue or a swastika drawing, or had someone reported one of the detailed, anonymous-but-obviously-Thad threats he left for other kids sometimes—*I'm going to choke you to death with your own entrails*, etc., lines always taken from other sources—he might have been sent to the guidance counselor, or the principal, now they called security to bring him there. He was always apologetic, contrite, and he had avoided getting expelled thus far. But at the same time he didn't see what the big deal was. One of the sickest bands, Cannibal Corpse, had half a million fans. If they all heard the same song, about eating a woman while you raped her, didn't that mean it was normal, by default? Wasn't most of Germany nazis at one point? Who were these people, to tell him what *normal* was? He didn't mean it, he always said. They were just words, pictures he had picked up along the way. But nonetheless he sometimes found himself wondering—along the way to what?

The Death Party was to be held the following day. The theme, or rather collection of associated symbols, was already there in the air, ready to be plucked: it was Good Friday—a string of public humiliations culminating in a big messy sacrifice, an unbelievably metal way to die. Thaddeus originated the text of the invitation, which he passed to Alex, Joel, and Amelia—his primary social contacts—and as usual, they edited it before it went out, passing it back and forth among them, stripping back a layer of TS—his initials, also "Thad Shit"—editing out some of the gore, the culty ritual stuff, the Norse symbols, which felt a little white supremacisty. It became, more or less, a party at the dead siblings' mansion in the White Knots. Then they sent it out to about forty people, who were encouraged to pass it on.

Tasks were assigned, and supplies. While Amelia, Joel, and Alex mostly focused on alcohol, Thaddeus, his version of the proceedings divergent, went to the hardware store and browsed: nylon rope, zip ties, duct tape, a bunch of trash bags. He wrapped up a couple of the largest knives from his kitchen. He went to the garage and checked the shotgun, the stash of shells. He would take it just before his ride came, he thought, to minimize the time in which it could be noticed missing. He scrolled through images on his phone of women impaled through the crotch by steel rods, stretched out on the rack; he saw another video and decided to make a bunch of masks; he didn't carve a specific plan so much as a broad series of signs to draw from. Who knew which way it would go? Didn't it make sense to be ready for anything, for whatever direction it might take?

In contrast to the power of information Sarah had possessed in the moments immediately following the accident, when the story was hers alone to control and relate, after Greg died she found herself on the outside looking in—no, she was banging on the glass. For all the friends she thought she'd had, Sarah felt abruptly like there was no one: Beth had been gone to her since the day they'd visited the hospital, and nothing Sarah did could repair it, and now Greg was dead, and Claire had literally slammed the door in her face. Her grief—if that was what it was, and she thought so—could find no outlet, no commiseration, and in its flux, she felt like she was drowning.

The following morning, Friday, the day after the funeral, a week after the accident, she set her phone alarm for an hour earlier than usual. She'd managed to get a ride with her parents since returning to school, but that day, for the first time since elementary school, she had to take the bus. As she slouched outside in the still-dark and walked to the corner to be picked up, Sarah felt like she was walking toward the first waypoint in a totally new life, set out for her by an unseen, clinical hand—like that of the government, she thought, an institution with no read on her emotional character, for whom she was just a parcel of data.

Gradually, as she stood there, rubbing her arms, blowing into her hands and inserting them into her pockets as if it was cold, though it wasn't cold at all, it was April, other kids walked up to wait for the bus and the corner filled. She recognized most of them from her neighborhood but not enough to know their names, not enough to want to talk to them. She felt uneasy, shamefully conspicuous, standing there on the sidewalk in a space she felt she didn't have a right to claim, at the edge of someone's private property, as if she'd figured she could just waltz up and follow this route along with the rest of them, could trust that a bus would eventually roll up and have an extra spot for her, the system she'd previously ignored would be waiting to seamlessly absorb her when she decided to take advantage of it.

But the bus did come, still mostly empty, and Sarah boarded behind the others, thanking the unfamiliar and surly driver. It was still dark outside. She stumbled down the aisle as the bus started moving again, the kids already huddled in the seats unrecognizable to her in their jackets and hoodies, faces angled into the windows in sleepy quiet, slumped and uncommunicative and unapproachable. *My peers*, she reminded herself. She slipped into an empty seat two-thirds of the way back, put her head against the window in kind, and tried to project the same indifference, as if she belonged here. She wished desperately for a hat to pull over her eyes. She worried she'd taken someone else's seat and would be called out, and when the bus stopped again, she flinched as the two kids who boarded walked past. She felt like a kindergartner again. *I'm seventeen years old*, she told herself. *I should not have these problems.*

As she sat there, trying to blend in, and the bus continued along its route, Sarah slowly became aware of a rotten smell hovering about her seat, egg and cinnamon and faintly shit, like a bad, sustained belch. When the smell didn't dissipate, an anxious wave passed through her and she adjusted, worried it was coming from her, a panicked scent her body had secreted in self-defense, but the smell grew less intense when she moved away from the window, it lingered at the far edge of the seat. She shivered. It smelled like food waste, she thought, food waste kept ripe by a human body, and she thought again of that party with Hannah, the house's matte of unplaceable odors, and her embarrassment spiked at whoever—at whatever—the smell was emanating from. The bus stopped again, loaded more. She considered moving seats, but that seemed too obvious, would draw attention she could ill afford. So Sarah resigned herself to living with it, she shimmied back to the window and leaned her head against it again. She searched her pockets for the gloves she knew weren't there, she put her backpack on her lap and sank her face into it, breathing in the nylon. She tried breathing through her mouth. She stared at her phone, and when that wasn't distracting enough she pulled out the pamphlet Claire had given her and studied it again, trawling for hidden meanings.

But there it was again, that current of air, almost nauseating in its ripeness, a yeasty note beneath it like spilled beer: private, like something she wasn't supposed to know about. She pulled on the scent of her backpack, on her own body odor. She scrubbed the roof of her mouth with her tongue and it felt filmy, as if the smell had settled there like a smear of fat, and she tried to ignore it, but every few seconds a whiff of it would wrap her face and then draw back, like a teasing scarf, and eventually she could take no more. In the pretense of adjusting her backpack, she peeked behind her, through the gap between her seat and the window: in the seat behind hers, a dark-haired girl sat leaned against the foggy glass, gazing vacantly out. Sarah turned back to face forward, confused, indescribably guilty, and then there it was again, the vaguely rotten smell. She covered her mouth with her hand, tested it, and then it hit her: it was the girl's breath. It was her bad breath against the window. Sarah felt a rush of new secondhand embarrassment, an awful shame at the triangulation her mind had made. Did the girl know? Did she know how much her breath stank?

She wished she hadn't made the connection, but of course now that she had noticed, she couldn't keep herself from speculating, from sinking into it, there was nothing to stop the guttural intimacy that filled the space between their seats, the small betrayal of the girl's body, this fetid pocket of air that filled and depleted with every breath like a speech bubble, which for their remaining minutes on the bus formed their universe. Sarah wondered if she should be the one to tell her, and how she would do it. She could take her aside privately when they got to school, maybe at her locker, could give her some friendly advice — here were some mouthwash brands she could recommend, some high-strength toothpastes. When did she brush her teeth? Was she brushing at night, too? It could all make a difference. She probably didn't even know the problem existed, this girl. In all likelihood, no one had worked up the nerve or sensitivity to say anything, though it had likely afflicted her for some time, as this wasn't the sort of breath that came from forgetting to brush your teeth one morning, this was a question of hygiene, of bad habits long held. Sarah felt confident she could come at it from the right angle: an easy correction, a quick change in routine. Sarah might be doing her a favor, even, because who knew how well known her bad breath was already? Maybe it was something people talked about behind her back, an undercurrent she didn't know existed, that traveled along with her person, slowly flecking her reputation, and which, with a few well-placed words, Sarah might be able to quell. Had she just never been taught to take care of herself? Hadn't her parents or guardian noticed? How much of it was her breath, and how much might be the rest of her body? Though she was disgusted, Sarah also felt fortunate, as if she'd been afforded this one small opportunity to effect valuable change, just by taking the bus and accidentally sitting near this girl.

She buried her face in the pamphlet again, *RED-PRINT*. She'd quickly put together that it was a product of Viceroy—the band Claire had brought her to see the night Greg died, the same band David had referenced in the message he'd sent her the night after they'd met up in her bedroom—or it had some relation to Viceroy, and she felt the text must be crucial in some way, held the key to understanding Claire's sudden transformation, what had happened that night to cause the turn, what had caused David to approach her.

Last night, she'd watched the video David had posted on Facebook the night he'd messaged her a couple weeks ago, which was still up, and it had disturbed her: a young man bashed his face into the wall until it was a bloody pulp. There were no cuts or edits away. The footage looked real, and the music tracked over it didn't fully conceal the sound of his face on the concrete—it was like the song had just been playing in the room. She heard it even when she turned off the volume. She had done some googling on the song, "Drawbridge," but had resisted taking it too far. Instead, she'd turned her attention back to the pamphlet, to a long paragraph on the last two pages, a text that had been typed over line for line with another layer of text to obscure it: at least the text was static, up to a point, even if it was illegible. It didn't peel itself open to her the way her phone did, the way her laptop did, to show the teeming depths beneath.

Except, suddenly, it did: as she was starting to fall asleep, her lamp still on, the lines in the pamphlet blurred and separated on the page, and suddenly it was clear: both layers of the text were the same, but one ran forward and the other backward, overwriting each other. She sat up, pulled a notebook from her bedside table, and tore a page free. Moving between the two versions, from the beginning and end, Sarah was able to map out what it said, which she transcribed word by word. She unfolded the paper and read it through again now, on the bus, as the smell of the girl's breath ate into her nostrils, another minor mystery she had solved:

Imagine an exchange between you and them. Every time you look at them, every interaction you have, no matter how small, every flicker of energy you direct their way, every look, every touch or thought, imagine putting a little bit of that pain—that difference—into them. Imagine you're crossing a drawbridge between you and them, and in the space of that moment you're pushing a fraction of your pain through the gate on the other side before it closes, before the bridge draws back up: this brief overlap when the elements align enough to make a connection. Doesn't it help? Doesn't it make them feel a little bit like you—even standing opposite them—before you turn away? Every moment a fist pulled back, a nocked arrow. You are a gun trained on the future: in time, across enough people, a large enough crowd, you can disperse it, all of it, into nothing.

There was the *drawbridge* again. The fact that it was written in her own loopy handwriting, on her notebook paper, made it especially unnerving. What was this pain that couldn't be borne? Who were "they"? Was that just everyone else, the non-pained? How did it connect with the video? She looked from the paper to the flaky greenish seatback in front of her, the bus squealing beneath her on its rusty twenty-five-year-old frame, the rest of the kids now chatting more animatedly as the sun rose and the bus filled. All noise. But the girl silent behind her, only breathing, an exchange of air between her seat and Sarah's. *Like a drawbridge*, she thought. She slowly breathed out through her mouth: who, then, was the narrator here, and who the "they"? Who the one who lived in the castle, and who the visitor stealing inside? The gun or the future? As the bus rumbled on, the longer she sat with the girl's breath, within it, Sarah could do nothing but start to breathe it in, too, to draw out its components one by one: egg, and orange juice, and a sugary cereal served with milk, along with whatever had come the day before, its own pocket of scents—a sweet tomato sauce, a whiff of yogurt—blended together and partially digested only to re-emerge later, gaseous, mixed with days of other lingering aftertastes, stiff onion and coffee, each a lilting note, all twining together again like melody as they crossed the distance between their seats. The calamities of the last week, the weeks before, all waned in the sensory power of the presence behind her, the silently resting figure and her terrible breath. She felt like she knew this girl: all it took was that one raw piece of her to reveal the whole, to split her wide open, as the text had done, as the boy's face had. She shivered.

The melody continued until they arrived at the school, when the morning light Sarah recognized had fully returned. She stood when the other riders did, and she let the girl behind her go out ahead. She was no more familiar to Sarah standing, and Sarah was convinced she'd never seen her before—she seemed glowery and was dressed all in black. Faded plush baubles dangled from her black backpack, and she had a shuffling, determined walk. She went forward down the aisle, head bowed into the morning, and Sarah followed. She inhaled at her back; she couldn't help it. The bus emptied onto the sidewalk.

As she approached the school, keeping close to the stranger from the bus, Sarah realized it was the first time in recent memory she'd entered Adena via the front doors where the buses let out, rather than from the parking lot in the back, where she wound through the narrow trophy hallways behind the new gym to get to her locker. And again, Sarah felt wildly out of place and overwhelmed, clinging to her quarry, absorbed in her bad breath, intimidated by the size of the building, towering over her in a way it hadn't before with its enormous brick wings and endless string of entrances, its diagram of tributary sidewalks: she felt like a pilgrim approaching a great temple. She held her hand over her face like a mask, she breathed in and held it there. The grass was loud with movement around them. Suddenly the mass of the student body was truly apparent to her—there were hundreds of them. Thousands, even; thousands of agendas apart from her own.

The girl took a sidewalk to the left, then next to the

right, then arced back to the left over the grass. Sarah followed a few steps behind. The girl finally entered the west unit through one of the secondary doors, which Sarah grabbed before it closed, and she tracked her across the cafeteria to her locker, plotting her approach: would she touch her shoulder? Would she speak? Only as she stood there at the end of the row, watching the girl spin the dial on the lock, only then did Sarah finally self-correct, something twisted in her gut, and she broke away. She sprinted to the nearest bathroom—one she had never used—banged into a stall, and fell to her knees as she vomited into the toilet, a hot and angry torrent, more than she'd consumed in the last week.

She knelt over the bowl afterward, breathing hard, her hands clenched on the porcelain. An acidic smell wafted back into her face, her backpack slumped forward into her neck, weighing her down, as if to force her further into it, into her own disgust. In its awful tang and muddy orange substance Sarah found herself recognizing notes from the girl's horrible breath, reflected grotesquely back at her, its heat and stench, filtering back into her nose and mouth, condensing on her skin, putrid egg and processed sugar and bile. She saw half-digested noodles and pulverized tomato glimmering sickly in the bowl, nothing she remembered eating. Her eyes shuddered at what had come from her body: it wasn't hers. It was this girl's guts conflated with her own, idly spiraling on the surface of the toilet water, *it was not her vomit*, and at this thought—its repulsiveness, its *wrongness*, like that phrase David had used, *Burst Marrow*—Sarah threw up again, until her shoulders ached, meal after meal she'd never eaten, she retched until she had nothing left inside of her, until her mouth was sore and bitter with the taste.

And she knew, somewhere apart from her, that the girl was empty, too, stealing her way back across the drawbridge.

Like she's put her pain into me, she thought.

"Were you following me?" came a voice behind her.

A knot pulsed up into Sarah's throat, like another piece of undigested food. She almost gagged. She turned, one elbow propped on the toilet, still on the floor. The girl from the bus stood before the open stall door, blocking her way.

"What? No, I—" She awkwardly tried to stand, for some reason unable to manage the dual processes simultaneously, the standing and the denial.

"That's bullshit," the girl said. "I saw you. You followed me to my locker."

She was stunned by the directness of the accusation. "No—" Finally standing, her head swimming in nauseous vertigo, suddenly angry at the interruption. "I was sitting in front of you on the bus. I hadn't seen you before. I just noticed—" She couldn't think of what to say. She tried to hide the view of the toilet behind her. But they were less than two feet apart, and the smell was back. "Nothing," she said. "It was nothing."

"No, tell me, what was it?" The girl moved slightly to the side; the implication was that she would keep Sarah from leaving the stall. "You noticed *what*?"

Sarah felt an aerated burp in her throat. "Your breath," she blurted. "It's rancid." Her hand flew to her mouth, as if to draw the delinquent words back. Where had she found that word?

The girl balked, as if slapped. Sarah saw her cheeks redden. "*You're* rancid," she said, shaking her head in disbelief. "I'm so sick of people like you. Your whole rich little clique. You're following people around, telling them how they *smell*? Are you fucking kidding? You're a fucking bully."

Sarah felt blindsided. She had only been trying to help, to offer the girl something. She had no stake in this otherwise. Was she supposed to recognize this random person? Standing there, Sarah took her in, she couldn't help it but she did, the girl's long dark hair, her faded black Led Zeppelin shirt, its design nearly washed out, her ill-fitting jeans, the soft ragged edge where they met her ankle, old Converse; she looked at her, as if for the first time, and couldn't help seeing the girl compared to herself, her person mapped against Sarah's. That word—*rancid*—like garbage. Like trash. Her eyes teared; she felt so stupid, but she couldn't help it. Her stomach rocked again, and she swallowed hard. She thought, *I know you*, but also, *We are so different*. She felt on the verge of throwing up again. She put one hand on the side of the stall. "I thought you would want to know," she barely said, not sure why she was still speaking.

It won her no sympathy. "Are you seriously crying right now?" the girl said. Her eyes were hard. "Un-fucking-believable." She shook her head. "Fucking Sarah Field"— she felt an icy chill hearing her name—"you don't even see it, do you?" she said, although Sarah suddenly did see it, could almost see too much of it, maybe that was the problem, and her throat closed like a valve. "You're just a stupid little rich girl. I'm not your fucking charity. I'm so sick of this—I'm tired of being *noticed* by people like you."

Sarah spun, she threw up again, falling to her knees, barely making it to the toilet.

Behind her, she heard the girl scoff and walk away, pushing the bathroom door open. She waited another minute, just breathing, until Sarah was sure she was alone again. She was shaking. How did that girl know her? What did she know about Sarah that Sarah didn't know about herself? She tried to exhale evenly; she wiped her nose, tucked the waylaid strands of her hair behind her ears where it had fallen. She climbed to her feet, brushed off her knees, and flushed the toilet—the bowl was sucked clean.

At the sink, she scrubbed her face until it was raw and devoid of feeling; she swilled hand soap from the dispenser until she gagged, until she felt it slime her throat. She spit mouthful after mouthful of soapy water into the drain but couldn't clear the taste completely. In the mirror, her skin was blotchy, her eyes puffy, her hair slicked around the perimeter of her face. She wiped the mascara from where it had smudged and stood watching the red gradually drain from her face, her hair drying slowly, as the interaction retreated with the blood to a deeper place inside her. Fifteen minutes later, she braced herself and walked across the school to the south unit in a daze, as if waking from hypnosis, as late as she had ever been with Greg; this random girl had risen up to consume her morning just as easily. What was wrong with her? Why couldn't she leave well enough alone? What awfulness could she possibly have in common with that girl, snarled up in their stomachs—what rotten information?

It wasn't us, pulsing acidic through her guts as she traversed the school we now knew well, its hallways suddenly empty of students, cleared by the bell. But it was a symptom of our dawning: she was drawing closer, closer to the point at which, when we arrived, she would recognize what we offered and be able to take it. She felt at the edge of a truth about herself she couldn't qualify intellectually but felt acutely in her body—it was something about where she stood in relation to other people, how they were part of her, but also *not* part of her, she wasn't sure. Close enough to taste it.

Despite everything, she arrived at homeroom and received her umpteenth tardy slip, which signaled a detention, in silence. The bell rang eventually, the morning began in earnest, and Sarah navigated back into her regular schedule, her typical routes across the school with its repeatable faces and hallways, which she traveled automatically, without thinking. But the foul taste in her mouth never faded, soap and vomit, it ran beneath this familiar map like a dirty stream, its sourness under her every interaction, bitterly the same. Sarah looked back on her life of a few months ago, which had felt rich with interaction and people, and reconciled her place in it. She found in actual fact she had operated around a few precious cruxes: Beth, David, Greg, Claire—they had been the current in which she traveled. *Her whole little club.* She had not thought to look beyond her, to raise her head above the water. She had let herself be immersed in them. Now, by contrast, it seemed as if they had all been methodically stripped away one by one, present but with their faces blacked out, unresponsive and blank; soon everyone would be gone, and then—like that—the future would pounce. She wondered if, given the space, the people in your life just expanded to fill it, they filled every crack like water, until there was no air left. She drew a line from Greg's changing behavior to his confusing death to David's fake cult to Beth's angry disappearance to Claire's suddenly frightening attention and then utter meanness, to the pamphlet in her backpack that suddenly seemed like the key to it all—a kingdom of drawbridges, all of them connected—but she couldn't put it together into any sort of reasonable-seeming pattern; it was this swirling vortex of angsts where she felt like she was the core, but felt selfish to feel like she was the core, but wasn't everyone their own core, and again, why should she be any different? Wasn't that what the girl had said?

—

Invitations to the Death Party quickly broke loose from the group of forty that Alex, Joel, and Amelia had curated, and rippled, like the best gossip, through the kids of Adena. The dead brother and sister. The mansion in the White Knots. Beth and Greg's names weren't included in the message—Amelia et al. had cut them out—and because Beth wasn't actually dead, the identity of the dead siblings couldn't be verified online, meaning that the grisly premise felt both obviously false and yet outrageous enough to be at least somewhat true: there was an address, after all. Down in the basement, both Tyler and Rhea got the invite, from different sources—Tyler deleted the message immediately without processing it, and Rhea read it, and then promptly forgot that she had—it wasn't relevant to their world. Two stories above them, David got it, but he didn't associate it with anyone he knew; he had never known where Beth and Greg lived. Claire, who no longer had any Adena contacts, and had a different number anyway, did not receive it. Neither did Sarah.

Beth herself, as she drove in dogged pursuit of her new light, as the suburbs gave way to country, as the car drifted gently back and forth against the center line, knew none of it, either: she wondered, looking out at the fields, what she would do when she found him, the light, what she would say to him if it was Greg. Would she tell him how much he had hurt her? Why was she the one left in the cavern of the house, while he had the rest of the world—while he could escape it? Why had it fallen to her to find him, to bring him back to earth? Why was it always her?

That afternoon, someone drove up to the White Knots and in memoriam tied white ribbons around the trees on either side of the road leading up to Beth's house, then took the effort to drive all the way up the driveway and leave a bouquet of white roses on the stoop, *For the departed.* Forces gathered.

And into Sarah's void stepped David. David, who as his bashed hand healed had steadily molded his routine to avoid the locked basement door, as surely as he'd modified his school route to avoid Sarah, who had quietly divested that portion of his life in favor of the top two floors of his house. He used the internet on his phone or via his mother's desktop in the office; he started watching TV with commercials in the den. He let his social media accounts go on without him, and subtly, in response, his classmates withdrew from his person. He did not try to investigate. It was like there were two Davids, the flesh-and-blood version and his digital shadow, which spread and shifted depending on how the light was cast: fundamentally out of his control. Equally, after a day David stopped checking to see if the basement was still locked; like the guest bedroom and dining room and patio, it simply became another unused piece of the house. His videogames quickly reverted to former habit. He figured one day he would have to make a concentrated effort to reclaim his laptop—break the lock and go down there—but as the days passed this became a more distant and futuristic goal, like the time he would have to learn to check the balance on the bank account in his name: it was on his to-do list, but he didn't actually anticipate doing it. He was surfacing, he felt; he was growing.

With the transition from the basement to the top two floors had come another, related shift. Since the afternoon he'd spent in Sarah's bedroom nearly three weeks ago, David had been thinking about her constantly. And though he had failed to convince her of anything but his own ineptitude, the fantasy he'd described to her still ran through his head, twining with the thought of her absence even after we'd left him, and together these narratives created a new picture: that there was someone who'd loved him (or who had seemed like she might love him), a feeling he hadn't known how to reciprocate at the time, but which, given his changing circumstances, his newfound lack of embarrassment at himself, even his injured hand (which though self-inflicted read to him like a war wound, like a difference he had also achieved), maybe he could reciprocate now. He sat on the couch in the living room off the foyer that Friday afternoon after school—it was spectacularly nice, the living room, it was rarely ever sat in—and he surveyed the neatness surrounding him. The sleek bookshelves across from the couch, decorated with tactfully chosen books and curios, the lamp and heavy upholstered chairs, the bay windows, the beige carpet, and the grandfather clock, everything so clean and impeccably selected and arranged—and he attributed it to himself. He slid his phone from his pocket—he was acting on his own at this point, taking an initiative that hadn't been explicitly offered to him—and called Sarah, out of the blue. What was thinking about the future, if not this?

She answered quickly. "Hello? David?"

"Hey, Sarah." Just saying her name, already things were different.

"Is something wrong?"

"No—I just wanted to see how you were." He paused, racking his brain for pretext. "I'm sorry about Beth's brother. I'm glad you're okay."

He heard her inhale through her nose on the other end of the line, and then exhale. "Thanks. That's really sweet of you. That means a lot."

"It's rough."

She sniffed again. "Yeah. You know, I don't think we've ever actually talked on the phone before."

"Oh, yeah. Maybe."

On her end, Sarah settled back into her bed, awash in

old sensations, a feeling of comfortable normalcy. Her body, primed for alarm since the phone had started ringing, uncoiled a bit; for a second she lost the taste in her mouth that had lingered since morning. "It's different. You sound adult."

He made the sounds of a chuckle, a single airy beat. "Ha, thanks."

"So, what's up with you? What have you been up to?"

David looked around the living room again. He couldn't remember communicating with someone in it or from it ever before. The grounds were untested, rife with opportunity. He felt a sudden desire to show it off. "Well, I was wondering if you might want to come over, to talk."

It sounded sinister the way he'd said it, but this was uncharted territory, and David believed in the power of intent.

Sarah hesitated. He could tell she was thinking about their last encounter but didn't want to bring it up. David felt on the verge of losing her into the cyberspace between them. "It just seems like you've had a lot going on lately," he said—he assumed this was what most people liked to hear, an acknowledgment they had problems that carried weight—"and I just wanted to say that I'm here, in case you want to talk." He was impressed by the way he pivoted, to make it about Sarah rather than himself—he reached out and felt the squat body of the lamp on the end table, glossy porcelain painted with irises, it probably cost, what, hundreds, thousands of dollars?

When Sarah spoke her voice flooded with affection; David pictured a bottle uncapped. It was just two syllables, but their length felt liquid and powerful. "Okay," she said, overflowing. "That would be great." He imagined her wet. "Are you around the rest of the day?"

"Yep, I'm here."

David wasn't sure where these phone calls were supposed to end. Neither was Sarah.

"I'm looking forward to seeing you," she said. He wanted to hear her keep talking, to keep that combination of emotions, whatever it was, he wanted her exactly this way. Was this how she had always been?

"Me too."

"I'll see you soon."

"Okay."

Their syllables ran out and they eventually hung up.

Sarah arrived thirty minutes later. In the doorway she collapsed forward and embraced him; she hugged with her whole body, as if she needed the support. When he'd first experienced one of these hugs he'd thought she must be easy. It occurred to him again now, this initial reading, and then he tried to put it back away. After he invited her in, she started walking immediately to the basement door, and he had to reach out and touch her shoulder to stop her. "Do you want to sit in the living room?"

"Oh—sure."

He walked ahead of her into that light-filled room and inadvertently smiled to himself, he offered her a seat on the couch and sat next to her on a separate cushion. The fabric was robust, rarely impacted. Even his posture felt different now, straighter, honed. The light was really good—it was natural.

"I don't know if I've ever been in this room," Sarah said, looking at the wall behind the couch, which David noticed for the first time had a painting on it, a large dawn or sunset. "It's nice."

David took the compliment as if it was directed to him. "Thanks. I've been spending more time here." He hoped this conveyed all of the information he wanted it to.

They fell into talking, which was mostly David listening. He heard about Claire's change-of-face, about the crash, about the way Beth had treated Sarah in the hospital, about her alienation. She didn't mention Greg specifically, and David thought she was avoiding him on purpose, that it said something about the frame of mind in which she had entered this conversation, it meant the door was ajar. He felt he was listening where he hadn't before, picking up new aspects of Sarah he somehow hadn't processed before: her deep insecurity coupled with her complete trust, the way things or people either rose up like mountains in her mind, occupying everything, or they receded into waves in the distance she couldn't even see. He felt that his new environs, the appointment of the living room was causing him to be more receptive, and that before, when he'd felt pressured and cut their relationship off, it had really been their surroundings that had doomed them, his dingy basement, his fellow teens, not David himself. He felt himself becoming one of the mountains again, breaking the surface of the water.

At a certain point she paused, her hands on her knees. "I guess I've been thinking about the last few months, about all the shit that's happened. I'm not really sure how to ask this."

He genuinely thought she was going to ask if they could try again. "Take your time," he said generously.

She dragged her palm down her face, like forcing something down or wiping it off. "Do you think, at school, do people . . . know me? Like, do you think I have a *reputation?*"

He felt like he'd missed something—this felt like a terribly basic question for Sarah, like she knew nothing, or everything, and was looking for a specific answer.

"I'm sorry," she said, before he could answer. She looked up—was she crying? "I'm not even sure what I'm asking. But sometimes I feel like—I don't know—like there are people out there who know me that I don't know. If that makes sense."

He tried to piece this together. It sounded so sinister—people *out there*. But maybe it was, to her? "I mean, you're popular," he said. "So people know who you are."

She looked up at him: she looked utterly terrified. "I am?"

"Yeah," he said, trying to reassure her, though not sure this was what she wanted. "Of course. You're the center of the universe." He smiled.

After a long moment, in which she seemed to sift her feelings, she smiled, too. "That's sweet." She looked away shyly. "I've been meaning to ask you something else . . ."

Here it was. He leaned forward minutely, his back still incredibly straight. "What is it?"

"The posts you made the night after we talked last, the message you sent me . . ." She trailed off as if expecting him to cut in. "I didn't get it. What did they mean?"

David felt unreasonably shocked, as if Sarah had asked him about an aspect of his life over which he had no control, like why he was rich or white. He did not want to talk about this, it was no longer a part of his purview. He had not seen the posts, nor, in fact, had he successfully logged in to any of his social media accounts or his email since the last time they'd seen each other, and he felt very clearly that while they might bear David's name, they were no longer David. "I got hacked," he said at last. It was amazing how easily he shrugged off any responsibility whatsoever, like writing off an old childhood grudge. "I got locked out of my accounts. I haven't posted anything in weeks."

"Were you trying to freak me out?"

"I didn't post them. I didn't send any messages. I don't know who it was."

She looked at him skeptically. "But the whole conversation we had that day, about that group, Burst Marrow." She shuddered. "I—what were you trying to do?"

Fragments of his desperate night drifted through David's head, where his plan to beguile Sarah had cohered under our direction—it felt like a dream, a dream he had somehow tripped into reality. He didn't know what to say. Did he tell her? Did he tell her he had been coached, what we had promised him as he lay prostrate on his bed muttering *Yes yes yes yes* into the palm of his hand? Did that make him even more pathetic, or did it vindicate him? Could he be blamed for being enthralled? It didn't seem like a conversation for the living room, for where David believed himself to be now: he saw their last conversation as part of the self he'd left locked in the basement—that easily tempted, easily manipulated self, the fringe theorist—now unacknowledged and forgotten. He decided to do what he'd done on the phone, to make it about her.

"I made it all up," he said, finally. A residual wave of cold crawled through his spine, a glimmer of what we had left behind, making him shift uncomfortably, which added to the effect.

She searched his face. She didn't seem surprised—a little dagger at his composure. "Why would you do that?" she said.

He looked at his lap. Tiny dust motes floated through the air, visible in the light through the windows, like a place resting he had disturbed. "Something got inside of me," he said quietly. He waited a beat for Sarah to respond, to help him find his next point. She didn't.

"They were like—it was like I needed a way to make you pay attention to me again," he said. "So I made all this shit up, about the group and everything, because I knew if I had this problem, you'd be drawn in to solve it." *You'd be drawn in*. It didn't sound like David.

"I don't understand. Who's 'they'? Like someone told you to do this?"

"No, it's like—" He waved his hands in the air, trying to articulate, whipping those minute flecks of dust and flakes of skin into flurries, cyclones of dead cells. He thought he might cry. He knew that his vulnerability, his demonstrative angst was something Sarah was attracted to, would try to soothe, and therefore that it was also a trap. Or maybe his awareness of its power was the trap. But if he truly felt vulnerable, torn, wasn't that real? "I don't know how to describe it," he said. "It was like an *awareness*, or a sense or something. Like there was a part of me that stopped seeing you as *you*, rather than just a—I don't know." *Just a tool*, that part of him silently finished.

She looked at him, chewing the inside of her mouth, waiting for more, and David realized that, try as he might, he could never explain it—this *awareness* he had—because Sarah didn't share it, she didn't have it in her like David did, that was the point, that was why he thought she could be manipulated, *be drawn in*—those weren't David's words—that was why he had brought her here again, *summoned her*, that was why she was sitting here right now on the opposite cushion, *willing*, waiting to fall open.

"I think," he continued, his blood surging, in power, in dread, "I think I was trying to impress you, in some perverted way. Like, after we broke up"—he carefully pluralized and felt satisfied by it—"I felt I had something to prove. I wanted . . . I wanted to matter to you again."

Sarah's face collapsed into understanding. "David. Of course you're always going to matter to me. You know you don't have to prove anything to me." Her hand bridged the border between her cushion and his and hovered in the air for a moment, level with the upper part of his arm, as if Sarah was deciding whether to rest it on his leg or his shoulder, to make what she'd just said about David's lack of sexual potency or just his general patheticness as a human.

Energies crackled somewhere.

At last, her fingertips dipped—David's heart leapt—and then they fluttered unexpectedly upward in a surge of resistance, landing on his shoulder. It was contact, but it was a different kind of contact, reassuring rather than sexual: it signaled there was a part of her that was now unavailable to him, that he had spoiled forever. David's posture demonstrably weakened, he felt his dignity slipping out through his fingers, pale from when he'd bandaged them, and trailing onto the hundred-grand carpet (what did he know)—the familiar residual chill of us came back, he looked up in acknowledgment and had to blink once to clear his field of vision, so there was a second when Sarah's figure swam before reclarifying itself, and though the moment passed almost instantaneously, there lingered in David the feeling that when he'd looked back up she hadn't really been there, that in the haze of his vision she had been merged together with the living room, like the couch on which they were sitting or that valued lamp, a part of his new context, arrayed for his convenience, awaiting his input: *a tool*. Like he'd wanted. Like we promised.

There is a part of you you have to slam shut like a door.

And he gave that input—he leaned into the space, into Sarah's panel (her arm folded like an accordion), and kissed her during this transitional moment, before it elapsed and she became fully human again. David figured he must have punched the right button, because she was responding to him (her eyes grew, and then closed), she was running both of her hands down his back. He opened his eyes and as he kissed her he watched her face, which had lost its alertness, gone slack, and he pushed under the hem of her shirt, and the sensation of his hands on her bare skin was unfamiliar for a second, and then he remembered it, it became old ground, it was the same, the difference was the light pouring into the room through the bay windows, the couch, the clock, the difference was the living room and what it ascribed, who he was now.

She slowly drew apart from him and a thread of saliva

joined them, momentarily. She cleared her bottom lip and lazily opened her eyes. "Should we go downstairs?"

For a second David considered the lexicon they shared, where downstairs was the default rather than his bedroom upstairs, the logical next step. It occurred to him that Sarah had never really let him go as a boyfriend; no matter how much time passed between them, they could come right back to this spot. But the basement was disgusting and the realm of all his past misdeeds—it was amazing they had lasted all the time that they did down there, where it stank of come and grease and weed, where nothing could really be hidden. He didn't want to go downstairs. "Let's stay here," he said.

She turned to the thrilling windows. "David, your— let's go somewhere private."

David sensed that if he didn't act now the opportunity would be lost, that every second they spoke her resolve was bearing back up. He stood and took her hand—this was him leading. "Let's go upstairs."

He led her out of the living room and into the house's more familiar compartments. They passed the basement door, and something about the way they turned the corner made him want to reach out and test the doorknob—a habit from almost three weeks ago, before he abandoned the basement completely—but he didn't, they sailed on away, they drifted upward, in the way one ascends stairs without considering the complexity of the motions involved, toward the room that was both new and old, which held—David realized suddenly—room for them both.

On the day of the accident, as Greg launched through the windshield, as he lay comatose in the hospital four miles away, as his visitors came and went in their rounds—all part of the same moment, as he experienced it—he dwelled within a memory: he was riding a school bus with his sister. He was in eighth grade, and Beth was in sixth. It was the first day of the school year, and Beth's first day in middle school. He sat at the aisle, and Beth was at the window, watching nervously as the bus moved along its new, unfamiliar route, picking up its older, unfamiliar faces that bore traces of what seemed then like adulthood: faint mustaches, heavier makeup, oily acne. It was the year, Greg remembered, that he finally stopped changing for gym class, because he could no longer comfortably wear shorts due to the scarring on his thighs, and he refused to wear sweatpants (the school's permissible alternative for boys), and so each day he didn't change for class he lost points, until he gradually started failing. Weird how a data point could be extrapolated like that, he thought, could dig a channel you couldn't easily pull yourself out of.

Beth, beside him, was scared by the concept of changing classes multiple times per day, that the four minutes between periods wouldn't be enough and she would get lost. Would she have to learn the names of all the kids in all of her classes? Fifth grade, at the top of the school, and then the world suddenly partitions, stratifies, and you're back at the bottom of the ladder. She'd missed her final two weeks of elementary school, too, sick with mono, so the new school was doubly intimidating, like she'd come back from the grave, from another town. Over the summer their father had driven them out to the school, and though they couldn't go inside, Greg had walked Beth around the perimeter of the building, showing her where the cafeteria was, the gym, to talk her through as best he could what her route might be, how to work a locker: she asked him these incredibly detailed questions he didn't even realize could be questions, like how to choose what to buy for lunch at the cafeteria, how to know which line to stand in, and he had felt, truly, for the first time like an older brother, the possessor of advanced specialist knowledge, the reassurance to her mundane concerns. But simultaneously, he was aware of how little thought he had given to those same day-to-day realities himself, that he hadn't thought to ask. Would it have changed his life, if he had considered the day's menu before he stepped into the cafeteria and, by default, asked for pizza? If he went to his locker after first period, rather than third? Maybe not all at once, but by degrees. He had offered to escort her first to her locker, then to her homeroom. Then, at the first bell, he would meet her again to walk to first period. After that, she was on her own—their lunches didn't overlap—until the end of the day, when they would meet at the front doors and board the bus (number 36) again together. It occurred to Greg now that Sarah had lived along their bus route, but she didn't enter the picture until later that year, and besides, he ought to have remembered, she didn't take the bus anyway. Where would she have been, in that moment?

He heard Beth whispering something under her breath, a string of numbers, like a mantra.

"Shut up, what are you whispering?"

"It's my lock combination. How do you remember it?"

He pondered this. Truthfully, he couldn't have told her his own combination. "After a while you'll just remember it."

"What if I don't?"

"You will. But if you're afraid you'll forget, you can write it on your hand or something."

She sat in silence, clearly worried. "I don't have a pen. Only pencils."

He unzipped the outer pocket of his backpack and dug around until he found one, and gave it to her. But until he'd felt the pen in his fingers, he hadn't known he'd been carrying it.

He closed his eyes, and when he opened them he heard the voice to his right, as if it had taken Beth's place: "Greg."

Over the summer, the voice had become unpredictable, but also routine, prone to breaking into his day at random times, though generally not aggressively enough to hijack it completely: in most cases, he could safely ride it out and answer the questions without anyone noticing. Still, he worried about how it would play into the school day, now that he was thrust back into public again, when he would rarely be alone. He was a year and a half into therapy, and the monthly psychiatrist had most recently put him on Risperdal in June, which he had learned—not via his doctor—was an "antipsychotic." The doctor had called it a "mood stabilizer." This was a data point, too. Would he be sitting here, entrusted with his younger sister, were he not stable? If he was psychotic? Wasn't she dependent on his knowledge?

"Greg," the voice said again.

"What?" he said aloud, his annoyance piqued. Beth looked to him from her hand, where he saw written in neat block print extending from her palm onto her left index finger, R TO 42, L PASS 42 TO 10, R TO 4. It was as confusing as it possibly could be. "What?" she echoed.

"Where is Beth?" the voice said.

The annoyance instantly subsided. She was here, accounted for. That was an easy one. "She's here," he barely articulated. He had *instincts*, that was it—he didn't have the same questions as Beth, because he unwittingly had an answer already. Did she have none? Those were data points, too, maybe, the spaces for those instincts: with each interaction she was learning how to react to the world, how she *should* react, when he'd been too caught up in his own machinery to notice the difference.

"Where are you going?" the voice asked.

He turned to the aisle to answer; they were about three-quarters along the route. "To school."

"Do you have everything?"

Everything? What was that? Greg didn't know, but it prompted him to do a mental inventory all the same. He had not brought his razors—he'd intentionally removed them from his wallet the night before. He was trying to limit their use at this stage, to minimize the potential triggers, though his legs were already fucked as it was. He was short a pen (Beth had moved on to absently barbed-wiring her wrist, which was cooler than hearts or whatever, but still likely to get her noticed). His bag was light today: after school, they would go to Staples to get the rest of their school supplies. *Everything.* What did that word even mean? Was he prepared?

"Yes."

They rehashed their plan again. Beth was nervous about being unsupervised for so much of the day. "You can text me if you get scared," Greg said.

"You're not supposed to text during class."

"You can go into the bathroom and do it. That's what everyone does."

She thought this over, and then looked up at him. "But won't you know anyway? If I get scared?"

He looked out the opposite windows as they passed the small farm adjacent to the middle school grounds. *Everything*. The voice was silent again. "Sure," he said. "I'll know."

As promised, when they arrived he walked Beth into the school, which opened like a cathedral, to her locker on the south wall of the cafeteria, where he stood behind her as she locked and failed to unlock, then unlocked her locker, and he masked his annoyance, which seemed to stress her out more, and finally he took her to her homeroom, which was in the art room—which felt appropriate, to him—and he left her there, feeling relieved, like a weight had dispersed. But by the time he hit his own locker and made it to his own homeroom on the other side of the school he was four or five minutes late, and when he stepped into the room, the math teacher, Mr. Daltrey, looked up and said, "So, Greg, not going to be any different this year, is it?" And he realized that it fundamentally wasn't. In that moment he understood: everything came at a cost. And what might have otherwise survived as a positive point of data—the satisfaction at successfully seeing Beth into her first day, at his ability to respond to her need—instead became a negative one, a symptom of his *bad habit*, his disrespect for the institution—a groove like the scars on his legs he could no longer capably hide.

And one thing led to another, over time, a constellation of those data points, a rippling wave of consequences that made him who he was, that eventually changed his relationship with Beth to its roots. Was that what the voice had been trying to make him notice, when it had changed? To see those points more clearly? Was that what it had wanted for Sarah—what we had wanted—to change her, as it had changed him?

What if it had been that sense of relief that he'd carried forward instead, Greg thought now, that sense of guiding his sister, that she needed him, that he was capable of reassuring her? If, rather than what came after, it had been the feeling of that endless bus ride on their first day, answering her questions, as the bus circled the school and parked out front, the twenty or thirty seconds they'd spent waiting to exit, moving down the aisle, when he felt like she was ready, and he'd helped her prepare? If that was what he'd cast out into the future—if that had been the moment that lasted, that rippled outward? How much would the trajectory have changed?

Where is Beth?

She was here, to his right, where she had always been, as he reached out and touched her arm, indicating it was time to go. So they stood, and he sensed her fear and put a hand on her shoulder, and for a second took her arm—her barbed-wire wrist—he squeezed it reassuringly, and together they slowly traversed the length of the bus toward the exit, the doors open to the morning light, and turned: this was where he stepped off.

Beth pulled the car to the gravel alongside the state road gutting the center of a town an hour north of her house. Her dad would have called it East Jesus—it was one of those little communities that bulb off the back highways of mostly rural states, towns with names like Bangs and Paris, notable only for the inconvenience of having to decelerate from sixty to thirty-five as you pass through them: a gas station/grocery store combo, chain-link fences housing brutal dogs, dismantled pickup trucks propped on cinder blocks. It was what you envisioned when you pictured the Midwest without ever having been there. This particular bulb was called New Grace, and comprised one stoplight and three stop signs. As soon as she passed the green welcome sign the light in her head zoomed up to greet her, and then it swung sharply to the left, and she knew she was close, she was practically on top of it.

She sat in the car thirty feet or so past the small white house from which she felt certain the light was emanating. It floated in back of her head, a presence over her shoulder, pivoting when she turned back. The house was unremarkable, like a child's drawing of a house, symmetrical with a steep roof, a single window in the attic space looking out like an eye; she mentally classified it as a farmhouse, for no reason other than that it seemed to sit isolated from its neighbor. White paint flaked from the siding, as if someone had rubbed it with a wire brush. The grass around the house was overgrown and patchy, and a mailbox jutted into the road at an awkward angle, the house number—12—painted on the tin. Beth watched the house through the rearview mirror, as if afraid to look at it directly for fear of being discovered. The light shifted through yellow-green and red-orange, maintaining its consistent purple undertone.

Now that she was here, Beth didn't know what to do. Should she go up to the front door and knock, to face her brother head-on, let him know she knew where he'd gone? Should she bide her time and see if he emerged? The shabbiness of the house and its lawn, this blister of a town, it surprised her for some reason, made her feel like she was trespassing—why would her brother have come to a place like this? But then, of course he had. Of course he had needed to go somewhere different. She felt pulled by conflicting impulses: to climb from her disproportionately nice car like a lost traveler and walk toward the quasi-farmhouse, and to start the car and race back the way she'd come. It was the same desire she'd felt at the hospital, to erase any evidence of her involvement. The compromise was sitting in the car, not moving at all, watching the light like a television, the image in the rearview mirror its screen.

She didn't have to wait long. The front door of the house opened and a short, older woman with a fluff of gray hair, enormous glasses, jeans, and a faded pink sleeveless top emerged, hoisting a folded wheelchair under one arm. She carried it down the three steps of the stoop and unfolded it on the sidewalk below. She paused, her hands on her hips, pulled her glasses up, and wiped off her face with the front of her shirt, then seemed to notice Beth's car. She craned her head as if to make out the license plate. Beth slid down in the seat, which was so big it masked her completely anyway. By the time she lifted her head again and peered through the rearview mirror, the woman had gone, leaving the wheelchair at the base of the steps. When she appeared again from the front door, she was supporting a young man at least a head taller than she was—older than Beth—with dark hair that hung over his face, glasses. Beth read him automatically as the woman's son. The light in her head moved as he did.

She blinked: the hair on her neck prickled, as if she'd taken a wrong step and only just caught herself from falling. *We knew him.*

It wasn't Greg. Beth realized this instantly, but she wasn't as crushed as she'd expected to be, not at this moment. It was as if a part of her had known all along it couldn't be him, as if pursuing this theory had been a method of building a wall between her and his death, so that when the moment inevitably arrived and she was proved wrong, there was already a buffer there. The young man had Greg's aspect, though—in a few turns, it could have been him. It could have been Greg three generations ago, or if Greg had grown up and his physical features had evolved to match his maturity. Was this really him, the owner of the purple light she had been following? Was he the one who never slept?

She watched the woman brace herself against the railing and negotiate the two of them slowly down the steps. Every motion seemed to cause the man extreme pain. He looked utterly wiped out. The light went bright orange and red with every step he took, but she didn't need its reassurance, as each movement telegraphed its associated pain through his entire body in a faint shiver, though he kept his back straight, his head bowed, and lips pursed. Beth realized the purple she'd noticed underlying the light must have been him masking the pain, biting it all down. She felt suddenly, unbelievably sad. Greg: he had never been purple. He had never been able to disguise it.

At the bottom of the steps the woman left the young man supporting himself on the railing and pushed the wheelchair forward. He slowly turned and she guided him with one arm as he sank into it. She swiveled the chair on the walk and pushed it onto the bare asphalt of the state road, then around to the old blue sedan parked in the gravel driveway twenty feet behind Beth. The young man kept his hands folded in his lap. The movement across the gravel was torturous; with each imperfection in the terrain, Beth would watch the light flicker reddish orange, so bright and sharp that she'd feel it herself, a blink of pain behind her eye. At the passenger side of the car, the woman had him brace against the door as she helped lift him out of the chair, but the maneuver looked unpracticed—she forgot to lock the wheelchair and it slid suddenly backward, the car shifted as they strained against it. Once he was finally in the passenger seat, the door closed, the wheelchair folded up and loaded into the trunk, and the woman had buckled herself into the driver's seat and started the car, only then did the tension Beth hadn't even noticed building in her shoulders and neck begin to relax. The car had pulled out of the driveway and begun its journey south before she caught her breath enough to realize that she ought to follow them. She started her car, hauled a U-turn in the center of the bleak, empty road.

She trailed them back the way she had come, gradually speeding back up to sixty, into middle-ground farmland—or what she assumed must be farmland, fields at least—and as she drove, Beth realized how apart she felt from the two people in the car ahead of her; their lives were distinctly different. If left to their natural courses, they would never have overlapped. There would always be people who were in power, Beth thought, and there would always be people who were below them: at this moment, she felt herself to be one of those people with power. She couldn't qualify it any further, this harsh thought, but it sat somewhere inside her, an emotional distance she was maintaining, despite the light connecting her to the young man, the same sense she'd held for the person who was supposed to be closer to her than anyone else in the world but who, in the end, had been completely inscrutable, as familiar as this perfect stranger.

The blue car suddenly swerved to the right and sailed into a parking lot splitting off the state road. The light pulsed orange. Beth jammed on her brakes—no cars visible behind her—and veered into the parking lot after them. She read the gold letters above the message board as she flitted by it: HOLY BLOOD COMMUNITY CENTER, and then the message on white below: WELCOME ALL / POST 638. A church? The lot held a few scattered cars; it looked like none of the drivers had wanted to park directly next to each other. The building was squat and had two distinct brick wings, a set of glass doors at their intersection. She mentally split the two wings into the community center and the sanctuary, the Holy Blood and its organs. The blue car pulled into a handicapped space near the front doors, and Beth drifted her monster car into a row on the opposite side of the lot, so she could keep watching through the rearview, as she'd watched the house, her car facing away from the church, looking out into the field.

The gray-haired woman unloaded the wheelchair from the trunk and they reversed the process getting out of the car. She propped open the glass door, bumped him onto the sidewalk, and they disappeared inside. They left the door open behind them. Beth exhaled. The sunset heat radiated down through her windshield, the sky going yellow. It was well past seven. She noticed a grouping of little American flags planted along the sidewalk out front of the building, a flagpole on the side of the building facing the state road. Explicit Americana made her nervous. What was she doing here?

A pickup truck pulled into the lot and parked a few spots away from her. A boy her age got out the driver's side and slouched his way inside the community center. A few minutes later a hybrid-looking car pulled in and paused out front; another kid jumped out and ran inside through the open door. The car circled the lot and left.

Beth watched the door of the community center as, one by one, more cars arrived and their drivers or passengers trickled into the building—all kids, she noticed. She surveyed the other cars in the parking lot around her: most of the cars she didn't recognize, but she picked out an Escalade in the far corner, elsewhere an Audi, the flared rear end of a sports car. She felt weirdly comforted at being able to identify them, like kindred spirits. Eventually, the older woman, who she assumed was the young man's mother, emerged from the building, stepped away from the door, and lit a cigarette. Again, her eyes wandered over to Beth's car. Beth cringed, she scooted down again, but so she could still see through the side mirror. The woman waved away a cloud of smoke, and suddenly she was walking across the parking lot toward Beth's ridiculous enormous car. Beth had the brief thought that she could back up and run her over.

The woman knocked assertively on her window. Beth

sheepishly scooched back up and pressed the button to roll it down. The gray-haired woman seemed very far below her. She said something, but Beth couldn't make it out through the accent. "What?"

"I saw you back in New Grace." There was no accent after all, she realized. "Are you lost?"

"Yes," Beth said.

The woman looked unconvinced. "This your first time here?"

Beth shifted in her seat. The smoke filtered in through the open window. Her parents would think she had been smoking. "Yes," she said.

"Don't you think you should be in there, then?"

She looked back to her rearview mirror, to the quiet double doors of the church, the light sheltered behind them.

"Are you hurt?" the woman persisted.

Beth shivered. "I don't know," she said.

The woman narrowed her eyes. "Are you a conspiracy theorist?"

Who was this woman? "No. I don't even know what that means."

The woman put her cigarette back into her mouth. "Okay. If you do want to go in after a while, I can take you."

"Thanks," Beth said shortly, and rolled up the window. The woman stood there a second before turning away and walking back across the parking lot. When she was far enough away, Beth cracked the window again to try to get rid of the smoke smell. What was this place?

She returned her attention to the community center via the rearview mirror, and she watched the light somewhere inside it, conversant yet edgy, orange and purple. As time passed, it slowly developed a rich violet ring, a color she'd never seen—she wondered if the young man was presenting or performing, if he was sharing his ills with a group. The ring slowly closed, turning the light fully violet. The color was almost as intense and pure as it had been the moment before the crash, or when Sarah touched Greg's arm in the hospital—she didn't know what it meant: something you felt with your whole body, your whole mind. A lie you didn't know was a lie any longer—what was that? Belief? Beth wondered what color she was right now. Was that violet hers, too? Had she ever felt something so purely? The fact that she couldn't clearly identify it—it wasn't sadness, not grief or anxiety, but something more distant and obscure—seemed like it proved the rule, that she hadn't. If she couldn't feel it when her own brother died, then obviously it wasn't part of her makeup. Maybe the woman was right: maybe she should be inside the church.

She thought of the video she'd seen on David's Facebook almost three weeks ago now, the people shutting down like machines, the man and woman scrabbling at the center of a circle, the figure standing at the edge of the frame, watching: the kind of scene provoked by a color like that, a place like this. She pictured a group standing in a circle, a group of people wounded in a similar way as the young man, who had all come here with a similar purpose, gathered in some anonymous assembly room inside the church. She pictured the young man in their midst, first seated in his wheelchair, and then rising impressively as he spoke. She saw him visiting each of the people gathered, speaking quietly to them in turn, making his way slowly around the circle, sharing his truth that was not quite the truth, but a belief he held deeply. At first he walked cautiously, unsteadily, like he had down the steps outside his house, but the more he spoke, the more his strength seemed to return. She saw him addressing the group as a whole, once he had visited everyone, once they saw what he did. She saw him standing in the center of the circle, all eyes drawn to him as he spoke. He planted something in your mind. He passed it to you. A cold wave prickled her shoulders. She saw him raise his arms, the violet light as violet as it could be, as singular and single-minded as was his focus. He gave an order that wasn't an order but an intimation. He clapped his hands. He watched the effect ripple. She saw it so clearly.

And, wrapped in this fantasy, Beth did what she'd been doing since she stopped going to school seventeen days ago: she watched, she waited, she acted as a receiver, she focused squarely on the light and let it fill her mind. Inside, those poor suckers were lured in by that deceptive light, its vibrant *conspiracy*, offering their deepest vulnerability to someone who only wanted it for himself, who drew on it for his own strength, while outside, Beth sat at a healthy remove, in the safety of her towering driver's seat, wise enough, she thought—having learned enough—to keep herself out of it. That distance, the detachment she'd felt as she followed the light in the blue car down the highway, that she felt growing as she sat here: maybe it was something Greg had left her with when he'd gone, a river carved into her over time that she'd finally taught herself not to cross. Maybe she couldn't get close to anyone again; she was too cynical.

Or maybe that was us. We let her spin out that fantasy, stranded out in the parking lot, looking at the church reflected in her mirrors; we let it expand and curdle because it held her there, it kept her from what was at its center; it drew her further apart from what was happening inside, because her alienation, her anger, her bitterness, her armored aloneness was where we wanted her. Because if she'd stepped inside, it could have been fatal to us. Her light wanted her in there. We didn't.

She watched the light glow, flicker in its intensity. She felt, suddenly, as if she'd outgrown it. She wondered if she even believed in the light anymore, if it was the power of her belief in it—in the light's accuracy, its intent—that allowed it to exist at all. She put her head back, to look at the orange sky. It, too, was tinged with purple. It had been everything to her. And now?

—

Earlier that afternoon, as Beth made her way north, Sarah scanned the heavily adorned walls of David's bedroom as he fumbled with her bra, and she realized there was a level they'd always been lacking as a couple: all this memorabilia—did he really like this stuff? She had spent countless hours down in the basement with him as he played videogames or mindlessly consumed television, but what did he actually enjoy? Did he read? He cupped her breasts in his hands and fell with her onto the bed—did he have taste? She had known him since middle school, before it really mattered, but she didn't know much about him, not really, and yet here she was. It was the second time someone had kissed her unexpectedly in three days, and this time she had followed it through. She wondered how different the two instances were mechanically, if the only real difference was that Greg was dead now instead of in the hospital, or that Claire was gone and Sarah knew it was because she had responded the wrong way and she didn't want it to happen again, didn't want another person to disappear, so she was grasping at Dave (had she ever called him that?) because he was the one who came for her, that it could have been anyone and she would have acted the same way, it could have been Claire at her front door, could have been the random girl on the bus, she'd let them fill her up her like vomit because she was sick, sick and didn't know what she wanted, and stupid for not listening to the people who told her what it should be. When they'd entered the room, David had automatically flicked on the overhead light, though the windows would have lent sufficient atmosphere on their own. What did he know about ambience?

He was unbuttoning her pants. "Do you have a condom?" she said.

He stopped. "Uh, no. I—I'm sorry." She saw him sinking toward the bottom half of the bed, still fully clothed, her own underwear pulled midway down one thigh, a stretch of pubic hair exposed. Their roles seemed to shift again—here she was, splaycd and vulnerable, and there he remained, buttoned—and she had to take responsibility, she again had to be the one to take them onward. She leaned forward—it felt like it took all her strength—and pulled him up by his waist and unzipped his pants.

"It's okay," Sarah said. "We'll figure it out." Her mind scrolled instantaneously through all their interactions over the past three weeks, up to this one, and she wondered if there was anything more horrible than being mean to a person—lying to them, manipulating them—and then pretending it had never happened. He had contrived this situation and he couldn't even follow it through. She thought if she went limp, just like that, if she stopped interacting with his body, then he would stop, too, he would not have the courage to proceed. But she didn't, because she was already doing it, the one thing she could give him—could give anyone—was encouragement. Because she had already driven Claire away. Because it was easier to see it through. Exhausted, her vision blurred into the ceiling above her, the fan with its three clustered light bulbs, one of them burned out: it was that yellow again, that light, the color David had planted in her when they'd reconnected, *marrow*, the color of botched ritual, the color of that house off the U of O campus, the party with Hannah, the school bathroom where the girl had followed her. He had somehow brought it back: the dynamics of the scene were the same.

And as she guided his hand, guided him into her, a moment abruptly returned to her. When she'd climbed from Greg's car after they'd hit the tree, her nose had been bleeding. And at the time she had absorbed it as part of the crash—it wasn't there in the minutes before the accident, and then afterward it was—but now that she tried, she couldn't remember the collision that had caused it, couldn't remember her head jarring forward into the dashboard. But she hadn't lost consciousness, hadn't hit her head on anything when the car crashed—it was only Greg's half of the car that had been decimated—and lying on David's bed she rewound the seconds in her head, frame by frame, the rivulet of blood creeping back into her nose, and then the car was whole again and careening, but she was still bleeding and starting to bleed, and she remembered it then: Greg had hit her. He had hit her in the face. On the bed, she separated from her body.

David fucked her. They all fucked her. It was the same contact, every way.

And at a certain point, Sarah looked to the right, out the window beside his bed, from the yellow of David's room to the filtered gray palette of the world beyond them. Through the shifting trees, the sky was a furious white, a single, impossibly dense color of equal violence within which she could sense movement, a swarming, the atmosphere out there as thick as language. She could have bellowed it into words.

We were out there upon that wind.

Picture a living room: a staging area, a calling ground, a place to which you've been gathered for a purpose you don't know yet. Imagine an exercise in synchronized breathing, like that preceding a dance, carried out for no other reason than because that's what all the participants have in common, at this point, their ability to breathe. Imagine a shared movement to a common purpose, bringing all this hot breath into the same room so it can circulate its furious potential, pass from mouth to mouth, from palm to palm, one set of lungs struggling to match its neighbor, a potential so great it condenses on the air. Imagine repeating this exercise until an intimacy is formed between you all, a familiarity of rhythm, until the pattern is so ingrained that when one person loses a breath you could catch it in your hands like a moth. Imagine, over time, a new understanding is formed, an awareness of the raw data—the blood, the breath, the smell riding its current, the relentless pulse of the body—all of which makes up the person next to you. Imagine this understanding deepening, through repetition, until all of that potential has resolved itself into a pattern, predictable and regular, a breathing template, until what stands beside you, before you, behind you comprises not a person but a course of possibility, a series of expected actions and their reactions, and their reactions in turn, mapped out in their component parts, waiting to be shaped: a course based not on instinct, not on emotion, but on ruthless, mechanical calculation. A closeness that reveals a distance, like the way a rush of blood can be traced back to a heartbeat, a gasp to a breath out of sync. And now picture yourself taking that intimate, internal rhythm and pulling it apart, isolating the pulse in your hands: imagine each heartbeat as a knot in a string that connects all of you, a drawstring waiting to be loaded, pulled taut, and released.

It was somewhere in that possibility swirling around them, David and Sarah, one whose edges we'd left sharp, the other who fumbled in the dark for something to hold, it was bursting at the walls of David's bedroom, of his house entire, clamoring for a way inside, it was in the air between their mouths—this closeness that had revealed a brutal distance—there, like the breath held in before a scream: that was us.

And as Beth drifted off outside the church, the church that was not really a church, that only had the bearing of a church, inside, sure enough, a pulse went from hand to hand, the young man traced it out in the shapes he'd known since childhood: shapes more than familiar to us, but which, in his hands, represented our opposition.

Collin was there that night, as he had been almost every night since September, practicing the technique he'd been given, trying to forget his dead sister, to disperse her memory into the noise of his reality enough to move through it. He, too, had been a breath held in: a chaos that over those months had become an order, and in that order, he'd finally learned to exhale. He hadn't known what was out there—or he had known, but so instinctively that it was impossible to articulate. But now something in him had changed: he'd begun to see how he could define it— the amorphous grief and rage that tracked him everywhere, the apartness, the emptiness, its whole incredible weight—and to exist within that definition. How others carried that weight, too, and how he could lessen it in himself by finding it in them. It was still hard, impossible at times, but on certain nights he glimpsed a method for getting out: the first step of a long staircase. He thought back to the version of himself first stranded on that empty state road—his clammy hands on the steering wheel, his gaping pores, his backpack full of sweaty clothes, literally directionless, obliviously marked for annihilation—he couldn't see it clearly, the pain he carried, where it sat out among the world. And then, after all these nights, he could.

"So where did you spend that night?" the man said, to his left.

"Woodburne Park. There's an amphitheater," the kid across the circle from Collin said.

"And the night before?"

"In the garage."

The kid looked down—a scrawny white kid, with burn marks on his arms—and bit his lip. Collin couldn't see them, but he knew his eyes were closed.

"Eyes up," the man said.

Collin had known he would say that.

The kid looked back up, and met Collin's gaze across the circle. "I didn't mean to hurt him."

"I know you didn't."

"I just want to be able to go home again."

Collin dropped his hands. The kid across from him blurred a little, and then clarified, as if his shadow had stepped away. For a second Collin felt lighter, almost faint, like he'd skipped a breath, and an abrupt sound escaped him—a sudden, guttural laugh. In the next moment, he had a fleeting, transitory memory—Rachael walking into her bedroom, closing the door—and then the heaviness sank over him again. The kid opposite him wobbled. He knew him. He recognized him. The specific story was unfamiliar, the detail of his circumstances; he couldn't have been more different from this kid in all the regular ways— but their shape was the same.

He tried again: he met his eyes, blurred them, and the kid's face doubled and split. He felt a sudden, bracing burst of cold garage air, a whiff of old gasoline—as if the memory had become his own. Tears ran down his cheeks. He understood.

He decided on the spot that he needed to be blackout drunk that night, as soon as humanly possible after he left this building. He decided to go to the party he'd gotten a message about, at one of the houses in the White Knots: this was how he could accomplish this goal as cheaply and efficiently as possible.

That night, Tyler and Rhea were sitting on the couch in the basement living room, a day after the weed had officially been spent. It was his nineteenth night, following the eighteenth full day he'd spent in David's basement. Typhus sat on the floor before them, and the TV was on, the volume low. A stagnation had come over the basement, an unacknowledged competition for who could go the longest without moving or speaking. He was wearing earbuds—he had more or less stopped using them when Rhea arrived, but over the last twenty-four hours he had picked them up again. He couldn't stand the tension of the silence among the three of them, he needed to fortify this atmospheric texture with another. He thought when he looked back on the time he'd spent here, he would not be able to describe what had happened, nor how this situation had come to be.

There had been a moment the night before, after the incident with the fake weed, in the early hours of the morning after they'd gone to bed, after he and Rhea had retired to the bedroom. Rhea had settled into the shared bed routine better than he had, and it was taking Tyler hours to fall asleep there. He would have to lie in a position of mounting discomfort until he simply grew exhausted at maintaining it and his mind gradually blurred off, or he would stare at the ceiling until the boredom of it was too much like the day that had preceded it, and his body caved to sleep. But that night he was lying in one of his uncomfortable positions on his side, head aloft, his arms knotted, one knee folded into his chest, his leg raised and muscles clenched, some kind of tortured yoga pose, staring into flattened space, when a shaft of light appeared on the closet door and then spread. He moved his head minutely and saw the door open silently, and someone was standing within it. By the figure's stature, he knew it was Marcy—that was the name that came to him first, not Typhus but Marcy—and he felt a sudden flush of fear grip him, a crippling dread, and he lay stiff in the bed next to Rhea like a gnarled sculpture, pretending to be unconscious, letting the seconds expire as he had every single one prior to this. She watched them for a minute without ever fully entering the room, and then silently closed the door. A minute after that, the living room light went out, too. It took another few minutes for his body to re-regulate, for him to calm down and his breathing to relax, for Tyler to fully reconstruct the scene and realize what it was, what domestic and benign thing it represented: it was a child checking in on her parents, he thought. It was the validation of a presence.

He awoke the next morning half expecting her to be gone, and half expecting her to be curled in the bed between them. But he found her where he always did, in the living room, not on the couch but lying on the floor, blanketless and exposed, as if she hadn't earned the furniture yet, as if she'd accepted the tacit punishment of the floor. He'd sat on the couch behind her and absently turned on the TV until she eventually awoke to the sound of it, startling up in alarm, as if she weren't permitted to be asleep. When she saw him sitting there she had scampered off to the bathroom, then returned without acknowledgment, freshly made up and dressed for the ostensible new day.

That day had passed into night, a day in which Tyler had absorbed nothing and expended nothing but his own silent agitation, a mounting restlessness combated by deep shame, a vague fear that he was being irresponsible, not in his life as such but as de facto leader of their trio, that their group's cohesion was slowly dissolving over a lack of anything to hold it together, even basic communication, that he should have planned this better—he should have planned something. The TV screen fuzzed out its images and the speakers their associated tones. It would be time to sleep again before long. Tomorrow, he told himself, things would change. He would change things. His heartbeat accelerated at the thought, at the anticipation of action. Tomorrow would come and it would bring with it a plan. They looked at the TV without seeing it, as if it was a part of the wall, their eyes wandering across it like a static, aimless canvas. And then into this silence—or what Tyler perceived as silence, though there was noise present—came four sharp knocks from the door in back of the basement.

His skin froze—all three looked up. In the seconds immediately following those sounds, the powerful mantle of leadership fell upon Tyler again. He felt attention turn to him. He took his earbuds from his ears in a way he hoped didn't signal alarm. He turned slowly to Rhea and raised his eyebrows as if to say, *Did you?* and she shook her head. The knocks came again, more insistently, with the sound of the door jostling; Tyler felt sure that after this there would be yelling, the sound was likely to be heard upstairs.

He looked at Typhus, who was already unfolding her legs and moving. Again, he summoned his tone, he chose his words carefully. "Could you deal with it?"

He realized instantly afterward he'd said the wrong thing. He would be regretting those words for the rest of his life.

Typhus disappeared into the back of the basement. He and Rhea looked at each other, and all at once Tyler felt like he had a million things to say to her where he hadn't before, there was an infinite amount for them to discuss, but he had to do it now, in these next few seconds, because their circumstances were about to change, they would never be in uniquely this position again. He suddenly thought of drapes—they could have supplemented the curtains over the bedroom windows with drapes or blankets, could have allowed themselves more light. They could have moved the couch. But before he could put thought to action, he heard the back door open, and then a commotion of voices. At first he thought there were three, but then he realized that one was Typhus, that he hadn't yet heard her communicate above speaking level. From the way the voices immediately erupted, he knew Typhus must know the person at the door, must have given them away. He stood, without knowing whether he was going to move farther than that, and thought, *Fucking*—

He heard a scuffle, the scrape of shoes on concrete, and then a quiet, stunned scream. He ran into the back of the basement, turned the corner to the hallway with the washing machine, and felt the sudden break in the air that meant the door to the outside was open. He heard rapid steps on the concrete stairs, a human collision. He sprinted down the hallway, whirled around in the doorway, taking his first breath of external air since Typhus had arrived three days ago.

The stairwell was empty. He waited a beat for sound to guide him, but there was nothing. He climbed the stairs in as few strides as possible, leaving the door open behind him. He emerged at the fringe of the backyard like an intruder. To his left, a yellow pool of light splashed into the grass through the windows in the kitchen, but to the right it was dark, there was a strip of black from the overhanging roof of the garage. A solitary figure staggered out from the shadowed space onto the moonlit lawn, clutching her side. She made a throaty sound and fell to her knees, then onto her stomach.

There was a second when Tyler's mind was just blank, when he stopped taking in information. And then he was running toward the fallen figure, tripping over his own feet, he was kneeling down and rolling her onto her back, blood seeping in blotches through her frayed shirt, her chest and stomach swiped frantically open, and Typhus was standing beside him. A new set of sensory experiences overcame him: the smell of grass and blood, a perverse breeze, wetness wherever he put his hands, the nearness and heat of Typhus's breathing, almost panting. He slid one arm beneath the girl's legs and the other under her shoulders, and lifted her up. Her head flopped back and in the moonlight he saw that there were cuts on her face and neck, too, random slashes just starting to bleed. He couldn't tell if she was breathing, he was shaking too much. He stumbled once under the weight, and then his body decided that he had the strength to carry her. He lurched back across the lawn to the basement steps with the body in his arms—the moon a searchlight, a flicker in the window—and as he moved he became aware of Typhus again, who was silent, who ran ahead, so small, and raced down the steps, something glinting in her hand, back from where they'd come, as if there had never been anywhere else to go, as if the only way through was to go deeper, and as he edged his way down the concrete steps he saw a burst of blood on the wall—a splotch and a crescent-like smear that almost seemed to cradle it. Typhus was standing in the open doorway below with her arms out, as if prepared to receive him, her front spattered in blood, and Rhea arrived behind her, one hand over her mouth. By their positions alone it was as if Tyler had gone out and brought this body back to ruin them all, as if it were his own body, part of a plan he'd made, and there was a horrified moan he couldn't let go of, that he could never let go of, and he could picture no end to this, literally no end—he saw the step before him, one treacherous step downward, and then another, and then another, and then silence.

It was just after dark when her phone buzzed and woke Beth in her car. She grabbed it from the cup holder, to silence it, and saw that she'd received an image from an unknown number. Unthinking, her mind still bleary, she thumbed it open. It was a screenshot of a block of text, some cryptic missive, and she was going to delete it when she suddenly recognized her own address. Her eyes scanned the message backward: THE DEATH PARTY. A date—today. Her heart started racing, she tried to read the text but couldn't make sense of it. *Come celebrate two souls taken too soon.* What the fuck? Two souls? Did this have something to do with Greg?

But the second she saw the address, we knew. We realized, at last, the full potential of Beth's role. We knew where she needed to be: we needed her *there*, back home, in the thick of it. That was where it would all happen, where we could come to fruition. So we took the light— that persistent fucking thing, her forever GPS—and we buried it.

Beth blanked the phone and tossed it away, frightened, unable to fully process what she'd seen, and only then did she see the glimmer of light reflected in the windshield and remember where she was and what she was doing; she paused to get her bearings again, to reorient herself around the familiar light in her head.

But in its place were two of them. Two lights. She blinked, expecting them to resolve into one, like a street-light stared at for too long, from too close. They didn't.

She detected movement behind her. Through the rearview mirror, she saw the door of the community center swing open and people spill out and disperse into the parking lot. Out of the corner of her eye she saw the old woman get out of her car to meet the young man at the door, and then escort him toward their car. The associated light moved to the right with them. Then she saw someone move past her back window, left to right, a boy with dreadlocks who looked around her age, who she felt she recognized in some way, or ought to recognize, and she twisted around in her seat to watch him go. The second light moved away with him. *Two souls.* Beth heard car doors shutting, and she turned back around with the two lights in her head, clearly distinct—one the purple she knew well and the other suffused with an amber-like brown, intense guilt, but also desire, like the color she'd seen in Greg toward the end: a decision made, but doubted. She felt their counterweights tugging her mind in opposite directions, alerting her that they were here, and *here, too,* and they needed her attention. She rubbed her neck, she felt sweat prickling at her forehead. She tried to count the number of doors slamming—two for each car, she averaged—but this only confused her more, like she'd been dropped onto a field in the midst of a game she had no idea how to play.

Cars were leaving the parking lot now, and she started hers in response, but she stayed sitting there, unable to move, paralyzed by the choices offered to her. Should she go home? If she did, what would she find there? Was it safe there—was it here? The two lights in her head rolled back and forth, they seemed to change positions—one car passed the other?—but she couldn't see either behind her in the mirrors, and a wave of dizziness hit her, her mind retreating with the strain, her center of gravity slowly tilting and then frantically recalibrating. The lights swooped again, as if to mock her, and her stomach did the same. She wrapped her fingers around the steering wheel and stared at the dashboard until she started crying, and then bit down on her tongue, bracing herself. The car jerked inadvertently forward and scraped onto the curb. Beth stomped the brakes. She closed her eyes, opened them, closed them, opened, and the lights were still there. What was happening? Was one of them Greg? Had he been hidden here, all along?

In the space of a minute she felt the bodies attached to the lights receding, they were moving in opposite directions, drawn rapidly apart by their two vehicles, and she thought if they kept going she would either be pulled apart or the lights would disappear forever. But she wasn't, and they didn't: her mind stretched to encompass them—she imagined each of the lights as a shooting star, tugging her into the infinity of space as they grew farther and farther away. She let herself sit for another minute, the rest of the cars exiting the parking lot. She huddled against the steering wheel as the two points rolled out, as the distance between them grew.

When the parking spaces around her were empty, she backed the car up (too wide), rolled across the lot, and turned back onto the state road. She automatically turned right, she drove south, the way she'd come, attaching herself to the second light like it was a passed baton, like it was Greg, his *soul*, and she was following it home, to the Death Party—it was the only place she could think to drive, that she had any idea how to get to. She didn't think to use her phone; the light was the only navigation she'd ever really known. Where else was she going to go?

She picked up speed, the sky now nearly dark. She kept her eyes trained on the road ahead, on the taillights ahead of her, an old maroon car; she was not going to do what Greg did, she would not end up like her brother. One light pulled out behind her in the distance, the purple one— the liar, she thought, or we told her—back to New Grace, while she gained slowly on the other, the guilty one, the two lights suspended beyond her eyes, passing on their information without information, their knowledge without knowledge.

She realized too far down the highway she wasn't using her headlights. She flicked them on, and at the same time a third light burst into her mind, milky yellow, and another locative sense with it, another point on her mental radar, somewhere ahead. She swerved—her coordinates did as well—but she managed to right herself smoothly. There were no other cars that she could see, beyond the maroon one ahead—just her and the night, it was her in this car and these lights. What was going on?

And then a fourth appeared, reddish brown, the color

of a family fight. And a few seconds later, another, blue with a fringe of yellow: pleasantly occupied. And then a sixth. One by one, they popped into her mind like bulbs as she drove, like flares, each one momentarily blinding her and each one tethered, swarming in the space of her mind like a room hung with illuminated baubles, blaring down at her. The smoke lingering from the woman's cigarette made it feel like the inside of her head was burning, singed by the heat of the lights. She felt as if the SUV was about to be compressed, or burst into flames. The road plowed on, and the lights continued to multiply, eight now, then ten, like balloons suddenly filled with air, crowding each other out, bumping up against the edges of her head. She turned on the radio to anchor herself and it sputtered out a stream of incomprehensible language, and it was all too much, too much information she couldn't keep track of, like the lights were intended purposely to overwhelm her, to crowd out the space for her to exist, like Greg had, to send her back to her tower, where she'd been trapped for years. Like that was all she knew.

She bowed her head and lifted it up again, took a long, tired blink. The faster she drove, the more she tried to un-crowd them, the farther the points in her skull dispersed, forming a constellation within her mind, a map of stars pressing behind her eyes, vibrating in her nasal passages, seeping out through her pores, and then other lights emerged to fill the gaps between them. She thought her head would explode. She closed her eyes for six seconds—

she counted—and when she opened them the road was unwavering, and she simultaneously saw civilization in the distance, real lights, but by then she had lost the critical part of knowing where she was driving, if that place was really what she was aiming for. She felt refracted in so many directions, like a broken mirror splitting light, like every light was equally Greg, or an aspect of him, every one was her dead brother beckoning her on, telling her to just end it, to choose one of these points and crash right into it.

Go home, Beth.

I'm trying, she said to herself. "I'm fucking trying!" She hit the ceiling of the car. She felt a red ball of anger glowing inside of her, finally, and she suddenly recognized that purity of feeling she'd thought was missing, it was searing, burning in her forehead: maybe it had been there forever, invisible until it was set alight. And yet she drove on, expandable Beth, she screamed into the car, into the night air, humming all around her, she dug her nails into the steering wheel to keep from wavering, and when the signs implored her to slow back down again she did, she dropped to a crawl. As she passed the first houses on the edge of the suburbs she felt points pulling her toward them, toward either side of the road, and ahead, and she knew everyone must have them, the lights, and these twenty or fifty or a thousand people were her siblings now, all of them marked and laid bare to her. Her head swam; she felt like she was underwater, staring at the sun from below the rippling surface. She could barely keep her eyes open. By now the maroon car had disappeared somewhere, but she could no longer pick out its light anyway. She followed the streets carefully to Meridian Circle, winding into the loop of manicured trees that contained her house on the hill, except she felt less like she was returning home than merely finding a place to stop. She didn't notice the white ribbons tied around the trees leading up to the house.

Unsure she could navigate the wraparound curves of the driveway, she pulled the car to the edge of the street across from it, stopping when she felt the front tire skip off the road. She tumbled out, crossed the street, and climbed the driveway—she wasn't sure if she had ever done it on foot before. She felt like she was making a pilgrimage to some distant mountain temple, dragging the lights in her wake like an offering to a forgotten god. Why had they ever lived here? What was the point of this giant dark house? At the top of the driveway, minutes later, she vomited, breathless and worn, and watched it inch down the driveway.

At the garage, she put in the code she barely remembered and covered her ears as the door lifted—the loudest sound she'd ever heard. The lights felt right on top of her now, like they moved with her, an enormous, vaguely pulsing mass—she couldn't have separated them if she wanted to, could not even hope to address their information. She tried to find the purple light within them, her guide, and then the orange one, but she couldn't, they had been subsumed or vanished among the others, or had otherwise shrunk away, their messages passed on, delivered like a chain letter, leaving her to fend for herself in this great empty house. She knew she was done. She crossed the garage, lit like laboratory death, and felt the lights around her, in this very room, as if there were others invisibly present, close at hand, as if they were bearing her body along. She thought if there was no relief inside the house then there was no relief anywhere, but at least it was familiar, at least there was somewhere she could remain quiet and still, in one position, while the lights did what they wanted to her.

She sealed the garage, closing herself in. But as soon as she opened the door to the house, she knew something was wrong. The lights shifted around her, they seemed to follow her in from the garage, to move ahead of her into the house. At the end of the hall off the garage, the lights inside the house were off, as she'd left them, but there was another hue supplementing the darkness, a faint glow cast not by lights in the house but which seemed to exist on the air itself. She walked slowly down the hallway, one hand trailing the wainscoting. She emerged into the kitchen, where this new, oily light coated the floor.

"Hello? Who's here?" she called out.

Her voice was met with a thick silence; the sound barely left the room. She crossed the kitchen into the foyer. Opposite, the doorway to the other living room—what her parents called the "parlor"—was a cloudy yellow, the light thick and material, like viscous fog: she followed it inside.

She followed the ugly glow and the lights in her head, re-arranging ahead of her, pulling her to that one room.

When she entered, Beth found the living room empty, but teeming with that light, with the gathered heat of its potential: arrayed before her, a dozen spheres of light radiated at eyeline, as if each was attached to an invisible body, a pair of eyes. They were all the same shade of watchful yellow, no purple or orange among them, all honed on her, a singular will. From the shelf to the right of the doorway, she took a glass ball the size of her fist, some random curio she'd never noticed before, and held it against her stomach, a little orb of coolness against the warmth of the air, as she walked into the center of the room. She turned, and the lights closed in behind her, circling her. They filled the house. They filled every room in every house, every living room and bedroom and basement. They filled the universe.

She dropped the glass ball, it clunked at her feet, and she dropped to her knees in the thrum of the lights, at the center of the room. She looked up at the halo of lights above her—a ring and, alongside it, an arc, a *conspiracy* of lights, she thought, peering down at her—and the air above them that same off-yellow seemed to turn, drifting like a toxic cloud, and she felt like she wasn't actually in the room herself, but some other version of her was, a pre-monitory, future Beth. A time would come, here in this room, when she would be surrounded, the Death Party would come upon her, close in, and here—before all of them—a choice would be made that changed them, that would rip through the room like a bomb.

Her body trembled, as if flinching from contact, and she realized how oppressively hot it was beneath the lights. The carpet smelled like it was burning. Her skin was damp, the inside of her nostrils crackled—she felt faint, feverish; all she wanted was relief, to take some of the weight off her, to relinquish the burden she'd been carrying for years, for as long as she could remember, the burden that refused to relent even after Greg was dead, that refused to allow him to be dead at all, that transmuted him into everything around her. She was cowed in that heat. Beth stood, and at the same time pulled her shirt over her head. The warmth of the light wrapped her bare skin. She peeled down her jeans inch by inch—the sweat was so thick on her it was like manipulating wet cardboard. She unfastened her bra and let it fall to the floor, stepped out of her underwear, and she stood there among the glowing bodies filling the room, that she felt ransacking her kitchen, charging up the stairs, dogpiling in her and Greg's empty beds, in her parents' rooms, the bathrooms, the closets, before coming to gather here, they could all see her, now and then, here and unspecifiably into the future. Her eyes tracked through the cloudy dark, through the threat of the old house, bearing down.

So let them come, she thought. Let them come and see what happened. She wobbled on her feet for a second, naked, before the turgid mass of the lights, a mucous yellow, the swollen bubbling version of it matched in her head, pushing itself tighter against her brain, colonizing her mind like yet another room. It was blinding. Let them come. See what— She blinked.

A line of vibrant red shot through the circle of lights gathered around her in a sudden wave, like an arc of blood—and they turned the color of charred bone.

Beth crumpled.

It was inevitable. We pushed her too hard, and she caved and pushed us out. Beth wasn't strong enough to bring it all to fruition, there in her living room—the magnitude of what we sought was too great for her, pitting her against a houseful of invaders; she was a fighter, but not a leader—and at that point, we couldn't carry her any further on our own, no matter how big her house.

So we left, again.

He got headaches. He'd gotten them as far back as he could remember. His first memory was from beneath a glass table, under which he must have crawled, peering up at his mother through the glass. She was looking down at him through the table's surface, and her face was divided neatly in half by the edge of the glass table, the beveled edge creating a strip of voided space down the middle of it, so half of her face was on the left side of the divide, and a darkened orb eclipsed the right (the underside of a bowl). This was the moment when the first headache hit, or so he recalled, and though Adam couldn't remember precisely the pain he'd felt then—only the image burned into his brain—he understood it was the same pain he felt now, the pain he'd felt all of his life, which had followed him through his years like a shadow. The pressure above his ears that slowly spread across his forehead like two search-ing hands, then tugged in opposite directions beneath his skin, as if trying to pry his skull open. Over the years, the level of pain varied: some headaches were mild enough he could suffer through them, blurry-eyed and sweaty, until the pain subsided; others knocked him out cold, and he awoke hours, sometimes a day later, a blank expanse behind him.

Adam's life was the spaces between these headaches, arbitrary stretches of time punctuated by unconsciousness. His eyes would clear and he'd be somewhere else, in another bed or room; his eyes would clear and the day would have gone, he'd have to start over again. The world moved at a different rhythm than his; he felt unable to match its speed, to exist within its prescribed cycles of day, school, night, weekend. He couldn't keep friends, because he couldn't keep pace with them. His every interaction was subject to its own independent clock, whose increments he did not know, only that they ran relentlessly down. He spoke too quickly, in great rushes of breath—in lurches— or not all.

And each time it happened, each time one of those headaches struck, the image would cut over his eyes—half of a face, like an arc, and the black orb—like a test pattern, like the spots of color following a bright flash, and down he would go. His affliction moved in phases, or seemed to, though its bounds were unknown to him: he could go a week or two feeling totally normal, or it could happen twice in a day, three weeks in a row. It was like he'd lived all his life under that glass table, Adam thought sometimes, watching the shapes of others move past, feeling the vibrations when they spoke or bumped up against the glass, gesturing for his response. For years, every time he had a headache his mother would take him to the same pediatrician, where they had the same conversation, and the doctor prescribed a new, slightly different pain reliever, and as Adam grew larger and larger in the kiddie-sized waiting room chairs, among the butterfly wallpaper, the great sigh that seemed to accompany every visit, he came to resent the ritual. He took the pills erratically, between headaches, to try to preempt them—because by the time the headache arrived it was too late for correction, the pills were not fast-acting enough—and their effects worsened the space between them, made it fuzzier: the only moments of clarity seemed to be when he woke up, after a headache, and stared down the next one.

Over time, the image that appeared every time he went under acquired a sort of mythic significance, like it meant something beyond his personal memory. He started seeing it elsewhere, those same visual elements, projected onto different surfaces by light or shadow, or in the setup of a room, or he'd register something in his surroundings that resembled their arrangement (in reality, it was two basic shapes, a half-moon and a circle)—and he would instinctively brace himself for an attack, could almost trigger it, essentially, through anticipation alone, by the map he laid on the world. There was nothing medically wrong with him, he was repeatedly told: just these shapes inside him, waiting to take hold. He lived beneath them, in thrall, his eyes downcast, until the day we found him.

He came from a town no one had heard of before we hit it: Lenape, the only incorporated city in the county. After he left, when people asked where he was from, he gave the name of a town twenty miles east, because Lenape was too charged and because anyone downstate didn't know the difference anyway.

There were more kids in the cafeteria that morning than there might have been. The vending machines had been installed over winter break, and so the area had become more of a hangout before school. Adam, sixteen at this point, didn't drink soda or eat processed sugar (both had been classified, at some point, as intensifying the headaches), nor did he carry money of his own, but the social draw was strong enough that he was there, too, hanging out, or at least standing, with the appearance of hanging out, biding his time until the first bell rang.

Matthew entered the cafeteria from the south entrance, from behind where Adam stood. Later reports indicated that Matthew had entered from the north door, the emergency exit leading to the parking lot, because people remembered him facing them—and there was an authoritative insistence that he could not have walked all the way across the school, through the halls and past the central offices without being detected, armed as he was—but Adam knew this wasn't the case because he remembered

Matthew walking past him, on his right side, and then walking almost halfway across the cafeteria, toward the less crowded half, before stopping. Adam didn't register it immediately—he didn't look at people's hands first, not yet—and only when Matthew was several feet past him did he see the black holster strapped to Matthew's olive pant leg, the handgun displayed there casually, where his hand hung.

It was a bright morning in February, around 7:45 a.m. The six circular tables nearest to the vending machines, generally eight-seaters, were nearly full. The air, antiseptic from last night's cleaning when the kitchen staff entered at 5:30, now hung thick with egg grease and potato, the product of the kitchen at the north side of the cafeteria. The cinder-block walls were painted the off-white of a gymnasium, and the fluorescent light above lent the same tone, of a space hastily converted. On this side, the side with the crowded tables and vending machines, were thirty or forty kids: a chunk of the football team, which Adam recognized from the scattered pieces of their uniforms; the kids waiting for the bus to the career center; and others, people like Adam, there because they were early and didn't know where else to go. Adam had no regular table and thus no seat unless he crossed the cafeteria, toward the kitchen, to where there were still empty tables, and because he had nowhere to sit, he felt his surroundings acutely, his lack of intent standing by the vending machines. He was contemplating pretending to buy food, or at least walking up and down the line to look at the options—when Matthew entered and Adam saw him walk to the center of the room, and stop.

Adam didn't know Matthew particularly, or even his name at that point; he would have idly associated him with the jocks, another white kid with a crew cut, which to him signified athlete or military, and carried for Adam, then a kid with allegiance to neither, the same connotation. (He didn't hate cops yet, either.) The face and name would be applied to his memory after the fact, when Matthew's blandly severe face filled every screen, but in the current moment, as he crossed the room, stopped at the center, they were a blank. Matthew's movements, the path he traced across the room, the lines drawn in the air, the choreography of it all became especially important to Adam in the years that followed.

He watched Matthew walk slowly past him, in the channel between the lockers and the cafeteria tables. Time had split into two realities in that moment: there had been the time before he'd noticed the holster—not just the holster, but then the gun, two distinct *noticings*—and the time after. His perception shifted, too, as if Adam was no longer himself, but a person watching himself. His eyes went from Matthew to one of the circular tables that he passed, a random table, and he lost him for a second. The left half of the table was filled with students, the other empty—an arc cradling a circle. Adam automatically blurred the shapes, and the sound around him slowly melded together: one of his headaches. If he held the image for a few seconds, it would come—the earsplitting pain, the passing out. He blinked away from the table, tried to find Matthew again, and did so just as Matthew arrived at the center of the room, and paused, his back to Adam, to the crowded part of the cafeteria.

No one else seemed to have noticed. The rest of the cafeteria, the seated students busied among themselves, the kids at their lockers, waiting in line or at the counter in the service area, at the vending machines, immersed in their own worlds, none of them reacted. Or, like Adam, they had noticed, but hadn't yet reacted, they were caught in this prison same as him, the space expanding between those two timelines, a reaction that somehow grew both more immediate and further away with every second. Matthew was just a kid standing by himself, like Adam was a kid standing by himself, that was part of the reason he had *noticed*, the crime was the *noticing*, not that anyone knew this, then or later.

The headache waited there, at the fringes of his vision, ready to take him. The pain, the blankness, the awakening or not in the aftermath, the damage done. Matthew stood at the center of the room. An energy laced Adam's perception, the possibilities of the room all endless, simultaneous, overwhelming. He could signal for help, somehow, for intervention, drop to the ground, try to find someone, an adult, a wall. He could attempt to cross the space between them. He could try to stop it. *It*—whatever it was.

Seconds evaporated between them. The headache: it wasn't like he had found it, but like it had been situated there, waiting for him to stumble into it, hanging in the air like a noose awaiting a neck. And maybe that had always been the inevitable outcome, long before this situation had come to be. Who would know, or even think to question it? In the end, it would be Adam's story to tell, it could be like this parcel of seconds—the *look*, the *noticing*, the slow walk across the cafeteria—it could be like this span of time had already been lost to him, processed into other shapes. A fortuitous accident. An act of God. There was the certainty of the headache, the erasure of his current moment, and then there was the uncertainty of the seconds before him uninterrupted, awake and present in the cafeteria, the spiral of the black future: it was as if he held them in either hand. He felt he and Matthew—the person later identified as Matthew—were two points of stillness in a flurry of movement, an axis around which the rest of the world moved. Each an arrow pulled back and held for release. A course of bodily possibility: run, duck, fall, scream, turn, look. Adam found the table again; his head went swampy. The person who was Matthew fumbled with what was later determined to be the iPod in his pants pocket, the earbuds running up under his shirt, disguised in a way the gun wasn't. He reached toward his holster.

The thought arrived to Adam, to his body: *He could choose.*

We did not enter the school with Matthew that day.

We had no hand in his plan, in the maps he'd drawn, the Glock G17 he'd stolen from the cabinet in his uncle's bedroom, in the nine-millimeter ammunition from the garage, in the holster he'd bought at Walmart for $8.99 (cheap nylon), in the playlist he'd made, which drew heavily from the *Donnie Darko* soundtrack—he'd watched the movie six times in the last week—nor in the numbers he'd scrawled on his arm in permanent marker, inspired but not explicitly connected to the above, 7:44:20, the time he anticipated to begin his mix and draw his weapon, six minutes before the bus to the career center arrived, when the cafeteria would be at its morning peak. He was a piece moving on his own. That wasn't us.

But we were the culmination of his trajectory. In the moment he drew the handgun from its holster and swung its sightline in a wild arc across the crowd, we found purchase: we stormed the cafeteria like a wave. We were the recoil in the second before the first shot rang out, the collective intake of breath before the air burst, the silent beat before the scream; we were in every single kid in that bone-white cafeteria, whose heads snapped to attention in the classrooms and bathrooms, the body-wide jolt, who froze in the hallway, who scrambled under desks, who cowered in place, who ran for the exits, who watched it happen then or watched it later, who had a part of themselves activated in that moment or in the seconds or hours or days or years after, and in those who carried it with them already, buried inside or out on their sleeves. We were the current of violence in the air, the recognition of its potential, seeking an aspect to exploit, a moment to turn, to burst; we were in the security footage from other schools that Matthew had studied for weeks beforehand, and the recordings that, in the aftermath of this one, made their way online; we were the lack of diegetic sound, what turned the cafeteria into colors and shapes, into movement he drove like a magnet, an image shifted purposely out of focus, rendered unreal to avoid your place in it; we were in the choice Adam made, in his understanding of that choice. We were the pulse surging out from that moment, from that point at its center, the wire braced through everything—the whole epidemic. A force like the wind, like the arming of a moment. We were there.

We came to Adam, in the shock of awareness that split his existence into two brutal options: he could let the headache take him, or he could push it away; he could try to intervene. *You could choose.*

Adam saw himself blacking out, and then he saw himself waking up. The cause, and the effect. The offer, and the promise. He would wake up again, when it was over. And so he let it take him, he let the familiar pain in his head mount and carry him away. As always, it was horrible, like the top half of his skull was being screwed off like the lid of a stubborn jar, grinding into itself.

Like I've been shot, Adam thought, and he blinked out and fell backward just shy of the first gunshot, which was swallowed somewhere behind him, and the cafeteria exploded into chaos and the town was catalyzed and we moved on and the world changed a little, again.

—

When he awoke next, he was in the hospital like the other victims. Eventually, Adam pieced the story together and formulated his place in it: three students had been killed on the scene, and five others wounded—of those five, three were in the Lenape hospital with him, and two others had been flown by helicopter to Cleveland. The shooter, Matthew Vann (whose name was released a day later), after firing wildly into the cafeteria until his gun was empty, had tried to flee through the exit to the parking lot, but was tackled at the door by a teacher, who had charged toward the scene when he heard the first shot from his classroom off an adjacent hallway. Matthew had plenty of ammo, three full boxes' worth, but they were stowed in his backpack, would have cost valuable seconds to access; it wasn't clear, when he fled, if it was to reload or for some other reason. The duration of the attack—from the first gunshot to when Matthew was tackled and disarmed—was less than forty seconds, short of the first chorus in the first song of his mix, "The Killing Moon."

One of the students who had been airlifted to Cleveland died sixteen hours after the shooting, bringing the death toll to four; the second student was left paralyzed from the neck down. In the first reports that circulated after the shooting, Adam was included in the list of gun-shot victims, nine, but later, after he left the hospital and was driven home that afternoon, and information about his condition was fed back into the machine, he was removed from the statistic, and the number was reduced. His name remained in early articles, when the details were uncertain; in the more extensive summaries that followed, he was deleted. He flickered in awareness for those twenty-four hours and then disappeared; in the names read off at assemblies, vigils, memorials, his was missing. He cemented his absence, or his non-presence, and he didn't return to school. There were no adult victims: that was a line he'd read in one of the articles. *There were no adult victims.*

A week later, surveillance footage from the Lenape High School cafeteria appeared online, and was shortly edited into a sixty-second clip, which was what circulated most widely. One version was given old-school time stamps, color-shifted, digitally granulated, and doctored to decrease the frame rate, so it better resembled the footage from Columbine; another was edited together using multiple angles from different security cameras, looped and annotated to emphasize certain movements, like a music video. Another was set to "The Killing Moon." It was the static, silent, relatively untouched version that Adam watched for the first time, on the laptop in the bedroom he had barely left since the shooting. In wide angle, from the camera mounted in the southwest corner of the cafeteria, he watched Matthew enter the cafeteria from the camera's blind spot and pass the vending machines, the rest of the cafeteria a dim ripple of movement, like disturbed water. It took Adam a second to pick out where the recorded version of himself stood on the screen. The quality of the video didn't let Adam see the holster. He couldn't tell from the video the exact moment when he saw the gun, or when recorded Adam saw it, but he estimated it at about ten seconds in, a quarter of Matthew's way across the room. Recorded Adam remained still as Matthew crossed to the halfway point, until just before the pillar at the center of the cafeteria, where he stopped. Adam paused the video. It had seemed arbitrary, but this must have been a strategic decision, since the pillar partially blocked Matthew from the kitchen and checkout line—it would take longer for the adults on that side of the cafeteria to figure out what was happening.

Adam studied the screen like a painting. The layout of crowded tables on the near side, the pillar marking the center of the cafeteria like the hub of a wheel, the tables beyond it almost empty, the kids clustered on the one side, as if to stay as far from the adults as possible. A pattern they hadn't realized they'd drawn. For the first time, Adam noticed there was someone standing a few feet behind him in the video, behind recorded Adam, a red-haired girl a head shorter than he, wearing a maroon hoodie. He went back to the start of the video and watched again. She collected a soda from the vending machine as Matthew passed, and then she lingered there. He paused the video at the same spot, Matthew at the center of the room, then played it, then in a few seconds stopped it again because he thought he'd left it on pause. How long had Matthew just stood motionless, looking the other way? He pressed play again. Matthew remained standing, his back to the busy half of the cafeteria, the gun at his side where Adam couldn't see it, waiting to be drawn. (He paused it again.) Adam, both versions, stared at Matthew. Had he planned something different? How long had Adam had to intervene, really? Was it those eight seconds, or was it longer? *Why was he so fucking still?* A chill worked its way up his shoulders; Adam wondered if he could see it in the video, the moment he'd recognized his choice. The moment we arrived. He tapped the space bar repeatedly on the keyboard so the video progressed frame by frame, as if in slow motion. Matthew spun, and at the same time raised the pistol, dragging an arc across that half of the cafeteria. As he did so, the kids at the table nearest to him—which had prompted Adam's headache and subsequent blackout—pulsed back from their seats at the table, separating from it, and their movement cascaded through the crowd, to the other tables. There was no intervention, no flash of insight, no cosmic hand swatting him out of harm's way: just the blurry gray blocks of reality. But that girl by the vending machine, reacting only enough to turn—where did he know her from?

In the footage, he found the shapes again, in the

curved line of students that had leapt up, their suddenly bare table. His eyes shifted the already grainy footage. He watched himself fall backward, as if in a trance, the nearly invisible, titanic issue of Matthew's gun, and then the girl behind him fell, too, in a sprawl, like a violent echo, like they were tugged down on a single thread. His twisted shadow.

Grace Dabrowski: the girl paralyzed from the neck down. That was her. He had fallen, *made himself* fall, and the bullet that might have struck him had buried itself in the person left in his place.

Adam stopped the video. A chasm opened in his chest in the shape of a moon: *You are a survivor*, a voice inside told him. *You did what you had to do.* He stared at the table, the arc of people, the shapes on the screen, until they swallowed him and the pain came again, and he blacked out, there on his bed.

We moved on, but we never left him.

In the weeks and months following the shooting, while the surveillance footage was scrutinized and interpreted, the contradictions and conspiracy theories quickly crawled out from the usual corners of the internet. Why had the police and school administration claimed that Vann had entered from the north door of the cafeteria, when the footage proved definitively he hadn't? Separate footage from the parking lot revealed that Matthew entered the school at 7:28—the gun already in its holster—and he had started his attack at 7:44. Sixteen minutes he'd spent inside with a visible gun. How had no one noticed it or reported it? How had he managed to walk across the entire school with a gun strapped to his thigh? Furthermore, other footage (uncovered separately from the cafeteria footage, and unauthorized) had triangulated Matthew's walk across the school to the cafeteria, a very public walk that took three minutes: but what was happening during the remaining thirteen minutes? Where was the footage from outside the offices, where he must have passed en route to the cafeteria? What other footage had been deleted? Convenient, wasn't it, that the only intervention came from a single teacher, after Vann had left the field of view of any camera—a teacher whose name, too, was not released by authorities, but only confirmed once a crowd-sourced internet operation had discovered it? And then Adam's name returned to the conversation. Who was this victim from the video whose name was scrubbed from the list of the wounded and deceased? Was he a student at Lenape at all, and if not, what cause did he have to be in the cafeteria before school? Were his school records merely fabricated after the fact? In fact, the argument went, if you studied the footage carefully, it was clear that he fell before the first shot was even fired. He had a clear sightline to the alleged perp as he entered. Was Adam Hollis a crisis actor, an agent planted to ensure the action was carried out effectively? Was Matthew Vann merely a pawn in a larger plan that had gone awry, and thus been aborted midway through? Some of the speculation was real, and some of it was noise. Adam started getting emails from burner accounts demanding answers, full of personal details about his life, his schedule, his mother's history, even his father's name—details Adam himself hadn't known. He was encouraged—required—to speak up, to explain his role in this. He was accused of being present at other shootings, in what they called "actions," in 2010, in 2008. They battered him with the names of the victims, the heart-wrenching details of their lives cut short, irreparably damaged. He should confess. He should kill himself. He should be killed. Threatening calls from unlisted numbers and a flood of letters without return addresses came to the house. He knew enough not to respond, but he couldn't keep himself from drowning in it, couldn't stop the sheer volume from coloring his thinking, from noticing the patterns and throughlines to the messages and calls themselves, the common points of entry, which felt like a coordinated effort, a code others kept insisting was buried there. There was the event itself, and then around it this cloud of data, like smoke from fire, like bad air he couldn't help but breathe in. *Was* there a code there, he wondered, to the shapes he'd known all his life? Was there a deeper order to it? Eventually, the online clamor reached a certain pitch and he was brought back to the police station for a second interview. His headaches got precipitously worse.

When he didn't black out, he would be nearly paralyzed by the pain, his muscles would seize up and he'd go rigid, unblinking on the ground like a sacrificial victim strapped to the altar, the pain from his head crawling down through his limbs, and for hours he couldn't move, couldn't think, he lay there staring at the ceiling like he was waiting for something, some vision, for a different face to appear. The blackouts were better.

Adam and his mother left Lenape that summer, after he turned seventeen. He never returned to school. They moved three and a half hours southwest, to an even smaller Ohio town, to escape the noise, the house calls and unwanted visitors. The headaches eventually affected his eyesight, and he started wearing glasses, which he'd never needed before. The shapes remained, but the triggers grew manifold: certain light, sound. He had trouble looking at screens. There were days following the headaches when he could barely walk, when he had difficulty standing and needed to use a wheelchair. It was like the gunshot he'd missed had returned, one way or another, to find him, had left this airless channel within him where it might have passed through. If he had known, he asked himself over and over, if he had known the cascading waves of *what happened*, of the kids dying and wounded, the girl paralyzed in his place—would he have changed his decision? Would he have been able to? The awareness of the choice, rather than the decision itself, seemed to him at times like the most severe consequence.

As the headaches grew to be a bigger part of him, of his physical presence and waking consciousness, his story changed in tandem; the headaches became the stand-in for everything else, the only part of his past worth remembering. He built a wall between himself and Lenape. He started going by his middle name, Graham. He learned how to deal with them, the headaches, the memories, the footage that ran ceaselessly through his head. In time he found others who carried a similar pain with them—or a similar kind of pain or trauma, a gap like the one we'd left in him, or which we had articulated, that had been growing since he was born—and he tried to define it, put words to it, to find its place within them and in the world outside. He channeled it into his body, his scarred voice, into the basements and blank halls his band played, to the pockets of kids like him. Together, he thought, they might be able to move beyond it.

We left, but we never left him. We cauterized that wound inside him; he spent the rest of his life trying to dig us out.

HOW LONG SINCE YOU'VE BEEN MISSING HOW
LONG SINCE YOU'VE BEEN MISSED HOW LONG
SINCE YOU REMEMBERED HOW LONG SINCE ANY-
ONE COUNTED FOUR NINE SEVEN ONE POUND

It was always going to be Tyler. Not David with his por-
nographic cult fantasies, not Greg with his voices, not
Claire and her masks, or Beth and her train of lights—it
was Tyler we'd needed this whole time. We rushed through
the basement door behind him at the base of the stairs, the
girl's body in his arms, in the second before he pulled it
shut, when he could see no farther ahead of him than closing the door, than breathing in again. He felt us like the
wind, a question breathed at his ear, a bargain offered, and
its return: *They could run.* They did not need to take responsibility for this. Wasn't that what he had always done?
Hadn't he always been running?

He saw the two options presented to him, as clear as
two doorways, where before there had been nothing. They

could stay, take charge of this girl and the consequences that sprawled into forever. Or they could go. He saw their escape, his escape, like an offer extended to him. *Let us in, and we will get you out of this.* And so Tyler turned his head sharply to the side; he assented, he chose the path that took it from his hands; he let us in.

And when he returned to himself and heard Rhea's shouts filling the cramped hallway, rebounding off the concrete walls, Typhus in front of her, a full head shorter, her arms out, as the slashed-up body bled endlessly onto his clothes, Tyler knew what to do. He reached behind him and twisted the dead bolt on the door. He said to Rhea in a sharp whisper, "Get the backpack from the bedroom," and she quieted, nodded once, and disappeared.

He turned so Typhus could take the top half of the body. The girl's head lolled against her chest, her blood-matted hair falling lank over Typhus's arms. She stepped slowly backward down the hallway, past the dryer, the sink. He saw that Typhus still had a blade clenched in her hand, some kind of utility knife or razor, bloody and gleaming darkly—where had she found it? Had she brought it with her? Either way: the weapon was accounted for. Her face, contorted with effort, had blood streaked across the cheek. Rhea would have been a better choice to help carry the body, but Typhus didn't know where the backpack was with her confiscated wallet and phone, with Tyler and Rhea's stuff. The things that could identify them.

One of the girl's hands trailed in the air, drawing a thin, wavering line of blood across the white surface of the washing machine, like the readings of a heart monitor.

Rhea circled the basement the opposite way and met them in the weight room. She clutched Tyler's backpack to her chest, her phone held at her side—as if waiting for his order. He jerked his chin and Typhus stopped, and they lowered the body onto the floor in the center of the room. As Typhus laid down the shoulders, Tyler noticed she was dressed in blood, too, her hands were red. The room smelled like iron and animal sweat, the slow rot of the trash bags they'd been stowing there, like terror. "Who is it?" he asked, as they put her down.

"It's my sister," Typhus said. Rhea moaned and put a stifling hand over her mouth. She turned away in disbelief, and in that second—when Tyler's eyes moved from Typhus's face to the body below them, to draw the connection—he noticed the girl was still breathing. It had been undetectable while they were in motion, in the desperate flurry of action, but she was breathing shallowly, expelling pulses of blood through the wounds crosshatched across her chest, face, and neck, like the breath of someone trying to go undetected, to stay hidden. Tyler scanned her face and couldn't tell if her eyes were open. Her chin trembled, the slightness of her movements disguised by the cuts to her body, by the amount of blood, dark marks on slick red. His eyes went to the razor still clutched in Typhus's right hand. Across from him, Typhus's face was absent of emotion, except her eyes, looking quaveringly to Tyler, waiting for him to register this new and bloody sight for her, to tell her how to react. Like she had no idea what she'd done.

He remembered her standing in the doorway of their bedroom the night before, after they'd gone to bed, checking in on them. She needed to put herself in someone, he thought, and she had chosen him. Or he had lighted upon her, by accident, at exactly the right time. It was clear to him now, the deathwish she had brought with her to the basement—she didn't want to exist as herself, but to enthrall herself to something that would take her completely. He knew the feeling well.

A shiver skittered across his chest, like a crack in ice. Rhea stood shaking in the corner, kneading the zippered bag in her hands. A part of him was crying out to her, screaming at her—*Call 911, call someone*—but that space in him, where we were, that space of cold calculation, it was telling him to forget the body at his feet, that it was no longer a part of the bigger picture; it was telling him this house was tainted now and what they needed, even more desperately, was to leave. He saw himself in a car, along an unknowable road, a sudden gray clip of unbridled sky like he hadn't seen in weeks—there was an endpoint somewhere, but it wasn't here. And he reached for it.

Without speaking, he drew their path out of the room: he found Typhus's eyes, and then Rhea's, and then, behind them, the open door to the living room—he looked from them to their exit and nodded once, decisively. It was three minute lines he traced in the air, left, up, and across, and then sharply down: *Leave her.* He would take the rest of himself from that room, but there was a piece of him— that arc he cut out with his eyes, a chink in his vision— that stayed behind forever.

He pushed himself to his feet, and across from him, Typhus did the same. Their joint motion spurred Rhea as well, she unfroze, and the three of them passed mutely through the door into the living room, leaving the body behind. Each step, each second folded into the one before it, propelling them from one reality into the next.

In the basement living room, beside the old couch where, until five minutes before, the three of them had existed indefinitely in some wildly different form, they stopped, as if a piece of each of them hoped they could just sit down again and resume where they'd left off, that the stasis would eventually return and they would be swallowed back into it. An acid panic roiled in Tyler's stomach, rising into his throat, and he swallowed it down; it seemed to brace the room before him into bitter reality. He put his hands on Rhea's shoulders, he looked into her eyes, and it occurred to him that this was the most intimate interaction they'd ever had together, a moment based on something deep and corporal—his bloody hands on her shoulders, the way she bit her lip, a little stab of pain to keep the emotion from erupting across her face, the fearful eyes refusing to cry, the spray of freckles beneath them, the backpack clenched in her hands—and he felt the weight of the moment even as he projected himself far beyond it, toward a future he didn't know. But a future. He felt its weight as he felt himself sinking into that sliver of space in the corner of his vision, what he had left barely alive in the other room. Beside Rhea, Typhus stood mutely, her breathing even, expectant. He felt like he was leaving them stranded even now, even as he took them with him; he had drawn them into the furious wake of a choice they didn't know he'd made, whose consequences would be forever unfurling. They had trusted him instinctively, and he had taken their lives and, by a series of small turns, he had unspooled them. They didn't know—they didn't know it could have gone any other way. He shoved it down—the panic, the fear and guilt—he shoved it down until it choked him.

"We need to leave," he told her, told them both.

Rhea nodded, slowly, and swallowed. "I know where we can go," she whispered.

Typhus turned to look at her—Tyler wondered if it was the first time she'd done so.

With a shaking hand, Rhea turned her phone toward him: it was a screenshot of a text, several paragraphs long, titled THE DEATH PARTY. "On April 11, two young lives were brutally ended . . ." At the end of it, a date and an address. He looked from the screen to Rhea. "It's a wake?"

"There's no one there," she said. "The house has been empty since they died."

Something leapt in his chest, a simultaneous relief and horror: they had somewhere to go. But also: how much further would it be, until they reached safety? He gathered his resolve again, or he buried everything that wasn't his resolve. He told them what to collect, their remaining identifiers; they were leaving. It felt almost natural to him. *They were leaving.*

———

David awoke late that night faceup in his bed, naked from the waist down. Sarah lay beside him, rolled away. She was barefoot, but otherwise fully clothed. David remembered Sarah stealing out of the bedroom with her clothes and the long while she'd spent in the bathroom, but he didn't remember going to bed, or inviting Sarah to stay—he wondered if he'd fallen asleep accidentally, if he had let the remarkable night slip away from him in the midst of something embarrassing. Either way, a shift had occurred. He had fucked Sarah; the two of them were something different now. He reached down and felt his penis—it was dry but still slightly sticky, it provided evidence. He sat up and, as quietly as possible, he rose from his side of the bed. His room felt different, like something he had abruptly outgrown. His twin-size bed, where Sarah lay at the very edge: too small for two fully grown people. He walked out of the room, through the hallway and down the stairs, past the closed basement door in the foyer (which he didn't even read as a real door anymore), and into the living room. Moonlight came through the bay windows, which gave the room a new richness, and his nakedness, of course, made it his. A silver car was parked on the street in front of his house, but he didn't take this in, he absorbed it as part of the nature of the street at night, where people stood naked inside their homes.

Two walls away, Tyler, Rhea, and Typhus stood crouched at the top of the stairs. They had changed out of their bloody clothes, swapping their shirts for three of the white T-shirts Typhus had brought, and stuffed the incriminating shirts into the backpack, which Rhea now shouldered. Tyler hadn't wanted to turn on the water, to leave more blood in the bathroom, so their hands and faces were still spattered with it. They'd taken nothing else. They paused in anticipation at the door, barely breathing. Ahead of them, the rest of the house, like another universe, lay quiet and dark. Behind them, the darkened basement, the girl bleeding out in the weight room, between two closed doors. Tyler couldn't bear to bring them out through the back, up those bloody concrete steps. He silently unlocked the door and placed his hand on the doorknob, turning it slowly, so the latch slid back. He took a long breath in, and let it out minutely, afraid that it would stagger, it would crack him open. He pushed the door open into the foyer and planted his bloody hand on the wall beside the light switch, leaving a gummy red palm print behind, a warning of what lay below.

As David stood there in the living room, tracing its new shapes in the dark, the basement door opened at his back and three figures emerged into the foyer. David turned when he heard the latch click on the front door. For a second he didn't register what he was seeing—he thought he was somehow witnessing an optical illusion, because how could there be three people *leaving* his house, rather than entering it?—and then a sound escaped him, which betrayed his presence.

At his exclamation, Sarah awoke upstairs, suddenly panicked, unaware of the day and time. The bed, the room around her, it all felt rigged, like a context into which she had been tricked—she felt like she was awakening from a trance, from the effects of a drug she'd been slipped. She remembered flashes of the hours before like something she'd watched on-screen: loud friction, flesh under her fingernails, hot breath on her shoulder. The door was ajar, and she knew David was out there somewhere, he would be back for her, inevitably, and when he arrived, she would be forced to put words to the night before or else her memories would be overwritten by David's, he would force his own narrative over them—why they did what they did, what had led them to this moment—and she would be tempted to take it for what he told her it was. She was standing before the strands had reconciled in her head, her intentions split as she left the bedroom, she didn't know how she felt yet, didn't know what she would do when she found

David. She thought it could depend on where he touched her, if he tried to, or which of them spoke first.

She came around the railing and saw the front door hanging open at the bottom of the stairs, like a moment she'd just missed, like she'd just stumbled into its charged aftermath. An urgent spike drove through her, and Sarah ran down the stairs because it felt like the situation was changing suddenly, like the open door created a runway—an *escape*—and she finally recognized it as such. There was movement to her right as she stepped into the foyer, and it was David, he was running across the living room toward the door, toward her, and the picture of it—of his nakedness, the startled expression on his face—registered in her mind as empty, inhuman, like startling a wild animal indoors, and instead of turning to him she ran across the threshold, through the open front door. When her bare feet touched the lawn outside, something switched inside her again, and she realized she was fleeing—she was running away, running from David—and she fell into this movement as she had fallen into the ones prior to it, completely, and she found herself racing for the closest sign of recognizable life, for the silver Lexus parked on the street as its doors slammed, waving her arms, screaming maybe, crossing the lawn and banging on the car doors, and the narrative of the last eight hours was already re-forming, details she heretofore hadn't remembered or which had laid dormant exploded into prominence in her mind, and the people in the car were opening the door and taking her in and spiriting her away, these three white-shirted figures of her age, bearing her into this future.

———

Instinctively, as soon as the door shut Tyler stamped on the gas and slicked away from the curb—the tires barely squealed, the car's powerful internal mechanisms designed for maneuvers like this. He frantically adjusted the rearview mirror, trying to spot David behind them, to see if he had given chase, but his house was dark, shadowed by the streetlight like a dead thing in the night, and the three in the back seat were twisted backward, too, blocking his view. The car shot blindly down the street, past a stop sign, and it was the tiniest, slightest little thing—there were no other cars on the road, there probably wouldn't be for hours—but it panicked him like nothing else had before. He had no idea what he was doing, where he was going, what they would do when they got there. They had made for the car automatically because that was the most apparent way out (it was Typhus's sister's, for which Typhus had furnished him the bloody keys), and now there were three people in his back seat, Typhus, Rhea, and this unknown girl, this fugitive from David's house. Where the basement had offered a series of neat constraints and closed circuits, a pattern he could reasonably predict and control, the world he found himself in now, for the first time in weeks, it was anything but—it was wild and out of control and infinite in its consequence. He felt his palms sweating into the steering wheel. He wanted desperately to be inside, to be safe again, unexposed, alone. The car just kept going straight, the suburban houses whipping past in a dark indistinguishable blur. Behind him, David's house long out of view, the girls in the back seat turned back around to address their driver. A stoplight, the first one they'd seen, screamed up at them from the distance, a shocking point of red light over a four-way stop, and Tyler slammed the brakes, throwing all of them forward, stopping the car a good fifty feet short of the intersection. The light dangled ahead of them, wobbling in the wind. It switched guilelessly to green, and still he sat there, his breath coming hard. What should he do? Where should he go? Where should he *go*?

A whisper inside him, so faint it might have been mistaken for instinct, offered a suggestion: *Left*.

The breath of relief that escaped him was almost a cry. He gently pressed the gas pedal, and turned left.

From the back seat, the new girl broke the silence that until now had filled the car, the silence that had seemed in deference to his own, in a small voice. "Where are we going?"

Tyler didn't answer. He continued down the new street until the question receded like the stoplight, until we nudged him right, and he turned right down another quiet, tree-lined avenue. Gradually, as he drove them down these streets that if he'd been paying attention he would have known well, Tyler felt his mind throwing up its numbing barriers, pouring his nervous endings into a vision of himself in the future, far from here, its details vague but its presence clear: he felt himself separating from his passengers, blurring them out, until it was just Tyler, alone, a body driving while his mind was elsewhere, until he was safely removed. Was that not how he'd made it this far?

That distance—the distance he held from his own life—had been within him for so long he'd forgotten it was there, that it was any different than the way everyone else was, but in the back room of the basement, he had realized—we had shown him—its pointed use: how this could protect him, absolve him even, how it could flatten this moment into nothing. He had slipped into it as easy as the clean white T-shirt he wore now. And we were there now, rooted in him, in that space, the arc-shape he had drawn in the air in the unfinished room of the basement, from the three of them to the door, away from the body they'd left for dead, away from what they'd done: the acknowledgment they were choosing to leave it behind. And if he followed for long enough, far enough, he could forget his agency in it, that it had ever happened. It would cease to be a part of him at all. Or so we told him.

He slipped farther away. They passed street signs, landmarks he might have recognized but chose not to. The houses flickered past, the trees shuddering in the night breeze, and we absorbed their data—the lights in their windows, the shapes of their living rooms, the depth of their basements—but Tyler noticed none of it. Slowly, the streets grew more affluent, and they hit areas Tyler himself had never been, but we guided him on, down roads we had learned well.

Behind him, the new girl, *Sarah* (he heard her and Rhea exchange names), broke the silence again, and then Rhea, in the middle seat beside Typhus—who sat squeezed against the door, looking out the window almost sleepily— with a glance toward Tyler in the mirror, said quietly: "What happened in there?"

Sarah's voice was unsteady. "He had me upstairs," she said. A sudden swoop in her stomach when she noticed her phrasing—it wasn't exactly true, but it nonetheless felt right, like she'd uncovered something she didn't realize was there, a sudden jolt of acid in her. "I—I just ran." That had been her instinct, she realized: to run. "I just ran."

Rhea touched her shoulder and felt Sarah flinch. "It's okay," she said. "We've got you now."

It was as if the basement didn't exist, as if they had just come driving by David's house at the exact right time to rescue this girl from the side of the road, on their way to somewhere else. As if the basement and everything that happened there had been paved over.

And as Sarah relayed what had happened in David's house that afternoon, that night, she was surprised by the narrative that emerged, by the way the pieces fit together in a way they hadn't before, as if her whole new experience with David over the last three weeks, the complete shape of it, finally resolved in front of her eyes. She had run from the house, across the lawn in her bare feet for the car idling there, and that stretch—from the bedroom to the top of the stairs to the foyer to their car—had activated something within her, had tripped her into a set of emotions she didn't realize she'd been feeling, but only reconciled when she was acting on them: desperation, fear—even rage. Why was it only clear to her in that moment, when she'd decided to run? Why hadn't those instincts kicked in earlier, before she went to his fucking house, before they even started dating? Because it was clear to her now that David had tricked her, lied to her, from his "society" onward, he had tricked her into his house, had brought her up to his bedroom—unfamiliar turf, awful light—and used her displacement, her open wounds, her *willingness*, her empathy for him as a means to fuck her. That his actions were alternately clumsy and devious only made it worse. The more she spoke, the angrier she got. It had been this way for as long as she could remember. The story with David, the story with Greg, Claire, the random girl on the bus, with everyone maybe—problems she somehow felt were her obligation to solve. And unfailingly, each time, once she had scaled that particular mountain, like she always did, trudging ceaselessly upward, wearing herself down to nothing, taking on their everything, leaving her insensate from their burned nerves, coated in their filthy emotional deposits, all that remained was a long, lonely fall, an inevitable horrifying, sprawling crash into the next person. She did not want to feel his fucking fingernails on her again, to smell his rank laundry pile, his come-stained bedspread: it had *become* her, like everything did, but no longer. It would never touch her again. She was sick of it, sick of all of it. She didn't want to hear David's story anymore, not anyone's—she did not want to be part of it.

Now she was in the darkened car with these three, dressed in identical white T-shirts, their only real visual signifier in the darkness of the car, like some kind of cult, with no idea where they were going, the girl next to her nodding quietly as she talked, the silent driver she thought she might recognize from school carrying them onward, the other girl smushed into the window like she was dead, and somehow Sarah felt more akin to these shadowy strangers, safer in this back seat in its recirculated, weirdly blood-smelling air than she had with anyone in the last month—they shared this pocket of the same desperation, fear, rage. A frantic careening into the future.

She was shaking. Outside their car, the streets had gradually become familiar to her again, blacker than she remembered, it seemed like the streetlamps in this neighborhood did a poorer job than they did elsewhere, so there were just these faint yellow patches of illumination they passed, little mist-like clouds that caught the leaves by their edges and made them vibrate. Like the world beyond them, too, was trembling. "That's fucked up," Rhea said, when she was done. "It's good you got out of there."

The road they were on undulated into Meridian Circle—Sarah started. This was Beth's street. Their car rounded the street's long curve as if on tracks, as if drawn along, hardly slowing—no one drove it that way unless they'd done it dozens of times. She had always hated this neighborhood at night, when the houses became gothic and imposing, the roads harder to navigate. Someone had told her it had been designed that way, like the infrequent streetlights, to minimize through-traffic, to bolster its sense of seclusion—its residents paid for it. In the dark, she made out white ribbons tied around the trees to either side of the road, like they were marked for chopping. She heard, improbably, the rustling of their leaves. They rounded the last bend before Beth's, and their headlights illuminated a dark outline on the wooded side of the road opposite the driveway, Beth's dad's SUV, sitting half-off the road, half in the ivy-covered embankment, its headlights shining mutely ahead, diffuse in the murky air, the driver's-side door open, as if the driver had fled from something, some monster in the woods. What the fuck? Panic spiked through her and she reached for her phone, then realized she didn't have it, it was stranded in David's bedroom.

A knot caught in her throat; it tasted like blood. They turned into the driveway and slowly wrapped their way up toward the house. It loomed over them as they pulled up toward the garage. She turned in her seat to look behind them—what were they doing here? Did they know Beth—had they known Greg?

The driver turned off the car and removed the keys from the ignition. He opened his door and the dome light came on. Was that—there was blood on his face, blood smeared like warpaint. He was nearly white-blond. "Wait here," he said, the first thing she'd heard him say. He stepped out of the car and closed the door. He walked up the driveway to the garage door, and pressed a series of buttons on the panel beside it. *How did he know the code?*

The garage door shuddered open, and automatic fluorescent light burst out at them. Like a spaceship, she thought dumbly. She turned to Rhea—marks of blood now visible on her face, too, on the other girl's face. She opened her mouth and closed it.

The boy returned to the car. "What are we doing here?" Sarah finally asked aloud, her voice suddenly pitching higher, as the door closed again. She looked to each of them for an answer. "What—why did you want to come here?" She grabbed the door handle, stopping her hand from trembling. "What are you doing? Why were you at David's? This is Beth's house. Beth and Greg Walker—they live here."

"Not anymore," Rhea said.

Her stomach dropped out. Tyler started the car again.

"What? What the fuck does that mean? Where's Beth? What did you do to her?"

"We'll be safe here," Tyler said, as if that meant something to her, and the car eased forward again, toward the light, drawn inexorably into the garage as if pulled by a magnet, and Sarah opened the passenger door enough to see a strip of asphalt scrolling beneath them—but the dome light betrayed her. Rhea's arm shot across her chest and pulled it closed, the car's pace unbroken. And though Sarah knew this house, knew it well, in many ways as intimately as she knew her own, there was something wrong with it now, wrong with the air, wrong with the light, wrong with the muted driver, and there was something overflowing from her besides, as they passed from the dark into the false light, as the house gradually enveloped them, her fear, her anger, the rage of being a passenger one too many times, of this constant exchange of houses, of bedrooms, of her weak lungs, of the world pressing, pressing, pressing her into nothing.

She screamed, and threw her weight against the door, which flung open, breaking Rhea's grip. Sarah fell stumbling from the car, caught herself on the driveway—her palms scraped the asphalt, she pushed herself up—and ran again. Toward the garage, toward the house—toward Beth.

And outside, around their little car, the big house, the air beat down its heavy messages, as old as the breeze.

A SICK FUCK WIND BLOWS IN FROM THE NORTH
FROM THE EAST THE SOUTH THE WEST THE OAK
SCREEN GLASS STEEL GARAGE DOOR IS THROWN
OPEN LIFTED TO THE PORCH THE LAWN THE
GARDEN THE ASPHALT THE WINDOWS TREM-
BLE SO HARD IN THEIR PANES THE PAINT FLAKES
OFF THE GLASS BREAKS THE WALLS SHAKE
THE AIR SINGS A BODY HURTLES STRUGGLES IS
DRAGGED DOWN THE STEPS IN BARE FEET IN
SNEAKERS IN HEELS IN COMBAT BOOTS ACROSS
THE LAWN OVER THE FENCE DOWN THE DRIVE-
WAY THROUGH THE GATE INTO THE STREET
STEPPING CLIMBING CARRIED SHOVED INTO
THE WAITING IDLING PASSING PARKED ESCA-
LADE DIRTY VAN TAURUS PICKUP THAT PULLS
FROM THE CURB THE SHOULDER OUT OF THE
DRIVEWAY THE PARKING LOT AS THE DOOR
SLAMS BEFORE TURNING LEFT TURNING RIGHT
PULLING OUT TEARING DOWN THE STREET THE
ROAD HEADED SOUTH OR WEST OR NORTH AND

DRIVES FOR TWO MILES FORTY MINUTES SIX
HOURS ACROSS THE STREET ACROSS TOWN INTO
THE CITY TWO COUNTIES OVER ACROSS STATE
LINES THROUGH WAVING FIELDS TREE-LINED
STREETS FARMLAND FLATLAND TERRACED
SPRAWL TAPERING AT ITS EDGES IN DISBELIEF IN
FAMILIARITY IN AWE IN INDIFFERENCE AT THE
POTENTIAL THE AWARENESS THEY SPILL STAG-
GER BOLT FROM THE DRIVER'S SEAT BACK SEAT
TRUNK TO THE PARKING LOT THE SIDE OF THE
ROAD ONTO THE DRIVEWAY THE EXIT RAMP
INTO THE CLEARING THE DITCH THE HOUSE THE
FLUORESCENT CANDLELIT DARK ROOM AND
VOMIT SPIT UP RETCH COUGH BLEED SCREAM
INTO THE PALM OF THEIR HAND INTO THEIR
LAP THE SINK ONTO THE GROUND THE ASPHALT
THE TILE FLOOR THE CARPET THE ALTAR AT THE
SUCCESS FAILURE BREAKING OF A DARE A BET A
KNIFE A BULLET A LIGHT A RITUAL A PROMISE
AT THE FORCE OF THE CHANGE THE GUT COR-
RECTION THE POTENTIAL THE CALLING VOICE
THE YELLING NO BECKONING OFFERING WEL-
COMING THEM TO THE CENTER OF THE WIND
THE UNIVERSE THE EYE THE SPIRAL TO WIPE
THEIR MOUTH WITH A SLEEVE THE BACK OF A
HAND AND CRAWL CLIMB TO THEIR FEET STAND
AND CROSS BURN SURGE ACROSS THE GRAVEL
TILE HIGHWAY DIVIDER HALLWAY ROOM TO

THE STALLED PARKED PASSING UNMARKED BUS
SEDAN LEXUS TAURUS THAT PULLS FROM THE
SHOULDER OFF THE GRASS OUT OF THE DRIVE-
WAY AS THE DOOR SLAMS BEFORE TURNING
RIGHT TURNING LEFT PULLING OUT TEARING
DOWN THE ROAD THE STREET AND DRIVES FOR
SIX HOURS FORTY MINUTES THIRTY SECONDS
TWO MILES ACROSS STATE LINES TWO COUNTIES
OVER OUT OF THE CITY OUT OF TOWN ACROSS
TOWN OCCUPIED LAND SUBDIVISION DISTANT
SKYLINES TREE-LINED STREETS WAVING FIELDS
WHERE THE SIGNS SAY LENAPE DAYTON CHAR-
DON COLUMBUS MIDDLETOWN JESUS HELL IS
REAL TAPERING AT THEIR EDGES IN DISBELIEF
IN FAMILIARITY IN AWE IN INDIFFERENCE AT
THE EDGE OF AWARENESS POTENTIAL THEY
SPILL STAGGER BOLT FROM THE DRIVER'S SEAT
SHOTGUN BACK SEAT TRUNK INTO THE PARK-
ING LOT THE DITCH AND CROSS THE EARTH THE
SCRUB THE DYING GRASS UP THE STEPS AND
PULL YANK FORCE OPEN UNLOCK THE STEEL
GLASS SCREEN MAHOGANY OAK DOOR OF THE
APARTMENT THE TRAILER THE CHURCH THE
ABANDONED BUILDING THE SCHOOL THE MAN-
SION AND CLIMB CROSS NAVIGATE DESCEND TO
A HALLWAY BEDROOM BATHROOM BASEMENT
GARAGE KITCHEN CLASSROOM GALLERY CAFE-
TERIA SANCTUARY CUPPED IN THE PALM OF THE

HAND STILL WATER MUCUS BLOOD SPIT YOU'VE
GONE AWAY STAYED COME BACK WOKEN UP SUR-
VIVED MOVED ON IN THE THICK OF WEATHER
RANK CHANGING COTTON FOR INCONSIDERATE
FLEECE AGAINST WARM SKIN AT THE HEIGHT OF
THE MEAN SEASON

In our wake, after leaving Lenape, an eleven-year-old at the middle school two miles over carries a 3-D map in his head—at little red pulses, the closets where he's been instructed to hide. When he thinks *school*, the image that comes to mind is no longer the building itself or the classrooms or the school bus, but the police officer out front, his black belt sagging with equipment, once present only on assembly days, now always.

Eighty miles south, a sophomore girl stops wearing headphones when she's out in public, when she's outside the house at all. The sound of footsteps behind her is always terrifying; she has to turn around as soon as she hears them, to check.

On the eve of his seventeenth birthday, a boy takes a bottle's worth of Ambien in one fell swoop at the bathroom sink. He's found ninety minutes later, and his stomach is pumped clear. Two months later, he locks himself in his bedroom when the house is empty and does the same.

Another girl fights back one night and leaves an angry

red stripe across her father's cheek. It lasts for days. A bow snaps.

At school, another boy starts sitting in the last row, in the corner along the wall adjacent to the hallway: from the doorway, it takes almost a full ninety-degree sweep to see him.

Another practices shooting with his older brother's gun in the woods beside his house. He's convinced that it will happen again—it always happens again—and he will be ready.

Three years later, yet another goes off to college three hours downstate: at a party, in his room, he tries to rape a girl he doesn't know. He never sees it in those terms, never consciously connects it to Lenape, but the connection is there nonetheless, in its long current.

A girl stops wearing her dangly earrings—she is afraid of someone ripping them out, using them to keep her from running.

He punches his younger sister in exasperation. It echoes down the generations.

She stops eating in the cafeteria.

A brace of cold haunts the air, always.

Another, Graham, one in whom we'd rooted particularly deeply, carried that space inside him until it sharpened into a blade. He sought to define us, to map us out onto the world, to outline our symbols, identify our presence in any given moment. He saw himself as a template. He figured if he found others damaged in the same way, he could pull them back from the edge, he could show them how he survived. He thought he could find us where we were. He started a band, and later his group at HBCC; he became a mouthpiece, and he put shape to it that way, or his shapes in any event.

In time others followed, people like Collin, they found him or he brought them in, and he showed them what he'd learned, offered a means of processing that pain, that damage before we could get to them, before we took root in them the same way we had in him. He worked the corporal circuits he knew, the back channels of support groups, hardcore shows, his tortured, methodical zine, his messages passed from hand to hand and mouth to mouth, like the hook of a song, like his three faithful chords, through the basements and event halls of the Midwest, always just at the edge of view, to keep himself from wider visibility, from letting the shadows of his past rise up and haul him, screaming, back into it.

A day would come, he believed, when he would look out and he would be able to see us, finally, as neatly as the headaches that had followed him all his life. He would bring us out, into the room, and he would see what was inside him. And in that, maybe he could let it go. And we might go, too, like a breath exhaled into a crowded room, a burden passed from one to many: if he could capture us in the moment of transmission, he could disperse us, all of us, into nothing. He could end us.

In the end, across it all, he hacked out something that

looked like us, or a version of us, like the sloppy Bad Religion covers he'd played with his band before he started writing his own lyrics. It wasn't us, as much as anything wasn't exactly *us*—we had our own names—but it was the earth of us: the air, the context we inhabited.

I was born in turbulent soil, he had written for a song, or a fragment of one, swiping characteristically broad. He might have been. But more accurately, he *was* the turbulent soil, and we its tiller.

But that wasn't it, either, exactly. Maybe he was the soil and the tiller both, and we were the season:

The little clutch of sweaty air that David exhaled in his bedroom on the night we found him, when he realized—we helped him realize—that Sarah's hurt could be useful to him. A shudder almost like a laugh.

The sound of Beth's muffled crying through the walls, so consistent and routine as to become ambient to Greg, like the clanking pipes of an old house. He learned to ignore it, as if it didn't involve him.

The sour breath filling her lungs in Sarah's bedroom as Claire withheld an answer: she watched a moment, absent of intervention, change its shape in the silence, into something she could use, hold in her hand.

The steam from the water so hot it blotched Beth's chest red, enough to conceal another bruise, for a moment at least, to obscure her in the mirror until the bathroom cleared again.

The iron-thick tang of a person becoming a body on the basement floor.

The way a crush of people, surging across a room, through a screen, becomes a shape.

A scream tumbling out of a car, breaking free of its bounds, drawn up and out into the whispers of the trees, into the ambient quiet of the night.

It was like Beth's house, the house whose garage Tyler pulled into, drawn by something beyond him, as his passengers bled out around it, surging toward the house, after Sarah. The house mattered more than anything, but it also didn't matter at all—it wasn't the act or the person, but the shape of its course. We were looking for a space where we could expand, for a culminating moment that could turn and then burst, could catalyze the people around it. It could have been anywhere, anyone, in any of these houses. In any room. Dayton, Pike County, Lenape. Why not Adena? Like Graham, in his ramshackle former church, we were merely waiting for the moment to hit.

And as it happened, something else was already snaking toward that house in Peak's Trace, independent of us, toward where Beth lay unconscious and alone after we'd left her. Another car weaved through the suburbs collecting passengers one by one, its trunk loaded with equipment. Separately, Collin, after killing three aimless hours at the Steak 'n Shake off Wellesley Pike (one hour inside, two out in the parking lot), started the Taurus and finally headed south, toward the same location. And wider, across an area that measured approximately thirty square miles, for their own individual reasons, sixty-one other kids made the same decision: to converge.

We felt it swinging inward, this set of trajectories—aimless, violent, indifferent, excited, all twined together—the lead-up to the moment when we could turn, and then explode, pulse through Adena like a shockwave. Beth had seen it, too, had seen that potential and watched its spread—we had shown her—but in the end, she fought it, it was too big for her; we couldn't get her there. And so we brought him instead, Tyler, we brought them all to where it was already mounting, to where the pieces were aligning for the final move, and simply needed a push.

And then we would move on, as we always had.

———

Outside Beth's house, as the garage door closed, guttering its light, Alex's mom's Prius came silently around the bend. Inside the car, the vanguard of the Death Party, the same crew as yesterday: Thaddeus, Alex, Joel, and Amelia. Behind them, another car, a Nissan, with two more—Ethan and Nate—who had been to the liquor store, the Meijer. Six of them, all told.

The hill where Beth's house sat lay dark and silent and empty. *I want to fuck that house,* Thad thought, in the front seat of the Prius. He didn't know exactly what they would do once they were inside, but he figured he would let the house guide them, the will of the group. By the time they left it, he reckoned, it would no longer be the same house; it could no longer be inhabited in the same way. A mark would be left that would outlast all of them. It would be cleansed, and then stained.

"Whoa, shit," Alex said. Their headlights illuminated the SUV slumped at the edge of the road across from the driveway, the driver's-side door hanging open, dome light still on: a tombstone marking the house's grave. Could it have been the very car Beth and Greg died in, dredged from the junkyard and dropped here to guide them in like a finger? He should have brought flowers to leave, a tribute.

Alex turned up the driveway, wrapped slowly around the hill, their collective anticipation building, and pulled to a stop outside the garage. The Nissan pulled in behind them. They all filed out of their cars. Three of them—Amelia, Nate, Ethan—went over to the front door, while Thad opened the trunk to evaluate the supplies he'd brought, spread across three paper bags, wedged inconspicuously alongside the beer. He looked behind him—Joel walked to the edge of the driveway, looking down toward the street, at the abandoned car. From up by the house, you could see farther around the curve of the road in either direction; from below, at street level, most of the house was hidden. From one package, Thad unwrapped the brown paper from his father's shotgun, examining it without lifting it from the trunk, not wanting to reveal what he'd brought. The night was quiet. He felt a breeze he had not noticed from down below. Rarefied air, up here. He felt an uncommon calm: everyone had their role. If you'd asked him, in this moment he would have said he'd brought the gun for protection, as an added safety. Who knew what kind of traps rich people left in their houses.

"Thad." From the front door. "Come over here."

He prickled; his *assistance* was needed. He crossed the driveway to the sidewalk and went to the front door he'd entered through yesterday, where Amelia, Nate, and Ethan stood. "It's locked," Alex said.

He felt an—unnecessary, he knew—irritated flush of anger. "What do you mean? It wasn't locked yesterday."

"I don't know what to say, it's fucking locked."

Thad tried the handle. It was locked. His mind cycled for possibilities—some caretaker had been here to lock it up? Whoever had left the car down in the street? He beat his fist against the door. The house didn't answer. He noticed a bouquet of flowers on the stoop. Someone else had been here. "I'm going to try the garage," he said, turning away. "Can you keep trying?"

"It's locked! What do you want me to do?"

"I don't know!" he shouted. "Look for another door. Break a—fucking window. I don't care."

He stalked back toward the car, his calm dissipated, leaving Ethan and Nate. Amelia hurried after him. "Thad, are you okay? Do you think—"

"Yo, Thad," Joel called, from where he stood, waving him over. Thad didn't want to hear his name anymore, suddenly edgy, but he walked over to meet him. Joel gestured over the edge of the hill to the street below. Below them, a row of three cars had appeared at the edge of the road, parked in a line behind the abandoned SUV, as if following its lead. Like a funeral procession. Thad shivered. As they stood there, a fourth car arrived and parked neatly behind the last. He returned to the open trunk.

"What do you want me to tell them?"

His hand hovered over the gun. "Tell them"—he said—"the house needs to be cleared."

Joel took out his phone and texted something, presumably that. Thad felt the message resound across all of the phones in their group, ripple down into the street below. He felt a rush of power. He'd given an order, and it was obeyed. Unconsciously, he reached into his pocket when his own phone vibrated. "Hold. The house needs to be cleared." For a moment Thad forgot the order had come from him. In the seconds after, as the rest of the group did the same and idly checked their phones, as they regulated the message from beyond, *The house needs to be cleared*, when they were all quiet enough to hear the quiet of the house, he heard, from the other side of the garage door, a sudden staccato beat of footsteps, followed by a muffled cry. Alex, Joel, Amelia—the three others by the car—their heads turned at once to the garage. And so it needed to be cleared.

Thad caught a human scent in the air, off the ground, a streak of vomit close at hand he hadn't noticed before. He looked down and saw a dark stain marking the asphalt, the shape of a tongue. "There's someone inside," he said.

Amelia, Joel, Alex—they looked over at him now. He peered back into the trunk. His hand hovered over the shotgun. He noticed his fingers were shaking. He closed them into a fist. "We'll let them settle," he said. He paused, considering. "We shouldn't speak until we're inside the house," he said. "Just keep moving forward."

He imagined it, this order, like a sacred text passed down into the street to the others, separate from his own voice. He opened one of the other bags and unraveled the long kitchen knife from the towel he'd wrapped it in. He admired the blade shining black in the automatic light posted as sentry above the garage.

"Dude. What the fuck is that?" Joel said.

Thad didn't answer, obeying the rule he had just set. He opened the last paper bag and drew out the gas can he'd lifted from his garage—a blossom of noxious air came with it. He handed it to Alex with a significant nod. He passed the coil of nylon rope to Joel, Amelia the metal bat. With each new item, a new iteration of their group presented itself, a new potential reality was offered, a new version of what was about to happen, building on either side of the garage door. Finally, he passed out the masks: Alex scoffed when he saw them, and Thad marked it. They arranged themselves across the mouth of the garage. He felt the procession growing in the street. That was how he thought of it: a procession. *We shouldn't speak. Just keep moving forward*, he repeated silently.

To their right, he heard a burst of glass, something hurtled through a window. So the house was breached, he thought. Beside him, a series of sounds from beneath someone's mask, like three notes up a scale: *What is it?*

It's a Death Party, Thaddeus said to himself. Which would it be, he wondered—which version of them? The sign, or its meaning?

Inside, five minutes before, it was Rhea who caught Sarah at the far side of the garage, at the door leading inside—she reached for her shoulder and Sarah shrieked again, and pushed her away. "It's okay!" Rhea shouted, trying to get her hand on her shoulder, to dull the panic, to hold her frantic movement. "Sarah—*Sarah.*" She tried her name. "Calm down—no one's going to hurt you!"

Sarah's back was against the garage wall, she was hyperventilating, in full-body panic. Tyler closed the door of the car and walked toward them, the Lexus now fully inside the garage. Sarah glanced at Typhus, who had followed Rhea, who still had not spoken and stood just feet from them, also breathing hard, staring at her with malice.

"What—" Sarah gasped, barely able to get it out, not

sure what she should ask, trying desperately to not give in to the fact that she was terrified. But it felt impossible to fight, to catch her breath. "What are we doing here? What's happening?"

Tyler reached past her—she flinched—and pressed the panel beside the door leading into the house. The garage door rumbled closed again, shutting them inside.

"The house is empty," he said, turning back toward her—and he realized how close Typhus had come to Sarah, how focused she was on her. A dagger of fear pierced his chest. He realized, terribly, that he didn't know what Typhus would do. Or, worse: he knew exactly what. The razor was still in her hand. Sarah didn't seem to have noticed it.

"There's no one here," he repeated, as evenly as he could, opening his body minutely, trying to keep the energy static, to hold Typhus in place. He wished she would look at him instead, that he could redirect her now, absorb her. "We'll be safe here, for a while at least."

But Sarah was still chaos. "What do you mean, it's empty? Do you even know where we are? This is Greg's—this is Beth's house," she said again. "Beth Walker."

He noticed she wasn't wearing shoes. "The kids are dead. The parents are gone. There's no one left."

"No, she—" Sarah's mind scrambled, struggling to put logic to it. She looked to Rhea and Typhus for support, but they looked back blankly. They didn't know any different from Tyler. "Beth is—she's not *dead*. Greg was killed in a car accident"—she wiped her eyes—"he died after a car accident, but Beth . . ." She thought of the SUV pitched at the edge of the road outside, the dozens of unanswered messages and calls; her stomach turned again. "She's my best friend. She lives here," Sarah insisted, suddenly unsure, her voice wobbling. How long had it been since they'd last communicated? "She's not dead."

Rhea was shaking her head. "You're wrong. I saw it. It was both of them. There's not supposed to be anyone here." She pulled out her phone, to verify it.

Sarah stepped away from the wall, edged another step away from them, one hand behind her, touching the wall. "I promise, she's alive—she *lives* here." The SUV's headlights illuminating the outline of the seatbacks in the window, the dense and aimless trees beyond—no sign of anyone. *Could* she be dead? She needed to get into the house, to try to find Beth, if she was in there. And to keep the others out of it—whatever they intended. She had climbed into their car as if they'd come driving up just for her—but in reality, she'd known nothing about these people. Where had they come from? "She's here," she said again, not sure how to convince them of it. "She's alive."

Beyond the garage door came the unmistakable sound of a car pulling up around the final bend of the driveway. "Fuck." Tyler looked toward the door. "Who is that? Who else lives here?"

"I don't know, it could be her parents, I guess. I—"

For the first time, she saw worry in his face. He closed

his eyes and opened them—a long blink. His eyes flicked away from her, and then back just as quickly. Sarah followed his look—Typhus stood to Sarah's left, feet away, slowly turning a razor in her fingers. Sarah choked down a gasp, felt her heart rate spike again, but she tried not to broadcast it in her body. How had Typhus gotten so close without her noticing? Sarah stepped back, away from Typhus, so she could see everyone at once.

Tyler looked at the garage door, then back at the house. "Let me think," he said. "Can we just—there must be a place where we can hide here for a few hours, right? Until everything calms down. We can figure out what to do."

"Until what calms down?" Sarah said. Typhus shifted— her face bloodier than the others'. "What are you running from? What did you do?"

Rhea suddenly looked up from her phone, to Tyler. Her face was ashen. "It's tonight," she said.

They heard car doors slam outside, voices.

"What's tonight?"

Rhea showed him her phone. "The Death Party. It's Friday," she said. "The fourteenth. It's tonight."

What is happening? Sarah thought. *The Death Party?*

Tyler felt his blood go cold. He had misread the date— he'd thought it was weeks away; he hadn't counted the time they'd been in the basement. A stupid mistake. He spoke quietly, almost to himself. "We're fucking trapped."

"We need to get out of here," Rhea said.

He tried to find the answer; something slipped in him and grew desperate, frantic. The thought of moving, of going somewhere else—it was impossible. Any sense of a plan he'd had, that we'd implied, fell to pieces. He felt lost—he had no idea what to tell her, to tell them; he had no idea. How did he tell her he was here, here in this garage, but also not here, that maybe he had never been anywhere? "No, we don't need to leave," he said, his voice suddenly unsteady. "We can—this can be our alibi, right? Like we were here the whole time. We can wait it out—we can wait inside. The same as before." He felt like he was throwing gibberish out between them, like he had no solution but to delay. Why had we led him here? To be trapped?

Rhea sobbed, as if her will had left her all at once. "I can't do this anymore," she said. "We have to go." He had seen her cry before, but it had never had anything to do with him. "I don't want to be here." She sniffed, wiped her nose. "Give me the keys. If you're not going, then I am. We"—she motioned at Typhus and Sarah—"we will go."

Typhus took a step closer to Tyler, as if to take his side, to attach herself to him. "Where?" he said. "Where would you go? What are you going to do?"

"I don't know," she said. "I'll figure it out. I always figure it out. We've always—" Her voice broke. "Just give me the keys." She heard someone yell outside, an indeterminate voice. "Tyler, please. Or come with me."

He took a step back. Her words buried into his chest:

after all of it, she was still trying to follow his lead, still asking him if there was a plan, she was waiting for him to give her an answer, to orient them here, to assign their circumstances meaning, significance, something. She did not want to go without him.

Around them, the walls were hung with equipment: a ladder, a rake, a leaf blower, an old bicycle—a father's tools, and these three figures with the potential of movement. Tyler was aware he had the keys in his pocket, that without them, the car couldn't be moved. And Rhea was in front of him, searching his face, asking him to account for something, for anything familiar, a measure of their past, which felt as old as they were, for something to justify all of this, for an answer that extended somewhere past him, beyond these walls. *Where are you?* She took the same step forward. She had been asking for years.

To his right, the door beckoned. What lay beyond it he didn't know, not precisely, only that it was another step deeper, another wall behind which he could hide: they could all hide, if they needed to, somewhere in there, in another basement. To survive to the next night, the next morning, or the next hour, and then take it from there. It was what he had always done. It was the only way.

We've brought you this far.

He suddenly found Rhea's eye—there was a distinct sensation of *grasping* it, like fumbling for a light switch in the dark—and he remembered when they'd been introduced in seventh grade, Rhea had been one of the first people to critique his drawings, she'd said from behind where he sat in the cafeteria, "That's cool, but how can he fly with such fucked-up wings?" and Tyler had turned from his heavily eraser-smudged drawing to Rhea, not exactly offended, and said, "The wings are vestigial," because he'd just learned that word in biology, "like a tailbone. They're left over from an earlier generation that knew how to fly." He remembered how in later years she would pester him about drawing, but at a certain point he had stopped taking her interest seriously, he figured she asked out of some residual obligation, like checking on a grandfather's health, and during all the days in David's basement where they'd had infinite time and she'd never brought it up, not once, that was the sign she'd finally given up on him, all those billions of moments later, and Tyler saw this moment suddenly as if on a map, a record of everything she'd ever done, could ever do, all of these moments exploding out from each other, the complete potential of her person, as vast and dense and complex as a galaxy. He had brought them here—had drawn them here—but for what? For their safety, or for his own? What had he done?

"Please," Rhea begged. "They're coming."

It was simple: he had unraveled them.

"I can't."

Sarah's attention moved across them; she felt the seconds winding down, her every possible movement a question, a question with a cascading series of unknowable answers. She was suddenly aware of the number of steps between her and everyone else. Typhus, two steps to her right; Rhea, three steps ahead; Tyler, two to her left; past Tyler, the door into the house. In the dark of the car, both Rhea and the younger girl had been unrecognizable to her, a set of symbols—Rhea's short haircut, the other girl's raccoon-like makeup and partially shaved head—but in the clinical light of the garage, Sarah realized she had seen the younger girl before, that she went to Adena, too, same as Tyler, Sarah saw her sometimes between home-room and first period, as she left the south unit for her first class. But it was not the same blood-spattered girl she saw now—she hadn't had the green hair, the intense makeup. The only reason Sarah had noticed her before was because she was so short. Something had changed in her since the last time she'd seen her—something permanent. Someone's blood on her face and arms, a red thumbprint under her eye, the razor in her hand, a secret level of experience Sarah didn't know—a deep and guttural wound. An hour ago, she had awakened in David's bedroom as if into a new and savage world, a world whose bounds, suddenly, had become this garage, its components like a stage, like a clock face, knocking forward with her heartbeat. Where had they come from? What did they want with Beth—with her?

She bolted. She broke past Tyler, toward the door to the house.

Typhus instantly followed, and Tyler shouted, "Wait!"—

to whom, he wasn't sure, he never was—and as he spun away from her, Rhea shoved her hand at his pocket, trying to take the keys. A bitter surge of betrayal coursed into his throat. He grabbed her wrist, viciously. At the door, Sarah slapped the button on the panel, to open the garage again.

The air filled with a grinding churn as the door drew up behind their silver car like the blade of a guillotine, like a drawbridge, the antiseptic white fluorescence of the garage meeting the inky, shifting blacks of the night. Their combined attention was drawn with it, the edge of their reality lifted to reveal the endless expanse of possibility beyond. Tyler looked not at Rhea, but past her.

"Please," she whispered, straining in his grip, somewhere far from him.

A group of figures stood at the edge of the driveway, blocking their way out. Sarah thought wildly it was a string of scarecrows, like mannequins stuffed with newspaper and strung along a fence at Halloween, and then she reconciled it: a line of people stood spaced across the mouth of the garage, four abreast, as if they had the house surrounded. Their faces were obscured by blank, oval-shaped cardboard masks. Her eyes went instantly to the most grotesquely armed: the figure second from the left, whose hoodie was drawn up behind the mask, an inverted white cross on his chest, held a long black knife at his side. The person to his left carried a red gas can; on his right, a coil of white rope around one shoulder; and the fourth, a metal baseball bat. The way the light from the garage brought their clothes into detail, a mess of mismatched off-blacks against the stark cardboard masks, perversely, only made the sight more unearthly. Sarah felt the air leave her. She didn't even think of trying to close the door again. A phrase she'd heard weeks ago suddenly came back to her: Half Blessed. Of course. The group Claire had mentioned, the same group David had lied to her about, by a different name. The Death Party.

They.

—

Beth awoke in the living room to no light: they were gone from her—the mass of yellow lights, and the purple one that had guided her—and somehow she knew it was for the last time. Maybe they had been gone, truly gone, since Greg had died, maybe that purple light had only been there to make the ending less abrupt. She lay faceup on the floor. She awoke to the sound of glass shattering to her left, on the far side of the room: something cracking into the floor hard, and then a patter of glass hitting the carpet, like a wayward gust of rain. She closed her eyes—it seemed almost lighter—and opened them. The beams in the ceiling slowly, faintly clarified in the dark, above the space where the phantom lights had gathered, like a drawing in single-point perspective, pulling her upward and in. She pressed her chest—warm, damp, and alive. A current of air nudged at her shoulder, a tendril of colder air into the room's dark, anticipatory heat. She reconciled it with the broken glass at the same time as another fist's worth of glass punched into the room, followed by a series of smaller blows, the clearing of a pane, a male voice, and then someone twisting the latch from inside. And finally, an awful grinding, the squeal of lacquered wood on wood as the window, unengaged for years, was shoved upward.

So this was it. As she had seen—as we had shown her. They had come.

───

Overhead, the garage door locked into place with two loud clacks, their echo fading into a silence that momentarily descended over the garage: the two groups seemed to survey each other, the four inside the garage for the four outside. The moment felt charged through as if by a rippling energy—everything perfectly still, but in anticipation of movement, as if a current passed from the figures at the edge of the driveway to Typhus to Rhea to Sarah in succession, Tyler saw them all connected like knots on a single thread, just before it was yanked. A wobbling note—a quiet, muffled moan rippled through the air, he didn't know from whom. Where had he brought them? To what end?

It happened faster than he could have imagined, like

dominoes falling. Rhea wrenched her arm from him and screamed; Tyler's fingernails dug into the skin of her forearm and ribboned it off. His phone and the keys clattered to the ground. In response, misreading Rhea's scream as the result of an attack, by some instinct, Typhus charged Sarah, who stood at the door. Tyler sprang forward, past where Rhea cowered, to try to keep Typhus and Sarah apart. Seeing Typhus charging at her, Sarah herself tried to run. For a second the three of them—Tyler, Sarah, and Typhus—were all converging on the same spot. As Tyler threw his hands out, to separate them, Sarah's bare feet squeaked and she slipped on the floor. In trying to correct her own course in response, Typhus tripped. Her forehead collided with Tyler's outstretched elbow with a sound like a cracked knuckle.

She stumbled backward, toward the middle of the garage. Her eyes flew to him—astounded. She made no sound. The razor clattered from her hand. Her other hand grasped in the air once, twice, a third time, and then she collapsed.

Rhea shrieked—a sudden, primal wail. She clapped her good hand over her mouth. Sarah, just gaining her balance, fell against the wall and slid to the floor. The image of Typhus's sister, bloodied beyond recognition, washed over Tyler like icy water: the same posture, an opposing choice. A choice he had made, and then chosen to put away.

I want to fuck you to death.

He couldn't believe it had been him; it had meant

nothing to him, among everything else—he couldn't even have conceived of an effect.

Does anyone know you're here?

It was as if he had no other memories besides these.

Could you deal with it?

By then he had known there would be consequences, and had done nothing to stop it, to intervene. Had he ended them?

———

And though Thad had braced himself for the moment the garage door would slide open, flooding his body with light, he had not anticipated how little he would be able to see through the slits in his mask, or the handle of dread that plunged into his stomach as he absorbed what was inside the garage, the bloodied kids and their flurry of movement: the bright muscle-red stripe of the girl's flayed arm as she twisted away, the other girl's head cracking and her body hitting the floor like dead weight, the scream and the sharp line of panic it startled in him, despite himself, at the way the fallen girl suddenly started to *shake*. Nor had he factored in the realization that rather than one united agenda, as he'd imagined, among his people standing there, the vanguard of the Death Party, instead of one singular will, there were four, united only by the two directives he'd given moments before: *We shouldn't speak until we're inside the house. Keep moving forward.* What did it mean, what he'd said? What would they do? He tasted his own sweat, trapped by the mask. He had left them with one choice. It was bigger than him now.

He gave a signal, a twitch with his knife.

His guts strangled themselves, and then, as he detected peripheral movement from his companions through the narrow gaps in his mask, loosed: a belch of oxygen.

They stepped wordlessly into the garage.

Collin had not journeyed into the White Knots before—the name itself was enough to steer him away, as a Black dude—and he would have been worried about getting lost had there not been a noticeable contingent of traffic on their way to the same destination. When he rolled up on the series of streets that split off Prior Hills, he knew which to take—the second on the left—only because two cars ahead of him did the same thing. He turned, following them, onto Meridian Circle, and then he paused, watching their taillights vanish around the curve, into the dark of the trees. When they were gone, he pulled forward.

He wasn't very deep into the trees when he began to feel like he was trespassing, like this was not a party for him, the neighborhood was too rich and alien. He knew Peak's Trace was nice, but he hadn't expected it to feel so isolated. His headlights illuminated the white ribbons looped around the trunks of the trees to either side of the road, knotted tight, their ends waving loose in the breeze, as if holding their necks in place, like a deep and ancestral evil, warding ghosts. He knew he was in the right place, and also the wrong one. He felt raw from the meeting at HBCC, but eager to subsume the rawness with rich-people alcohol. He had smoked a bowl at the Steak 'n Shake, too, but looking at those trees, he thought he ought to have waited. Was it not a party like this where Rachael had gone, the night she died—the night the world *killed her*? Her own Death Party. *Stop*, he told himself. *Enough of this.*

He followed the road as it curved, slowing to a stop under each infrequent streetlamp, to gather his wits beneath its cone of light before moving on, into the adjacent darkness. One hand over the other—a constant, gentle turning as he followed the road. Maybe White Knots was a generous nickname, he thought: the road was shaped more like a noose. *I should go*, he thought. *I should just go now.* But then, he routinely thought that. And also: he would've had to go home.

He came finally around the bend, and before he noticed the house, he saw the line of cars parked along either side of the road, wrapping this curve of the street. He watched as the car ahead of him shifted over, like those in front of it, and parked. Without thinking, he did the same. After a minute, he cut the engine, and then the lights. The inside of the Taurus was totally black as his eyes adjusted— the only light he saw came faintly from the house, its upper half visible through the trees on the hill. From where Collin sat, he could just see the entrance to the driveway, where the cars had left a gap. But the cars hadn't gone up, it didn't look like. He tried to count; there must have been twenty cars—fifty or sixty people at least, he guessed.

Quiet as it was out here, he thought at first they must all be inside already, that he had arrived to find the party in full swing. But then he realized he hadn't seen anyone get out of the car in front of him. Were they waiting for him? He looked around, to the cars on the other side of the street, those parked farther ahead, and he saw glimmers of movement from within them through the windows, occasional lights. They were all just sitting arrayed at the base of the house, as if waiting to storm it. As if waiting on a command.

He took out his phone. He saw a message from a few minutes ago, posted in the group to him and 112 other people. "Hold. The house needs to be cleared." An icy prickle moved across his shoulders. Was that what they were all waiting for—a *clearing*?

He stared up at what he could see of the house, one of those big colonial-looking places you saw in the rich parts of Adena, that could have been there two hundred years. He tried to place the light he saw—was it from the garage? The rest of the house looked dark. So they weren't inside yet. Who was up there, trying to get in? What was being *cleared*? He shifted, looked around again at the quiet street. The car felt thick with her. It was here, a house like this one, a dumb high school party like this. She had been out, drinking happily with her friends; there had been coke, they'd gone to the Steak 'n Shake afterward for four-dollar burgers at 3:00 a.m., or so her friends reported. She had come home and gone into her room and never come out. They had had to break down the door. Why was he suddenly afraid?

A simple answer: well, lots of reasons.

But he didn't have the energy for deference, not tonight. He wiped the tears from his eyes and opened the door, stepped out into the street.

The moment he interrupted the silent, anticipatory air, he felt the gaze of the kids in their cars on him, watching as he walked down the corridor of cars toward the house. He crossed a pool of light from a streetlamp, then went out of it. Eyes everywhere. Six months ago, he never would have done it, put himself in front of all these people, dragging the weight of their vision behind him, like some kind of spectacle. But he needed to know.

He started up the driveway, where there were no cars. It wrapped in almost a circle as it ascended—another knot—before it revealed the house to him: he saw two cars parked by the garage, a group standing before them, at least four black silhouettes against the garage door, lit from above. He blurred them out. It may as well have been Rachael, locked in there, waiting to be cleared—to be broken free. He continued up the driveway, right at its center, toward the garage. "Take me," he whispered. He imagined himself framed the same as they were—an outline against the night. *Obliterate me.*

Do you ever think of following her?

So what if he did? So what if he always did?

He lifted his arms to either side, to make himself obvious, and walked up to them.

But they didn't see him, or acknowledge his presence. As he reached the cars, Collin noticed there were indeed four kids, but they were turned away from the driveway; they stood facing the garage, standing in an ominous row, like supplicants to the house, waiting for it to open to them.

He made his way to the Prius. The trunk was open, and several cases of beer were laid out on the asphalt. He looked down. A shotgun lay undisguised in the trunk. The same instant he saw it, he heard the sound of glass shattering, to his right. Instinctively, Collin ducked out of sight, behind the car, as if it had been the sound of the gun. *Fuck.* All white people, as far as he could tell, a mansion in the secluded woods, a fucking shotgun. He shouldn't be here. He heard his own breathing, put his hand over his mouth. For the first time in an hour, he noticed he was sweating again. He was amazed he'd lasted this long. Maybe he was changing, in some way. He crept to the edge of the driveway to look down to the street from the hill, wondering if he should go back the way he'd come.

Where it had been empty before, the road and the opening of the driveway were swarming with people, pulled by Collin's example, maybe, or merely tired of waiting, spreading like a slow tide up the hill. He started to hear kids' voices below, like a distant radio.

He turned back to the garage door, to the four figures blocked against it like shadows—like cutouts—like incinerated bodies. He hid behind the Prius.

With a loud, metallic sound, the door lifted.

Her back to the wall, beside the door leading inside, Sarah watched the four masked figures divide and bleed into the garage. In the center of the room, Typhus convulsed on the floor, her eyes rolled back, her head slamming into the composite concrete, her foot scuffing repeatedly in a dumb punctuated squeak. Rhea on the floor, too, coiled into herself, holding her wounded arm to her chest, inching herself backward, away from them, her blood smearing across the floor. And Tyler between them, as if searching for his own reaction to the bodies suddenly at his feet, laid low by either hand. He raised his arms slightly, took a slow step back, until he was even with the apparent leader, the boy with the knife. Sarah saw Typhus's razor lying on the ground beside her, Tyler's phone, the keys. A haze of associations came back to her again, like a wave of information bearing purposely up to swallow her: the *blood rituals*, the *blind fires*, the inverted cross on the leader's shirt, their weapons. Of course—Tyler had led them here. He was a part of it, too. David had delivered Sarah right into his hands, from his front door to the car waiting in the street. Was this what she'd been led toward all along, since Greg, even? Since Claire? *How did they keep finding her?* Her stomach pitched; she felt like she might vomit, but she had nothing left inside her. She thought back to that party with Hannah, to the presence that had felt just like this: opaque but intentional, a group in thrall to a system, a social order she didn't understand, that toyed with her ignorance of it, that preyed off the fact that everything could be a threat. That she was vulnerable, open, willing—and allowed herself to be. She remembered Beth had once told her she couldn't wear headphones because it left her too unaware of her surroundings—not that she didn't want to, but she *couldn't*—and Sarah had never understood it. She hadn't needed to. Should she run? Should she run now? *Half Blessed*, *Burst Marrow*, the *Death Party*, whatever it was called—they were all the same thing.

And equally, as the Death Party entered, the garage looked to Thad like nothing less than a massacre in progress. The door had opened, and almost instantly he saw the boy cut two people down. And Thad felt his group's numbers suddenly, an instinctive charge bolted through him, and he intervened. *We are at war,* he thought: the Death Party and the kids in the garage. He raised his knife like a machete and sank it into Tyler's shoulder, as easy as anything.

Rhea screamed again. At the sound, Sarah's heart automatically went out to her, a jagged line of empathy, so she started toward her, and for a moment her mind froze—she didn't know which side she was on. And then, with perfect clarity, she realized who she was here for, and made a decision. She grabbed the razor off the floor and kicked the keys toward Rhea as Tyler dropped to his knees, the knife in his shoulder. She turned and bolted to the door—into the house.

They were in the living room: two of them. Beth heard them drop through the window one after the other, which slammed after them, sending more glass to the floor. They made their way slowly across the room, crunching over the glass, toward where she lay motionless. She saw the doorway to the foyer, open, ahead of her, and through the foyer the front door on the left, the kitchen beyond, the hallway, all dark—she calculated her quickest way out of the house, which doors might be locked, might take more than a turn to get through. The front door in the foyer was the closest— through one wall, one handle. They were close enough she could smell their body odor.

The far wall of the living room was suddenly cut with white light—the flashlight on his phone. A second light joined. They scanned across the room—the decorated walls, the furniture, the vaulted ceiling. She felt a light illuminate her body, and then just as quickly move away, as if in embarrassment.

"Fuck, man. Is that her?" A whisper—ridiculous, after smashing in the window. A kid.

"*Fuck*, man. Is she dead?"

Was she? He crept the light slowly back toward Beth, as if gaining confidence, until it highlighted her again. The glow lingered on her chest, her face dropped in shadow, her eyes narrowed against it. She looked down her collar-bone, trying to breathe as little as possible, to make herself like the body they thought she was. A faint shine, where her sweat had dried and then, slightly, returned.

She felt them step closer, as the lights held on her, the heat of their own bodies nearing, then beside her, on her left. One closer, and the other behind him. He crouched, or knelt, at her shoulder. Despite herself, she thought of Greg. Had anyone else ever been this close to her?

The way he was crouched, the way the phone light sheered his athletic shorts, she could tell he had an erec-tion, could see it through his shorts. She saw her stomach clench, a rotten line pulse up to her throat. Was this what it would take, from now on, to know what someone was feeling, what they wanted? He adjusted his phone: she thought she saw him tap it, take a photo.

It hadn't been Greg, in those moments, she decided. When he'd betrayed her or hurt her or left her alone. It had been someone else, no matter what his light said. There was what she knew—what the light told her—and what she *knew*.

She tracked for her arm in the dark, and the fingers of

her right hand found the cold of the glass ball lying beside her. Until this night, she had never ascribed any meaning to this object, hadn't known of its existence in her house at all. Like it had been waiting here for her, all of these years. Silently, outside the perimeter of light, she wrapped it fully in her palm.

The kid beside her leaned forward, over her, blocking, briefly, the light behind him.

Beth swung it up, up into the material darkness above her.

At the crack of glass against jaw, Thad pulled the knife from Tyler's shoulder. An arrow of blood spit across the garage floor. On his knees, below him, as his pulse hammered out through his left arm, Tyler remembered a friend he'd had when he was a kid, Alan Smallwood, who Tyler had only realized in retrospect was a bully. He and Alan were close for several years; they'd hung out from third grade almost all the way through sixth, and he'd spent most afternoons and weekends at Alan's house, playing videogames and eating Pop-Tarts in secret (both of which, at the time, he'd been denied in his own house). He rode home with Alan and Alan's mom almost every day after school, where he would stay for a few hours before she drove him home.

After third grade, where they'd met and become

friends, the two were in different classes, and Alan was an athlete, destined for football, and thus even then he had a group of friends isolated from Tyler's. As a result, most of Tyler and Alan's contact took place outside of school proper. They would meet after the bell to be picked up by Alan's mom, and when they hung out they didn't talk about school, and so Tyler mostly knew Alan outside the context of other people his age: a silly, physically inclined kid with a goofy sense of humor, an invisible military dad, and a doting, nervous mom, whose house came equipped with privileges that Tyler's own lacked.

But Alan had a violent streak, or what at the time Tyler saw as an angry streak, which showed itself occasionally, even in their tiny world: he would wrestle the controller out of Tyler's hands when he was losing too badly, or punch him in the shoulder hard enough to sting; he screamed at his mother when she tried to counter him and would slam his door so hard things fell off the bookshelves. In those moments Tyler got scared and silent, he let his body go limp and didn't react, like an animal playing dead, until Alan had settled. The spikes in Alan's temper were always brief, he would be suddenly violent and then docile and sweet, and over time Tyler unconsciously adjusted to the routine. He didn't challenge Alan, he didn't ever raise his voice, and when there were arguments or cruelty to his mother Tyler just kept quiet and let the moments pass until balance returned. He never considered how these outbursts might bleed into Alan's school life, that they existed at all outside of their bubble—he didn't even really notice they had an effect on him, Tyler—they were just the wrinkles of his friend.

One day, in fifth grade, Alan failed to appear at their usual meeting spot in front of the school. Tyler waited as the school emptied out, the buses loaded up and left, and still Alan did not show. Eventually, after almost an hour of waiting, pacing in circles around the parking lot, Tyler wandered back into the school, unsure of what to do, and he walked up and down the hallway until a teacher found him and brought him to the office, where he used the phone behind the desk to call his mother. By the time she arrived to pick him up she was furious, as she'd had to leave work early, and all the way home she'd berated him, blaming him for what was clearly Alan's folly, for a problem that was not in Tyler's control, and for the first time he resented Alan for it.

Improbably, by some logistic confusion, the same thing happened the next day: Tyler assumed the problem would autocorrect, as Alan typically did, and so he showed up at their spot again, and for the second day in a row Alan did not arrive. Befuddled, he called his mother again, who this time refused to pick him up until her shift was over, and by the time she found him that evening—two-and-a-half miles from the school in the wrong direction, four miles from home—she was seething and violent. And Tyler regulated it the same as he did Alan's moods, and again he blamed Alan for his inconsistency, for opening up this space in which he could be harmed.

The following day, he heard by rumor that Alan had been suspended because he beat up this girl, Courtney Macau. That afternoon, Tyler diligently went to their meeting place again, despite having no indication that Alan would be there, almost out of spite, to punish himself for Alan's lack of contact, and when Alan finally showed— without any acknowledgment of his absence the previous day—Tyler went sulkily along with him to Alan's mother's car without question. It was only later that afternoon, while they played videogames in Alan's bedroom, slung out on bean bags in front of the TV, that Tyler's courage bubbled up and he asked for clarification. "I heard you got suspended," he said.

A moment passed, and Tyler's stomach lurched in anticipation. Would Alan hit him?

"Yeah," Alan finally said noncommittally.

Tyler didn't look at him. "I heard you beat up Courtney Macau."

"I didn't beat her up," Alan said immediately, his attention fused to the screen. "I slugged her."

Tyler didn't ask anything else, and the conversation lapsed as their characters hunted each other down in split screen and Alan joyfully decimated him again. But the word stayed with him, *slugged*, coupled with his resentment that Alan hadn't shown up for two days and Tyler had been the one punished for it, and yet Alan seemed to have no remorse for the position in which he'd left his friend, no awareness of it even. Later, Tyler thought about the way Alan had reframed the story, even in that brief conversation, maybe without even knowing it, how he obfuscated what he'd done to Courtney, adjusted its weight, as if it had been a clerical misunderstanding, or how it proved that some kind of dichotomy or hierarchy already existed within him at age ten, where *slugged* meant something different or less severe than *beat up*, had its own distinct characteristics that Alan understood intuitively enough to seek to correct, like a shot versus a graze, there were violences that meant less than others to him, or that in his perception didn't even mean violence at all, but merely physical reactions, like when he hit Tyler's shoulder, slugged it, like when he grabbed his mother's arm, squeezed it.

But in the moment, in the fifth grade, Tyler had no vocabulary for it, only the word and his resentment, and that night Tyler had a dream in which he beat Alan unconscious in the tiled halls of the school, and it was vivid in the dream the way he felt his blows connect with Alan's chest and arms, the places where Alan was already muscled, the flesh tense but giving beneath his fists, and the moment he knew Alan was unconscious was when a slug spit from his mouth, landing with a smack on the floor by Alan's face, that was the barrier at which Tyler stopped.

When he awoke he felt deeply guilty, and was relieved when he saw Alan that day, no worse for wear, no knowledge of Tyler's nightmare attack. He'd felt weirdly bonded to Alan in the weeks thereafter, deferent and submissive, as if he had something to make up to him, some long-unspoken apology for his psychic badness as a friend, and it was like that all the way up to the trip to the library.

The specifics of the trip were lost to him now, but at one point several classes of their grade had taken a field trip to one of the local public libraries. He and Alan had been assigned a task, to locate some material in the library, and that was how they had come upon Henry Ballinger in the stacks.

Henry was a short, slight kid with glasses, a lisping, high voice, an unchanging yellow-striped shirt with a white collar like Arnold from *The Magic School Bus*, and had moved to their school at the beginning of the year. None of this had ever meant anything independently to Tyler, but when Alan sauntered over to Henry and said, towering over him, *"H-hey, H-Henry, howth it going?"* Tyler suddenly understood: these traits were all weaknesses. And, because he had approached Henry alongside Alan, Tyler was by default the opposition to those weaknesses. He couldn't remember what was said, but he didn't interpret Alan as being anything other than Alan, his silly and occasionally gruff self, and he remembered thinking that Henry ought to keep this in mind, too, that Alan was generally friendly but he had a temper, that angry streak, as Tyler always had in the back of his own mind. And Tyler made sure to laugh at what Alan was saying, because Alan liked it when his funniness was acknowledged, and when Henry shrank away Tyler thought it was foolish of him to do that, because when Alan got worked up it was best to be still rather than respond, not to show you were affected; and Henry's face got red and he started to tremble, which Tyler again thought was an inadvisable response, when they were clearly joking around, because Alan might interpret this as another weakness. Likewise, when Henry slowly, pathetically raised his hand like a flag, as if to ask a question in class, Tyler didn't read it in the moment as Henry trying to signal for help, and Tyler didn't know why he did it—maybe because he still felt guilty for his dream, or assumed his friend was not directly capable of causing harm, only Tyler himself was, unconsciously—but Tyler grabbed Henry's wrist and thrust his arm back down, harder than he'd intended, so Henry fell to the floor, to his bare knees, and cowered there, and Tyler felt Alan's presence spread to him, like the two of them were a wall over the other boy.

The rest of the memory was lost to him, but it must not have caused a noticeable interruption, since he didn't remember being reprimanded and he and Alan remained friends for another year afterward, until Alan's athletic commitments gradually drew him elsewhere. But this sequence—the slugging, the dream, Henry Ballinger—settled within Tyler like a dormant seed, a triptych that culminated at the library, a moment where Tyler had been given a choice, to pick a side, and he had instinctively sided with violence.

In that desperate moment at the basement door of David's house, the bloody body in his arms, when he'd been raw and terrified, we had found this seed, the place where Tyler had branched one way, a calculation Tyler hadn't known he'd made, when he'd set aside a part of himself in service to his own momentary survival, trading it to a form of power he didn't recognize at the time, a power that was both screen and shield, that protected him by obscuring his role in it, where he could look at Henry and see only someone else, someone who was not Tyler.

As Thaddeus bore down over him, the mask blank beneath the synthetic light of the garage, the scene in the library came rushing back to Tyler, a gristle of memory he thought he'd long chewed to nothingness. Beside him, Typhus's head continued to hit the floor, so relentlessly he thought it would split open. Rhea dragged herself away from him, toward where Typhus lay, palming the keys. He saw the intruders separate, to block them from each other, to wall them in, and he couldn't find Sarah. His shoulder seared, he felt blood leaking through his fingers, the edges of his vision starting to flicker. He heard his own breathing, Rhea's hoodie dragging across the floor, the hiss of the lights, and beyond them, a murmur of voices, of whispers, like a chorus, storming on the air, bearing down on the garage. He cast his eyes up, to the long tubes of fluorescent light blaring out from the ceiling, refracted and multiplied in his eyes, blotting his vision with drifting, ropy shapes, like a language he didn't know how to speak but understood by its tone, like an ambient scream, and he saw us there, he felt us within him. He recognized a moment balanced on its edge, his former self at the bottom of the basement steps, covered in blood, a boy plummeting into his future, waiting desperately for an order—a clarity, an escape—to arrive. We had given it to him, and it had brought him here.

Typhus's body went quiet, slack like a snapped cord. At the sudden silence, Tyler turned to see her head loll to one side. A line of drool glimmered on her chin. Rhea cried, "No—"

He felt us. And he let us go. We sprang from him, into the current of light, into the blood-rich air of the garage.

Tyler felt us go, too, like a wire twisting in his gut, a sudden lightness, and simultaneously, an oily horror in his stomach, as if his center had been punched out. His eyes teared—in light, in relief—and he stuttered out a single, gasping syllable, like a gate cracked open, like the plunge of a missed step, like a throat cut short, and then he realized what was happening: in the moment he had thrown us off, we were trying to move between the kids in the garage, to jump to someone else, through that rank air, so thick with potential you could have choked on it, could have sliced it with a knife.

Three walls away, Sarah charged through the darkened house: it was warm in the hallway, body-heat-warm, like a packed room in the summer without air conditioning, and she cut through this busy air, a tangy smell that was almost familiar, toward the other end of the house—toward a crack, a shout, a crash. The living room. When she crossed from the kitchen onto the polished wood of the foyer—her usual point of entry—she abruptly remembered she wasn't wearing shoes or socks; she was barefoot and bloody and armed with a razor in this pristine house like a savage. A streak of light swung past the doorway of the living room— she followed.

Behind his mask, Thad breathed hard, the cardboard moist against his face. He wanted to tear it off. The knife was heavy in his hand, thick with blood. He kept thinking, *That wasn't the plan, that wasn't the plan*, but what *was* the plan? Why had he swung like that? He saw Amelia cross behind Tyler—who was bloody and clenching his shoulder, on his knees—to straddle Rhea and swing the bat into her side with a metallic crack. Beside Thad, in response, Alex roared and uncorked the gas can, and before Thad could properly react, could get him fully in his sights— and hold on, Joel, where was he?—Alex thrust the can forward, dousing Tyler with an arc of gasoline. No, he—what was this? Where was Joel? Where was that other girl? Behind him, he heard the sound of a crowd, a mash of voices, he heard it like a growing chant, but he couldn't see them without turning all the way around. This was what he'd started: it was like he'd pulled a lever, set them off, and now it was unfolding and unfolding, action after action—he was attacking. His group was attacking. He had struck Tyler once already. And so Thad followed his own example: he raised the knife once more.

—

Over a handful of seconds, ducked behind the Prius, Collin watched. The garage door opened, and—he didn't quite know how to describe it—two waves of violence surged both outward and inward at the same time, crashing into each other. A line of screams, a shock of blood, two kids on the ground, and almost instantly the masked group had attacked. At his back, Collin heard the chatter of kids making their way up the driveway, rounding the bend like he had, into view of the garage, he felt them *mounting*, and within seconds they would see him, hiding there, watching it all.

He couldn't explain why he did it. Maybe because the world was pressing him to action, or because he was out here in the White Knots where his very existence felt threatened but also like a threat itself, maybe because Rachael had gone from him and he wanted to know, *was she here*, because he would be spotted anyway. Maybe it was because he had chosen a side, even before he'd gotten here, or because he wouldn't be found cowering there, behind the car. Maybe it was because he'd seen the gun in the trunk and a narrative had sprung up around it, an answer to a question he didn't realize was being asked. But he stood, he lifted the shotgun from the trunk of the Prius, startled by its weight—he didn't consider whether it was loaded or not, the thought simply didn't occur to him—and swung it with both hands toward the masked kid at the center of the garage, no more than ten feet from him, as he raised the knife again before the boy who was bowed at his feet.

Sarah didn't resolve the scene in the living room immediately—she saw only fragments. The moonlight streaking through the windows on the southern side only reached halfway across, so the whole left half of the room was in darkness. She heard a muffled cry, bodies in conflict. Stepping inside, she saw a bloom of light up from the ground, from a phone lying faceup. A shape barreled past her, into the dark half of the room, taking with it another phone light clenched in a fist, and collided with the shelves on the wall. She felt glass on the carpet beneath her bare feet as she ran toward the crash, toward the movement on the far wall, and she remembered Claire had asked her, during the heady building of their friendship, the relentless exchange of data, *What would you do if someone followed you home?* and the question had taken her so off-guard that Sarah laughed it off, gave some absurd answer, but now she realized the question had been loaded, a setup, and that her first, automatic answer, *I don't know*, had been the real answer, because she didn't, she'd never considered it, had never needed to consider it, had not trained for it, but now it had come, and she felt Typhus's blade tight and sweaty in her own hand and she wanted to smell it, to stick it into her face. Another dark shape shot past her, kicking the light on the floor, so the beam juddered and shifted, casting a line across the room that illuminated, pinned against the shelves, a ripple of bare torso, and Sarah almost choked on her own heart, it was *Beth*, trapped there. Sarah's attention raced among them in a jagged line, and the question presented itself again, was being asked now, as she crossed into that dark and seized the figure by his shoulder, crooking her right arm around his neck—feeling the other person step back, too, realizing her presence—and she searched for the answer in her roiling stomach, in her body, and it came to her with her reaction, as she dragged him backward, revealing Beth against the shelves, and again it wasn't precisely her answer, but one she'd been handed, working through her, a line from the pamphlet Claire had given her, written out in her own handwriting: *You are a gun trained on the future.*

It was Collin. It was always Collin. Collin Reyes, whose sister Rachael killed herself last year, who had come so close to following her, who coursed with rage and grief that took her shape merely because it was a convenient vessel for something much larger, deep and generations wide, an age of violence the size of this state, this goddamn country, who had come here to answer it, who had gathered the audience to hear him finally speak. He had brought them here, as Beth couldn't, he had brought them here in an arc at his back. This was it, the culminating moment we had been building toward—to take root, to burst open—it was not in the living room, as we'd expected, but here at the edge of the garage, a kid with a gun in front of a crowd—classic image, wrong image, we ought to have known—standing there at the precipice of the rest of his life, the rest of their lives, at the edge of a choice. It was him. It was Collin. We stormed from Tyler toward him, through the air, the atmosphere sang out a metallic hymn, it seemed to scream, MAKE THIS HOUSE AN EXAMPLE A PYRE A WRECKAGE AN ENDING—

We anchored in the coldness of him, the part of him that hated this house, these people, everything they represented. His fingers seemed to slide into position on the gun, to slot neatly around the trigger, to regulate his trembling hands. He flicked off the safety—he wouldn't have even known it was there.

Do it, came an urge in him. *You're here, and she isn't. Take what they took from you.*

Then he saw the bloodied face of the white-blond boy on his knees, before the masked figure with the knife, and he remembered the kid from HBCC, the crack in his voice when he'd talked about how he slept in the garage—the way Collin had cried, too, despite their difference. He hadn't known the moment, but had recognized its shape, and a part of him had gone out to that kid. The sense memory he'd caught from the kid there, as if it was his own—the whiff of gas, cold garage air—it was here now, too. In that fraction of a second, in that bloodied face, Collin recognized himself—and then he recognized Tyler.

His rage dropped out of him: all he felt was horror.

Outside, Collin dragged the shotgun to the left, clear of the garage, and fired it: to shatter the moment.

Inside, in the burst of sound, Sarah plunged her blade into the cheek of the attacker.

We recoiled into the air, again, as the shotgun blast exploded into the night, and Thad whirled, his knife arm dropping, to see where the shot had come from, to reconcile Collin, the crowd behind him—and we churned through the air, for Thad's reaction, the crowd's reaction,

Alex's, Joel's, Amelia's reaction, we crackled up with the warmth of the buckshot in one stalled and corrosive instant, seeking purchase, a new place to take root.

Tyler saw us, then. Or he didn't see us, exactly, but he sensed us there, like a change in the air, like a breath we waited for someone to draw, to let us back in—to let us try again. He saw the line that connected them all—Rhea and Typhus and Collin and the Death Party and the kids whose faces were suddenly visible in the light from the garage, who had come to see it—he felt it pulled tight, nocked in his chest, the cusp of this violence at which we waited, spinning above them, ready to descend. It was him, he knew, or it would be someone else, a massive violence he could tear off at the root by taking it into himself, by making it his responsibility. He saw it like a diagram, like a tossed coin, like a split down the center of a branch, held by its last fibrous tendons: a branch toward violence, to take us, to keep us with him—and a branch away. He stood in the midst of the same transformation that had gripped him beside Alan, momentarily, all those years ago. It could have been him, behind that mask. It had been.

He threw himself at Thaddeus, and we flooded back into him like a rush of foul air. As Thad turned, Tyler grabbed his waist, yanked the slack knife from Thad's hand, and jammed it into the back of his knee as far as it would go. Thad screamed as he fell, and we strained against Tyler, as the sound saturated the night, as we tried to disperse with it, to reach the kids gathered there. But Tyler held us tight—he wouldn't let us go.

His head dropped, and then he hoisted it, smearing a black arc across the periphery of his vision like a scrawl of dirt on a windshield. An orb spotted over his vision and disappeared. The scream dissipated, as if he'd swallowed the echo. We were part of him again. We always would be.

Thad hit the ground on his knees, another crack that resounded in Tyler's teeth, and he toppled onto his back. As Amelia looked on, Rhea, wincing to her feet, swung at her with her uninjured arm, the keys out between her knuckles, her fist colliding with Amelia's collarbone, and Amelia went down, the bat rolling across the floor. Trying to charge them, or to step back, Alex slipped on the gasoline-slick floor and fell hard onto his back. At the sound of Alex's tailbone splitting, Joel, who was already nearly into the crowd—who seemed to be fleeing—ran back to him. Rhea lurched to Typhus, tried to lift her by the shoulders, to drag her across the garage, toward the Lexus.

Tyler pulled himself forward, over Thad, who writhed on the ground, a pool of blood spreading beneath his bent knee, his leg trembling. He howled in pain from beneath his mask, the cardboard mottled with spit and perspiration. Tyler ripped it away and Thad's hair spilled from the hoodie tightened around his bright red face, his eyes sparkling with tears. Gasoline dripped from Tyler's face onto Thad's wet cheeks. He was a kid, maybe the same age as Tyler was. They were all just kids. Thad grasped at Tyler's back, digging his fingernails into the skin, to pull him closer. Tyler slammed his forehead down, their skulls cracked and the bridge of his nose split, and Thad's grip relaxed. His head slumped backward, his knee still twitching. Tyler felt blood under him, at the heel of his hand, his knee, and looked up: for the first time, he saw the crowd gathered just outside the garage, around the two parked cars, maybe twenty people, watching him, watching them as they writhed on the floor. He tracked for the gun, for the shooter he hadn't seen—he couldn't find anything. Acknowledging the crowd seemed to break open the garage like a jar, and suddenly sound was everywhere: panicked breathing, crying, a commotion of voices, footsteps racing forward—a set of shattered pieces.

A second of silence, and then the boy in Sarah's grip screamed, an anguished, grating cry from his throat, through the blade crammed between his teeth, into his tongue, keeping him from opening his mouth any wider without tearing it, from expressing the scream fully: a sound she felt in her arm against his neck, in her own mouth, and the burble of blood that popped, spilled from his mouth onto her hand, the smell of an old iron gate—a voiced, rattling moan into the dark of the room, trapped within its walls.

For a second Beth was fully illuminated against the

bookshelves, from the phone light in his hand, her breathing panicked, her pupils pinned, and then the light dropped to the carpet. Sarah heard the other boy, who she couldn't fully discern in the dark, who had shrunken into a corner, let out a quiet, terrified cry—more of an exhalation.

She pulled the blade out, and stepped back, loosed her grip from the boy. She heard blood hit the carpet—*like rain*, she thought—a pained, sibilant moan from the area where his mouth was.

Holding the razor out in front of her, though she wasn't quite visible, Sarah picked up the phone and turned the light toward the two invaders, broken before her.

———

Outside, in the garage, Rhea opened the back door of the Lexus, struggling to hoist Typhus. Tyler climbed off Thad, who rocked quietly back and forth, trembling, and climbed to his feet, using his right arm for leverage, his left shrieking at the shoulder, useless to him. Then someone from the crowd, a girl with long dark hair he didn't recognize, stepped forward, and went to Rhea: she took Typhus's legs and helped load her into the back of the Lexus. Rhea nodded; she closed the door with her left arm and climbed into the driver's seat.

As she did, others from the crowd began to come forward as well, separating themselves from the group, to cross the invisible threshold into the wreckage, to the kids wounded in the garage. The engine started, and the white headlights flicked on, throwing their hunched shadows into the wall. A jagged puddle of gasoline pulsed across the floor, twining with the blood.

The Lexus slowly reversed from the garage, and the crowd moved away from it, seemed to channel around it. There was a loud crunch as its back end struck the Nissan, parked perpendicular to its route, shunting the smaller vehicle into the back of the Prius parked beside it.

Tyler stumbled bleeding out into the driveway, his head pounding. There were no other houses visible from up here, just the shaggy black outlines of trees and the driveway disappearing around the bend, down to that solitary streamer of road, wrapping out of view in both directions. Ahead of him, Rhea eased the Lexus backward down the hill, away from the chaos of the garage. She moved slowly through the kids still on their way up the driveway, who wondered what was happening, what had broken the night; through those who stood watching, or who were already on their way down, unactivated and quiet, bumping their way home. She turned the wheel slowly, consistently, looking over her shoulder, as she wound down the road, parting them. Tyler felt the spectators watching him as he staggered past, too, holding his arm, streaked in blood; he felt us in the back of his head, pulsing against his vision, blinded by the descending headlights. He felt the car's residual heat, the lingering exhaust where it had passed, the smell of gas clinging to the air, his skin. When his eyes finally cleared, Typhus's sister's car had reversed into the street, itself pulled back and then sent away from him, back the way they'd come, drawing its sound into the distance.

The street was filled with cars lined on either side of the road. He followed alongside them. He was leaving it behind, all of it: he was leaving this fractured group of strangers, broken where they'd begun, the crowd of onlookers, he was leaving the house they had meant to storm, the house he knew was supposed to be the center of it all, to which he felt attached by that invisible vector, pulling tighter the farther he walked. He was leaving Rhea, and Typhus, in their car moving away; he was leaving her sister, sprawled in David's basement. He heard shouts behind him, up by the house, and he knew they were leaving, too. He lost his footing; he put his hand out to steady himself against the window of a Camry. When he pulled it back, a red palm print left behind, he saw a face looking mutely out at him through the glass. And then he saw others.

It was Rhea who carried Typhus now, who would carry her to the next point—after that, he didn't know. When she awoke, if she awoke, would she be better? Would they both be? He gritted his teeth until his mouth filled with saliva and blood, until his tongue swilled copper. He focused on that dizzying taste, on the physical act of his walking, the motion of his feet, the cluster of matter under his fingernails, the faint pump of blood from his left shoulder, collecting at his elbow and traveling down his forearm to his palm, the counterbalanced warmth and coolness, the associated peaks and valleys in the pain, the pulse in his ears, his forehead like a cracked windshield, held together by internal pressure, his broken nose, the scribble of white pain at the center of his back where the skin had been wrung open, the pace of his blinking, the effort of staying upright despite his exhaustion, the nauseating smell of gas, the blood loss—he didn't let his mind stray from these details.

As soon as Rhea was out of view he'd forgotten which way the car had gone, and he appreciated not knowing. He chose the direction he was facing, the erratic streetlamps hovering ghostly in the heavy air like an ethereal gate, floating over the silent line of cars, the arc-shaped stain nestled at the edge of his vision, like blood in the corner of his eye. He noticed it only when he blinked. At some point the wounded Nissan sped past him—he had to get clear of the road—slamming on its brakes before the curve, scraping one of the parked cars as it went, but neither acknowledged the other, they were on their way gone like he was. He moved off along the side of the street toward that vague distance, and out, and out, and out. A breeze followed him, rustling the treetops, until it ran out, too.

Across town, when the unknown car had vanished down the street and David turned back to his house, it no longer felt familiar to him: it was no longer safe. The aura of adult magic with which it had been imbued for the past two weeks had suddenly dissipated. The house seemed polluted to him, spoiled by the invasion, as if the structures that made it up—the extensive basement, the spotless living room, the expanding kitchen and back patio, his den of a bedroom, structures he'd once admired—had now come to betray him. All this time, and he had never even known the alarm codes. He put on pants—to do so he had to go back upstairs, to face his bedroom again, which now felt like a massive deception, a room where he'd been broken open and rifled around, come out with his insides rearranged. From the way Sarah had run to the car, he assumed she'd known the invaders somehow, that she had accepted his invitation to come over in order to distract him while her friends robbed the house. It was her revenge on him, revenge he undoubtedly deserved. Her forgotten or discarded shoes, her backpack lay by his desk. He knelt and unzipped it, poking through for a hint of her plans. He found her phone, which he couldn't unlock, and then drew out a white pamphlet: the title, *REDPRINT*, above a stark black symbol. He had seen the symbol before. He turned the pamphlet over. On the back, an address and a proposition, or a command: *ARE YOU ASKING THE SAME QUESTIONS*.

David turned on all the lights in the top two stories of the house.

When he was finished, he stood at the point at which the three others had emerged. The door to the basement hung open, its darkness gaping up at him. He was vaguely aware that there was an emergency protocol he ought to be following, there was a system in place for things like this. He switched on the light at the top of the stairs, resigned to seeing what they'd stolen. On the wall to the right of the door, below the light switch, a bloody handprint—the moon-like heel of a palm, a blot from the base of the thumb. The same symbol. His stomach turned over. He had not known it was within him—to be cruel, to be calculating—but now it was. He couldn't argue it: he had tried to trick Sarah, to take advantage of her, to assert some kind of control. How could he blame her for fighting back? Was that the question—*THE SAME QUESTION*? As he descended the stairs, dread building in his stomach, he felt like he was reentering a once-familiar place he hadn't visited in years, as if the basement was some primitive part of his past, an ur-place from which the primordial David had evolved.

It was his no longer. The disarray was approximately the same, but everywhere there were signs the basement had been occupied for much longer than tonight, maybe even since he'd first been locked out of it, that the three people he'd seen in the foyer had been all over here, sleeping in the bed, eating from the refrigerator, fucking on the couch. With every new piece of evidence he found—a backpack stuffed with clothes and toiletries, a bag of oregano, a quarter-loaf of wheat bread in the fridge, a wet toothbrush at the bathroom sink, a tube of eyeliner, the crumpled sheets on the bed—David felt a little piece of his composure slipping away, a pit of fear growing in his stomach, a tremendous uncertainty. There was no protection in this house, not really, in this neighborhood of houses, their walls were nothing but wood and brick and plaster. They belonged to no one: even David himself, his body—he remembered pulling out of Sarah, unable to control himself, bursting into the room—it wasn't his. He thought of the jar of emergency money in the pantry—was it still there? Should he hide it somewhere? Bury it? A heaviness fell over him, and he went to his knees, he pressed his forehead into the vinyl skin of the couch, took in the petrified odors of dried sweat and fast food and weed, and let himself cry, folded over. He had nowhere to go.

David stayed there until the smell dissipated, until his senses regulated the still air, and eventually he gathered himself enough to stand, to complete his survey of the kingdom that had once been his. He took a deep, shuddering breath. He walked across the room and opened the door to the weight room. He smelled the body before he saw it—a thick, iron-like wave that swept out when he opened the door, mixed with garbage—and then he saw her lying there, this body splayed out in the center of the room, blood everywhere. Her skin was so unanimously red, her clothes so soaked through, that for a second he thought she had been skinned. He recoiled, pressed his hand over his mouth to keep from vomiting, and then he was racing inside, he was falling to his knees again and bowing his head, he was inhaling the scent of a person, registering the random, vicious cuts across every part of her upper body, and she was still breathing faintly, breathing and bleeding, and he was breathing, too, following her lead like a trail in a forest. He took one of her hands in his; the fingers were still warm. He didn't know how to fight any of it, so he just held it there, he ran his thumb down her fingers to the knuckles, and he repeated it, this minute gesture, his heat into her, skin over bone, a frail bridge between them. With his other hand, he reached into his shorts for his phone. He called 911. When they asked for the address, David hesitated—he pictured a string of numbers and letters—and then he remembered.

Tyler walked through the night at the edge of the road, long after the private streets ended and the grid returned again, the streetlights regulated. He pulled against us, resisting the line in his chest that sought to pull him back, that tightened with every step. Eventually, he figured, the line would either snap or it would bring him down, and he was fine with either scenario. Pain laced through his head, at his temples, down the top half of his face, gathering at the broken cartilage suspended in his nose. He breathed in the fumes of spilled gasoline until his nasal passages went numb. His shoulder throbbed. He could barely keep his eyes open. Every once in a while, he would blink and his vision spotted, a blackness flickered at the edge of his eyesight like a Rorschach blot, like a light stared at too long, a flash of the dreams that awaited him when he finally fell asleep. When it got to be too much, all of it, he would stumble, and the jolt would return him to his senses enough to rebalance, to find his feet again. Blood soaked through his white shirt, joining the blood that had come from Thad, stiffening his clothes as it dried. The wound on his arm gradually stopped bleeding and dried over.

One way or another, in the deep of the night, he approached the strands of I-75, and the remainder of his directional sense brought him back to his own house, where he hadn't set foot in almost three weeks. He hopped the chain-link fence to the backyard, crossed the scrubby lawn, and entered through the sliding glass door in back that was never locked. The house smelled like burning tinfoil. He crossed the living room, lit blue from the muted TV, and dug his fleece-lined hoodie from the pile in the laundry alcove where he'd deposited it several lifetimes before. He wanted his headphones, desperately—even though he had no phone, nothing to use them with, he felt naked with his ears uncovered—but he didn't want to risk going any deeper into the house. The pressure in his head urged him to sit down, to collapse on the floor, to go to his bedroom and quietly bleed out, but he couldn't. He couldn't. If he ended, it would be the same as letting go— another would follow. It would find someone else. We would.

He was opening the back door to leave like a thief, the hoodie bunched in his arms, when he noticed a presence standing on the other side of the couch, where it hadn't been before, blocking the light of the TV. A chill went all the way through his body.

"Where have you been? You're never home anymore," the man said.

Tyler turned back to the door, his hand shaking involuntarily.

"Hey," the man said, closer than he had been, though not trying to stop him. "You leave here again now, you're not coming back."

You can't do that, Tyler didn't say. He slid the glass door open and left, the same way he'd entered a thousand times before, ever since his house key had been revoked. He slid it shut behind him.

He pulled the hoodie over his clothes in the shadow of the tree in the backyard, where the tire swing still hung. The motions of pulling it over his head, fitting his arms through the sleeves, felt needlessly complex and exhausting. The ruptured skin on his back screamed as he pulled it over his chest. He drew up the hood. It was too hot, but he didn't care; the material was thicker, harder to bleed through, and he could sweat off the gasoline. He hopped the fence again, his wounds masked, for the time being. The urge to anonymize himself was almost mechanical. And he kept walking, indefatigable Tyler; as his house shrank and disappeared behind him, he turned, out of his block, out of the neighborhood. He turned right before the train tracks, and then drew an unwavering line northeast. He passed chain restaurants, auto dealers, low ugly sprawl, and eventually a golf course, then another.

As morning arrived, somewhere north, when the houses jumped in size and cobblestones appeared, as the sky shifted white, he passed another person on the sidewalk jogging in the opposite direction, a blond girl around his age, the only human he'd seen on the street since the night before. What time was it? The girl turned her head and their eyes met as they passed each other, she stumbled briefly in alarm at the sight of his bloodied face, and Tyler recognized something there for a split second, he saw a familiar bearing in her eyes, an aspect he knew, a notch in her like there was a cut in him. He tried to look back, but both of them were moving on, the distance between them widening automatically, and it was clear their paths would never cross again. Two hundred feet later, it dawned on him that it had been Claire, totally transformed. He turned back, which felt like a superhuman feat—she disappeared over the hill, and was no more. The name was there, and then it was gone with her. He turned left, and continued that way.

———

As the strangers scattered, Collin had scattered, too. In the chaos, he dropped the gun where he'd found it and shrank into the crowd. When he was sure that it was over, when the masked group had fallen apart and disbanded, he made his way back down the hill; as he encountered people, he summoned his whitest voice. "Nothing going on up there," he said with a shrug. "Someone set off fireworks or something." And he slouched away, back to his car. He prayed to be forgotten, if he could be. He pulled the car out—the process was surprisingly complicated, and he couldn't turn around—so he followed Meridian Circle forward until, eventually, it looped and spit him back out onto Prior Hills.

And somewhat to his own surprise, he found himself

driving home, through the quiet back roads of Adena. Twenty minutes later, after 2:00 a.m., he turned onto his street, clicked the lights off, and pulled into the driveway.

He cranked down the window and sat there, in the dark within the dark, as the night gathered and, piece by piece, caught up with him. He had stopped something, he thought, even if he didn't know exactly what. Or he had changed it for one person, at least. It was like the planets— they each had neared the other enough to change both of their orbits, if only briefly. If only once.

He got out of the car and let himself in through the front door. He dropped his keys in the bowl on the table and went to the kitchen, still in his shoes. He turned on the lights, opened the cabinets, and took out a box of cereal, one of the bowls from the stack. He poured the cereal from a height, so it rattled in the bowl. He opened and closed the fridge for the milk, and then noisily put the ingredients back away. He set the bowl down, got a spoon from the drawer, and dragged a chair out from the table: only when he saw his mother standing in the kitchen doorway in her nightgown, still blond but looking older than usual, shorter, too, only then did he sit down, silently.

It was Rhea's first time in a hospital as far back as she could remember. She waited because she assumed she wasn't allowed to leave, because someone had to be there when Typhus woke up, someone had to tell her something. (And this had been the only name Rhea could give the hospital at the time, Typhus, she didn't know anything else, she had not thought to open the backpack at her feet and look for the wallet.) But even with the fake name and Rhea's tripped-up recollection of events, her half lies, they'd taken Typhus away and they'd intubated her, and when they asked about the blood on Rhea herself, she said it was because when Typhus started convulsing she'd accidentally hit her in the face and caused her nose to bleed, and had scratched her up pretty bad; Rhea said she didn't need it looked at, she thanked them—she didn't know how these kinds of services were exchanged, what she needed to provide in order to receive them. Later, a nurse had seen her arm by accident and insisted, and they'd wiped it with an antiseptic and given her stitches and bandaged her up and now she was rooted here, additionally in debt. She nursed the bruise on her ribs, where the girl had hit her with the bat; the staff hadn't uncovered that yet. She figured at some point they would come for her, hospital security or the police or whoever, she would have to pay for this. The car she and Typhus had arrived in—Typhus's sister's Lexus—sat unattended in front of the emergency room, blood all over the seats, and this, too, she worried she would have to answer for. All of it.

They wouldn't allow her in to see Typhus, so she sat in the hallway, in a cushioned chair. She ran her hand continuously down her bandaged arm, the stinging breaks in her skin where Tyler had grabbed her. She couldn't quite sit up straight. Part of her refused to believe it was Tyler who had done it, and a darker part wondered if it was the only real part of Tyler she'd ever seen. Would she see him again? Shouldn't she have known him well enough to know? She watched the middle-of-the-night trickle of visitors and staff pass through the waiting room and lobby, old and frazzled-looking people, tired nurses in sneakers. When Rhea had pictured hospitals she'd always thought of white tile, but Shawnee Valley was like being in a hotel; there was carpet in the waiting room, a grand piano in the lobby, wood paneling, there were planters in the corner. All the times she'd driven past its landscaped grounds, she had never thought she'd see inside. Across the waiting room from her, on the wall inside a glassed-in office, there was a painting of old-timey surgeons in scrubs operating on someone's chest, and a long-haired, robed man stood among them, holding his hand over one of the surgeon's hands, guiding his work. Rhea felt like a speck in the midst of it all, as the forces above her moved about and beyond, pulling information from Typhus's physical symptoms, from the hospital and government's elaborate records and computers and diagnostics, triangulating her condition with her medical history, her allergies, her name. Was Typhus a murderer? Or was she just defending herself against a threat to her existence? Weren't they all doing that, all the time? Could anyone be blamed for fighting back?

Rhea was there until the end; she was there until, unbeknownst to her, Typhus's sister was brought into another room nearby; until Typhus woke up and was no longer Typhus.

———

And in Beth's living room, the night before, with the light from the phone, Sarah drew the two intruders out of the shadows—the other kid ran up to keep his friend from collapsing, blood pouring through his fingers from the wound in his face, air hissing out from the channel the razor had dug. Beth slid down the wall, covering herself in shadow. Sarah flashed the phone light across their eyes. She thought she might have recognized them, but then she put the impulse away. She walked them to the foyer, the razor held at their backs. When they struggled with the front door, she shoved them aside and opened it herself. She was greeted by the smell of gasoline saturating the air. She inhaled it and felt instantly nauseous; her head spun. "If I see you again," she said to them, surprising herself, "I'll fucking kill you."

Outside, it was as if the world, the garage had been blown apart. Kids milled about the driveway, in the grass, by the cars parked there—the Nissan had been hit by another car. From the stoop, Sarah saw streaks of blood at the edge of the garage, saw someone pulling up the kid who had stabbed Tyler from a long trail of red, dragging him toward the Prius, another girl sitting in the grass, holding her neck. No one wore masks anymore. The Lexus was gone from the garage. Crushed beer cases and weapons lay scattered about the driveway and garage. Tyler, Rhea, Typhus—she couldn't see them. She saw no bodies, no one motionless on the ground. Just the ripples of an aftermath, the charged air, smell of smoke and gasoline, kids' voices, getting the wounded into cars to take them elsewhere. When the two kids from the living room reached the driveway, someone ran to them, helped them limping into the Nissan. She memorized the plate number. The scene was carnage, but equally felt like a moment cut off before its peak, a moment that had broken before it truly began.

A lanky boy with long hair standing at the Prius seemed to notice her standing on the stoop. He closed the door and walked toward where she stood. Again, she wondered if she recognized him. She remembered something David had said, another lie about Half Blessed, or Burst Marrow, or whatever—these kids: they were all from Adena.

He stopped at the edge of the driveway, maybe ten feet from her. "I'm sorry," he said, his voice cracked. "We thought you were dead." He looked down.

They didn't even know who Beth was.

In the living room, Beth sat on the carpet against the bookshelves, curled into herself in the dark. When she entered, Sarah felt for the light switch by the doorway, and turned on the lights. In an instant, the black shadows, the moonlight, the shrouded textures of the room were oblit-

erated, thrown into bright, high relief, and in that bright-
ness, their real viciousness was revealed: the glittery spray
of glass across the carpet from the broken windows, a
cracked glass ball, thick clots of blood spotted across the
floor, the traces of footprints within it, some nearly black,
all leading up to Beth, naked, herself misted with blood,
trembling, her body faintly shimmering with sweat.

The violent remnants of the night finally hit Sarah in
that moment, ricocheting through her in a quaking spasm,
as if her body was finally registering it, coming to terms
with itself, with her complicity in it, as if she hadn't been a
part of it—or she hadn't been aware of her part in it—and
then, all of a sudden, she was.

She flicked off the light, almost as quickly, in sympathy, in sudden fear, as if she couldn't contextualize the violence past a certain point, couldn't cope with its full
extent. She crossed the room again, in the dark, turned on
a lamp—warmer, forgiving light—and dropped her blade
and sat down beside her friend, against the bookshelves.

For some reason, she thought of Hannah; she remembered the hour she'd spent alone in Hannah's car outside
the house in the fall, during the party. It occurred to her
now that something had been happening to Hannah
while Sarah sat there bored, thumbing the volume knob
on the dormant radio, something Sarah had missed, something that conditioned Hannah to shriek so fiercely when
she turned the keys in the ignition and the radio ripped
out at earsplitting volume before she pitched it down to

nothing. It was a different Hannah who had gone into the house than had come out of it. Sarah couldn't put it all together—there was a dissonance where the revelation should be, a gulf she was just shy of crossing—but she knew there was violence there, there was violence all around them, buried in those shadows.

Along Beth's neck she saw a string of faint bruises, a sickly purple against her skin, and for the first time Sarah thought, *Someone did that.* Beth was sitting there beside her in the lamplight, making herself as small as possible, and she was intact, but also: she was terribly wounded. *We thought you were dead.*

Sarah pulled her lips into her mouth and imagined how big this house must feel with just one person in it, how devoid of sympathy. The smell: old breath, blood, and ripe sweat—it was fear. She took Beth's shoulders into her arms, fit Beth's smaller body alongside hers, wrapping it as best as she could. Despite the lamplight, ambient darkness returned to them both. Beth startled at the initial contact, and then she settled into it.

Next to her, Beth imagined a light flickering: an orange base, a bluish purple tinge. Maybe a ring of residual red. She knew it wasn't real—she knew she had no brothers or sisters left. But it was enough for her. She recognized that it was Sarah holding her, and human warmth was human warmth, but at the same time, she felt like she was finally, mercifully alone.

They, too, were there until morning.

The following evening, Claire braced herself outside the double doors leading to the dining room. It had been years since she'd been in this position, outside this door at this traditional, appointed time, but here she was. She heard voices through the doors, laughter, a hum that was years of Saturday nights old but which all of a sudden felt new to her, as if she were a rededicated convert to a church she'd attended when she was younger, where the rituals were familiar but still felt intimidating and foreign, cut with the same fear as when she'd experienced them as a child. She turned the handles and pulled the doors open, where they were arrayed waiting for her. They were all waiting for her.

When he had outlasted the limits of the suburbs, Tyler walked along the shoulder of the state road in the channel between the road and the fields, long into the heat of the day. He was desperately tired. His entire body ached, his face stiff and numb, as if it had frozen in place. His sweat smelled like gas. He put himself forward one step after the other, same as ever, a walking torch waiting to be lit, but he knew it was only a matter of time until the exhaustion brought him down, when his body just stopped working altogether and his vision spotted over completely, when the darkness took him for whatever was left.

Late that afternoon, along a desolate patch of road—the only sign of life was power lines, farmland—a car pulled over to give him a ride. By that point, Tyler's concentration was too narrow to see the car as it approached, and he didn't notice until it had slowed and followed alongside him for a period of time, until the door slammed—an interruption in the air, he didn't read it as a car door—and the driver appeared in front of him, blotting out his surroundings. The figure braced Tyler's upper half as his legs, finally, gave out beneath him, and he collapsed into the stranger.

As the man helped him to the passenger's side of the car, basically carrying him, Tyler focused on the hemp bracelet the man wore on his wrist, the central bead patterned with a shape like a lidded eye, and this one detail seemed totally out of place against the shifting fields behind him, the cascading sheaves of wheat in their—what was the lyric—in their *turbulent soil*, high in this season, almost ready for harvest. The bracelet quickly shifted out of his view and he forgot about it. The car was faded maroon, and though he only saw the side of it he recognized that it was a *Taurus*, he knew this with certainty, and he prized this fact, this secret knowledge, stowed it away like treasure. Tyler fell inside when the door opened, the man shut it gently beside him and returned to the driver's side. He felt the vague rumbling of the engine beneath him. He slumped automatically in the seat, his head settling against the window. The car was old, the window had a crank. His gaze flicked upward to the windshield and stayed there.

They had driven for twenty minutes or so in that direction, Tyler hovering just at the edge of sleep, his sight pinholed into a surface of plummeting blue through the windshield—this infinitesimally changing color like a reel of film endlessly unwinding—before Tyler realized that he hadn't spoken, neither of them had spoken. He didn't know where he was going, or where he was being taken. His vision pulsed at the perimeter of that patch of blue sky, tinged dark at its edges, like the rhythm of his own blood. He wondered how long he had lived with it inside of him, that arc, that space, if it had really been forever, just waiting for the right time and place to activate and define itself. He thought of Rhea and Typhus, together as far as he knew. The girl who lay in the basement, the bloody marker he'd left at the top of the steps. Claire, jogging among mansions. Would they be better? he asked himself again. If they had it in them, too? Would he? The sky gradually shifted colors, to pale yellow with a trace of orange. He didn't know how long they had been driving, where this road led. It didn't matter to him.

As if in response to his thoughts, Tyler's insides pitched as the car slowed and then turned to the left. The sky pivoted on its fulcrum, drifted, drawing a line, and then the car paused. Tyler emerged from his drowsiness. He recognized somewhere in the stalled motion that he was required to act. He dragged himself up in the seat, which all of a sudden he smelled: weed and old cigarettes. He looked at his lap and, for a second, didn't recognize his left hand—it was dyed red, all the way down to the fingernails. He scratched minutely on the upholstery, on a resin-like stain. Tyler looked over at the driver, for the first time. The man was looking away, out the window, his hands still on the steering wheel. He had dreadlocks pulled into a pony-tail, stretched earlobes. A little halo of loosed curly hairs around his head glared in the setting sun. Tyler felt he rec-ognized him from somewhere, indefinably, that his bear-ing, his outfit, the Taurus were familiar to him: he tried to remember the names of people he knew but could only think of Rhea, Typhus, David, Sarah—his life before the basement seemed like a cover story he had poorly memo-rized. He thought if he could see the driver's face, he could make a determination. They were in a parking lot in the country, it was almost dusk: these two facts arrived like brilliant flashes of insight, like he'd just run a wet rag across the filthy surface of his perception. The man turned off the engine, which seemed like another signal. Tyler was sweating in concentration in his thick hoodie, in the stale air of the car.

After a minute, when Tyler didn't move, the man in the driver's seat turned and looked at him—he was a kid, not an adult. They made eye contact for a second and again Tyler thought he was so familiar, there was a kind of buried history between them, some routine contact he couldn't call up, he was familiar but there was that space in him, too; Tyler could have reached over and outlined it in marker. How long could one go, Tyler wondered, until they felt it, knew it was there? Forever? Tyler pulled his red hand into the sleeve of his hoodie, concealing it. What was the value in knowing?

The young man's eyes flicked down at the movement: Tyler noticed that the olive sleeve of his hoodie was spotted dark brown, a blobby trail that went all the way to his elbow.

Their eyes met again, and Tyler remembered his broken nose, too, his bloody mess of a face. The driver turned and reached into the back seat. Tyler's defenses spiked— *Should I react?*—and then, a few seconds later, the driver came back with a navy-blue hoodie. He handed it across the seat. A set of syllables occurred to Tyler, a name: *Cameron—Kevin—Connor—Collin.* Collin. Of course. He had known Collin since middle school. He knew David's basement, too.

"Keep it," he said. "It's clean."

Tyler bunched the sweatshirt in his lap, caught the scent of detergent.

"Whatever you're carrying, you don't have to hold on to it," Collin said. "You can let it go." He paused. "You can let yourself breathe."

He didn't realize he hadn't been. Tyler nodded to him, letting a breath out slowly, and finally he pushed the car door open, and in what felt like an entirely unrelated, draining set of motions pulled himself out of the car. He wrung the hoodie in his hands like it was a task he'd been given. He felt the wound in his shoulder break open again, a line of coldness inch back down his arm. He took a few faltering steps across the parking lot before he felt the driver at his back, an arm out to guide him. He hadn't heard him get out of the car.

He had been brought to a church, or a place that was like a church. He caught the message board as he stepped up to the sidewalk, HOLY BLOOD COMMUNITY CENTER, but he couldn't lift his head enough to see if there was a steeple. Tyler couldn't remember the last time he had been to a church—not since his infancy at least, if ever—though the building reminded him less of a church than of the VFW hall in Owl Creek where he and Rhea had used to go to hardcore shows. He noticed a string of little American flags along the sidewalk. *Was* it a church? A warm glow came through the glass doors, there was a light on somewhere deeper inside. He limped toward the glass doors, the driver behind him, not touching, but present, and the walking was unfamiliar, like a skill he'd let atrophy over months, that he'd failed to keep up, but eventually he reached them. The driver pulled open one of the doors and they stepped inside.

A placard greeted him on the opposite wall: AMERICAN LEGION POST 638. He felt a gust of familiarity, instinctively tried to remember if he had any weed on him that might get confiscated. The building branched, and in the lobby, or the foyer, or anyway at the building's joint, he peeled off his sweaty hoodie, the sleeve stiff with drying blood. The smell—gas and blood and sweat—hit him in a wave and made him gag; he coughed and spit a wad of something vile into the trash bin, and stuffed the hoodie in deep after it. The relief was immediate. He gingerly slid his arms into the new sweatshirt, the one he'd been given, and zipped it up, concealed again. He turned back to offer some version of his thanks, to test out the name, but the driver had gone.

He turned left, because that hallway went deeper, because he knew he was winding down and whenever the trail stopped, he, too, would stop. He passed a line of closed doors. GONE BUT NOT FORGOTTEN: that was what the placard over the stage at the VFW had said. He dragged a finger along the wall, tracing his path in red: ironic, he thought, nothing more basic than blood. Was that what made something holy, its irreducibility? His footsteps echoed on the tile—it was a reminder of his erratic pace, lacking in precision—and then when he hit carpet, the echo stopped. It dawned on him: of course—for years as a kid, he had gone to church every Sunday morning. He passed through another set of double doors, and emerged into an empty multipurpose room, a circle of metal folding chairs set out in the center. The lights above were all on, in expectation. Tyler found his way to an open chair. He sat down to listen.

ACKNOWLEDGMENTS

Thanks to my parents, Martha Moody and Martin Jacobs, who are very much part of my story, and to my brothers, Eli, Michael, and Jack (in order of age), for being the best siblings.

Thank you to my wife, Sam Skurdahl, for her love, her encouragement, her persistence, and her patience. Despite my best efforts, she is still funnier than I am.

Thank you to the other earliest readers of this book (2017!), who helped me "light the lamps," as Jeanne might say, to see what else was possible: Alyssa Bluhm (whose four-year-old notes I still refer to), Joey Holloway, Jeanne Thornton, and Ross "the Vacuous Spider" Wagenhofer. Thank you to Graham Nissen, intellectual and artistic lodestar and wise, wise man. Thank you to Ben Kopel and Brandi Wells. Thank you to John Baren.

Thank you, in a fundamental way, to Bill Clegg, who saw a shimmer of promise in the book way, way back and helped me chase it, relentlessly, and who became the book's most tireless and fiercest advocate, even in the midst of global collapse. Without him, this project would have stalled out long ago. Alongside Bill, my sincere thanks go to the chorus of the Clegg Agency: Marion Duvert, David Kambhu, Lilly Sandberg, and Simon Toop, each of whom has offered indelible insight, warmth, and enthusiasm throughout this book's long life.

And thank you to Daphne Durham and Lydia Zoells, whose sage, incisive, and steady counsel helped crack the book open, filling it with light and new shadow. I'm grateful to you both for your faith in the vision of this weird book, and for your creative insight, tough questions, and unanimously good ideas.

Thank you to Clara Spars for translating Viceroy's lyrics into something truly special, to Na Kim and June Park for the perfectly uncanny cover design, and to the production, publicity, and marketing teams at MCD/FSG for their support of this book and others of its kind.

Thank you to the other writers who have helped bolster this book on its journey toward publication, especially Mona Awad, Rachel Eve Moulton, and Kira Jane Buxton, and to the many other artists whose work shaped the writing of this book in tone and form.

—SIMON JACOBS
October 2021, Portland, OR